# THE WIZARD WAR

Rollant squeezed the trigger. His crossbow bucked against his shoulder. All around him, bowstrings twanged. Quarrels hissed through the air. Several blue-clad soldiers fell. "Die, traitors!" Rollant shouted, reloading as fast as he could.

"Steady, men," Lieutenant Griff called. "Make every shot count," he urged. "We can lick them."

Did he really believe that? Rollant didn't, not for an instant, not while the company was standing out here in the open, trying to hold back the gods only knew how many of Thraxton's men.

A couple of soldiers not far from Rollant went down, one with a bolt in the leg, the other shrieking and clutching at his belly. But then, although quarrels kept whizzing past the men in the company and digging into the dirt not far from their feet, none struck home for a startlingly long time. That was more than luck. That was. . . . Behind Rollant, somebody said, "A mage!"

Rollant turned his head. Sure enough, a fellow in a gray robe stood busily incanting perhaps fifty yards behind the company's skirmish line. "I'll be a son of a bitch," Smitty said. "A wizard who's really good for something. Who would've thunk it?"

"As long as he can keep the bolts from biting, he's worth his weight in gold," Rollant answered. "And as long as he can keep us safe like this, *we're* worth a brigade."

Then the mage let out a harsh cry, loud even through the din of battle. The wizard was staggering, as if pummeled by invisible fists. He grabbed at his throat. Someone might have been strangling him, except that nobody stood anywhere close by. The northern wizards had found the mage. With another groan, he fell. His feet drummed against the ground. He did not rise.

An instant later, a crossbow bolt struck home with a meaty slap. A man only a few paces from Rollant howled. Whatever immunity the company had enjoyed died with the man in gray.

# SENTRY PEAK

# HARRY TURTLEDOVE

SENTRY PEAK

This is a work of fiction. All the characters and events portrayed in this book are fictional, and any resemblance to real people or incidents is purely coincidental.

A Baen Books Original

Baen Publishing Enterprises
P.O. Box 1403
Riverdale, NY 10471
www.baen.com

ISBN: 0-671-31846-2

Cover art by Carol Heyer

First printing, November 2001

Library of Congress Cataloging-in-Publication Number 00-033722

Distributed by Simon & Schuster
1230 Avenue of the Americas
New York, NY 10020

Production by Windhaven Press, Auburn, NH
Printed in the United States of America

# PROLOGUE

Now it came to pass when Avram succeeded his father Buchan as King of Detina that those in the north would not accept his lordship, anointing his cousin, Grand Duke Geoffrey, as king in their lands. For Avram had declared even before old King Buchan died that he purposed freeing the serfs of Detina. The subtropic north was a land of broad estates, the nobles there taking the fruit of the labor of their fair-haired tenant farmers while returning unto the said serfs but a pittance. By contrast, merchants and smallholders filled the south: men who stood four-square behind Avram.

Declaring he had inherited the whole of Detina from King Buchan, Avram would not suffer Geoffrey

1

to rule unchallenged in the north, and sent armies dressed all in gray against him. Geoffrey, in his turn, raised hosts of his own, arraying them in blue made from the indigo much raised on northern estates that they might thus be distinguished from the southron men. Now Avram had the larger portion of the kingdom, and the wealthier, but Geoffrey's men were the bolder soldiers and, taken all in all, the better mages. And so the war raged for nigh unto three years, until Avram's general named Guildenstern moved against the northern army under Thraxton the Braggart, which held the town of Rising Rock close by Sentry Peak. . . .

# I

Sweat streamed down General Guildenstern's face. Hating the hot, muggy summer weather of the north, he took off his broad-brimmed gray hat and fanned himself with it. The unexpected motion spooked his unicorn, which sidestepped beneath him. "The gods curse you, you miserable creature," he growled, and fought the animal back under control. It took a little while; he knew he was something less than the best rider in King Avram's army. *But I hold the highest rank.* The warmth of the thought was far more pleasant than the warmth of the weather.

Beside him, Lieutenant General George shed his hat, too, and wiped his wet forehead with the sleeve of his gray tunic. *His* unicorn stayed quiet under him. Guildenstern noted that with a stab of resentment, as if it were a reproof of the way he handled his own

mount. He saw slights everywhere, whether they were
there or not. His thick, dark eyebrows came down
and together in a fearsome scowl.

Lieutenant General George squinted into the
westering sun, which glinted off the silver streaks in
his black beard. "Do you know, sir," he said, "now
that we've forded the river, I don't see how in the
seven hells old Thraxton's going to keep us from
running him out of Rising Rock."

Now Guildenstern's eyebrows leaped upward in
astonishment. His second-in-command was most often
known as Doubting George, sometimes even to his
face. He worried about everything. "That's . . . good
to hear," Guildenstern said cautiously. If Doubting
George thought Thraxton the Braggart couldn't hold
Rising Rock, he was very likely right.

And if by some mischance the army didn't take
Rising Rock even after Doubting George thought
the town ought to fall, who would get the blame?
Guildenstern knew the answer to that only too well.
*He* would, no one else. Not his second-in-command,
certainly.

He reached for the flask of brandy he wore on his
belt next to his sword. He took a long swig. Peaches
and fire ran down his throat. "Gods, that's good," he
rasped—another warmth obviously superior to the
local weather.

"Nothing better," Lieutenant General George
agreed, though he didn't carry a flask in the field.
He nodded to himself. "We're coming at Rising Rock
from three directions at once, and we outnumber
Thraxton about eight to five. If he doesn't fall back,
he won't have much to brag about once we're through
with him."

"Count Thraxton is a sorcerer of no small power."

Guildenstern knew every officer within earshot was listening for all he was worth. He didn't want any of his subordinates thinking the attack on Rising Rock would prove a walkover, just in case it turned out not to be.

"Oh, no doubt," Doubting George said. "But we gain on the northerners in wizardry, so we do, and the Braggart's spells have already gone awry a time or two in this war. I wouldn't fall over dead with surprise if it happened again."

Was he really as guileless as he seemed? Could anyone really be that guileless? *Or is he laying traps beneath my feet?* Guildenstern wondered. Had he been Doubting George's second-in-command, that was what he would have done. He took another swig of brandy. He trusted what he carried in his flask. That was more than he could say of the men who served under him.

*But I'm advancing*, he thought. *As long as I'm advancing, as long as I drive the traitors before me, no one can cast me down.*

A haze of dust hovered over his army, as it did over any army marching on roads that had never been corduroyed. Because of the red-tinged dust, Guildenstern couldn't see quite so far as he might have liked, but he could see far enough. The ordinary soldiers weren't out to betray him. He was . . . pretty sure of that.

Regiments of crossbowmen made up the biggest part of the army. Save that they wore King Avram's gray, many of them hardly looked like soldiers at all. They looked like what they were: butchers and bakers and chandeliermakers, tailors and toilers and fullers and boilers, grocers and farmers, woodsmen and goodsmen. Not for nothing did false King Geoffrey

and the rest of the northern bluebloods sneer at King
Avram's backers as a rabble of shopkeepers in arms.
Shopkeepers in arms they were. A rabble? In the first
year of the war, perhaps they had been. No more.
They'd never lacked for courage. Now they had discipline as well. The crossbow was an easy weapon
to learn, and could slay at long range. That they were
here, deep in the Province of Franklin whose lord
had declared for Geoffrey, spoke for itself.

A fair number of the heads under those identical
gray hats were blond, not dark. Serfs—former serfs,
rather—had been free to bear arms or take on any
other citizen's duties in most of the southron provinces for a couple of generations. That accounted for
some of the blonds in the ranks. Others had fled from
their northern overlords. Avram's orders were to ask
no questions of such men, but to turn them into soldiers if they said they wanted to fight.

Even through the dust the marching army raised,
the sun sparkled off serried ranks of steel spearheads.
Archers were hideously vulnerable if cavalry—or even
footsoldiers with pikes and mailshirts—got in among
them. Posting pikemen of one's own in front of them
forestalled such disasters.

General Guildenstern's smile turned as amiable as
it ever did when he surveyed the spearmen. Far fewer
blonds served among them. They were real soldiers—
professionals, not conscripts or zealots. If you told
a man who carried a pike to do something, he went
out and did it. He didn't ask why, or argue if he didn't
care for the answer.

The sun also gleamed from the iron-shod horns of
the unicorn cavalry. Guildenstern sighed. The riders
he commanded were far better at their trade than they
had been in the early days of Geoffrey's attempted

usurpation. They still had trouble matching their northern foes, for whom riding unicorns was a way of life, not a trade.

And, of course, unicorns bred best in the north. "I wonder why," General Guildenstern murmured.

"Why what, sir?" Doubting George asked.

"Why unicorns thrive better in the north than in our part of the kingdom," the army commander answered. "Hardly anyone up here is virgin past the age of twelve."

His second-in-command chuckled, but said, "That's just superstition, sir."

"I should hope so," Guildenstern growled. "If it weren't, every bloody one of our riders'd go on foot." He sent Lieutenant General George a baleful stare. Was the seemingly easygoing officer trying to undermine him by pointing out the obvious? When Doubting George muttered something under his breath, Guildenstern's ears quivered. "What was that?" he asked sharply.

"I said, 'The enemy is weak,' sir." Doubting George's voice was bland.

That wasn't what General Guildenstern thought he'd said. Gods knew it had sounded a lot more like "Unicorn Beak." Guildenstern's left hand came up to stroke his nose. It was of generous, even noble, proportions, yes, but no one had presumed to call him by that uncouth nickname since he'd graduated from the officers' collegium at Annasville. He'd hoped it was years forgotten.

Maybe he'd misheard. Maybe. He tried to make himself believe it.

Asses—unicorns' humbler cousins—hauled the wagons that kept the army fed and supplied. They also brought forward the stone-throwers and the dart-flingers that made the footsoldier's life so unpleasant in this war and that sometimes—when the gods chose to smile—made siegecraft move at something faster than a glacial pace.

A company's worth of men in long gray uniform robes also, to a man, rode asses. General Guildenstern's lip curled as his eye lit on them. "Why is it," he demanded of no one in particular, "that we can't find a wizard— not a single bloody wizard—who knows what to do when he climbs on a unicorn?"

"I don't much care about that, sir," Doubting George said. "What I want to know is, why can't we find a single bloody wizard who knows what to do when he opens a grimoire?"

"Demons take them all," Guildenstern muttered. That was, of course, part of the problem. Demons *had* taken a couple of southron wizards in the early days of the war. Down in the south, mages were more used to using sorcery in business than in battle, and military magic was a very different game, as the elegant and arrogant sorcerers who served Grand Duke Geoffrey had proved several times.

"We do need them," Lieutenant General George said with a sigh. "They are up to holding off some of what the enemy's wizards throw at us."

"Some," Guildenstern granted grudgingly. He kept on glaring over toward the mages, though. As if his gaze had weight, it drew the notice of a couple of them. He would have taken pride in the power of his personality . . . had he not misliked the way they looked back at him. Like any man of sense, he wore an apotropaic amulet on a chain around his neck. His left hand stroked it, as if reminding it to do its job. Measured against the mages who fought for Geoffrey, most of King Avram's wizards were less than they might have been. Measured against a man who was a soldier and not himself a mage, they remained intimidating.

Doubting George said, "I wonder what sort of hellsfire Count Thraxton's cooking up over there in Rising Rock."

Now General Guildenstern glared at him. "You were the one who said his spells kept going wrong. Have you changed your mind all at once?"

"Oh, no, sir." His second-in-command shook his head. "I think we'll lick him right out of his boots." Yes, he could afford to be confident; he wouldn't have to explain what had gone wrong if the army failed. "But it's always interesting to try and figure out what the whoresons on the other side'll throw at us, don't you think?"

"Interesting." It wasn't the word Guildenstern would have used. Rather to his relief, he was spared having to figure out *which* word he would have used, for a scout came riding toward him, waving to be noticed. More often than not, Guildenstern would have let the fellow wait. Now he waved back and called, "What's your news?"

Saluting, the young rider answered, "Sir, some of our pickets have run the traitors out of Whiteside. The little garrison they had there is falling back toward Rising Rock."

"Splendid." Guildenstern brought a fist down on his thigh in solid satisfaction. "I'll spend the night there, then." The scout saluted again and galloped back off toward the west, no doubt to warn the men who'd taken the hamlet to have ready a lodging suitable for the army commander.

They didn't do a perfect job. One of Grand Duke Geoffrey's banners—red dragon on gold—still floated above Whiteside when General Guildenstern rode in as the sun was setting. At his snarled order, troopers hastily replaced it with Detina's proper ensign— gold dragon on red. The general doffed his hat to the kingdom's banner before dismounting and striding into the village's best, and only, inn.

The innkeeper served up a decent roast capon and a tolerable bottle of white wine. He'd likely favored Geoffrey over Avram, but did a fair job of hiding it. By their blond hair and blue eyes, both the serving wenches who brought Guildenstern his supper were serfs, or rather had been till his army entered Whiteside. The wine—and, no doubt, the brandy he'd put away before—left the general feeling expansive. Beaming at the wenches, he asked them, "And how do you like your freedom?"

"Oh!" they exclaimed together, like characters in a comedy. Their names were Lindy and Vetty; Guildenstern wasn't quite sure which was which. Whichever the younger and prettier one was, she said, "Hadn't thought about it much, your lordship, sir. I guess it'll be pretty good—money of our own and all, I mean."

By his scowl, the innkeeper didn't think it would be so good. Now he'd have to pay them wages instead of hiring them from whichever local noble controlled their families. "Freedom," Guildenstern said, quoting King Avram, "is worth the price."

He wasn't altogether sure he believed that; he'd never had any great liking for yellow-hairs himself. But he enjoyed throwing it in the innkeeper's face and watching the fellow have to paste on a smile and pretend he agreed. "Just as you say, General," he replied, as if each word tasted bad.

"Just as I say?" Guildenstern echoed complacently. "Well, of course."

When the innkeeper took him up to his bed-chamber over the dining hall, he found it a rough match for the supper he'd had: not splendid, but good enough. "Won't find anything finer this side of Rising Rock," the innkeeper said.

"No doubt." Guildenstern's voice was dry; there weren't any more towns between Whiteside and Rising Rock. But he put that out of his mind, for something else was in it: "Send me up the prettier of your girls, the one with the freckles, to warm my bed tonight."

"With the freckles? That's Lindy." The innkeeper's smile went from deferential to rather nasty. "Can't just send her up, now can I, sir? Not if she's free, I should say. She'll have to decide all by herself if she wants to come up here."

"By the gods!" General Guildenstern exploded. "That's taking things too far, don't you think?" The innkeeper just stood there. "Oh, all right," Guildenstern said with poor grace. "*Ask* her, then."

He wondered if he'd made a mistake. If the girl said no, he would never live it down. But Lindy knocked on his door a few minutes later. As soon as he closed it behind her, she pulled her shift off over her head. Guildenstern enjoyed himself. If she didn't, she was a reasonably good actress.

Afterwards, she leaned up on one elbow beside him, so that the soft, pink tip of her bare breast poked him in the shoulder. "You trounce our lords," she said earnestly. "Trounce 'em good, and every blond girl in the kingdom'll open her legs for you."

"One more reason to win," Guildenstern said, and caught her to him again.

If Count Thraxton had ever been happy in all his born days, his face didn't know it. He was tall and

thin and lean, beard and mustache and eyebrows
going gray. His features might have come from one
of the masks tragic actors wore so even people in the
highest rows of the amphitheater could see what they
were supposed to be feeling. His eyes were large and
dark and gloomy, the eyes of a sorrowing hound.
Harsh lines of grief scored his cheeks. His thin-lipped
mouth perpetually turned down at the corners.

He'd looked mournful at his wedding, to one of
the loveliest and wealthiest women in all of Detina.
He'd looked mournful after their wedding night (wags
said she had, too, but never where he could hear
them: along with his skill at magecraft, he was uncommonly good with a sword). Now, with real disaster
looming up from the south and east, he looked no
worse—but no better, either.

A servant—a serf, of course—came up behind
Thraxton, his footsteps obsequiously soft. "Supper is
ready, your Grace," he murmured. "The others have
already taken their places."

They hadn't presumed to start eating without
Thraxton. He wondered how long even that minimal
courtesy would last. Not long, unless he started winning victories against the rabble of merchants and
peasants who fought for scapegrace Avram and not
Geoffrey—a man who, by the gods, knew *how* to be
king. But Thraxton saw no victories around Rising
Rock—only the choice between losing another battle
and abandoning northwestern Franklin without a
fight.

His stomach knotted. How was he supposed to eat,
faced with such a dismal choice? But not appearing
would only affront the generals who served under
him. He nodded to the hovering serf: a sharp,
brusque motion. "I'm coming," he said.

His subordinates sprang to their feet when he strode into the dining room. All three of them bowed low. "Your Grace!" they chorused.

"Gentlemen." Thraxton returned the bow, not quite so deeply. He sat down in the empty chair at the head of the table. Once he was comfortable, the other officers sat down again, too.

"May I pour you some wine, your Grace?" asked Leonidas the Priest, who sat at Thraxton's right hand. Instead of the blue tunic and pantaloons that uniformed Geoffrey's men, Leonidas wore the crimson vestments of a hierophant of the Lion God, with a general's sunburst over each shoulder. Not only did he worship his chosen deity, he fed him well.

"Blood of the grape," Thraxton said, and Leonidas smiled and nodded. Thraxton nodded, too. "If you would be so kind." Maybe wine would let him see something he couldn't see sober. Maybe, at the very least, it would help ease his griping belly.

On Thraxton's left, Baron Dan of Rabbit Hill filled his own goblet with red wine. He was younger than either Thraxton or Leonidas, and waxed the tip of his beard and the ends of his mustache to points, as if he were a town dandy. Fop or not, though, he made a first-rate fighting man. Dan offered the bottle to the officer at the foot of the table, who commanded Thraxton's unicorns. "Some for you, General?"

"No, thanks," Ned of the Forest answered. "Water'll do me just fine." The harsh twang of the northeast filled his voice. Thraxton wasn't altogether sure he could read or write; one of his lieutenants always prepared the reports he submitted. He was a gentleman only by courtesy of his rank, not by blood. Before the war, he'd been a gambler and a serfcatcher, and highly successful at both trades. Since the fighting broke out, he'd proved nobody could match him or his troopers—most of them as much ruffians as he was, not proper knights at all—on unicornback.

Baron Dan withdrew the wine bottle. Leonidas the Priest clapped his hands a couple of times in smiling amusement. "Any man who drinks water from birth and lives," he observed, "is bound to do great things, much like one who survives snakebite."

"Oh, I got bit by a snake once," Ned said. "Any snake bites me, *it* dies."

He might have meant he killed snakes with his knife or with a boot. By the way he made it sound, though, he thought his blood more poisonous than any venom. And he might have been right. He was the biggest man at the table, and without a doubt the strongest. His face was handsome, in a hard, weathered way. His eyes . . . His eyes worried even Thraxton, who had seen a great deal. They were hard and black and unyielding as polished jet. *A killer's eyes*, Thraxton thought.

A lot of men were killers, of course. The world was a hard, cruel place. But most men pretended otherwise. Ned of the Forest didn't bother.

The serf who'd led Thraxton in began carving the pork roast that sat in the middle of the table. He also served Geoffrey's commanders baked tubers. Thraxton, Leonidas, and Dan ate in the approved manner, lingering over their food and chatting lightly of this and that. Ned's manners proved he'd been born in a barn. He attacked his food as if he were a wolf devouring a deer he'd pulled down. In an astonishingly short time, his plate was empty. He didn't bother asking the serf for a second helping. Instead, he stood up, leaned forward to grab the knife, and hacked off another big slab of meat. He slapped it down on the plate and demolished it with the same dispatch he'd shown at the first helping.

"A man of appetite," Dan of Rabbit Hill said, more admiringly than not. He waved to the serf, who gave him a second helping about half the size of Ned's.

"We are all men of appetite," Leonidas said with another smile. "Some have a passion for spirituous liquors, some for the ladies, some for our meats, some for arcane knowledge and enlightenment." He inclined his head to Count Thraxton, who acknowledged the compliment with another of his curt nods.

"This here is just supper," Ned said, helping himself to still more pork. He took a big bite, then went on with his mouth full: "What I've got me an appetite for—a passion for, if you like—is killing those stinking southrons who reckon they've got some call to come up here and take our serfs away."

"That is well said," Thraxton murmured, raising his wine goblet in salute.

Had he been dealing with another proper gentleman, the lower-ranking officer would have drunk wine with him and graciously changed the subject. Ned of the Forest did not drink wine and had few graces. Staring across the table at Thraxton, he demanded, "Then why did we let those sons of bitches run us out of Wesleyton, southwest of here? Why are they running us out of Rising Rock, too?"

Leonidas the Priest coughed. Turning to Thraxton, he said, "What the distinguished soldier commanding the unicorns meant was—"

"I said what I meant," Ned ground out. "I want a proper answer, too." Those black, black eyes of his held Count Thraxton's.

*He is trying to put me in fear*, Thraxton realized. Ned wasn't doing a bad job of it, either, though the army commander refused to show that. Thraxton said, "The unfortunate truth, sir, is that General Guildenstern commands more soldiers than I do. We shall withdraw—I see no other choice—regroup, and strike back toward Rising Rock as opportunity permits."

"Guildenstern's got more men than we do, sure enough." Ned nodded. "That's *an* unfortunate truth, no doubt about it. Way it looks to me, though, *the* unfortunate truth is that nobody figured out what in the seven hells the bastard was up to till after he got his whole army over the Franklin River and started coming straight at us, and that was a lot too late." He snapped his fingers. "So much for all your fancy magic. Sir."

"Really, General." Leonidas wagged a finger at Ned of the Forest. "You forget yourself."

Thraxton waited for Dan of Rabbit Hill to come to his defense against the border ruffian, too. Baron Dan sat staring at his goblet as if he'd never seen such a thing before. He said not a word. From his abstracted silence, Count Thraxton concluded he agreed with Ned.

Realizing he would have to speak for himself, Thraxton said, "I confess, I thought Guildenstern would turn north after crossing the river instead of making straight for us. Perhaps I let myself be distracted by the enemy's demonstration toward Wesleyton."

"Demonstration?" Ned made the word into a reproach. "What they demonstrated was, we couldn't hold the place."

Leonidas the Priest and Dan looked at each other. Then they looked at Thraxton. And then they looked at Ned. After coughing a couple of times, Leonidas said, "What Ned meant was—"

"I said what I meant," Ned repeated. "We didn't hold Wesleyton, and we aren't going to hold Rising Rock. And it's a shame and a disgrace that we aren't, if anybody wants to know what I think." He stared straight into Thraxton's eyes again.

Thraxton glared back. His temper was slower to kindle than Ned of the Forest's, but it burned hot when it did catch fire. "Now you see here, young man," he growled. "We may have lost Wesleyton. We may lose Rising Rock, and in part that may even be my fault. But I tell you this." He pointed a forefinger across the table at Ned, and his voice rose to a shout: "We may have to fall back now. But we *will* take back Rising Rock. We *will* take back Wesleyton. We will! *My* army will! And that's not all. We *will* rout General Guildenstern and the invaders out of Franklin. And we *will* rout them out of Cloviston south of here, too. We'll push them over the River and back among the rabble of robbers who sent them forth. By all the gods, we *will*! *My* army!" He slammed down his fist. Silverware jumped on the linen. Wine jumped in the goblets.

Dan of Rabbit Hill's lips shaped a word. He didn't speak it out loud, but Thraxton, among his other arcane skills, had learned to read lips. He knew what that silent word was. Dan might as well have shouted it. *Braggart.*

King Avram's men called him Thraxton the Braggart. He'd sworn a great oath to beat them at Pottstown Pier, back when the war was young. He'd sworn it . . . and events—bad luck, really; nothing more—had left him forsworn. He'd chased Guildenstern back into the Province of Cloviston, chased him almost to the Highlow River, and sworn an even greater oath to drive him out of Geoffrey's realm altogether. He'd sworn that second oath . . . but the hard battles of Reppyton and Reillyburgh, somehow, had gone no better for his cause and Geoffrey's despite the savage sorceries he'd loosed.

Braggart? He shook his head. He didn't see himself so. If anything, he felt put upon, put upon by fate and by the blundering idiots it was his misfortune to have to endure as subordinates. *If only I led men worthy of me*, he thought. *Then everyone would know me for the hero I know I am.*

Meanwhile . . . Meanwhile, Ned of the Forest stared steadily back across the table at him. "All right, your Grace," the backwoods ruffian said. "Remember you said that. I aim to hold you to it."

*Arrogant dog*, Thraxton thought. He muttered to himself. Not all sorcery was showy. Not all of it required elaborate preparation, either. He waited for Ned to leap up and run for the commode. The spell he'd just cast would have kept a normal man trotting for a couple of days.

But Ned of the Forest only sat where he was. For all the effect the magic had on him, he might have been carved from stone. Thraxton ran over the spell in his mind. He'd cast it correctly. He was sure of that. *He's been drinking water all his life*, he remembered. *His bowels might as well be made of cast bronze.*

*His head, too.* That piece of malice helped ease Thraxton's bile-filled spirit. So did the words of Leonidas the Priest: "So long as we all stand together, we *shall* drive Guildenstern back into the southron darkness whence he sprang. Rest assured, the Lion God will eat his soul." He made a certain sign with his fingers.

Thraxton, who was an initiate in those mysteries, made the answering gesture. So did Dan. Ned of the

Forest kept on stolidly sitting. Scorn filled Thraxton. *But why should I be surprised? The gods must hate him.*

The serf brought in a honey cake piled high with plums and peaches and apricots. "A sweet, my lords?"

Count Thraxton took a small helping, more for politeness' sake than any other reason. Dan of Rabbit Hill and Leonidas matched him. Ned attacked the honey cake with the same gusto he'd shown with the pork roast. "Sir, you have crumbs in your beard," Leonidas remarked after a while.

"Thank you kindly," Ned replied, and brushed at his chin whiskers—a surprisingly neat adornment—with rough, callused fingers.

"How is it," Thraxton asked, "that your whiskers remain black while your hair is going gray?" Did fearsome Ned of the Forest resort to the dye bottle? If he did, would he admit it? If he didn't admit it, what clumsy lie would he tell? How ridiculous would he look in telling it?

Ned's smile was the one Thraxton might have seen over dueling sabers. But the ruffian's voice was light and mild as he answered, "Well, Count, I reckon it's likely on account of I use my brains more than my mouth."

Silence fell in the dining room, silence broken only by the serf's smothered guffaw. Thraxton turned a terrible look on the fellow, who first blushed all the way up to his pale hair, then went paler than that hair himself and precipitately fled.

"Any more questions, sir?" Ned asked with another carnivorous grin.

"Enough!" That wasn't Thraxton. He said nothing, reckoning Ned of the Forest would not listen to him if he did. But Dan of Rabbit Hill's voice commanded attention. Then Dan said, "Enough, the both of you."

"Sir?" Thraxton sounded winter-cold, the cold of a bad winter. "Do you presume to include me?"

"I do," Dan said stubbornly. "If you get people quarreling with you—if we quarrel among ourselves—who wins? Avram the serf-stealer and the stinking southrons, that's who. Nobody else but."

"You're right," Ned said at once. "I'll let it lay where it's at. Count?"

"Very well." But Thraxton's voice remained frigid. It might not have, had Dan phrased his request a little differently. King Avram was the worst foe, true. But that did not mean no wretches, no enemies, marched behind King Geoffrey. And now Dan of Rabbit Hill had chosen to add himself to that list. *Your time will come, Dan*, Thraxton thought, *yours and Ned's and everyone's.*

"Up, you lazy sons of bitches!" somebody shouted. "Think you're going to sleep all bloody day? Not bloody likely, let me tell you."

Rollant's eyes flew open in something close to panic. For a horrid moment, he thought he was back on the indigo plantation outside of Karlsburg, and that the overseer would stick a boot in his ribs if he didn't head out for the swampy fields on the dead run.

Then the escaped serf let out a sigh of relief as full awareness returned. His pantaloons and tunic were dyed gray, not the blue of the indigo he'd slaved to grow. The traitors wore blue, not King Avram's men. And that wasn't the overseer screaming at him, only his sergeant. As a matter of fact, Sergeant Joram had more power over him than the overseer ever had, but Rollant didn't mind. When he joined Avram's host, he'd chosen to come under the rule of men like Joram. He'd never chosen to do as his one-time northern liege lord and overseer told him to do. He'd expressed his opinion of that relationship by fleeing to the south the first chance he got—and then again, after the serfcatchers ran him down with dogs and hauled him back to his liege lord's estate.

All around him, his squadmates were stirring and stretching and yawning and rubbing their eyes, as he was doing. Sergeant Joram roared at them as loudly as he roared at Rollant, though their hair was dark. Joram treated everyone like a serf—or rather, like a free man in the army.

No, Rollant hadn't had to join King Avram's host to return to the north country to make war against the baron who'd chained him to the land—that was how he thought of the fight, in purely personal terms. He'd been making pretty good money as a carpenter down in New Eborac. He'd married a pretty blond girl he met there; her family had escaped feudal ties a couple of generations before. They had two towheaded children.

Norina had wept when he took King Avram's silver bit. "I have to," he told her. "Geoffrey and the northern nobles are trying to make sure we never get our place in the sun."

His wife hadn't understood. He knew that. Norina took for granted the freedom to go where she wanted when she wanted and do whatever she pleased once she got there. Why not? She'd enjoyed it all her life. Rollant hadn't, which made him realize exactly how precious it was.

Right now, that freedom consisted of standing in line along with a lot of other poorly shaved, indifferently clean men and snaking toward the big brass kettles

hung above three fires. When Rollant got up to the fire
to which his line led, a bored-looking cook slapped a
ladleful of stew down on his tin plate. Rollant eyed it
with distaste: barley boiled to death, mushy carrots,
and bits of meat whose origin he probably didn't want
to know. He'd eaten better back on the baron's estate.

"You want pheasant and asparagus, blond boy, you
pay for 'em out of your own pocket," the cook growled.
Rollant went off and sat on the ground to eat. The
cook snarled at the dark-haired fellow behind him, too.

One of Rollant's squadmates, a youngster named
Smitty, sat down beside him. He ate a spoonful of
the stew and made a face. "The crocodile they threw
in the stewpot died of old age," he said.

"Crocodile?" For a heartbeat or two, Rollant
thought Smitty meant it. His horizons had expanded
enormously since he'd escaped his liege lord, and
even more since Norina taught him his letters, but
he remained hideously vulnerable to having his leg
pulled by men who'd been free to learn since birth.
He took another spoonful himself. "Just a dead jack-
ass, I think, or maybe one of the barons who live up
here."

Smitty grinned at him. "Bet you'd like to see every
traitor noble from Grand Duke Geoffrey on down
boiling in a pot."

"That's what we're here for," Rollant said simply.

"And to keep the kingdom from breaking in two,"
Smitty said. "If Geoffrey gets away with this, Detinans'll
be fighting wars among themselves forever."

"I suppose so." But Rollant couldn't get very excited
about the idea. Smashing the nobles who held down
serfs like him—that was something he understood in
his belly.

He went down to a little stream to rinse his tin

plate, then stuck it in the knapsack in which he carried most of his earthly goods. Along with the meager contents of the knapsack, he had a shortsword on his right hip (he always hoped not to have to use it, for he knew nothing of swordplay but hack, swing, and hope for the best), a quiver full of crossbow quarrels, and the crossbow itself.

He patted that crossbow as he took his place in the ranks for the day's march toward Rising Rock. It was a splendid weapon. All you had to do was pull to cock it, drop in a quarrel, aim, and squeeze the trigger. Thousands of flying crossbow bolts made battlefields very unhealthy places for unicorns—and for the men who rode them. A quarrel would punch right through a shield, right through chain, and right through plate, too.

Smitty came up to stand beside him. "Did you ever shoot one of these things before you joined the host?" Rollant asked.

"On my father's farm, sure—you know, hunting for the pot," Smitty answered. "How about you?"

Rollant shook his head. "Never once. Northern nobles don't want serfs knowing how easy crossbows are to use. They're afraid we'd find out how easy they are to kill. And do you know what?" He grinned a ferocious grin. "They're right."

"Why do you say 'we'?" Smitty asked. "You're not a serf any more. You haven't been one for a while."

"That's true," Rollant said in some surprise. "But it's not just something you can forget you ever were, either." The way he talked proved as much. Having grown up tied to his liege lord's land had marked him for life—scarred him for life, he often thought.

Sergeant Joram strutted up in front of the men. "Let's go!" he boomed. "Next stop is Rising Rock."

Rollant cheered at that. So did most of the soldiers with him. They all knew Geoffrey and his forces couldn't afford to lose the town. They all knew he couldn't keep it, either, not with the small army he had there. Joram went on, "Any traitors get in our way, we smash 'em into the mud and march over 'em. That's all I've got to say about that."

More cheers rose. Rollant yelled till his throat hurt. The chance to smash the men who'd mistreated him was all he wanted. He'd dreamt of revenge for years, ever since he fled the north for New Eborac. In a way, he was almost grateful to Geoffrey and the other high lords who were trying to carve their own kingdom from the flesh of Detina. If they hadn't, he might never have got the chance to hit back.

Thin in the distance, trumpets blared at the head of the column. As with an uncoiling snake beginning to crawl, that head began to move before the tail. Rollant's company was somewhere near the middle. He breathed the dust the men ahead of him kicked up marching along the dirt road, and his feet and his comrades' raised more dust for the men behind them. His toes wiggled inside his stout marching boots. He'd rarely worn boots, or shoes of any kind, on Baron Ormerod's estate near Karlsburg.

Through the haze of reddish dust, Sentry Peak punctuated the skyline to the northwest. Most of the countryside hereabouts was pretty flat; were it otherwise, Sentry Peak would have been named Sentry Knob or some such, or perhaps wouldn't have been named at all. Rising Rock lay by the foot of the mountain. West of Rising Rock swelled the lower elevation of Proselytizers' Rise, named after the bold souls who'd preached about their gods when Detina was first being colonized from the west. Rollant's early relatives hadn't cared to listen; they'd had gods of their own, and the proselytizers had got no farther than the rise.

Rollant knew the names of the gods his forefathers had worshiped, and some of their attributes. He believed in them, but didn't worship them himself. The settlers' gods had proved themselves stronger.

*And so has our southron army*, he thought. Most of the war had been fought in the traitors' lands. They'd mounted a couple of invasions of the south, but had been beaten back each time. When Rising Rock fell, they'd be driven out of Franklin altogether. Rollant's hands tightened on the crossbow he carried. He wanted the northern nobles to pay for everything they'd done.

Where was his own liege lord? Somewhere in one of Geoffrey's armies—Rollant was sure of that. Baron Ormerod wouldn't be a great marshal; he hadn't owned estates wide enough for that, and he was no mighty mage. But he was convinced the gods said he had the right to keep serfs on the land whether they wanted to stay there or not.

A farmer looked up from the field he was cultivating as Rollant's company marched past. He was old and stooped with endless years of labor; otherwise he probably would have been fighting for Geoffrey, too. Shaking his fist at the men in gray, he shouted, "By the seven hells, why don't you sons of bitches get on home and leave us alone? We never done nothing to you."

Rollant pushed his way to the edge of the company so the farmer could see him. "Say that again!" he called to the northern man. "Go ahead—try and make me believe it. I could use a good laugh."

"You!" The fellow shook his fist again. "Wasn't for

your kind, we wouldn't have no trouble. I hope the Lion God bites your balls off, you stinking runaway."

Rollant started to bring up his bow and pull back the string, then checked himself and laughed instead. "What's funny?" Smitty asked him. "Nobody would've blamed you for shooting that bugger."

"I was just thinking—he hasn't got any serfs of his own," Rollant answered. "He couldn't dream of a farm big enough to work with serfs. Look at his homespun tunic. Look at those miserable pantaloons—out at the knees, a patch on the arse. But he thinks he's a duke because his hair is brown."

"A lot of these northerners think like that," Smitty said. "If they didn't, Grand Duke Geoffrey would have to fight the war by himself, because nobody would follow him."

"Conquerors," Rollant muttered darkly. His own people had had real kingdoms in the north when the Detinans landed on the coast. They'd had bronze spearheads and ass-drawn chariots—which hadn't kept them from going down to defeat before the iron-armored, unicorn-riding invaders, whose magecraft had proved more potent, too. In the south, blonds had been thinner on the ground, and more easily and thoroughly caught up in the kingdom that grew around them.

Such musings vanished from his head when a troop of unicorns ridden by men in blue burst out of the pine woods behind the farmer's fields and thundered toward his company. "Geoffrey!" the riders roared as their mounts galloped over and doubtless ruined the crops of the northerner with the ragged pantaloons and the lordly attitude.

General Guildenstern's army had unicorn-riders, too. They were supposed to keep enemy cavalry off

King Avram's footsoldiers. But Geoffrey's riders had proved better all through the war. They looked likely to be better here, for no gray-clad men on unicorn-back were in position to get between them and Rollant and his companions.

"In line to the right flank! Two ranks!" shouted Captain Cephas, the company commander. "Shoot as you find your mark—no time for volleys."

Close by, another officer was yelling, "Pikemen forward! Hurry, curse you! Get in front of those uni-corns!"

The pikemen did hurry. But the troop of riders had chosen their moment well. Rollant could see that the pikemen wouldn't get there fast enough.

Because he'd gone over to the side of the road to shout at the farmer, he was among the cross-bowmen closest to the on-thundering unicorns. That put him in the first rank. He dropped to one knee so his comrades in the second rank could shoot over him. Then it was the drill swearing sergeants had pounded into him: yank back the crossbow string, lay the quarrel in the groove, bring the weapon to his shoulder, aim along the two iron studs set into the stock, pull the trigger.

The crossbow bucked against his shoulder. Other triggers all around him clicked, too. A unicorn crashed to the ground. Another fell over it, sending its rider flying. A northerner threw up his hands and slid off his mount's tail, thudding to the ground as bonelessly as a sack of lentils. A wounded unicorn screamed and reared.

But most of the troop came on. They smashed past the pikemen before the wall of spearheads could fully form. Rollant had time for only two shots before he had to throw down his crossbow and snatch out his sword. He might not be very good with it, but if it wouldn't save his life, nothing would.

A unicorn's horn spitted the crossbowman beside him. The fellow on the unicorn slashed at Rollant with his saber. Rollant got his own sword up just in time to turn the blow. Sparks flew as iron belled off iron. The unicorn pressed on. When the northerner slashed again, it was at someone else. He laid a crossbowman's face open, and shouted in triumph as the fellow shrieked.

Rollant stabbed the unicorn in the hindquarters. Its scream was shrill as a woman's. It reared, blood pouring from the wound. While the rider, taken by surprise, tried to fight it back under control, Rollant stabbed him, too, in the thigh. More blood spurted, astonishingly red. Rollant could smell the blood. That iron stink put him in mind of butchering day on Ormerod's estate. The rider bellowed like a just-castrated bullock. Then a pikeman ran up and thrust him through from behind. Ever so slowly, he toppled from his mount.

Surviving northerners broke free of the press and galloped away. King Avram's unicorns came up just in time to chase them as they went. Smitty said, "They paid a price today, by the gods." He had a cut over one eye, and didn't seem to know it.

"That they did." Rollant rammed his shortsword into the ground to clean off the blood. Baron Ormerod had always screamed at his serfs to take care of their—his—ironmongery. Rollant looked at the bodies strewn like broken dolls, and at the groaning wounded helped by their comrades and by the healers. Even as he watched, a healer cut the throat of a southron too terribly gashed and torn to hope to recover. "They paid a price, sure enough," Rollant said. "But so did we."

✧   ✧   ✧

General James of Broadpath was a belted earl. The northern noble needed a good deal of belt to span his own circumference, and had to ride a unicorn that would otherwise have made a career of hauling great jars of wine from hither to yon. Despite his girth, though, he'd proved a gifted soldier; few of the commanders who fought under the Duke of Arlington had done more to keep Avram's larger host from rampaging through the province of Parthenia and laying siege to Nonesuch, the town in which Grand Duke Geoffrey— no, King Geoffrey—had established his capital.

*With a little more luck*, James thought, *just a little more, mind you, we would have been laying siege to Georgetown, and hanging Avram from the flagpole in front of the Black Palace. We came close.* Sighing, he stroked his beard, which spilled in curly dark ringlets halfway down his broad chest. *Close* counted even less in war than any other time.

Now the struggle in Parthenia seemed stalemated. However much mead the southron commander swilled, he'd beaten back Edward of Arlington's invasion of the south and followed him into Geoffrey's territory when he had to retreat. Neither army, at the moment, was up to doing much.

Which meant . . . Earl James studied the map pinned down to the folding table in his silk pavilion. He rumbled something down deep in his chest. His beard and soup-strainer mustache so muffled it, even he couldn't make out the words. That might have been just as well.

He shook his head. He knew better. And what he knew had to be said, however unpalatable it might prove when it came out in the open.

Muttering still, he left the tent and stepped out into

the full muggy heat of late summer in Parthenia. He'd
known worse—he'd been born farther north, in Palmetto Province—but that didn't mean he enjoyed this.
No one of his build could possibly enjoy summer in
Parthenia.

The sentries in front of Duke Edward's pavilion
(rather plainer than James'; Edward cared little about
comfort, while the Earl of Broadpath relished it) stiffened into upright immobility when they saw James
drawing near. Returning their salutes, he asked, "Is
the duke in?"

"Yes, your Excellency," they chorused. One ducked
into the pavilion. He returned a moment later, followed by Duke Edward.

James came to attention and tried to make his
chest stick out farther than his belly—a losing effort.
Saluting, he said, "Good evening, sir."

"And a good evening to you as well, your Excellency," Edward of Arlington replied. In his youth,
he was said to have been the handsomest man in
Detina. These days, his neat white beard proved
him nearer sixty than fifty, but he remained a
striking figure: tall and straight and, unlike Earl
James of Broadpath, slim. "What can I do for you
today?"

"Your Grace, I've been looking at the map," James
said.

Duke Edward nodded. "Always a commendable
exercise." Back in the days before war broke Detina
in two, he'd headed the officers' collegium at
Annasville for a time. Even before then, he'd been
known as a soldier who fought with his head as well
as his heart. Now he went on, "Perhaps you'll come
in with me and show me what you've seen."

"Thank you, sir. I was hoping to do just that,"

James said. Duke Edward held the tentflap wide for him with his own hands—till one of the sentries, scandalized that he should do such menial service, took the cloth from him. Grunting a little, James bent at what had been his waist and ducked his way into the pavilion.

A couple of rock-oil lamps burned within, one by Edward's table, the other next to his iron-framed camp bed. The stink of the oil made James' nostrils twitch. The sight of the camp bed made him wince. He wouldn't have cared to try to sleep in anything so . . . uncompromising. Not for the first time, Duke Edward put him in mind of a military saint: not a common breed in Detinan history. James, never modest about his own achievements, reckoned himself a pretty fair soldier, but he was willing to admit sainthood beyond him.

Putting on a pair of gold-framed spectacles, Edward said, "And what have you seen, your Excellency? I presume it pertains to our army?"

"Well, no, sir, or not directly," Earl James answered, and his superior raised a curious eyebrow, inviting him to continue. He did: "I don't expect we'll be doing much fighting here in southern Parthenia for the rest of this campaigning season."

"That has something to do with what the mead-swiller who commands Avram's army has in mind," Edward observed, "but, on the whole, I believe you are likely to prove correct. What of it?"

"We're hard pressed in the east, your Grace," James said. "By all reports, Count Thraxton will have to fall back from Rising Rock, and that's a heavy loss. We've already lost Wesleyton, and Ramblerton and Luxor fell early in the war. Without any toehold at all in the province of Franklin, how can we hope to win?"

"Sometimes the gods give us difficulties to see how we surmount them," Duke Edward said.

As far as James was concerned, that was more pious than helpful. He said, "By himself, I don't see how Thraxton *can* surmount this difficulty. He hasn't got enough men to hope to beat General Guildenstern. Who was it who said the gods love the big battalions? Some foreigner or other."

"A gloomy maxim, and one we have done our best to disprove here in Parthenia—but, I fear, one with some truth in it even so," the duke said. "Do you have in mind some way to get around it?"

"I hope so, sir," James replied. "If you could send my army and me to the east, we would be enough to bring Count Thraxton up close to even in numbers with the accursed southrons. If we match them in numbers, we can beat them on the battlefield." He spoke with great conviction.

Duke Edward frowned—and, in frowning, did indeed look a great deal like a sorrowing saint. "I should hate to weaken the Army of Southern Parthenia to the extent you suggest. If that mead-swiller should bestir himself, we'd be hard pressed to stand against him."

"I do understand that, your Grace," James of Broadpath persisted. "But he seems content to stay where he is for the time being, while Guildenstern presses Thraxton hard. If he weren't pressing the Braggart hard, our army wouldn't have to pull out of Rising Rock."

Edward of Arlington's frown deepened. Maybe he didn't care to hear Count Thraxton's nickname spoken openly. Or maybe, and perhaps more likely, he just wasn't used to anyone presuming to disagree with him. King Geoffrey was admired in the northern realm. Duke Edward was admired, loved, almost worshiped. Had he wanted the crown, he could have had it. He'd never shown the least interest. Even Geoffrey, who mistrusted his own shadow, trusted Edward.

Earl James trusted Edward, too. But he didn't believe Edward was always right. Usually—no doubt of that. But not always.

"Holding our army between the southrons and Nonesuch is the most important thing we can do," Edward said.

Most of the duke's subordinates would have given up in the face of such a flat statement. James, perhaps, had a larger notion of his own self-worth. Or perhaps he'd simply spent too long brooding over the maps in his own pavilion. He stuck out his chins and said, "Your Grace, we can lose the war here in Parthenia, yes. But we can also lose it in the east. If Franklin falls, if the southrons flood through the gaps in the mountains and storm up through Peachtree Province toward Marthasville—well, how do we go on with them in our heartland?"

"Surely Count Thraxton's men and his magecraft may be relied upon to prevent any such disaster," Duke Edward said stiffly.

"If Count Thraxton were as fine a soldier as the king thinks he is, if he were as fine a wizard as *he* thinks he is, he wouldn't be falling back into Peachtree Province now," James replied. "He'd have Guildenstern on the run instead."

One of Edward's gray eyebrows rose again. "It would appear you are determined to do this thing, your Excellency."

"I am, your Grace," James said.

"You do realize that, even if you were sent to the

east, you would serve under Count Thraxton, he being of higher rank than you," Edward said.

*You would serve under the man you've just called a blunderer*, was what he meant, though he was too gracious to say any such thing. James of Broadpath sighed. "The good of the kingdom comes first," he declared. "It is my duty" —*my accursed, unpleasant duty*— "to serve its needs before mine."

And there, for the first time in the conversation, he touched a chord with Duke Edward, who bowed to him and said, "Duty is the sublimest word in Detinan. You cannot do more than your duty. Prepare a memorial proposing this move, and I shall submit it to his Majesty with the recommendation that it be approved."

"Thank you, your Grace," James replied, bowing in return. He wondered why he was thanking the duke. Serving under Edward was sometimes humbling but more often a pleasure and always an education. Serving under Thraxton, by everything James had heard, was an invitation to an apoplexy. Hesitantly, he said, "Tell me it isn't true, sir, that Count Thraxton once picked a quarrel with himself."

"I believe that, as regimental quartermaster, he refused to issue himself something to which, as company commander, he believed himself entitled," Edward said—which meant it *was* true.

James grimaced. "I wish the king would have found someone, anyone, else to command our armies in the east. Thraxton . . . is not a lucky man."

"He is the man we have," Duke Edward replied. "As I told you, he is the man under whom you will serve if your army fares east. Bear that in mind, your Excellency. Also bear in mind that, from all reports, Count Thraxton requires prompt, unquestioning obedience from those under his command."

"I understand, your Grace," James said. Unquestioning obedience didn't come easy to him. The duke had to know as much; James had never been afraid to tell him he was wrong when he believed that to be so. And James had been right a couple of times, too. If the charge hadn't gone up that hill by Essoville in the face of massed stone- and dart-throwers and whole brigades of crossbowmen sheltered behind stone walls . . . It had been grand. It had been glorious. It had also been a gruesome disaster. James had warned it would be. Duke Edward had thought one more push would carry the day against the southrons. If it had . . . But it hadn't.

To his credit, the duke had never shown the least resentment against James for proving himself correct. "Do always bear in mind," Edward said now, "that Thraxton will do as he will do, and that he makes all the vital decisions for his army himself." He was still driving home that same point.

"Rest assured, sir, I shall never forget it," James of Broadpath replied. "But I also know that we here in the west have learned more about how to fight a war than they know in the east. Let me get my men there and I will show Count Thraxton and everyone else how it's done." He bowed to Duke Edward. "After all, I've studied under the finest schoolmaster."

Courteous and modest as always, Edward murmured, "You do me too much honor, your Excellency," while returning the bow. He went on, "As I told you, I shall forward your request to King Geoffrey with my favorable endorsement. I do not promise that that will guarantee his approval, of course."

"Of course," James said. Even more than Count Thraxton, King Geoffrey was a law unto himself. Maybe that was why he left Thraxton in command in the east: one kindred spirit recognizing another.

"Even so, however," Duke Edward continued, "you might do well to keep your men ready to move to a glideway at a moment's notice."

"Yes, *sir*!" James said. The duke bowed again, this time in dismissal. More pleased with himself than he'd expected to be, Earl James left his commander's pavilion.

On the way back to his own, he met Brigadier Bell, who commanded a division of his army. With his flowing beard and fierce, proud features, Bell had been called the Lion God enfleshed. These days, he looked more like a suffering god; he'd had his left arm smashed and ruined two days before the charge up that ill-omened hill by Essoville. The wound still tormented him. The shrunken pupils of his eyes showed how much laudanum he used to hold the pain at bay.

"Will we go, your Excellency?" he asked James. Wounded or not, drugged or not, he was always ready—always eager—to go toward battle.

"Duke Edward will endorse the proposal and pass it on to the king," James said. "The decision is Geoffrey's, but the duke thinks he will approve." Bell whooped. James asked him, "General, *can* you fight?"

"I can't hold a shield, but what of it?" Bell replied gaily. "So long as I am smiting the foe, the foe can't very well smite me."

"Stout fellow," James of Broadpath said. He made as if to pat Bell on the shoulder, but arrested the motion, not wanting to cause the man more pain. Bell was like a falcon: take the hood off him at the right time, fly him at the enemy, and he'd always come back with blood on his claws. *And if King Geoffrey uses me as I use Bell . . . well, fair enough,* James thought. *It is the duty I owe the kingdom.* A moment later, he had another thought: *Duke Edward would approve.*

Ned of the Forest preferred camping out with his unicorn-riders to going into Rising Rock to sup with Count Thraxton. Ned had nothing in particular against Rising Rock, or against any other town. He'd served on the burghers' council in Luxor before Avram became king, and he liked the luxuries only town living afforded. But supping with Thraxton was another business altogether.

"You ever go to a dinner where you wished you had yourself a taster on account of you wonder if the fellow who invited you put something nasty in the food?" he asked one of his regimental commanders.

To his surprise, Colonel Biffle nodded. "Happened once, sir. The fellow who invited me was afraid one of the other gents there was too friendly with his wife. If he'd wanted to poison him, he might've botched things and poisoned some other folks, too—me, for instance." Ned had trouble imagining anyone wanting to poison Biffle, who was as good-natured a man as had ever been born.

Thraxton, on the other hand . . . "The serf who nursed our army commander, Colonel, must've been a wench with sour milk."

Biffle laughed, a big, comfortable laugh from a big, comfortable man. "I expect you can handle him, Brigadier," he said. He was a viscount and Ned a man of no birth, but he deferred to the commander of unicorns as if it were the other way round. Most men did.

But Ned's shrug was anything but satisfied. "I shouldn't have to try and *handle* him, Colonel," he said. "Guildenstern and the gods-accursed southrons should be the ones who have to *handle* him. I tell you, I spoke frankly to him this evening, and I'd take oath he tried to magic me afterwards."

At that, Colonel Biffle's round, pleasant face did take on a look of alarm. "Are you sure you're hale, sir? Whatever else you may say about him, Thraxton's a formidable wizard."

"Not formidable enough," Ned answered. "Miserable old he-witch has had a whole pile of chances to kick Avram's men right in the slats. Has he done it? I'll tell you what he's done—we're going to have to clear out of Rising Rock, on account of he didn't see Guildenstern coming till he was almost here."

"We really are going to have to leave, sir?" Biffle asked unhappily.

"No doubt about it. Not even a tiny piece of doubt," Ned said, more unhappily still. "If we stay where we're at, the southrons'll run roughshod over us in spite of the great and famous Count Thraxton the Braggart's mighty sorcery. They've got cursed near twice the men we do—of course they'd run roughshod over us. Then they'd bag the whole stinking army, and Rising Rock, too. This way, they just get Rising Rock. Happy day! And once we're done running, Thraxton'll make it sound like a victory to King Geoffrey. He always does." He spat on the ground in disgust.

"What can we do if they run us on into Peachtree Province?" Biffle asked.

"Hit back some kind of way, Colonel. That's all I can tell you," Ned replied. "You want to know how, you'll have to ask Thraxton the Braggart. It'll be a fine thing, him commanding the Army of Franklin when it's really the army that got run clean *out* of Franklin." He spat again.

Colonel Biffle wandered off, shaking his head. Ned of the Forest didn't wander. He stalked. He'd eaten his fill with Thraxton, but he checked the cookpots from which his riders ate to make sure the cooks were doing their job. Count Thraxton, no doubt, would have turned up his nose at the food—but then, Count Thraxton turned up his nose at just about everything and everyone. This was what Ned ate most of the time. Not least because he ate it most of the time, it wasn't bad.

His troopers, those of them still awake, tended their unicorns, currying the white, white hair or picking pebbles out from between their hooves and the iron shoes they wore or doctoring small hurts. Ned nodded approval. "Way to go, boys," he called. "Take care of your animals and they'll take care of you."

"That's right, General," one of the riders answered. "That's just right."

"You bet it is." Ned nodded again, emphatically this time, and the rider grinned at having his commander agree with him. Ned grinned, too. *What a liar I'm getting to be*, he thought. Oh, he took good care of his unicorns when he wasn't riding one of them into a fight, too. But when he did take saber in hand . . . He tried to remember how many unicorns he'd had killed out from under him since he went to war for King Geoffrey. Eighteen? Nineteen? Something like that. The generals who were known for their mounts— Duke Edward of Arlington, for instance—didn't take their beasts into battle.

Ned shrugged. He didn't care about any one unicorn nearly so much as he cared about licking the southrons. He could always get himself another mount. If King Avram prevailed, he couldn't very well get himself another kingdom.

There was his pavilion, and there were the serfs who took care of the cavalry's baggage wagons and the asses and unicorns that hauled them. The big blond men—some of them bigger and stronger than Ned, who was a big, strong man himself—gathered round the general. They were all his retainers—not quite *his* serfs, since he had no patent of nobility, but he looked out for them and they looked out for him.

They all carried knives. Had they wanted to mob him and melt off into the countryside or run away to the southrons afterwards, they could have. They didn't. By all appearances, it never entered their minds. One reason for that, perhaps, was that Ned never let it seem as if it entered his mind, either.

He ruffled the pale hair of the biggest and strongest serf. "Well, Darry, what do you hear?" Folk with dark hair often ran their mouths as if serfs had no more notion of what was going on than did horses or unicorns. Ned had taken advantage of that a good many times. His drivers and hostlers made pretty fair informal spies.

This time, though, Darry answered, "Is it true we've got to skedaddle out of Rising Rock? Don't want to believe it, but it's what people say."

"They say it on account of it's true, and may the gods fry Thraxton the Braggart for making it true," Ned answered. His serfs already knew what he thought of his commander. They chuckled and nudged one another, vastly amused to hear one dark-haired lord pour scorn on another.

A sly blond named Arris asked, "How will we keep Franklin if we can't stay in Rising Rock?"

"That's a good question," Ned answered. "Drop me in the seven hells if I know. Drop Thraxton in the seven hells if he knows, either. And drop him past the seven hells if the thought ever got into his tiny little mind before he let Guildenstern flank him out of this place." That set the serfs nudging and chuckling again.

Arris asked, "But how will we get our farms, boss, if those gods-hated southrons keep pushing us back?"

In the days when the war was young—days that seemed a thousand years gone now—Ned had promised to take the bonds from all the serfs who served him through the fighting, and to set them up as yeomen with land of their own. Free blond farmers weren't common in the northern provinces of Detina, but they weren't unknown, either, especially in the wild northeast from which Ned himself had sprung.

Now he shrugged. "One way or another, boys, you'll get yourselves farms. If I can't give 'em to you, you'll have 'em from the southrons. King Avram says so, doesn't he? And if King Avram says something, it must be so, isn't that right?"

Just as the serfs might have mobbed him and fled, they might have said yes to that and put their hope in the southron king rather than in Ned. But they didn't. They cursed Avram as fiercely as any other northern man in indigo pantaloons might have done. Ned laughed to hear them, laughed and ruffled their yellow hair and punched them in the shoulder, as a man will do among other men he likes well.

"If you people haven't given up on King Geoffrey, I don't reckon I can, either," Ned said. He nodded to Darry. "Saddle me a unicorn. I'm going to ride out and see exactly where the southrons are at." He tossed his head in fine contempt. "It's not like anybody'll know unless I go out and see for myself, I'll tell you that for a fact. Thraxton's the best stinking wizard in the world, right up to the time somebody really needs his magic. Then he flunks."

"Yes, Lord Ned," Darry said. "I'll get you a beast." As Ned ducked into his pavilion, Darry and the other serfs spoke in low voices full of awe. Ned chuckled to himself. The blonds, back in the days before the Detinans came from overseas, had worshiped a pack of milksop godlets that couldn't hold night demons at bay. They still walked in fear after the sun went down. Ned, now, Ned feared no night demons. With the Lion God and the Thunderer and the Hunt Lady and all the rest on his side, any demon that tried clamping its jaws on him would find it had made a bad mistake.

Outside the pavilion, one of the serfs said, "Ned, he could go up against a night demon without any gods behind him, and he'd still rip its guts out."

"Of course he would," another serf answered. "He's *Ned*."

Ned grinned as he tested the edge of his saber with his thumb. The blade would do. And he wasn't so sure the blonds were wrong, either. Fortunately, he didn't have to find out. He knew the strong gods, and they knew him.

When he went out again, the unicorn awaited him. He would have been astonished had it been otherwise. Handing him the reins, Darry said, "You make sure you come back safe now, boss." Real anxiety filled his voice. If Ned didn't come back safe, how many northern officers were likely to honor his pledges to the men who served him? Would Count

Thraxton, for instance? Ned laughed at the idea, though Darry wouldn't have found it funny.

None of Ned's pickets challenged him when he rode east toward the enemy. None of them knew he'd gone by. He didn't think of himself as a mage. Soldiers who did think of themselves so usually made him bristle—Thraxton sprang to mind. But he was Ned of the Forest. However he got it, he had a knack for pulling shadow and quiet around himself like a mask. Few could penetrate it unless he chose to let them.

Owls hooted. Somewhere off toward Sentry Peak, a wildcat yowled. Mosquitoes buzzed and bit. Ned slapped and cursed. He might cloak himself from the minds of men. Mosquitoes had no minds, not to speak of. They didn't care who he was. They probably bit Thraxton with just as much abandon. *Or maybe not*, Ned thought scornfully. *Why should they like sour wine any more than people do?* That made him want to laugh and curse at the same time.

The moon, low in the east, came out from behind a pale, puffy cloud and spilled ghostly light over the fields. Forests remained black and impenetrable, even close by the road. Maybe night demons really did den in them. If so, none came forth to try conclusions with Ned. Confident in his own strength, he rode on.

Ahead in the distance, lights twinkled like fireflies: the campfires of Guildenstern's army, King Avram's army, the army of invaders. "Why can't they just leave us alone?" Ned muttered under his breath. "We weren't doing them any harm. We weren't about to do them any harm."

But the southrons were pushing close to Rising Rock, close to driving King Geoffrey's men out of Franklin altogether. To force them back, to make sure

Geoffrey's kingdom stayed a kingdom, someone would have to strike them a blow. Ned of the Forest shook his head in frustrated fury. Count Thraxton wasn't going to do it. Count Thraxton was going to tuck his tail between his legs and skedaddle up into Peachtree Province.

"And he's a great general? He's a great mage?" Ned of the Forest shook his head again, this time dismissing the idea out of hand. Thraxton bragged a fine brag, but the proof of those lay in living up to them. Had Thraxton done that even once, the southrons could never have come so far.

Ned rode through open woods toward the campfires. The fires lay even closer to Rising Rock than he'd thought they would. He shook his fist at them. He'd grown rich and important hunting down runaway serfs and hauling them back to their liege lords. If Avram broke the feudal bonds that held serfs to their lords' estates, how would he stay rich? How would he stay important? He saw no way—and so he fought.

He was musing thus—dark thoughts in dark night— when a sudden sharp challenge rang out from ahead: "Halt! Who comes?"

"A friend," Ned answered, reining in in surprise. He usually came and went as he chose, with no one the wiser. Maybe his dark mood had let his protection falter—or maybe the nervous sentry had a mage close by. Putting an officer's snap in his voice, Ned asked, "What regiment is this?"

"Twenty-seventh, of the third division." That came at once, followed a couple of heartbeats later by a grudging, "Sir."

It told Ned what he needed to know. The southrons, merchants and bookkeepers in their very souls, numbered their regiments. King Geoffrey's were known by their commanders' names. The "friend" ahead was an enemy. Ned said, "I am going to ride on down a little ways and find a better crossing for the stream ahead."

He steered his unicorn into deeper shadows, and then away. The southron sentry didn't shoot. As Ned headed back to his own encampment, he cursed under his breath. He'd found out what he needed to know, but he didn't much care for it.

# II

"Come on, boys," General George boomed. "You'll never catch up with the traitors if you don't move faster than *that*."

"Why didn't *you* turn traitor, the way Duke Edward did?" one of the crossbowmen in gray returned. "You're from Parthenia, just like him. And if you were fighting on the other side, whoever'd be leading us now wouldn't march us so stinking hard."

"Oh, I doubt that," George said, and all the soldiers who heard him laughed. He knew they called him Doubting George. He didn't mind. They could have called him plenty worse—one brigadier in King Avram's army was known, though not to his face, as Old Bowels. George went on, "Any officer worth his pantaloons would push you hard now, because we're going to run Count Thraxton clean out of this province."

"You don't think he'll fight us, sir?" asked another crossbowman, this one a yellow-haired fellow whose liege lord was probably still looking for him.

"I hope he does, by the gods," George answered. He'd had some serfs on his own family lands in Parthenia, but holding Detina together under the rightful king came first for him. "If he doesn't run away himself, we'll run him out, and we'll smash up his army while we're doing it."

"What about Thraxton's magic, General?" a soldier asked him: another blond likely to have come out of the north. He sounded a little nervous. Serfs, even escaped serfs, often had reason to be nervous about northern nobles' magecraft.

But George just laughed—a deep, rolling chortle that made everyone who could hear him look his way. "I doubt you've got much to worry about," he said, which made the crossbowmen and pikemen close by laugh again, too. "If Thraxton's magic were half as good as he brags it is, those bastards in blue would be down in the Five Lakes country by now, instead of us pushing on them. Besides, it's not like we haven't got mages of our own."

He waved to the gray-robed contingent of scholarly-looking men on assback accompanying the long columns of crossbowmen and the blocks of pikemen and the squadrons of unicorn-riders at the army's front and wings. Most of the soldiers nodded, relieved and reassured.

George wasn't so sure he'd reassured himself. The southron mages just didn't look like men of war. They looked as if they would be more at home as healers or stormstoppers or diviners or fabricators who helped the manufactories in the southwest turn out the crossbows and quarrels and spearheads and catapults without which a modern army couldn't go about its murderous business. And the wizards had excellent reason for looking that way. Almost all of them *were* healers or stormstoppers or diviners or fabricators. They'd had to learn military magecraft from the ground up after Grand Duke Geoffrey chose to contest Avram's succession.

Things were different up in the north. The tradition of military magecraft had never died out there, as it had in the south. Instead, northern nobles used the sorceries that had helped their ancestors win the land to help hold down the serfs those ancestors had conquered. In the early days of the war, they'd embarrassed Avram's armies again and again.

Doubting George knew one reason he'd risen swiftly through the ranks was that, as a Parthenian who'd held serfs, he'd known some of the northern spells and how to block them. He'd never systematically studied sorcery, as Count Thraxton and some of the other northern commanders had, but he'd never panicked when it was used against him, as, for instance, Fighting Joseph had when Duke Edward's magic cast a cloud of confusion on the southrons and let him win the Battle of Viziersville despite being outnumbered worse than two to one.

A scout on unicornback rode up to General George. Saluting, he said, "Sir, there are stone fences up ahead with northern men behind them. They started shooting at us when we got close."

"Are there? Did they?" George said, and the scout nodded. The general rapped out the next important questions: "How many of them? Is it Count Thraxton's whole army?" Eagerness coursed through him. If Thraxton wanted to make a fight of it this side of Rising Rock, he'd gladly oblige the Braggart.

But the rider, to his disappointment, shook his head. "No, sir, doesn't look that way, nor even close. If I had to guess, I'd say they were just trying to slow us down a bit before we go on into Rising Rock."

"It could be." George looked ahead, to Sentry Peak in the northwest and Proselytizers' Rise due west but farther away. "Maybe they're buying some time to let their army pull out. All right." Decision crystallized. "If they want us to shift them, we'll do the job." He pointed toward the center, off to his right. "Go tell General Guildenstern what you just told me, and tell him we're moving against the foe."

"Yes, sir." With another salute, the rider pounded off to obey.

*Now*, George thought, *how long will it be before Guildenstern sticks his long, pointed nose into my business? Not very long, or I don't know him—and I know him much too well.* With Thraxton the Braggart in command of Geoffrey's armies in the east, King Avram's men should long since have smashed this treason. With General Guildenstern in command of the southrons, George supposed he ought to thank the gods that the traitors hadn't long since smashed the armies loyal to the rightful king.

Meanwhile, before Guildenstern could get his hands on this fight—which Doubting George duly doubted he would handle well—the army's second-in-command decided to take charge of it. "Deploy from column into line!" he shouted. Lesser officers echoed his orders; trumpeters spread them farther than men's voices readily carried. "Pikemen forward! Crossbowmen in ranks behind! Cavalry to the flanks to hold off the enemy's unicorns." He didn't really expect Thraxton's men to make any sort of mounted attack, but he didn't believe in taking chances, either.

The soldiers under his command went through their evolutions with precision drilled into them by scores of cursing sergeants on meadows and in city parks and sometimes on city streets all through the southern provinces of Detina. Hardly any of them had been soldiers before King Avram began levying troops from his vassals and from the yeomanry of the countryside and from the free cities and towns that had stayed loyal to him. But they moved like veterans now. Most of them *were* veterans now, and had seen as much hard fighting as professional soldiers often did in a lifetime's service during quieter days.

And then George shouted another order: "Mages forward! Cavalry screen for the wizards!"

Some of the gray-robed men on assback nodded and urged their small, ill-favored mounts up to the best trot the beasts could give. Others looked startled and apprehensive. George wanted to laugh at them. In many cases, they'd been in the field as long as the footsoldiers, who knew exactly what was expected of *them*. But the mages never stopped acting surprised.

George spurred his own unicorn. With an indignant snort, the beast bounded forward. George always wanted to see for himself; one of the things that had won him his nickname was his reluctance to trust other people's reports. He'd seen too many things go wrong because scouts brought back mistaken news or because a senior officer, not having examined the situation or the ground for himself, gave the wrong orders.

As George rode up to the top of a low hill and looked ahead, he found that things to the west did look much as the scout had described them. Not a lot of northerners were delaying the army's advance, but they had stone fences—the likely border markers between two farms—to hide behind. One crossbowman shooting from cover was worth several out in the open.

A moment later, George discovered the enemy didn't have only crossbowmen slowing up his advance. Trailing smoke, something large and heavy flew through the air toward his forwardmost unicorns. When it hit the ground—farther from the foe than even a crossbowman could shoot—it burst in a ball of fire. That was half artisans' work, half mages'. The flame caught one unicorn and its rider. They dashed off, both screaming, both burning.

"Catapults forward, Brigadier Brannan!" Doubting George shouted. "If they want to play those games with us, we'll make 'em think the seven hells start just behind those fences."

His army had more and better missile-throwers than did the men who followed Grand Duke Geoffrey. The northerners had looked down their noses at the mechanic arts till they discovered they needed them. But serfs and artisans could not match manufactories, no matter how they tried.

Up came the catapults. Brannan was a good officer. Doubting George kicked himself for not having ordered the engines forward with the cavalry. The northerners, surely, would not rush from cover to attack the catapults. They would be asking for massacre if they did. They might be brave—they undoubtedly *were* brave—but they weren't stupid.

Firepots flew through the air toward the catapults as they deployed. So did large stones: altogether unsorcerous, but highly effective. A stone smashed one machine, and several of the men who served it. Another catapult sent a cloud of dirty black smoke into the sky. The rest of the crews stolidly went about their business. In mere minutes, they were flinging missiles back at the northerners.

Some of their stones smashed against the fences. Some of their firepots burst in front of or against the fences, too. That was spectacular, especially from George's hilltop view, but accomplished nothing. But most of the missiles made it over the fences and fell among the enemy soldiers beyond. The northerners stirred and boiled, like ants when their hill was disturbed.

"That's the way to shift them!" George shouted, and ordered a runner to go on down to the catapult crews and tell them so. "Those buggers won't be able to stand against us for long if we keep dropping things on their heads."

Other catapults turned the business of pelting the foe with crossbow quarrels into something that might have come straight from a manufactory rather than out of a general's manual of stratagems. An operator at the right side of each dart-throwing engine worked a windlass connected to the engine's cocking mechanism by means of flat-link chains each turning on a pair of five-sided gears. Another operator fed sheaf after sheaf of arrows into a hopper above the launching groove. When the devices worked well, each one was worth several squads of crossbowmen. When they didn't—and they often didn't—their crews spent inordinate amounts of time attacking them with wrenches and pliers.

Today, they were working as well as Doubting George had ever seen them. Their operators had them angled high so their darts plunged down over the fences and onto the enemy crossbowmen just beyond. George smiled and called for another runner. "Order the pikemen and crossbowmen to advance on the walls there," he told the youngster. "They'll be able to get up to them and over without too much trouble, or I miss my guess."

But before the second runner could carry that command to the footsoldiers, lightning struck from a clear blue sky and smote one of the dart-throwers. The great ball of flame that burst from it made George's hands involuntarily fly up to protect his eyes. As the roar from the blast thundered by half a heart-beat later, his unicorn snorted and sidestepped in fright. With automatic competence, he fought it back under his control.

Doing that made his wits start working again. "Hold!" he shouted to the second runner. That worthy wasn't going anywhere anyhow. Like everybody else, he was staring in horrified astonishment at the ruination visited on the catapult. Even as he stared, another flash of lightning wrecked another engine. Doubting George was horrified and astonished, too. But he was also furious. He pointed to the runner. "No, by the gods! Get yourself gone to our so-called mages. You tell them that, for every catapult wrecked after you reach them, one of them will end up shorter by a head."

The runner sprinted away. George doubted he had the authority to make his threat good. With luck, the mages wouldn't realize that. If he had to terrify them into doing their job better, he would, and without thinking twice.

Another thunderbolt crashed down among the catapults. When George stopped blinking, he saw that this one had punished bare ground, not one of his engines or its crew. He nodded. Slower than they should have, his mages were casting counterspells. The next bolt didn't reach the ground at all. Doubting

George nodded again. The southron sorcerers *could* do the job, if only they remembered they were supposed to.

And then, when lightning struck *behind* the stone fences from which Geoffrey's men fought, George did more than nod. He clapped his hands together. "Go it!" he shouted to the mages in gray. They were too far away to hear him, but he didn't care. He shouted again: "Make the traitors think the seven hells aren't half a mile off!"

His officers knew what wanted doing. They had a better, more certain idea than the mages. That was plain. As soon as the catapult crews could work their stone- and firepot- and dart-throwers again without fear of being crisped from the innocent air above, his company and regimental commanders sent their footsoldiers forward against the stone fences without waiting for orders from him.

A few of the soldiers fell; neither bombardment nor magecraft had forced all the northerners away from those fences. They were stubborn and brave, sure enough. The war would have ended long since were that not true. Their bravery didn't help them here, though. Southrons gained the fences and started scrambling over them. Some northerners died where they stood. Some fled. Some came back captive, with upraised hands and glum faces.

"Lieutenant General George!" a rider called, galloping over from the center. "General Guildenstern's compliments, and do you need help from the rest of the force?"

Doubting George shook his head. "Give him my thanks, but I need not a thing. Only a skirmish here, and we've won it."

❖   ❖   ❖

Captain Ormerod was not a happy man as he trudged west, back toward Rising Rock. The mages had promised they would do dreadful things to the ragtag and bobtail of gallowsbait from the southern cities and runaway serfs who filled out the ranks of false King Avram's army. Mages' promises, though, were all too often written on wind, written on water. What one mage could do, another—or several others—could undo. The southrons didn't have great mages, but they had a lot of them. Ormerod didn't think the little delaying action at the stone fences had done enough delaying. It certainly hadn't done as much as his superiors had hoped.

And he had more reason for being unhappy than that. His left leg pained him, as it always did these days when he had to march hard. He'd taken a crossbow quarrel right through the meat of his calf in the frigid fight at Reillyburgh. The wound hadn't mortified, so he supposed he was lucky. But he had two great puckered scars on the leg, and less meat than he'd had before he was hit. Hard marching hurt.

"Come on, boys," he called to the footsoldiers in the company he commanded. "Keep it moving. Those southron bastards aren't chasing us, by the gods. We showed 'em we've still got teeth."

He put the best face he could on retreat. He'd had practice retreating, more practice than he'd wanted, more practiced than he'd ever thought he would get. Like so many northern nobles, he'd joined King Geoffrey's levy as soon as war broke out: indeed, Palmetto Province had been the first to reject Avram and proclaim Geoffrey Detina's rightful king.

Baron Ormerod wondered what kind of an indigo harvest his wife and the serfs would get from his estate when he wasn't there to keep an eye on things.

Bianca's letters were all resolutely cheerful, but Bianca herself was resolutely cheerful, too. What all wasn't she telling him? How many serfs had run off these past few months? How many of the blonds still on the land dogged it instead of working?

His first lieutenant came up to him, making him think of something besides his estate. "Sir?" the man asked.

"What is it, Gremio?" Ormerod asked. "By your sour look, something's gone wrong somewhere."

"With this whole campaign, sir," Gremio burst out. "Truly the gods must hate us, if they watch us bungle so but do nothing to help. . . . Why are you laughing, sir?" He sent Ormerod a resentful stare.

"Because if I did anything else, I'd start to wail, and I don't care to wash my face with tears," Ormerod said. "And speaking of faces, what would they say if they saw yours in the Karlsburg law courts looking the way you do?"

"Sir, they would say I've been serving my sovereign and my kingdom," Gremio answered stiffly. He had no noble blood, but had had enough money to buy himself an officer's commission: he was one of the leading barristers in Palmetto Province's chief town.

And now, no matter what he was, he looked like a teamster who'd had a hard time of it: filthy, scrawny, weary, in plain blue tunic and pantaloons that were all over patches, with black marching boots down at the heels and split at the front so his toes peeped out. Ormerod would have twitted him harder, save that his own condition was no more elegant.

And the footsoldiers they led were worse off than they were. The company—the whole regiment—had come out of Karlsburg and the surrounding baronies full of fight, full of confidence that they would boot the southrons back over the border and then go home and go on about their business. They were still full of fight. They still had their crossbows and quivers full of quarrels. They had very little else. They were all of them lean as so many hunting hounds, leaner than Ormerod, leaner than Gremio.

Sensing Ormerod's eye on him, a sergeant named Tybalt grinned a grin that showed a missing front tooth. "Don't you worry about a thing, sir," he said. "We'll give those whipworthy bastards what they deserve yet, see if we don't." Some of the men trudging along beside him nodded.

"Of course we will," Ormerod answered, and did his best to sound as if he meant it. The men he led had little farms on the lands near his estate. None of them had serfs to help plant and bring in a crop: only wives and kinsfolk. They'd given up more than Ormerod had to take service with King Geoffrey and fight the invaders, and had less personal stake in how the war turned out. The least he could give them was optimism.

Unfortunately, optimism was also the most he could give them. In the third year of a war he'd hoped would be short, in retreat in the third year of that war, even optimism came hard.

Lieutenant Gremio asked, "What do you know that I don't, your Excellency?" He made Ormerod's title of nobility a title of reproach. "*How* are we going to give the southrons what they deserve?"

Though he spoke with a barrister's fussy precision, he did at least have the sense to keep his voice low so the troopers couldn't hear his questions. Ormerod replied in similar low tones: "What do I know? I know that, if the men start believing they can't give Avram's armies the kick in the arse they ought to get, they'll all go home—and what will King Geoffrey do then? Besides take ship and flee overseas, I mean."

He watched Gremio chew on that and reluctantly nod. "Appearances do matter," Gremio admitted, "here as in the lawcourts. Very well—I'm with you."

Earl Florizel, the colonel of the regiment, rode up on unicornback. He waved to Ormerod. Back home in Palmetto Province, they were neighbors. Ormerod kept hoping Florizel would look his way when their children reached marriageable age. The earl said, "You fought your company well back there, Captain— as well as could possibly be expected, considering how outnumbered we were."

"For which I thank you, sir," Ormerod replied. "I hoped for rather more from the mages, and I'd be lying if I said otherwise."

"We usually hope for more from the mages than we get," Florizel said with a sour smile. He was in his late thirties, and a good deal lighter and trimmer after a couple of years in the field than he had been on his estate, where he'd let himself run to fat. "The trouble is, those bastards who fight for Avram the Just" —he turned the nickname into a sneer— "have mages, too."

"Ours are better," Ormerod said stoutly.

"No doubt, or our hopes would already be shattered," Florizel said. "But they have more. Many little weights in one pan will balance a few big ones in the other. That leaves it to the fellows who go out and hack one another for a living."

"King Avram's got more soldiers, too," Lieutenant Gremio said.

Ormerod and Florizel both pursed their lips and looked away from him, as if he'd broken wind at a fancy banquet. It wasn't so much that Gremio was wrong—he was right. But saying it out loud, bringing it out in the open where people had to notice it was there . . . The warriors who fought under King Geoffrey's banner rarely did that, as it led to gloomy contemplations.

To avoid such gloomy contemplations, Ormerod asked, "Colonel, where are we stopping tonight?"

"Rising Rock," Florizel answered, which gave rise to other gloomy contemplations. "And take a good look around while you're there, too."

"Why's that?" Ormerod asked.

Lieutenant Gremio was quicker on the uptake. "Because we're not bloody likely to see it again any time soon, that's why," he said.

"Oh." One mournful word expressed an ocean of Ormerod's frustration.

"He's right." Florizel sounded no more delighted than Ormerod felt. "We'll be some of the last men into Rising Rock, too, and it looks like we'll be some of the last ones out as well." *Out* meant retreating to the northwest. Colonel Florizel pointed in that direction. Sure enough, Ormerod could see the dust men and unicorns by the thousands raised as they marched along the road through the gap between Sentry Peak and Proselytizers' Rise, the gap that led up into Peachtree Province.

Closer, Rising Rock itself looked deceptively normal. The sun played up the blood-red of the painted spires on the Lion God's temples, and glinted from the silver lightning bolts atop the Thunderer's shrines. Ormerod sighed. The southrons worshiped the same gods he did, but they would send the local priests into exile for speaking out against the perverse belief that serfs were as good as true Detinans.

No sooner had that thought crossed Ormerod's mind than he saw a blond young man in ragged pantaloons—no tunic at all, and no shoes, either— making his way east with a bundle at the end of a stick on his shoulder. The serf was moving against the flow of soldiers on the road, toward the advancing southrons.

"Runaway!" Ormerod shouted, and pointed at him. He was amazed nobody'd pointed and shouted at the serf before he did.

The blond young man ran for the cover of the trees that grew close to the road. He dropped his bundle so he could run faster. Ormerod cursed; he couldn't send men after the runaway without disrupting the company's march.

Then he stopped cursing and pointed again. "Shoot him!" he yelled.

Some of his men hadn't bothered waiting for the order. They were already cocking their crossbows and setting bolts in them. Triggers snapped. Bowstrings thrummed. Quarrels hissed through the air. With a meaty *thunk!*, one of them caught the fleeing serf in the small of the back. He shrieked and fell on his face.

Ormerod trotted after him. The serf kept trying to crawl toward the woods. He wasn't going to make it. Ormerod saw that right away. If a crossbow quarrel didn't hit a bone, it could punch right through a man. By the trail of blood the serf was leaving, the bolt that hit him had done just that.

Drawing a knife from the sheath on his belt, Ormerod stooped beside the blond man. The fellow stared at him out of eyes wide with hate and pain. "I'll cut your throat for you, if you want, and put you out of your pain," Ormerod said. He did what needed doing with runaways, but he wasn't deliberately cruel about it.

"Red Lady curse you," the serf ground out. "Death Lord pull you under the dirt and cover over your grave."

"Serfs' curses. Serfs' gods," Ormerod said with a shrug. "They won't bite on a Detinan. You blonds ought to know that by now. Last chance: do I finish you, or do I walk away and let you die at your own speed?"

Blood dribbled from a corner of the serf's mouth. He'd bitten his lips or his tongue in his torment. His eyes still held hate, but he nodded up at Ormerod and said, "Get it over with."

The noble caught him by his yellow hair, jerked his head back, and drew the knife across his throat. More blood spurted, scarlet as the Lion God's spires. The serf's expression went blank, vacant. Ormerod let his head fall. The blond lay unmoving. Ormerod plunged his knife into the soft earth to clean it, then thrust it back in its sheath.

His men had kept going while he finished the runaway. He quickmarched after them, and was panting a little by the time he caught up. "Dead?" Lieutenant Gremio asked him.

"I didn't go after the bastard to give him a kiss on the cheek and tell him what a good boy he was," Ormerod answered. "Of course he's dead."

"His liege lord could bring an action against you for slaying him rather than returning him to the land to which he's legally bound," Gremio observed. "It falls under the statutes for deprivation of agricultural resources."

"His liege lord could toast in the seven hells, too," Ormerod said. "As far as I'm concerned, that sort of action falls under the Thunderer's lightning bolt."

"I merely mentioned what was legally possible," Gremio said with his annoying lawyerly precision. Baron Ormerod spat in the dirt of the roadway to show what he thought of such precision.

As Colonel Florizel had said it would, his regiment camped just outside Rising Rock that night. Florizel said, "Ned's unicorn-riders are supposed to keep the enemy away from us till we fall back, too." He eyed Ormerod and the rest of his captains. "Ned is an able officer, but I wouldn't put all my faith in his riders, any more than I would put all my faith in any one god."

Ormerod had already planned to post double pickets to make sure his company got no unpleasant surprises from the east. After hearing that, he posted quadruple pickets instead. But the southrons didn't trouble his men, and the regiment, along with the rest of Count Thraxton's rear guard, passed a quiet night.

"Ned knows his business," Ormerod remarked the next morning.

"Nice that somebody does," Lieutenant Gremio answered. He looked around to make sure nobody but Ormerod was in earshot, then added, "It'd be even nicer if some more people up above us did."

Ormerod grunted. "And isn't that the sad and sorry truth? But there's not one cursed thing we can do about it, worse luck." He raised his voice so the whole company could hear him: "Come on, boys. We've got to move out. I wish we didn't, but we cursed well do." Along with the rest of the regiment, the rest of the rear guard, he and his company marched out of Rising Rock, out of the province of Franklin, and into . . . he didn't want to think about what they were marching into. *Into trouble*, was what crossed his mind.

"General?" someone called outside of Earl James of Broadpath's pavilion. "Are you in there, General?"

"No, I'm not here," James answered. "I expect to be back pretty soon, though."

As he'd hoped it would, that produced a fine confused silence. When he strode out of the pavilion, the runner who'd come up was on the point of leaving. He brightened when he saw James. "Oh, good, your Excellency," he said. "Duke Edward's compliments, and he'd like to see you at your earliest convenience."

"Would he?" James of Broadpath said. "Well, of course I'll see him straightaway. He's in his pavilion?" He waited only for the runner to nod, then hurried over to the rather mean tent housing the commander of the Army of Southern Parthenia. He was panting and sweating by the time he got there, though the walk wasn't very long. His bulk and Parthenia's heat and humidity didn't go together. As Duke Edward's sentries saluted, James asked, "Is his Grace here?"

"Yes, your Excellency, he is, and waiting for you, too—or I think so, anyhow," one of the sentries answered. He raised his voice: "Duke Edward? Earl James is here to see you."

"Is he?" Duke Edward of Arlington came out of the pavilion. James saluted. Punctilious as always, Edward returned the courtesy. Then he plucked a folded sheet of paper from the breast pocket of his indigo tunic and presented it to James. "This may possibly be of interest to you, your Excellency."

"Ah?" James rumbled. The paper was sealed with

a dragon's mark stamped deep into golden wax. "That is King Geoffrey's seal," James breathed, and Edward nodded. Only a king would or could use the dragon's mark, and Avram's sealing wax would have been crimson, not gold—not that Avram was likely to send a sealed letter to a general in his rival's service.

With his thumbnail, James broke the seal. He opened the paper. The spidery script within was King Geoffrey's, too; James had seen it often enough to recognize it. The missive read, *In regard to the proposal to send the army under the command of General James of Broadpath, the said army presently constituting a wing of the Army of Southern Parthenia commanded by General Edward of Arlington, to the aid and succor of the Army of Franklin commanded by General Thraxton, the aforesaid proposal, having been endorsed by the aforementioned General Edward of Arlington, is hereby accepted and approved. Let it be carried out with the greatest possible dispatch. Geoffrey, King in the northern provinces of Detina.*

"You know what it is, your Grace?" James asked.

"I don't know, no, but from your countenance I should guess his Majesty has chosen to send your soldiers east," Duke Edward replied.

"He has." Earl James of Broadpath bowed to his commanding officer. "And I am in your debt, sir, for your generous endorsement."

"Hard times require hard measures," the duke said. "I am not certain this action will answer, but I am certain inaction will not answer. Go east, then, and may the gods go with you. I trust your men are ready to move at short notice?"

"Yes, sir," James said. "All we need do is break camp, march to the glideway port at Lemon's Justiciary, and off we go eastward."

"Not quite so simple as that, I fear," Edward said, "for it is reported the southrons have lately wrested from us the most direct glideway path leading eastward. But the wizards in charge of such things do assure me a way from here to Count Thraxton's army does remain open: only it is not so direct a way as we might wish."

"Then I'd best leave without any more delay, hadn't I, your Grace?" Without waiting for Duke Edward's reply—although Edward might not have had one; he approved of men who took things into their own hands and moved fast—James bowed, spun on his heel in a smart about-face, and hurried back toward his own pavilion.

As he neared it, he shouted for the trumpeters who served him. They came at the run, long, straight brass horns gleaming in their hands. "Command us, sir!" one of them cried.

Command them James of Broadpath did: "Blow *assembly*. Summon my whole army to the broad pasture."

The trumpeters saluted. As they raised the horns to their lips, one of them asked, "Your Excellency, does this mean we're heading east, to whip the stinking, lousy, gods-detested southrons out of Franklin?" Rumor had swirled through the army for days.

Getting King Geoffrey's army back *into* Franklin would be a good first step toward getting the southrons out. But James just waggled a finger at the trumpeter and said, "You'll hear when everyone else does. I haven't the time to waste—the kingdom hasn't the time for me to waste—telling things over twice."

Martial music rang out—the call for Earl James' army to gather together. As the trumpeters played, they eyed James reproachfully. He knew why; Count

Thraxton's army wouldn't have fallen to pieces had James given them the news before anyone else got it. He wagged his finger at them again. One of them missed a note. That made the others eye their comrade reproachfully. They took pride in what they did. James nodded at that; anything worth doing was worth doing well.

Soldiers in blue tunics and pantaloons—and some in blue tunics and in gray pantaloons taken from southrons who didn't need them any more—hurried from their tents and huts to the meadow where they gathered to hear such announcements as their commander chose to give them. They formed by squads, by companies, by regiments, by brigades, by divisions. At the head of one of the three divisions stood Brigadier Bell, a fierce smile brightening his pain-wracked face. Unlike the trumpeters, he had a pretty good notion of what James would say.

James strode out in front of the crossbowmen, the pikemen, and the unicorn-riders he commanded. As he ascended to a little wooden platform, he was very conscious of the thousands of eyes upon him. That sort of scrutiny made most men quail. Whatever else James was, he wasn't modest. He relished the attention.

When he held up a hand, complete and instant silence fell. Into it, General James boomed, "Soldiers of the Army of Southern Parthenia, soldiers of my wing, King Geoffrey has given us the duty of coming to the rescue of our beset comrades in the east. As you will know, Count Thraxton has been forced from Rising Rock, forced from Franklin altogether. He is—the kingdom is—counting on us to come to his aid, to help him drive the invaders from our sister province. The Army of Southern Parthenia is the finest force of fighters in Detina—in all the world. When we go east, shall we show Thraxton—shall we show General Guildenstern, may the gods curse him—how soldiers who know their business make war?"

"Aye!" his troopers roared, a great blast of sound.

"Good," James said. "Tomorrow morning, then, at dawn, we march to the glideway port at Lemon's Justiciary. From there, we fare forth to Peachtree Province, and from *there* we help Count Thraxton bring Franklin back to its proper allegiance. Is it good?"

"Aye!" the men in blue roared again.

Earl James saluted them as if they were his superiors, which made them cheer louder than ever. But when he raised his right hand, the cheers cut off as if at a swordstroke. *They're fine men*, he thought. *No commander could ask for better. More, perhaps, but not better*. "Dismissed!" he called to them. "Be ready to move when your officers and underofficers give the word."

As the soldiers streamed back toward their encampment, Brigadier Bell came up to James. The lines of agony from Bell's crippled arm would probably never leave his face, but his eyes shone. "A new chance," he breathed. "A chance to strike the southrons the blow we've been looking to strike since the war began."

"A new chance," James of Broadpath agreed. "Maybe our best chance."

"Yes!" Bell said. "We have never shifted men from the Army of Southern Parthenia to the east. Guildenstern won't expect it." His lip curled. "Guildenstern hasn't the mother wit to expect much."

"Maybe our best chance," Earl James repeated. His spirit wanted to soar. Bell's eagerness and the way the men responded to the transfer order tried to make it soar. But the war—the war he, like so many of Geoffrey's followers, had gaily assumed would be won in weeks—had ground into its third year with no end in sight. And so, instead of scaling his hat through the air in glee, he added, "Maybe our last chance, too."

The divisional commander stared at him. "Your Excellency, this is your scheme," Bell reminded him. "Have you no faith in it?"

"With the way the war has gone, my view at this stage of things is that any man who has faith in anything but the gods is a fool," James answered. "What I have is hope, a more delicate, more fragile flower."

He might as well have started speaking the language of the camel-riding desert barbarians of the western continent, for all the sense he made to Brigadier Bell. Well, that was the advantage of being a superior officer. Bell didn't have to see the sense in his words. All he had to do was obey. And he could be relied upon for that.

Getting James' effects ready to move took some doing: he had a great many more effects than his troopers did. Even with some serfs from Broadpath helping knock down the pavilion and load it and its contents into a couple of wagons, he felt rushed and harried. But he couldn't very well require of the men what he did not match himself. And so, mounted on his big-boned unicorn, he led the march out of camp at sunrise the next morning.

Lemon's Justiciary was named after the stone fortress where an early Count Lemon had had his courthouse. A little town had grown up around the fortress after the local blonds were subdued, a little town that had got bigger when the glideway went through and the port was built a stone's throw from that frowning stone keep.

For ages, men had dreamt of flying. Those camel-riding desert barbarians had tales of flying carpets. But that was all they were: tales. Modern mages in Detina and in the kindred kingdoms back across the Western Ocean had finally persuaded carpets to rise a couple of feet off the ground and travel along certain sorcerously defined glideways at about the speed of a galloping unicorn. It wasn't what poets and storytellers had imagined—but then, the real world rarely matched poems and stories. It was a great deal better than nothing.

Or it would have been, had any carpets waited at the Lemon's Justiciary glideway port. James and his men were there. Their conveyances?

James set hands on hips and roared at the portmaster: "Where are they, you worthless, stinking clot?"

"Don't blame me, your Excellency," the portmaster answered. "By the gods, you can't blame me. Something must have got buggered up somewheres further north—in Nonesuch its ownself, or up in Pierreville north of there. I can't give you what I don't got." He spread his hands. He went further than that: he pulled out the pockets of his pantaloons to show he had no traveling carpets hidden there.

Cursing did no good. James cursed anyway. Setting his hand on the hilt of his sword did no good, either. That didn't stop him from half drawing the blade. He said, "I can't travel on what I haven't got, either. And if I can't travel, I can't save the kingdom. The longer I have to wait here twiddling my thumbs, the longer the army has to wait here twiddling *its* thumbs, the greater the risk the war in the east will be lost past fixing. Well, sirrah, what do you say to *that*?"

With a shrug, the portmaster answered, "Only one

thing I can say, your Excellency: I can't do nothing about it."

The fleet of carpets finally glided into Lemon's Justiciary nearer to noon than to sunrise. By then, James of Broadpath was about ready to murder the mages who piloted it. But that would only have made him later still getting to the northern border of Peachtree Province. And those mages, once he got a good look at them, proved plainly weary unto death. The southrons, being tradesmen ever ready to ship their goods now here, now there, had gone into the war with far more glideways and far more wizards able to exploit them than was true in the provinces that had declared for King Geoffrey. They'd got good use from them, too. Till he had to do it, Earl James hadn't really worried about how hard it was to move and feed large numbers of soldiers. Glideways and their mages helped.

A few days before, he could have got to Peachtree Province by a relatively straight route through eastern Parthenia. But, as Duke Edward had said, one of Avram's armies now bestrode that glideway path, which meant James' men had a far more roundabout road to go. Once all his troopers—and their animals, and their catapults, and the fodder for the beasts and the darts and firepots for the engines—were finally aboard the carpets, they had to travel north through Parthenia, through Croatoan (which was supposed to mean something filthy in the language of the blond tribes that had dwelt by the shore of the Western Ocean when the Detinans first came from overseas), and into Palmetto Province before finally swinging east toward Marthasville in Peachtree Province . . . from which they would finally be able to go south toward the border and Count Thraxton's waiting army.

The journey would have tried the patience of a saint. James doubted whether even Duke Edward could have stayed calm through its beginnings— especially through the half-day delay occasioned by ferrying men and beasts and impedimenta over a river whose bridge had collapsed for no visible reason save perhaps the malignity of the gods. James didn't try. He bellowed. He cursed. He fumed. He consigned whoever had made that bridge to some of the less desirable real estate in the seven hells.

"Will we be in time, your Excellency?" Brigadier Bell asked once they got moving again.

"We'd better be," Earl James of Broadpath growled. "In spite of everything, I think we will be. And when we get there on time, we're going to make a lot of southron soldiers late." He rubbed his beefy hands together in anticipation.

A gold dragon on red flew in front of every company as General Guildenstern's army triumphally entered Rising Rock. "Show these traitors why they lost," Captain Cephas told Rollant's company. "March so you'd make King Avram proud of you." He couldn't have found a better way to make Rollant do his best. Serfs and ex-serfs cared more for Avram than did most free men.

Sergeant Joram added, "March so you'll make *me* proud of you, or you'll end up wishing you'd never been born." Hearing that, Rollant changed his mind. Keeping his sergeant happy was ever so much more important than pleasing King Avram. The king was far away, in the Black Palace in Georgetown. He would never have anything directly to do with Rollant. Joram, by contrast . . .

At the head of General Guildenstern's army, a band

struck up the royal hymn. Beside Rollant in the ranks, Smitty murmured, "That's pretty stupid. Grand Duke Geoffrey uses the same air as Avram."

"Silence in the ranks!" Sergeant Joram shouted. The end of his pointed black beard twitched in indignation. "Rollant, you can haul water for the squad tonight for running your mouth."

"But—" Rollant began. Then he bit down on whatever he'd been about to say. He wouldn't make Joram change his mind, and he would make his squadmates hate him. Being a blond in a dark-haired world wasn't easy. He had to keep swallowing injustice, and he never got the chance to give any out.

"Forward—march!" Captain Cephas called as the motion of the column finally reached his company. Off the soldiers went, always beginning with the left foot. Rollant hadn't had an easy time learning that; it was the opposite of what he'd been used to doing on Baron Ormerod's estate. Beginning with the right foot was the serfs' way of doing things throughout northern Detina; nobles and strawbosses hadn't bothered trying to change it. But Detinans themselves began with the left, and King Avram's army was profoundly Detinan even if it included some blond soldiers.

"Left—right! Left, right, left, right!" Sergeant Joram's cadence count underscored the difference.

Behind the kingdom's banner—the banner whose colors the northern traitors reversed—Rollant strode into Rising Rock. Back in the days when he was a serf, this collection of clapboard and brick buildings, some of the latter rising four or even five stories high, would have awed him. He remembered how astonished he'd been when he sneaked through northern towns on his way south after fleeing Ormerod's estate. Now he put on a fine southron sneer. You could drop Rising Rock in the middle of New Eborac and it would vanish without a trace. Even the gray stone keep by the river wasn't so much of a much, not when set against the southron city's temples and secular buildings that seemed to scrape the sky.

Up ahead, the band switched to the kingdom's battle hymn. Rollant's lips skinned back from his teeth in a fierce grin. The northerners hadn't kept that one; they had their own martial music. The battle hymn of the kingdom belonged to King Avram alone, to him and to the serfs he was freeing from their long-standing ties to the land.

A lot of the people lining the streets to watch Avram's soldiers go by were blonds. They were the ones who whooped and cheered and clapped their hands. They cheered hardest, too, when they saw fair heads among the brunet Detinan majority. A very pretty girl of his own people caught Rollant's eye and ran her tongue over her lips in what would have been a promise if he hadn't swept out of sight of her forever a few seconds later. He sighed, partly for the missed chance and partly because he missed his wife.

The dark-haired Detinans who'd come out to look over General Guildenstern's army looked less happy. "Did you ever see such a lot of vinegar phizzes in all your born days?" Smitty asked. "They never reckoned we'd get all the way up here. Shows what they knew when they backed Geoffrey the traitor."

"What do you want to bet some of 'em'll sneak off to tell Count Thraxton everything they can about us?" Rollant answered. Smitty scowled, but nodded.

"Silence in the ranks!" Sergeant Joram boomed again, and then, "At the beat, we shall sing the battle hymn of the kingdom."

"How can we do both of those at once?" Smitty asked, which struck Rollant as a reasonable question.

It struck Joram rather differently. "You, Smitty— water duty tonight," the sergeant snapped. He checked himself: "No, wait. I already gave that to Rollant. You can dig the latrine trench for the squad, and cover it over tomorrow morning."

Smitty winced. He didn't sing the battle hymn with any notable enthusiasm. Rollant did. Some sergeants would have put Smitty on water duty and handed *him* the nastier latrine detail. Even in the south, not everybody gave blonds a fair shake—not even close. Rollant tried not to fret about that. Compared to being bound to the land, with even less hope of getting off the land than an ox or an ass—which might be sold—the life of a carpenter in New Eborac wasn't bad at all.

"To the seven hells with King Avram!" somebody in the crowd shouted.

"Hurrah for good King Geoffrey!" someone else cried.

"Arrest those men!" Half a dozen officers and sergeants from the Detinan army yelled the same thing at the same time.

Soldiers went into the crowd to do just that, but came back emptyhanded. They couldn't tell who had shouted, and no one pointed a finger at the guilty men. *No blonds must have seen them*, Rollant thought. A moment later, he shrugged. That was not necessarily so. Maybe some of his people had seen, but were keeping quiet because they would have to go on living in Rising Rock along with the Detinans. A man who opened his mouth at the wrong time was liable to have something unfortunate happen to him, even if King Avram's troopers did occupy his home town.

When the leading regiments of General Guilden-stern's army marched out of Rising Rock heading west, the troops at the tail end of the column hadn't yet reached the east side of town. That said something about the size of the army. It also said something about the size of Rising Rock. Sure enough, the place could fall into New Eborac and never get noticed.

The field to which Captain Cephas led his men had plainly been used as a campground by Thraxton the Braggart's army not long before. The grass was trampled flat. Black patches showed where fires had burned. A lingering stench suggested that the northerners hadn't been careful about covering all their latrine trenches.

"Smitty!" Sergeant Joram pointed. "You dig a fresh trench there, among the old ones."

"Have a heart, Sergeant," Smitty said pitifully.

Asking a sergeant to have a heart was like asking a stone to smile. You could ask, but asking didn't mean you'd get what you wanted. Joram didn't even bother shaking his head. All he said was, "Get a shovel." He turned to Rollant. "Gather up the squad's water bottles. Looks like the ground slopes down over behind those bushes. Probably a creek somewhere over there. Go find it."

"Right, Sergeant." Rollant knew better than to say anything else. Some of the bottles he got were of oiled leather, others of earthenware. Most, though, were stamped from tin, and almost identical to one another. The manufactories in the south might not make very interesting goods, or even very fine ones, but they made very many. That counted, too; King Geoffrey's domain had trouble matching them.

Joram must have grown up on a farm: as he'd

predicted—and as Rollant had thought, too—a stream wound on toward the Franklin River. He wasn't the only man in Avram's gray filling water bottles there; far from it. "These stinking things are light enough to carry when they're empty," said a dark-haired soldier with a scar on his cheek, "but they're fornicating heavy once they're full of water."

Several troopers laughed. "That's the truth," Rollant said, and they nodded. But if *he'd* complained about having to carry the water bottles, one of them would have been sure to call him a lazy blond. If he wanted the Detinans to think him even half as good as themselves—if he wanted them to think he deserved to be reckoned a Detinan himself—he had to show he was twice as good as they were.

Out in the middle of the stream, a red-eared turtle stared at the soldiers from a rock. Had Rollant seen it in his days as a serf on Ormerod's estate, he would have tried to catch it. Turtle stew was tasty, and serfs didn't always have enough to eat after paying their liege lords the required feudal dues. He'd learned, though, that most southrons not only didn't eat turtles but were disgusted at the idea that anybody would. This one slid into the water undisturbed by him.

Not far from where he was filling the water bottles, a mossy stone bridge spanned the stream. One glance at it told him it had been there since before the Detinans crossed the Western Ocean: it was the work of his own people. Detinan arches used proper keystones; this one didn't.

*We were something*, he thought. *We weren't as strong as the invaders, but we were something, all by ourselves. Whatever we were becoming, though, the gods—our gods, the Detinan gods, I don't know which gods—didn't let us finish turning into it. Now we're part of something else, something bigger, something stronger, and I don't know what we can do except try to make the best of it.*

He was putting the stoppers in his water bottles when the bushes on the far side of the stream rustled. He didn't have his crossbow with him, but a couple of men close by did. If a few of King Geoffrey's soldiers still lingered, they would have a fight on their hands.

"Come out of there, you gods-hated northern traitor son of a bitch," rasped one of the troopers with Rollant.

More rustling, and out of the bushes came not northern soldiers but a scrawny blond man and woman in filthy, tattered clothes and four children ranging in size from almost as tall as the woman down to waist high on her. The man—plainly a runaway serf—said, "You're Good King Avram's soldiers?"

That made the Detinans laugh. The one who'd called the challenge answered, "If we weren't, pal, you'd already have a crossbow quarrel between the ribs."

"Gods be praised!" the serf exclaimed. "We're off our estate for good now. The earl'll never get us back again." He led his wife and children across the bridge toward the soldiers. They were halfway across when he noticed Rollant. "Gods be praised!" he said again. "One of our own, a soldier for the southron king." Then, pointing at Rollant, he let loose with a spate of gibberish.

"Speak Detinan," Rollant answered. "I don't understand a word you're saying." Back in the old days, blonds in what was now Detina had spoken scores of different tongues. This one sounded nothing like the one Rollant's ancestors near Karlsburg had used. That language was nearly dead these days, anyhow, surviving only as scattered words in the Detinan dialect the serfs of Palmetto Province spoke.

The runaway looked disappointed. In Detinan, he said, "I want to be a soldier for King Avram, too, and kill the nobles in the north."

"What about us?" the woman with him asked, pointing to the children and herself as they finished crossing the bridge.

One of the troopers in Detinan gray had a different question: "What do we do with 'em?"

"Let the blond fellow here deal with them," another veritable Detinan answered. "They're his, by the gods."

Rollant would have bet a month's pay one of the dark-haired men would say that. He'd already escaped to the south. He had not a word of this serf's language. But his hair was yellow, not brown. To a man whose forefathers had crossed the Western Ocean— or even to one who'd crossed himself—that made all the difference.

And, Rollant had to admit, it made some difference to him, too. He waved to the serf and his family. "Come along with me. I'll take you to my captain. He'll decide what to do with you." He pointed to the water bottles he'd filled. "You can help me carry these, too."

That set the other soldiers laughing. "He's no fool," one of them said. "Doesn't feel like working himself when he can get somebody else to do it for him." Had he used a different tone of voice, he would have been mocking a lazy serf. But he sounded more admiring than otherwise: one soldier applauding another's successful ingenuity.

"Come on," Rollant said again. The escaped serf ran forward and picked up almost all the water bottles. For him, bearing burdens for King Avram's soldiers was a privilege, not a duty—and a nuisance of a duty at that. Rollant smiled as he grabbed the couple of bottles the runaway hadn't. "When I finally got into the south, I was the same way you are now," he told the fellow.

"My liege lord can't tell me what to do any more," the serf said simply. "He can't come sniffing after my woman any more, neither."

Rollant led the whole family of runaways back to the encampment. Sergeant Joram glared at him. "I sent you after water, not more blonds," he growled, and then, before Rollant could say anything, "Take 'em to the captain. He'll figure out what to do with 'em."

Since Rollant had intended to do just that, he obeyed cheerfully. Captain Cephas eyed the newcomers and said, "We can use somebody to chop wood. You handy with an axe, fellow?" The escaped serf nodded. Cephas turned to the woman. "Can you cook? The fellow we've got could burn water."

"Yes, lord, I can cook," she answered softly.

"I'm not a lord. I'm just a captain," Cephas said. "We'll put the two of you on the books. Half a common soldier's pay for you" —the man— "and a third for you" —the woman. Their delighted expressions on realizing they'd get money for their labor were marvels to behold. Rollant understood that. He'd felt the same way. Only later would they find out how little money they were getting.

Count Thraxton knew a lot of his soldiers had expected him to fall back all the way to Marthasville after retreating from Rising Rock. Of all the towns in Peachtree Province, Marthasville was the one King

Geoffrey *had* to hold, for it was a great glideway junction, and most of the paths leading from the long-settled west to the eastern provinces passed through it. Falling back closer to it—to Stamboul, say, halfway there—might even have been prudent.

But, after his vow to Ned of the Forest, Thraxton would have reckoned himself forsworn—and, worse, the officers serving under him would have reckoned him forsworn—had he retreated that close to Marthasville. And so he didn't go very far to the northwest, but made his new headquarters at a little town in southern Peachtree Province called Fa Layette, not far from the picturesquely named River of Death.

Death suited Thraxton's present mood. Nor was that mood improved when a fellow who'd escaped from Rising Rock after the southrons seized it was brought before him and said, "They paraded right through the town, sir, the whole scapegrace army of 'em, all their stinking bands blaring out the battle hymn of the kingdom till your ears wanted to bust."

"May the Hunt Lady flay them. May the Thunderer smite them," Thraxton said in a voice so terrible, his informant flinched back from him as if he were the Thunderer himself. "May their torn and lightning-riven souls drop into the seven hells for torment eternal. That they should dare do such a thing in a city that is ours . . ."

"A city that *was* ours," the fellow from Rising Rock said. Thraxton fixed—transfixed—him with a glare. He didn't just flinch. He spun on his heel and fled from the chamber where he'd been speaking with Thraxton.

"Shall I bring him back, sir?" asked the young officer who'd escorted the refugee into Thraxton's presence. "Do you think you can learn more from him?"

"No: only how great an idiot he is, and I already have a good notion of that," Thraxton answered. The junior officer nodded and saluted and also left the chamber in a hurry.

Count Thraxton hardly noticed. He set an absent-minded hand on the front of his uniform tunic. His stomach pained him. It often did—and all the more so when he contemplated the spectacle of General Guildenstern, a man with neither breeding nor military talent, parading through Rising Rock, through the city Thraxton himself had had to abandon.

*I am the better soldier.* Thraxton was as sure of that as he was that the sun was shining outside. *I am the better mage.* That went without saying. No general in either army could come close to matching him in magic. *Then where are my triumphs? Where are my processions?*

He could have had them. He should have had them. Somehow, they'd slipped through his fingers. Somehow, he'd ended up here in Fa Layette, a no-account town if ever there was one, while Guildenstern, his inferior in every way, victoriously paraded through Rising Rock.

It wasn't his fault. It couldn't possibly have been his fault. He was the one who deserved that parade, by the gods. *And I shall have it*, he thought. He always knew exactly what he was supposed to do, and he always did it, but somehow it didn't always come off quite the way he'd expected. Since the mistakes weren't, couldn't have been, his, they had to belong to the officers serving under him.

Slowly, Thraxton nodded. That was bound to be it. Had any general in all the history of Detina—in all the history of the world—ever been worse served by his subordinates? Thraxton doubted it. Even now, the men who led the constituent parts of his army were not the warriors he would have wanted. Ned of the Forest? A boor, a bumpkin, a lout. Leonidas the Priest? No doubt he served the Lion God well, but he had a habit of being tardy on the battlefield. Dan of Rabbit Hill? *Better than either of the others*, Thraxton thought, *but not good enough*. Dan had a fatal character flaw: he was ambitious. Thraxton tolerated ambition only in himself.

A mage with the winged-eye badge of a scryer next to his lieutenant's bars came in and saluted Thraxton. "May it please your Grace," he said, "Earl James of Broadpath and his host have passed out of Croatoan and into Palmetto Province. They should go through Marthasville in a couple of days, and should reach us here the day following."

"I thank you," Thraxton said. The scryer saluted again and withdrew.

Alone in the chamber once more, Thraxton scowled. His stomach gave another painful twinge. Earl James' imminent arrival pleased him not at all. What was it but King Geoffrey's declaration that he couldn't win the war here in the east by himself? And James of Broadpath would prate endlessly of Duke Edward, and of how things were done in the Army of Southern Parthenia. Thraxton could practically hear him already. He himself cared not a fig for Duke Edward or his precious army.

James' men *would* let him meet Guildenstern on something like equal terms. "And I will meet him, and I will beat him," Thraxton said. He knew what he had to do. Figuring out how to do it was another matter. Until James of Broadpath got here, he remained badly outnumbered. If General Guildenstern pushed matters, he could erupt into southern Peachtree Province and force Thraxton from Fa Layette as he'd forced him from Rising Rock.

Guildenstern, fortunately, was not given to pushing things. Few of the southron generals were. Had Count Thraxton been fighting for Avram, he wouldn't have wanted to push things, either. But he couldn't stomach Avram at all, any more than any of the northern nobles who'd backed King Geoffrey could.

He studied a map of the territory through which he'd just had to retreat. Slowly, he nodded. He might have smiled, had his face not forgotten what smiling was all about. After a little more contemplation, he nodded again and shouted for a runner.

"Sir?" the young soldier said. "Your Grace?"

"Fetch Ned of the Forest here," Thraxton said. "Fetch him here at once."

"Yes, sir." The runner saluted. Even as he turned to obey, though, his eyes widened. The whole Army of Franklin had to know about the quarrel between the two generals. Thraxton shrugged. Beating the southrons, beating Guildenstern, came first. After that, he could settle accounts with the backwoods scum on his own side who failed to have a proper appreciation for his manifest brilliance.

Ned of the Forest came fast enough to give Count Thraxton no excuse to criticize him. His salute was sloppy, but it had never been neat. "What do you want with me, sir?" he asked—on the edge of military courtesy, but not over the edge.

"Come to the map with me," Thraxton said, and Ned obeyed. Thraxton went on, "You have always claimed that your unicorn-riders can cover twice as much ground as footsoldiers, and that they can fight as well as footsoldiers once they get where they are going."

"It's the truth, sir," Ned answered. "Not only just

as well as footsoldiers, but just like footsoldiers, too. You can do a lot more harm to the fellows you don't like, and do it from a lot further ways away, with crossbows than you can with sabers."

*This man knows nothing of the glory of war*, Count Thraxton thought scornfully. *He might as well be a potter—it is only a job, a piece of work, to him.* But then Thraxton gave a mental shrug. *He is the tool I have ready to hand. I can use him. I will use him. And if, in the using, I use him up . . . so what?*

Aloud, Thraxton said, "You shall have your chance to prove it, sir. I require you to take your riders south to the line of the River of Death" —he ran a bony finger along it— "and patrol it. And, at all costs, I require you to keep General Guildenstern's army from crossing the river and marching on Fa Layette."

Ned frowned. "Don't reckon I can do that, if he throws his whole army at one place. Unicorns, footsoldiers, what have you—I haven't got the men to stand against him. Way it looks to me, this whole army hasn't got the men for it, or why would we be waiting for the troopers from the west to get here?"

He had a point, worse luck. Count Thraxton had to backtrack, as he'd had to backtrack from Rising Rock. "Very well," he said with poor grace. "I shall revise my command, then. Here, do this: *cross over* the River of Death, if that should please you, and make the southrons think you are everywhere in greater force than is in fact the truth. Delay them till Earl James reaches Fa Layette, and you shall have achieved your purpose."

Ned of the Forest's eyes gleamed. This time, he saluted as if he meant it. "Fair enough, sir," he said— now he'd been given a task he liked. "I'll run those southrons ragged. By the time I'm through, they'll reckon everybody in our whole army is scurrying around south of the river."

"That would be excellent," said Thraxton, who doubted whether Ned could accomplish any such thing. True, the general of unicorn-riders had done some remarkable work down in Franklin and Cloviston, but mostly as a raider. Facing real soldiers, and facing them in large numbers, Thraxton thought him more likely to suffer an unfortunate accident.

*And his loss would pain me so very much*, Thraxton thought, and almost smiled again.

Ned nodded to him. "You just leave it to me, your Grace. I'll give you something you can brag about. And then, when James' men finally get here from Parthenia, I'll help you make your big brag come true, even if you did aim it right at me. As long as it helps the kingdom, I don't much care." He nodded one last time, then turned and, without so much as a by-your-leave, strode out of the house Thraxton had taken for his own.

"Insolent churl," Thraxton muttered. He rubbed his hands together. With any luck at all, the insolent churl would hurl himself headlong against the southrons and come to grief because of it.

But what if Ned's luck ran out too abruptly? What if Guildenstern's men smashed up the unicorn-riders and decided to press north with all their strength? That would without a doubt prove troublesome. Thraxton called for another runner.

"Your Grace?" the youngster said, drawing himself up straight as a spearshaft. "Command me, your Grace!"

He might have thought Count Thraxton was about to send him into the hottest part of a desperate fight, not simply to run an errand. Thraxton said, "Ask

General Leonidas if he would do me the honor of attending me." He summoned Leonidas far more courteously than he'd ordered Ned of the Forest hither.

"Yes, sir!" The runner hurried off as if King Geoffrey would be overthrown unless he reached Leonidas the Priest on the instant.

Leonidas, on the other hand, took his own sweet time about reporting to Thraxton's headquarters. Ned had come far more promptly. When at last Leonidas did appear, resplendent in the crimson vestments of a votary of the Lion God, Thraxton snapped, "So good of you to join me."

Leonidas gave him a wounded look, which he ignored. "How may I serve you, your Grace?" the hierophant asked.

"By coming sooner to find out what I require of you, for starters," Thraxton snapped. He had heard that his underlings complained he was hard on them. *With such fools for underlings, what else can I be but hard?*

Stiffly, Leonidas said, "Your messenger found me offering sacrifice to the Lion God, that he might favor us and close his jaws upon the accursed armies of our opponents."

"Let the Lion God do as he will," Count Thraxton said. "I intend to close *my* jaws on the southrons, and to do that just as soon as Earl James' men reach me."

Leonidas the Priest looked shocked. "Without the support of the gods, your Grace, we are as nothing, and our plans as vapors. I shall pray to the Lord of the Great Mane that he put this wisdom in your heart."

"Pray later," Thraxton told him. "I require you to move your army down to the northern bank of the

River of Death, and to stand in readiness to repel the southrons if by some mischance they overwhelm Ned of the Forest, whose riders will be harrying them south of the river."

"Very well, sir," Leonidas said, though his voice remained stiff with disapproval. "I shall of course do as you require. But I also suggest that you offer up your own prayers and sacrifices to the Lion God, lest he grow angry at you for flouting him. We would not want his might inclined toward the southrons, after all."

"No, indeed not." Thraxton could not imagine the Lion God—or, for that matter, any of the other Detinan gods—inclining toward King Avram and his misguided followers. The gods had led the Detinans to victory over the blond savages who'd once had this splendid kingdom all to themselves. If that wasn't a sign the gods wanted the Detinans to go right on ruling the blonds, Thraxton couldn't dream of what such a sign might be. He nodded to Leonidas the Priest. "Go now. Set your men in motion, as I have commanded."

"Very well, sir," the priest of the Lion God repeated. "Again, though, I urge on you suitable prayer and sacrifice."

"Of course," Count Thraxton said. Leonidas left, though he didn't look as if he believed the general. And he was right to disbelieve, for Thraxton had no intention of sacrificing. *Why should I?* he thought. *I am right, and the gods must know it.*

# III

As Lieutenant General George had known he would, General Guildenstern made his headquarters in the finest hotel Rising Rock boasted. As George had feared he would, Guildenstern grew less diligent about going after Thraxton the Braggart than he had been before Rising Rock fell. George suspected the army commander had found something lively in the female line here, but judged coming right out and asking would only make Guildenstern's always uncertain temper worse.

At supper a couple of days after King Avram's army paraded into Rising Rock, Doubting George did ask General Guildenstern when he intended going after Count Thraxton. "The sooner the better, sir," George added, "if you care for what I think."

By Guildenstern's expression, he didn't care a fig—

not even a moldy fig—for what his second-in-command thought. But he did his best to make light of his feelings, waving his hand and speaking in airy tones: "I don't think we need to worry about Thraxton for a while now. By the way he scuttled out of here with his tail between his legs, he's skedaddled down to Stamboul, and that's if he hasn't gone all the way to Marthasville. We'll settle him in due course, never you fear." He lifted a glass of amber spirits to his lips and gulped down half of what it held.

"If he's skedaddling, we ought to push him," George said stubbornly.

"And we will." General Guildenstern finished the spirits and waved for a refill. A blond maidservant— *not a serf any more*, Doubting George reminded himself—hurried up with a corked jug and poured more of the potent stuff into the glass. Guildenstern's eyes followed her as she swayed away. Doubting George sighed. *He's more interested in what's between her legs than in the tail he thinks Thraxton has between his.* But Guildenstern did bring himself back to the matter at hand: "In a few days, we will."

"Why wait, sir?" George asked. He'd already seen more than one victory count for less than it should have because the general in charge of Avram's army failed to push hard after winning the initial battle. And he doubted his superior's sincerity here. "If we've got the traitors in trouble, shouldn't we do everything we can to keep them there?"

General Guildenstern looked down his long, pointed nose at George. "Eager, aren't you?" By the way he said it, he didn't mean it as a compliment.

But George didn't care how he meant it. "Yes, sir," he answered. "If we've got 'em down, we ought to kick 'em."

Instead of answering right away, Guildenstern took another swig of spirits. "Ahh," he said, and wiped his mouth on the sleeve of his gray tunic. "That's the real stuff." George could only nod; Franklin was famous for the spirits it distilled. After yet another gulp, something kindled in Guildenstern's eyes. It didn't look like something pleasant. George hoped he was wrong, but—again—he doubted it. His superior said, "So you really want to go after Thraxton the Braggart, do you?"

"Yes, sir!" Lieutenant General George didn't hesitate, no matter what the gleam in General Guildenstern's eye meant. "If we chase him, we'll catch him, and if we catch him, we'll lick him."

"Here's what I'll do, then," Guildenstern said. George leaned forward. He was sure he wouldn't get everything he wanted. For him to have got everything he wanted, General Guildenstern would have had to set the army in motion day before yesterday, or even the day before that. Guildenstern breathed spirituous fumes into his face, fumes potent enough to make him marvel that the commanding general's breath didn't catch fire when it passed over the flame of the rock-oil lamp on the table. "I'll give you half the army, and you go after Thraxton with it the best way you know how. I'll follow behind with the rest."

"Half our army is smaller than the whole of his," George said slowly. "Not a lot smaller, mind you, but it is."

"So what?" General Guildenstern answered, airily once more—or perhaps the spirits were starting to have their way with him. "If I've told you once, I've told you a dozen times: my guess is that he's hightailing it for Stamboul."

"I'm still not sure you're right about that, sir," Doubting George said, in lieu of some stronger and less politic expression of disagreement.

"So what?" Guildenstern repeated. That struck George as a cavalier attitude even for a cavalier. But then the commanding general went on, "Suppose I *am* wrong. Suppose Thraxton the Braggart's lurking in the undergrowth just outside of town here. Suppose he hits you when you come after him."

"I am supposing all that, sir," George replied. "I don't suppose I like any of it very much."

"By the gods, why not?" Guildenstern said. "You said it yourself: half our army isn't much smaller than all of his. Suppose he does attack you. Don't you think you can keep him in play till I come up with the rest of our troopers? Don't you think we can smash him between us, the way you'd smash a hickory nut between two stones?"

Now Lieutenant General George was the one who said, "Ahh." He took a pull at his own glass of spirits. Maybe Guildenstern wasn't the best general in the world (as long as Duke Edward of Arlington kept breathing, Guildenstern surely wasn't the best general in the world). But he wasn't the worst, either. The move that flanked Thraxton the Braggart out of Rising Rock had been his idea. And this ploy here . . . *It puts me in danger*, Doubting George thought, *but it gives me the chance to show what I can do, too . . . if Thraxton really is hanging around not far north of here*. George nodded. "That just might do the job, sir."

"I think so myself," Guildenstern said complacently. "How soon can you have your half of the army ready to move?"

"Sir, I can put them on the road tomorrow at

sunrise," George answered. "I know you'll be ready to follow close on my heels."

He knew nothing of the sort. And, just as he'd expected, the commanding general looked appalled. "That strikes me as too precipitate," Guildenstern said. "The army should have at least two or three days more to recover itself before plunging on."

"We've already had all the time we need, sir," Lieutenant General George said. "Why, just today I had a delegation of soldiers asking me why we weren't already up and doing." That was fiction of the purest ray serene. George didn't care. If it got General Guildenstern moving, he was of the opinion that it benefited King Avram and the whole Kingdom of Detina.

"Insolent rogues!" Guildenstern rumbled. "I hope you gave 'em what they deserved." If he wanted to be up and doing, it was more likely in a bedchamber than anywhere else.

"Why, yes, sir," Doubting George said. "I gave 'em each two silver crowns from my own pocket, for being true Detinan patriots."

What General Guildenstern gave him was a harassed look. Guildenstern might have outmaneuvered Thraxton around Rising Rock, but George had just outmaneuvered the commanding general here. "Very well," Guildenstern said. "If you set out tomorrow, you may rest assured I'll follow the day after."

"Thank you, sir," Doubting George said. "I knew I could rely on you. I knew the kingdom could rely on you."

He knew nothing of the sort. What he did know was what a devilish liar he'd turned into. He hoped the Thunderer would have mercy on him. *It's not for my own advantage*, he thought apologetically. *It's for*

*Detina*. No lightning bolt crashed through the roof and smote him where he sat. He chose to believe that meant the god knew he was telling the truth.

"Yes, we must save the kingdom," Guildenstern said, as if the idea had just occurred to him. He got to his feet. "And, if I'm going to be marching out of Rising Rock day after tomorrow, I have some urgent business I'd best attend to now." He bowed to Doubting George and departed.

George suspected the urgent business resided in the commanding general's pantaloons and nowhere else but. He shrugged as he rose, too. Even in his jaundiced opinion, Guildenstern *wasn't* the worst general around. Now that George had succeeded in reminding him of his duty, he would probably do it well enough.

*And I have business of my own to attend to*, George thought as he left the hotel and hurried through the twilight toward the encampment of the brigades he himself commanded. Sweat ran down his face and down his back and dripped from under his arms. Even though summer was on the point of turning to fall, Rising Rock's muggy heat made it a place where nobody in his right mind wanted to hurry. Doubting George hurried anyway. Unlike his commanding general, he needed no one to remind him of his duty.

He was shouting for runners as he got to his own pavilion of gray canvas. The young men appeared as quickly as if a military mage had conjured them up. That was their duty, and they would have heard about it had they failed. "Sir?" one of them said, saluting.

"Hunt down Brigadiers Rinaldo, Brannan, Negley, and Absalom the Bear," George said. "Inform them all that they are to be ready to move at first light tomorrow morning. We shall march on Thraxton the Braggart's army then, our purpose being to bring him to battle and hold him in place so that General Guildenstern, following behind us, may fall upon him and destroy him altogether."

The runners stared. Whatever they'd expected, that wasn't it. After they took it in, though, they whooped and scattered. Reddish dust flew up from under their boots as they ran. The commanding general might be distracted, but they wanted to close with Thraxton.

Before long, the encampment started to stir like a just-kicked anthill, only with rather more purpose. Lieutenant General George chuckled a little and rubbed his hands together, as if he were an evil wizard on the stage in New Eborac. When word reached the half of the army that wasn't going forward, the half General Guildenstern had kept for himself, that this half *was*, he suspected Guildenstern wouldn't be able to stay in Rising Rock for even a few hours, no matter how much he might want to. He also suspected the commanding general hadn't figured that out for himself. *Well, too bad for the commanding general*, he thought.

Colonel Andy, Doubting George's aide-de-camp, came bustling up to him. Andy was a small, plump, fussily precise man, hopeless leading soldiers in the field but brilliant when keeping track of all the things they needed to do to reach the field with everything they had to have to fight well. "Sir, are we moving?" he asked, reproach in his voice. "You didn't tell me we were moving. How can I be ready when I don't know what to be ready for?"

"If I'd known, your Excellency, I would have told you," George said, and set a reassuring hand on Andy's shoulder. The aide-de-camp was only a baronet, hardly a nobleman at all, but despite that—or perhaps because of it—touchy about the way people used him. "I didn't know it myself till General Guildenstern gave me the order less than half an hour ago."

"He should conduct his business in a more businesslike manner," Colonel Andy said with a sniff. He bowed to George; if he expected punctilious politeness, he also returned it. "What precisely—or even what approximately—are we expected to do, if the commanding general has any idea of that?" His opinion of Guildenstern was not high.

"We're going after Thraxton the Braggart," George answered. "The commanding general is of the belief that he's falling back on Stamboul, or maybe even all the way to Marthasville."

"What utter nonsense," Andy said, a view that marched well with George's own. "Thraxton's an arrogant boor, but he's not an idiot." He added something under his breath. It might have been, *Unlike some people I could name*, but it might not have, too.

Doubting George didn't ask. Instead, he said, "Be that as it may, we're going after the traitors. If it turns out they're closer, we'll hit them, and then General Guildenstern will come up and finish them off."

"And what route shall we take?" his aide-de-camp demanded. "I have been given to understand that knowing where we're going is considered desirable in these affairs. This may be only a rumor, but I do believe it holds some truth."

"Er—yes," Lieutenant General George said. "The only real route we have starts in the gap between Sentry Peak and Proselytizers' Rise. Once we get up into Peachtree Province, what we do will depend on where Thraxton really turns out to be, don't you think?"

"Improvisation at the end of a campaign often leads to victory," Colonel Andy said, sniffing. "Improvisation at the beginning of a campaign often leads to disaster. The gods grant that this one prove the exception."

"Your Excellency, we are going after Thraxton the Braggart," George said. "I don't know where we'll find him, but I expect we will. When we do, we'd better be ready to give him a kick right where it'll do the most good. I rely on you to help us do that."

"You expect me to make ham without a pig," Andy said. "I shall do what I can, but I could do more if I knew more."

"I intend to move along the western slope of Sentry Peak," Doubting George said. "That way, if the traitors try to strike at us, they'll have a harder time hitting us from the flank. Past that, we'll just have to see."

His aide-de-camp sniffed again. "Not good enough. Not nearly good enough." But off he went, to do his best to make pork-free ham for George's army.

Ned of the Forest urged his unicorn across a stream in the forest north of the River of Death. The animal's every step took him farther from Fa Layette, and from Thraxton the Braggart. The farther he got from Thraxton, the happier he became.

A squirrel peered out from behind the trunk of an oak and chattered indignantly at him and at the rough-looking men in faded indigo riding behind him. Ned chuckled and spoke to Colonel Biffle, who followed him most closely: "If we weren't in such a rush, somebody'd bag that little fellow for the supper pot."

"Somebody may yet," Biffle answered.

But Ned shook his head. "We don't slow down for anything. We don't slow down for anybody. One of my men tries to make us slow down and I find out about it, he'll be one sorry so-and-so, and you can bank on that."

"All right, Ned," Colonel Biffle said hastily. "Everybody knows better than to get your angry up—everybody this side of Count Thraxton, anyway," he added in lower tones.

"People had ought to know that," Ned said. "I'm a peaceable man, but . . ." He normally spoke in a quiet voice, so quiet one had to listen closely to him to make out what he was saying. But when his temper rose, an astonishing transformation came over him. His eyes flashed. He shouted. He cursed.

"But . . ." Colonel Biffle echoed, and let out a nervous chuckle. "When your angry *is* up, your men are a lot more afraid of you than they ever could be afraid of the graybacked lice who fight for King Avram."

"Good," Ned said.

They went on for a while in silence. The road they followed hardly deserved the name. It was little more than a game track. But Ned's scouts had already traveled it from one end to the other, as they had most of the paths in the woods, and they knew just where it hit the main road leading north from Rising Rock.

After splashing through another small stream, Ned held up his hand and reined in. "Column, halt!" Colonel Biffle called from behind him, and the column did halt. Biffle asked, "What is it, sir?"

"I want to be sure the pack animals are keeping up with us all right," Ned answered. "Pass the word back, and then send it forward to me again. We can all use a little blow till it comes."

"Yes, sir," Biffle said, and back the word went. In short order, it returned: the laden asses—and even a few unicorns—were where they were supposed to be.

"Fine." Ned of the Forest nodded. "When we bump into Guildenstern's men, we'll need 'em. Every one of 'em'll be worth its weight in gold, matter of fact."

"Yes, sir," Colonel Biffle repeated, though he didn't sound altogether convinced. He did say, "You think of everything, don't you, sir?"

"I'd better," Ned answered. "We'd be in a fine way if I counted on Thraxton to do it for me, now wouldn't we?" His regimental commander giggled— there was no other word for it—deliciously scandalized. Ned didn't see that he'd made a joke. Thraxton wouldn't do him any favors. Nobody except the men he led—the men who'd seen for themselves what he was worth—would ever do him any favors. He didn't care. He expected none. "Forward!" he called, and rode on.

Forward they went. As they moved on, Ned wondered what he would do if Guildenstern's men suddenly and unexpectedly attacked from the south. It wouldn't happen, not if he could help it. He had scouts out not just ahead of his riders but off to the flanks as well.

But the forest between Rising Rock and Fa Layette was often thick and tangled. He liked setting ambuscades, and knew he could fall into them, too. If he did, he wanted to have a plan ready. Some men—even some soldiers of high rank—went through life perpetually surprised. Ned of the Forest had no desire to be among their number.

A scout came galloping back along the game path toward him. "Lord Ned! Lord Ned!" he called, reining in.

"What is it?" Ned leaned forward, like a hound

who knew he was about to be released from his lead line. "It must be something, by the gods, or you wouldn't ride hells-for-leather to get me word of it."

"Something, yes, Lord Ned." The scout nodded. He was a lean, weatherbeaten man in his early thirties: not a fellow who'd owned an estate full of serfs before the war, surely, but not one who'd take kindly to anyone who told him he couldn't dream of acquiring such an estate one day, either. His sharp northeastern accent wasn't much different from Ned's own. "Herk and me, we spotted southron riders heading up the road from Rising Rock. Unless we're daft, there's a whole big army behind 'em."

"Is that a fact?" Ned said softly, and the scout nodded again. Ned scratched at the edge of his neat chin beard. "They're not moving as fast as I would have, but they're not sitting on their hands down there, neither." His eyes narrowed. "They didn't spy you?"

"Lord Ned!" The scout both looked and sounded affronted. "You think me and Herk are a couple o' city men, can't walk across ground with grass on it without we fall over our own feet?"

"No, no." Ned of the Forest waved in apology. "Forget I said that: the Lion God swallow up the words. To business: tell me exactly where you and Herk were at and how fast the southrons were moving. Soon as I hear that, I can reckon up where we'd do best to pay 'em a call."

"A social call, like," the scout said, and grinned— showing a couple of missing front teeth—when Ned nodded. The rider spoke for a couple of minutes, at one point dismounting to sketch in the dirt to make his words clearer.

Ned scratched at the edge of his beard again.

clinging close to the west side of Sentry Peak, are they? That's not stupid. I only wish it was. But we'll have a harder time hitting 'em from both flanks at once this way."

If General Guildenstern had his whole army on the move, he would outnumber Ned's men eight or ten to one. Just for a moment, Ned wondered how he had the nerve to think about attacking the southrons from two directions at once. Then he shrugged and laughed a little. *I might have a better chance of licking 'em that way*, he thought.

But it didn't seem practical, not with the dispositions the scout said the enemy was making. Ned abandoned the idea without remorse. "Let's get down to business," he said again, and started giving orders.

When the path along which his troopers were riding forked, he chose the more northerly branch. Before he found out where Guildenstern's men were, he would have kept pressing as far south as he could. Now, though, he knew where he and his men had to be before the southrons' scouts got there.

He reined in when the track ran into the main south-north road. A couple of hundred yards south of the junction, the trees came down close to the main road on either side. A slow, nasty grin spread over Ned's face. The riders close enough to see it started grinning, too, and nudging one another. "He's got something up his sleeve besides his arm," one of them said. Everybody who heard him nodded.

Although Ned of the Forest did hear that, he hardly noticed. His mind turned like a serf woman's spinning wheel. And then, all at once, it stopped, and he knew what he had to do. "You men!" he barked to the unicorn-riders nearest him. "Take some axes and knock down enough trees to make a barricade across the road. Quick, now—don't sit there playing with yourselves. Get your arses moving right now!" He never cursed, except when action was near.

The troopers dismounted and fell to with a will. Chestnuts and oaks and pines came crashing down. Meanwhile, Ned shouted more orders. His voice changed timbre at the prospect of a fight. It belled forth, loud and piercing enough to stretch over a battlefield and urgent enough to make men obey first and think afterwards.

One man in eight stayed behind to hold unicorns. In most cavalry forces, it would have been one man in four. Ned wished he could do without unicorn-holders altogether. He didn't have that many men. He needed to get all of them he could into the fight.

At his command, the troopers who'd built the barricade crouched behind it, their crossbows cocked. Along with Ned himself, more men moved into position among the trees to the west of the road. In country less wild, one of the local nobles would have had his serfs trim the trees back out of bowshot from the roadway, to make life harder for bandits. No one had bothered here: here the road was the intruder, with the trees the rightful inhabitants.

Ned had just got things arranged as he wanted them when a warbler whistled cheerily—once, twice, three times. He nodded: that was no natural bird, but a scout at the southern end of the line he'd formed. The southrons were in sight. "Pass the word along: nobody shoots till I give the order," he said. "Anybody spoils our surprise, I'll cut off his balls and feed 'em to my hounds."

His men chuckled, not because they thought he was kidding but because they didn't. And he wasn't—at least, not when his temper was upon him. Along with the dismounted riders, he waited for the foe. The indigo uniforms in the shadows under the trees made his soldiers and him next to invisible.

The gray-clad outriders from King Avram's army rode north up the road without so much as glancing into the forest. They were well mounted—better mounted than a lot of Ned's men—and carried themselves with the arrogance that said they thought they could whip any number of northern men. A lot of southrons thought that way till they'd been in a couple of fights with the men who followed King Geoffrey.

When the southron scouts saw the barricade across the road, they stopped, then rode forward again. Ned of the Forest nodded to himself. He would have had his men do the same thing. If the barricade had been left behind as an annoyance by the retreating northerners, they could just haul the tree trunks off to the side of the road and free it up for the men under General Guildenstern to continue their advance.

If. When the men in gray dismounted and started walking over to the felled trees, Ned's troopers behind them popped up and started shooting. A few riders in gray fell. Others ran back out of range or started shooting, too. And still others rode back toward the south, to bring reinforcements to get rid of what looked like a small nuisance. *Me, I aim to be a* big *nuisance*, Ned thought.

The southrons wasted no time in bringing more men north to deal with the dismounted troopers who harassed them from behind the fallen trees. Ned nodded again. It was a smart piece of work. Had those men behind the trees been the only ones who were bothering them, they would have driven off King Geoffrey's soldiers in short order.

Ned filled his lungs and shouted one word: "Six!" Instantly, his officers and sergeants took up the cry. Every sixth soldier hidden among the trees stepped out into the open and started shooting at the southrons. Ned stepped out into the open himself. He would not order his men to do anything he wouldn't do himself. He was a good shot with a crossbow, although he preferred the saber at closer quarters.

With crossbow quarrels suddenly smiting them from the flank as well as the front, the southrons yowled in dismay. They went down one after another. Some few of them, with more courage than sense, tried to charge Ned's men. The charge withered like a garden in a drought. Some of the southrons drew their swords, but nobody got close enough to use one.

Again, of course, Ned's men couldn't slay everybody. More of the soldiers in gray ran back toward the south. "Shouldn't we chase 'em, Lord Ned?" one of Ned of the Forest's men asked—one who didn't get the point. "They'll bring all of Guildenstern's soldiers down on our heads."

"No, not all of 'em," Ned said. "They'll bring back enough to deal with what they see—and a bit more besides, in case some little thing goes wrong. So let the gods-damned sons of bitches run." Sure enough, the heat of battle also heated his language. "They're doing just what I reckoned they would."

This time, he heard unicorns and footsoldiers coming before he spied them. The pounding of hooves, the drumroll of marching feet, soaked into his body through the soles of his own feet as well as through his ears. And when the southrons came into sight, he nodded to himself once more. They'd sent plenty to overwhelm what he was showing—and that he might not be showing everything never once crossed their minds.

A great shout rose from the enemies in gray when they saw Ned and his men still in line of battle out in the open, waiting for them. The unicorn-riders outdistanced the crossbowmen and pikemen who advanced with them. Ned's crossbowmen, waiting there away from the cover of the trees, were the sort of target cavalrymen dreamt about.

Lances and sabers and iron-shod unicorn horns gleamed in the afternoon sunlight. "Bide your time, boys," Ned said. The onrushing unicorns thundered nearer. Here and there, Ned's men began to shoot in spite of orders. Then he shouted, *"Now!"* and all his men, both those in the open and the far larger number concealed under the trees, shot a volley at the unicorn-riders that broke their charge as if it had run headlong into a stone wall. Unicorns tumbled. Men pitched off them. Unhurt beasts fell over wounded ones. Ned's men kept right on shooting; thanks to those pack animals, they had bolts to spare.

Cries of "Magecraft! Black magecraft!" rose from the southrons. Ned of the Forest threw back his head and laughed out loud. And General Guildenstern's footsoldiers, seeing that the unicorns had failed but not seeing why, kept coming forward till they too took a couple of volleys from his massed dismounted force of riders.

"We'll lick 'em all!" one of his troopers cried.

But he shook his head. "Next time, they'll bring up enough to deal with the lot of us," he said. "The idea is, not to stick around here to get dealt with. Back in the woods, boys. Back to the unicorns. We'll be gone, and we'll hit 'em again somewheres else pretty soon—doing what we want, not what they want us to." He clapped his hands together. "That's what this here war's all about, ain't it?"

"Forward!" General Guildenstern cried grandly. Horns blaring, drums thumping, the part of the army he hadn't given to Doubting George marched out of Rising Rock, heading north toward the border with Peachtree Province. Guildenstern wished the army— or at least he—could have stayed longer. One of the blond serving girls—a serf no longer, of course, but still a servant—at the hotel had served him as delightfully as he'd ever imagined a woman doing. He sighed, then loosed another shout: "Forward! Duty calls!" He wasn't just telling his men. He was reminding himself, too.

Having reminded himself, he used his knees and the reins to urge his unicorn forward. Its every step took him farther from the blond girl. He wished he hadn't reminded himself of that. To keep from thinking about it, he loosed the brandy flask he wore next to his sword and swigged from it. Maybe the peaches from which the potent stuff was brewed had come from the province toward which he advanced. That was some consolation for leaving the wench behind. Some, yes. Enough?

*Probably plenty of willing blond wenches up in Peachtree Province*, he thought. That notion, possibly sparked by the brandy he'd poured down, went further toward consoling him for leaving Rising Rock.

*And they'll all fall at my feet—or into my bed— once I smash up Thraxton the Braggart's army once for all. I can do it. I will do it. Once I get clear of these woods, I'll outflank him again and again, the same way I flanked him out of Rising Rock, out of*

*Franklin altogether. He can flee or he can fight. If he flees, I throw more wood on King Geoffrey's pyre with every mile of land I take back for King Avram. If he fights, I crush him.* Guildenstern nodded and took another nip from his flask. The sun shone down brightly, as if on him alone. The breeze smelled sweet, at least to him. Victory made a better perfume than flowers or spice.

*Let me crush Thraxton,* Guildenstern thought. *Let my scryers send word to King Avram that Marthasville is his again, that the gold dragon, the true dragon, has driven out the red. What will that mean? Earl Guildenstern? Count Guildenstern? Even Duke Guildenstern, by the gods? Duke Guildenstern. I like the sound of that.*

He came from a family of merchants and artisans. No one except a couple of worthless cousins had ever gone hungry. Some of his kin enjoyed more wealth than most nobles. He'd never lacked for anything in all his days—anything except respectability. He shook his head. That was the wrong word. In the bustling south, merchants and artisans were perfectly respectable. He'd lacked . . . prominence.

He nodded. That fit. Becoming an officer had given him some of what he wanted. Becoming a noble would give him the rest.

"Duke Guildenstern," he murmured, and nodded again. It had a fine ring to it.

Doubting George, now, Doubting George was already a baron over in Parthenia, though King Geoffrey—Geoffrey the traitor—had seized his estate when he stayed loyal to King Avram, just as Avram had declared Duke Edward of Arlington's lands forfeit to the crown when Edward chose Geoffrey over him. Guildenstern was sure George scorned him because his blood wasn't higher. *Let me settle Thraxton, and it will be. Let me rescue George, in fact, and it will be.*

His second-in-command had stuck close to the western flank of Sentry Peak. General Guildenstern— *I outrank Doubting George, no matter how blue his blood is*—moved his slightly larger force north along roads farther west still. If Count Thraxton was rash enough to have lingered in the neighborhood, Guildenstern and George would smash him between them.

But Guildenstern didn't really believe Thraxton had done any such thing. No matter what Doubting George thought, he remained convinced Thraxton had hightailed it for Stamboul. If anything, George's belief that the enemy might be closer made him sure Thraxton wasn't.

He turned to Brigadier Alexander, who commanded one of the two divisions in the part of the army Guildenstern still led personally. "I say we have them on the run," he announced.

"Hope you're right, sir," Alexander answered with a smile. His face usually wore one; he had a bright, easygoing disposition.

His smile was enough to make General Guildenstern give one back—which meant it was sunny indeed. Expansiveness perhaps fueled by brandy, Guildenstern said, "No wonder you're a brigadier—your family's given King Avram a brigade's worth of men."

"Oh, not quite, General." Alexander chuckled at the commanding general's quip, even if he'd surely heard the like before.

"How many kinsfolk of yours *have* come out of Highlow Province, anyhow?" Guildenstern asked with genuine curiosity.

"Seventeen in all, sir, if you count my father," Alexander said proudly. "They wouldn't let him come north with us—said he was too old. But when John the Hunter led his unicorns south of the Highlow River to stir things up in our part of the kingdom last year, Father went out against him. They killed him in one of the little fights down there, the bastards." For a moment, his smile faded. But then it returned, though tinged with sorrow. "Not many of them got back over the river, and Geoffrey hasn't tried anything like that since."

"Seventeen." Even Guildenstern hadn't thought it was quite so many. "Not all brothers, surely—or your father was an even mightier man than I would have reckoned. Mightily beloved of the Sweet One, anyhow." He extended his middle finger in the gesture sacred to the goddess.

"Well, she did smile on him, General—there are ten of us sprung from his loins," Alexander answered. "The rest are close cousins. My brother Niel is one of your colonels of foot, and Cousin Moody leads one of your cavalry regiments. If Geoffrey wants to win this war, he'll have to lick every one of us, and I don't suppose he's got enough men to do it."

"I like that." Guildenstern took another swig of brandy. After the spirits seared their way down to his belly, he liked it even better. And he put it to his own purpose: "No wonder Thraxton's probably scurrying back toward Marthasville right this minute."

"No wonder at all," Brigadier Alexander said agreeably. "After the way you flanked the Braggart out of Rising Rock, what else could he do?"

"Not a thing. Not a single, solitary thing, by the gods." General Guildenstern smiled again. Yes, he liked the way Alexander thought.

"No wonder about what, sir?" asked Brigadier Thom, Guildenstern's other division commander.

"No wonder Thraxton the Braggart's on the run," Guildenstern replied. He gave Thom a wary look. The brigadier's father, Count Jordan of Cloviston, had done everything he could to keep Detina a single kingdom. Count Jordan had done a great deal to keep Cloviston loyal to King Avram, too, but the divisions in the realm also split his own family, for Thom's older brother, George the Bibber, had served as a brigadier under Geoffrey till cashiered for drunkenness. Even now, Guildenstern wondered about Thom's loyalty.

But the dark, shaggy-bearded officer nodded without hesitation. "No wonder at all," he said. "We've got him where we want him, sure as sure."

"Well said. By the gods, Brigadier, well said!" Guildenstern boomed. He leaned over to clap Thom on the shoulder. He almost leaned too far, far enough to fall off his unicorn. Only a quick shift of weight saved him from that ignominious tumble. Having righted himself, he did his best to pretend nothing had happened. "Sure as sure, as you put it so well, Count Thraxton must ingloriously flee, or else see himself ground like wheat between the millstones of our victorious army."

"A pretty figure, General," Thom said, "and one we shall make true." If he would sooner have been serving under Thraxton the Braggart, he did conceal it well. Of course, from everything Guildenstern knew about his immediate foe, even a man who might sooner serve King Geoffrey than King Avram was apt to have second thoughts about serving under Thraxton.

As General Guildenstern had during the advance on Rising Rock, he admired the concentrated might of the army he led. Crossbowmen, pikemen, unicorns cavalry, dart- and stone- and firepot-throwers, mages . . . He sighed, wishing mages were less necessary. But if the northerners had them—and they did—he needs must have them, too, and so he did.

On paced his unicorn. On marched the army. Rising Rock vanished in the distance behind him, obscured by bends in the road, by forest, and by the red dust boots and hooves and wheels raised. He sighed again. He would sooner have stayed back there sporting with that yellow-haired wench. She'd fit him very well, in every sense of the word. Well, no help for it—and there *would* be other women ahead.

He was musing thus when a courier shouting, "General Guildenstern! General Guildenstern!" rode toward him, fighting his way south against the northbound stream of soldiers in gray.

"Here!" Guildenstern called, and he waved for good measure. Both call and wave were probably needless: a swarm of banners and gold dragons marked his place in the line of march. But he didn't care to seem to be doing nothing.

The courier brought his unicorn up alongside Guildenstern's and saluted. "Sir, I'm Captain Menander, one of Lieutenant General George's guardsmen. You need to know, sir, that we had a sharp little run-in with Ned of the Forest's troopers late yesterday afternoon."

"*Did* you?" Guildenstern said, and Menander the guardsman nodded. "Whereabouts was this?" Guildenstern asked. "How far had Doubting George got before they jumped you?"

He didn't notice he'd used George's disparaging nickname till too late. Captain Menander was in no position to take offense. The courier answered, "Sir, our vanguard had got within perhaps six miles of the River of Death."

"Had it?" Guildenstern said—George was wasting

no time in moving north. "And what precisely happened?"

Menander looked disgusted. "If you want to know the truth, sir, Ned suckered us. I hate to say it, but it's true."

Guildenstern wasn't altogether sorry to learn of Doubting George's discomfiture—not even close. But showing that too openly wouldn't do. He said, "Ned of the Forest has managed to sucker more commanders more often than we'd like to admit. How did he do it to George?"

"He felled some trees to block the road and shot at our vanguard," Captain Menander answered. "Then, when we brought up more men to deal with his skulkers, he showed some of what he had hiding in the woods. We sent up still more men—and his whole force showed itself, gave us a black eye, and then ran away."

"His whole force, you say? Are you sure of that?" Guildenstern asked.

Menander the guardsman nodded. "Sure as can be, sir. I was up there at the edge of the fighting. As a matter of fact, it seemed like Ned had twice as many men as we thought he could. They handled us pretty roughly." He took off his hat and looked at it. So did General Guildenstern. Up near the crown, it had two small, neat holes through it. Captain Menander said, "A couple of inches lower, sir, and somebody else would be giving you this report."

"I see." Guildenstern nodded. He plucked at his beard as he thought. "I wonder if Thraxton left Ned of the Forest behind to harass our advance while he retreats with the rest of his army."

Captain Menander didn't answer. Guildenstern would have been affronted had he done so. Judging strategy wasn't a captain's place. *King Avram gave* me *that job*, Guildenstern thought.

"Wherever Thraxton the Braggart is, we have to find him and beat him," Guildenstern said. Menander nodded at that. He could hardly do anything else. The commanding general went on, "I still do believe he's running away as fast as he can go." He raised his voice: "Brigadier Alexander! Brigadier Thom!"

"Sir?" the two division commanders chorused.

"I intend to pursue Thraxton on a broad front, as broad as possible," General Guildenstern said. "Brigadier Thom, you shall take your men north up roads farther west. Brigadier Alexander, you shall continue on our present route, and hold the center between George and Thom. I'll come with you, and stay in touch with each wing through messengers and scryers."

"Yes, sir," Thom and Alexander said together. Guildenstern nodded. They were subordinate to him. They couldn't possibly say anything else.

As Captain Ormerod strode along the northern bank of the River of Death, he shook his head in frustration. "This would be miserable country for fighting a battle," he said.

"Sir, this is miserable country whether we fight a battle here or not." As usual, Lieutenant Gremio was more exact than he needed to be. That didn't mean he was altogether wrong, though. The woods, mostly pine with oak and elm and chestnut scattered through them, were thick and hard to navigate. Bushes and brambles grew in riotous profusion under the trees, making things worse yet.

"What's that?" Ormerod raised an eyebrow. "You wouldn't care to have an estate hereabouts?"

After the words were out of his mouth, he

wondered if Gremio would take offense. Living in Karlsburg, the lawyer didn't have—and didn't seem to want—a proper landed estate. But Gremio just said, "The only thing this country would be good for is burying my enemies. May it bury a lot of them."

Ormerod peered south, as if expecting to see King Avram's gray-clad villains bursting out of the trees in division strength or more. All he saw were more woods, identical to those on this side of the river. He said, "I hear Ned of the Forest buried a good many southrons a couple of days ago."

"The Lion God grant it be so," Gremio said. "Ned's no gentleman, but he fights like a round sawblade— there's no good place to get a grip on him."

"They say he almost fought Count Thraxton before we pulled out of Rising Rock," Ormerod remarked.

"He wouldn't be the first," Gremio said. "He won't be the last." His opinion of Thraxton was not high. Since Ormerod's wasn't, either, he nodded.

Before he could say anything, a gong chimed. "The call to worship," Ormerod said. He raised his voice to a shout: "Come on, men! Time to pay our respects to the Lion God."

"Time to keep Leonidas the Priest happy," Lieutenant Gremio said with a sneer. "I wish we were in Dan of Rabbit Hill's division, so the gods wouldn't hit us over the head every sixth day."

"You're nothing but a citified scoffer," Ormerod said, to which his first lieutenant nodded emphatic agreement. Ormerod went on, "The gods will recognize you, whether you recognize them or not."

"I'll take my chances," Gremio replied. "And ifsobe I'm wrong, and end up toasting in the seven hells— why, I'll save you a spot by the fire, Captain."

"Avert the omen!" Ormerod exclaimed. His fingers twisted in a sign the Detinans had borrowed from their serfs so long before, only a few scholars knew they hadn't brought it over the Western Ocean with them. Ormerod's own piety might not have been profound, but it was deep and heartfelt. He'd been a young man when a wave of proselytizing swept through northern Detina twenty years before, and he'd sealed his soul to the gods then.

Colonel Florizel had consecrated himself during that wave of proselytizing, too. "Up!" the regimental commander called. "Up, you Detinans! Let the gods know you care for them, and they'll be happy to care for you!"

Soldiers in indigo tunics and pantaloons made their way toward the altar Leonidas the Priest had set up in a clearing not far from the River of Death. Baron Ormerod and Earl Florizel accompanied their troopers. So did Lieutenant Gremio; he might be a scoffer, but he didn't advertise it to the men.

Again and again, the gong rang out. Florizel's regiment wasn't the only one assembling in the clearing; several more joined it. Off in the distance, more gongs belled. Leonidas couldn't be everywhere at once, but he made sure the men he led had every chance to worship.

When the southrons were closer, Ormerod had sometimes heard their gongs calling the faithful to prayer. All Detinans followed the same gods. All Detinans were convinced those gods favored them. Some Detinans would end up disappointed. Not a man usually given to deep thought, Ormerod simply assumed the southrons would prove the disappointed ones.

Florizel poked him in the ribs with an elbow. "Isn't

that a splendid altar?" the regimental commander said. "You couldn't find better in a proper temple back in Karlsburg, not hardly."

"No, sir, you surely couldn't," Ormerod agreed. The altar, gleaming with gilt, stood on a platform of new-sawn boards so more soldiers could see it. Also gilded were the bars of the cage in which the lion prowled, thrashing his tufted tail back and forth. Even the chain securing the frightened lamb to the altar had been slapped with several coats of gold paint.

Leonidas the Priest prowled the platform as the lion prowled the cage, waiting for the worshipers to gather. His vestments were partly of gold, but more of scarlet, as befitted a hierophant of the Lion God. Ormerod was proud to serve under such a holy man. He would have been prouder still had he reckoned Leonidas a better officer.

At last, the gongs stopped chiming. Leonidas the Priest raised his hands in a gesture of benediction. "We are gathered at the River of Death to fight for the life of our kingdom," he said. "Death and life are brethren. The Lion God knows as much. So does the lamb, his victim." He stroked the woolly little animal. It let out a desperate-sounding bleat.

An acolyte in crimson robes somewhat less magnificent than Leonidas' held a deep red-glazed bowl under the lamb's neck. Leonidas himself drew a knife from his belt and cut the lamb's throat. The acolyte caught the spurting blood in the bowl. "It is accomplished!" Leonidas cried.

"It is accomplished!" Ormerod echoed, along with the other soldiers reverencing their god. "Death and life are brethren. Such is the wisdom of the Lion God."

When the lamb was dead, Leonidas unchained the little carcass, lifted it, and gave it to the lion. With a soft grunt, the great beast began to feed. As the hierophant served the living symbol of his god, the acolyte passed the bowl of blood down to the waiting soldiers.

Ormerod stood near the portable altar. The bowl did not take long to reach him. He dipped the tip of his right index finger into it, then touched that finger to his forehead. "I am washed in the blood of the lamb," he murmured, and put the finger in his mouth to lick off the blood. "Like the Lion God, I taste victory. So may it always be."

Ritual accomplished, he passed the bowl—still warm with remembered life—to the soldier nearest him. In the worship of the Lion God, all brave men were equals. Even the southrons who worshiped him were Ormerod's equals in that way . . . which didn't keep him from wishing every one of them dead.

The last trooper who received the bowl brought it back to the acolyte, who, bowing gravely, returned it to Leonidas the Priest. Bowing in return, the hierophant accepted it from him and set it in the lion's cage. The lion, a veteran of countless such services, walked over and flicked out his tongue, drinking from the bowl.

"Go forth, my fierce friends," Leonidas called to the men who had come to worship with him. "Go forth and triumph over the wicked thieves who seek to steal everything we have, even our way of life."

As Ormerod and Lieutenant Gremio walked back toward their encampment, Gremio remarked, "It's nice to feel the gods are on our side. The way things look, I wonder if anyone else is."

"We'll whip the southrons yet—see if we don't." Ormerod spoke in ringing tones, not least to still his own unease.

"Do you know what I wish the gods would give us?" Gremio, on the other hand, was all but whispering. Ormerod shook his head. Still in that half whisper, the barrister from Karlsburg went on, "I wish they'd give us leaders who could count past ten without taking off their shoes."

"Leonidas is a very holy man," Ormerod said.

Gremio nodded. "No doubt of that, sir. But, once you've said it, you've said everything you can say to recommend him as a soldier." He lifted a forefinger; Ormerod saw a tiny bit of lamb's blood clinging to the cuticle and the crease between nail and flesh. "No, I take that back. He *is* brave, but how much good is bravery without wisdom?"

"I don't know," Ormerod answered. "I'd sooner have that than wisdom without bravery."

"In a commander?" Gremio's eyebrows rose. "I wonder." Whether he wondered or not, he changed the subject, at least a little: "And as for Thraxton, he'd serve King Geoffrey better if anyone could stand him."

"He's a mighty mage," Ormerod said.

"So he is—mighty enough to terrify his own side as well as the enemy," Gremio said.

Ormerod snorted; that was scandalous, but hardly untrue. The company commander said, "King Geoffrey dotes on him. The gods must know why, even if no one else does."

"It could be that no one at all knows why, the gods and King Geoffrey included," Gremio remarked. Ormerod snorted again, on a different note this time. That was too cynical for him to stomach easily. Maybe his unease showed on his face, for Lieutenant Gremio said, "Go into the lawcourts often enough, Captain, and you stop believing in everything."

"I suppose so." Ormerod didn't feel any happier. He wanted the men who fought under him to believe in what they were doing. He might have said more, but Gremio, whether he believed or not, had proved himself both brave and capable.

Back at the camp, a couple of serfs were tending to the company's asses. The blonds looked up from their work when the soldiers returned from the worship service. Seeing the Detinans with the bloody mark of the Lion God on their foreheads, the serfs muttered back and forth. They worshiped Detinan gods, too. How not, when those gods had proved superior to their own pantheon? But they still recalled the deities they'd once followed. Ormerod gave the serfs a suspicious look. Wouldn't they love to get some of their own back, after Avram loosed them from their feudal obligations? In their place, Ormerod knew he would have.

"They aren't as good as we are," he muttered. "Their gods aren't as good as our gods are, either."

"Well, their gods aren't as strong as our gods are, anyway," Lieutenant Gremio said. "In the end, that's what counts, isn't it?"

"I suppose so." Ormerod knew he didn't sound altogether happy about that. Strength mattered, of course. Without it, the Detinans never would have overthrown the blonds' kingdoms after coming across the Western Ocean, never would have bound the natives to the soil. But if strength was the only thing that mattered . . . King Avram's army had driven the one Count Thraxton commanded out of Franklin. Unless something splendid happened, the stinking southrons would drive Thraxton's army farther north still. Ormerod wished he knew how something splendid might be made to happen. For the life of him, though, he didn't.

As if his gloomy reflections were a cue, a scout came pelting back to him, calling, "Captain! Captain! The southrons! The southrons are coming up to the River of Death!"

Ormerod didn't hesitate. "Forward, men!" he called. "Get your crossbows, get your pikes, and forward! We have to keep them from crossing the river."

"Sir, our company's not going to be able to do that all by itself," Gremio said.

"Of course it won't." Ormerod pointed to the scout. "Go on to Colonel Florizel. Tell him what you just told me. If he doesn't send you on to Leonidas the Priest, I'm a serf. Go on." The scout pelted away. Ormerod raised his voice to a battlefield roar: "Forward!" He lowered it again. "No, we can't hold the southrons off all by ourselves, but, by the gods, we've got to try."

He waited for more argument from his lieutenant. After all, Gremio made his living by being argumentative. But now he only nodded. "Of course, sir. Let's go fill the southrons full of holes."

Along with the company, Ormerod hurried down toward the northern bank of the River of Death. Sure enough, a few unicorn-riders in gray had come up to the southern bank. They were peering north, as if wondering what awaited them.

Despite its fearsome name, the River of Death wasn't a great stream. The far bank lay within easy crossbow range. Before Ormerod could even start giving orders, his men started shooting at King Avram's troopers. A unicorn screamed as a quarrel went home. A man in gray toppled, clutching his belly.

"Well shot!" Ormerod said. "By the gods, well shot!"

A moment later, he discovered he might have been wiser not to draw notice to himself. Buzzing like an angry wasp, a crossbow quarrel zipped past his head and buried itself in a tree trunk. It would have buried itself in his flesh, too. He knew that all too well. He usually tried not to think about it. But when the Soulstealer's cloak brushed by him, he couldn't pretend he didn't feel the breeze of its passage.

Brave as if they fought for a cause Ormerod held dear, the southrons tried to charge across the river and get in among his men. But quick, fierce archery slew some, wounded more, and drove them all back to the southern bank. They started fighting as dragoons then, dismounting to give battle on foot.

Ormerod grinned. "They won't advance that way," he said. Since his job was to hold them south of the River of Death, he'd done exactly what he was supposed to.

Earl James of Broadpath felt like kicking someone, or perhaps several someones. The pox-ridden cretins who'd designed and created the chaotic jungle of glideways in the northern provinces of Detina would do in a pinch. No, he wouldn't have minded pinching them at all, preferably with red-hot pincers.

Everything had been tolerable till he'd brought his army over the Veldt River from Palmetto Province into Peachtree. He'd thought he would get to Marthasville soon afterwards, and down to Fa Layette soon after that. His scryers had told Count Thraxton as much.

Coming into the town of Julia, though, on the Peachtree side of the Veldt, had begun his education into just how complicated glideways could be.

An indigo-uniformed officer awaited him at the glideway port there. The fellow saluted and said, "Very good to see you here so soon, your Excellency. You must have made splendid time coming up here from southern Parthenia."

"Not splendid, but good enough," James agreed, more than a little smugly.

"Excellent," the officer said. He wore a broad smile, but not one of the sort that prompted Earl James to trust him. He'd seen that kind of smile on the faces of rivergalley gamblers and unicorn thieves. It didn't match whatever was going on behind the fellow's eyes.

When the officer didn't say anything more right away, James of Broadpath asked him, "Why did you call me out onto the pier here? I would sooner have headed straight east towards Marthasville with my army."

"I'm sure you would, sir," the officer said, his nod as false as his smile. "And as soon as your army transfers from these carpets to those waiting to take them to Marthasville, so you shall."

"As soon as my army does *what*?" James dug a finger into his ear, as if wondering whether he'd heard correctly.

"As soon as it transfers, sir," the other officer said again. No, James' ears hadn't betrayed him.

That didn't mean he understood what the other fellow was saying, or why he was saying it. "What's wrong with the carpets we're on?" he asked. "We've come this far on 'em. I don't see much point in changing for the couple of hundred miles from here to Marthasville."

"There is a point, I'm afraid," the officer said. "You've come this far on the Northern Glideway. The route east is over the Peachtree Glideway." Earl James' bushy eyebrows rose. The other officer, a captain supercilious enough to be a general, condescended to explain: "They use different sorcerous systems, sir. A carpet that will travel with ease on the one will not, cannot, move a finger's breadth on the other."

As northern noblemen went, James of Broadpath had a mild temper. But he felt that temper fraying now. "What idiot made that arrangement?" he growled, wondering how much time this unexpected difficulty would cost him. However much it was, he couldn't afford it.

"It isn't like that, General," the local captain insisted. "By the Thunderer's prick, sir, it isn't." For once, he seemed sincere. "The fellows who made the Northern Glideway had the low bid for that stretch of the route, and the fellows who created the Peachtree Glideway came in with the low bid there. The two outfits worked with different sets of mages who favored different sets of sorcery. Simple as that."

"Simple?" Earl James turned the word into a curse. "If things were simple, I wouldn't have to change glideways here. They all ought to run on the same system."

"They don't even bother with that down in the south, sir." The officer's shrug said that, if even the gold-grubbing merchants of the southern provinces who backed King Avram couldn't see the point to standardizing glideways, it wasn't worth doing.

James thought otherwise. "If they all ran on the same system, Captain, I wouldn't have to move my men off these carpets and onto the new ones. That sounds mighty fine to me."

"Nothing to be done about it," the local fellow said

with another shrug. "Do I hear rightly that your men'll be heading south from Marthasville?"

"What if you do?" James asked suspiciously. This fellow was without a doubt a son of a bitch, but that probably didn't make him a southron spy. Probably.

"Well, your Excellency, if you'll be going by way of the Northern Provinces and Western Ocean Glideway, you'll have to change again once you get into Marthasville," the captain said.

"*What?*" James of Broadpath's bellow made heads whip toward him all over the glideway port. Curses cascaded from him.

"It can't be helped, your Excellency," the other officer said. That was bound to be true, but did nothing to improve James' temper.

When he gave the necessary orders, his subordinates cursed as loudly and foully as he had. Brigadier Bell said, "We've come round three sides of a square, seems like. We might have done better just to march it."

Reluctantly, Earl James shook his head. "No, I didn't think so," he replied. "Say what you will about glideways, but they're faster, a lot faster, than shank's mare."

"I suppose so," Bell agreed. "But I hate even to seem as if I'm moving away from the enemy when what I really want to do is close with him." His right hand folded into a fist. His left hand twitched, as if it wanted to make a fist, too. But, hanging on the end of his ruined arm, it was all but useless.

"You'll have your chance," James assured him. The eager smile Bell gave in answer briefly banished the eternal pain from his face.

But when James' army, having disembarked from the carpets that had brought them to Julia, made its way over to the far side of the glideway port and the carpets that were to take them on to Marthasville, the general wondered if he'd spoken too soon. Not nearly enough carpets waited on the Peachtree Glideway's route toward Marthasville. "Where are the rest of them?" James demanded of the local captain. "I can't fit my force onto what you've got here."

"This is just about all the gliding stock on the Peachtree line, sir," that worthy said. "We've got so many men fighting, we're hard pressed to do anything else."

"How am I supposed to fight if I can't get to the battlefield?" James demanded.

"Oh, you will, sir—eventually," the captain said. "How much difference does it make whether you fight tomorrow or the next day, though?"

"My friend" —James freighted the word with heavy irony— "it might make all the difference in the world."

"It might," the other officer said. "On the other hand, it might not mean anything at all. More often than not, it won't."

James was tempted, mightily tempted, to argue that with him. The only reason he desisted was the point-lessness of it. "What do you expect me to do, then?" he asked. "Take half my army to Marthasville, send the carpets back, and wait for the other half to catch up?"

"Sir, the only other choice you have is leaving all your army here in Julia," the local officer told him. "If you want to do that, I don't see how I can stop you, but I don't suppose you'll make Count Thraxton very happy."

That, unfortunately, held altogether too much truth. James heaved a long, heartfelt sigh. "I don't think I'll make him happy letting him know I'm going to be late, either. But, as you say, I haven't got much choice." He raised his voice: "Brigadier Bell!"

"Sir!" The division commander hurried up to him.

"Brigadier, you are in charge of that part of the force which is compelled to remain behind in Julia until we free up carpets to bring it on to Marthasville," James of Broadpath told him. "Bring on the rest of the men as fast as ever you can. We'll wait in Marthasville— or, possibly, we won't. If Thraxton orders us forward, we'll go on as fast as we can. Scryers will keep you informed."

Bell saluted. "I understand, sir."

"Good." Earl James nodded approval. "And, because this delay is in no way our fault, the men need not suffer for it. Feel free to let them forage on the countryside hereabouts while they're waiting for the carpets to return."

At last, he succeeded in piercing the local captain's sangfroid. "What?" the fellow yelped. "You can't do that! They can't do that!"

"Oh, yes, we can." Brigadier Bell sounded as if he was looking forward to it. His good hand dropped to the hilt of his sword. "Just try and stop us."

The captain didn't try to stop him. The captain couldn't try to stop him, not when even the force Bell had left far outnumbered the tiny garrison in Julia. Earl James of Broadpath was something less than astonished when several more glideway carpets from the Peachtree line slid silently into the local port. There still weren't enough for him to take his whole army on to Marthasville at once, but the fraction left behind shrank from half to about a quarter.

At James' command, a scryer sent word to Count Thraxton that he would be delayed. A few minutes later, the fellow came back with Thraxton's answer: "His Grace, sir, is more than a little unhappy."

"You may tell him I'm more than a little unhappy myself," James said. "If he's such a mighty mage, he's welcome to conjure the army and me from Julia here all the way to Fa Layette." He held up a warning hand before the scryer could hurry away. "You don't need to tell him that."

"All right, sir," the scryer said. This time, James let him go.

Earl James soon discovered why the men who'd created the Peachtree Glideway had come in with the low bid: they'd done as little as they possibly could to make it worth traveling on. Their spells left a good deal to be desired. The whole glideway was sluggish; in the poorly maintained parts, the carpets barely moved at all. Watching the Peachtree Province farms and estates crawl past, James wondered if he would get stranded halfway to Marthasville. *That captain's head will roll if I do*, he thought.

One of the directing mage's assistants strode from one officers' carpet to the next and spoke reassuringly: "We're having just a little trouble with the sorcery on this stretch of the glideway, but it's nothing to worry about. Pretty soon we'll be going along sweet as you please."

"We'd bloody well better be," James said. The placating smile on the face of the directing mage's assistant never wavered. Maybe that meant he believed what he was saying. James of Broadpath hoped so. The other alternative was that he was lying and had no shame whatever.

Before long, the carpets did begin to move more briskly along the glideway. That didn't mean they ever got going as fast as those on the journey from the

Army of Southern Parthenia's encampment up to Julia had gone. James drummed his fingers on his knee, as if wishing could make the carpets speed up. Magecraft, unfortunately, didn't work like that.

Brisk movement or not, the glideway carpets didn't get into Marthasville till after nightfall. James scowled at the officer waiting on the pier to greet him. "All right, what are *you* going to tell me's gone wrong?" he growled.

"Why, nothing, sir," the fellow answered. "I'm here to guide you to the carpets to take your army south, that's all."

"That's what the chap in Julia said." James raised a bristling eyebrow. "Then he found me half the carpets I needed."

"On my honor, your Excellency, I don't think you'll have to worry about that here," the officer said. The captain back in Julia had promised no such thing. James suspected he hadn't because he had no honor.

This fellow kept his word, too. All the glideway carpets James' army needed—and more besides— waited on the southbound glideway path. James called for a scryer. "Be so good as to let Count Thraxton know we've arrived in Marthasville with something close to three quarters of our force," he said. "The rest is about a day and a half behind, back in Julia. Ask him whether he wants me to go down to Fa Layette straightaway, or whether he would sooner have me wait till everyone's with me."

"Yes, sir," the scryer said, and hurried away to do what needed doing with his crystal. A couple of minutes later, he returned. "Count Thraxton's compliments, your Excellency, and he says you may use your own judgment. I am also to inform you that he's trying to bring General Guildenstern to battle between Rising Rock and Fa Layette."

"He's doing what?" Earl James demanded. "Did you hear that right? He's trying to bring the southrons to battle now, before I can get there with my reinforcements?" Has he—?" He broke off. *Has he lost his mind?* was what he'd started to say. He couldn't very well ask that of a scryer, no matter how loudly and vehemently he was thinking it.

The scryer nodded vigorously. "Sir, the sorcerous link was very clear. I have told you exactly what Count Thraxton's scryer told me."

"All right," James said. It wasn't all right, but he couldn't do anything about it. He plucked at his bushy beard. "In that case, we'd better press ahead with the men we have here and let Brigadier Bell bring up the rest as fast as he can. Tell Count Thraxton's man we shall hurry on toward him, and tell Brigadier Bell to wring as much speed from the Peachtree Glideway as he can. I don't care if he has to start shooting people to do it—we're going to need him."

"Yes, sir." Off the scryer went again. James of Broadpath sighed. He'd heard Thraxton was difficult, but he'd never dreamt the eastern general could make himself so difficult so fast.

# IV

"Smite them!" Count Thraxton told the messenger. "You tell Leonidas the Priest he is to smite them! He is not to delay, he is not to dawdle, he is to smite the foe in front of him with all the strength he commands. If he will only smite them, victory shall assuredly be ours. Tell him that. Tell him that in exactly those words."

"Yes, your Excellency." The messenger's lips moved silently as he went over Thraxton's order. Like most in his service, he had a well-trained memory. After a moment, he nodded to himself and hurried away.

"He is not to delay even an instant," Count Thraxton called after him. The messenger nodded to show he'd heard and slammed the door on the way out.

Thraxton's lips moved silently, as the messenger's

had. He wasn't committing anything to memory. On the contrary: he was cursing Leonidas the Priest. *A terrible thing, to curse a hierophant of the Lion God*, he thought. *Very likely a useless thing as well: the god is bound to protect his votary. But what a pity if he is. And what must I do to make Leonidas move?*

His long, pale hands folded into long, furious fists. He'd done everything he knew how to do this side of riding up to the front from Fa Layette and kicking Leonidas the Priest in his holy backside. He'd blistered the ears of Leonidas' scryer. The scryer, presumably, had blistered Leonidas' ears. But Leonidas, instead of going forth to fall on the foe, had stayed in camp.

"Why am I afflicted by blundering bunglers?" Thraxton howled; his own inner anguish was too great to let him keep silent. Others looked down their noses at him for losing battles. He looked down his nose at the subordinates who would not give him victory even when it lay in the cupped palms of his hands.

And it did. As sure as the sun would rise in the east tomorrow, it did. His deep-set eyes swung toward the map. His shaggy eyebrows came down and together in a fearsome, anguished scowl that furrowed his forehead as if it were crossed by the gullies seaming the eastern plains.

"We *have* them," he whispered. "We need only reach out, and we *have* them."

The map plainly showed it. General Guildenstern had split up his army to pursue the one Thraxton commanded. When massed, Thraxton's forces were greater than any one part of the southron host. He could fall on one enemy column, destroy it, and then turn on the next, and then on the third.

He *could*. He didn't even need James of Broadpath's men to do it. The southrons still didn't believe he'd stayed so far south in Peachtree Province. They'd been sure he would scuttle up to Stamboul, or even to Marthasville. He'd laid his trap. They'd stumbled into it. And now . . .

And now his own generals were letting him down. He didn't know what he had to do to make Leonidas the Priest go forward against Guildenstern's invaders. Baron Dan of Rabbit Hill had a reputation as a splendid soldier, but he didn't seem inclined to assail the southrons, either. And, as luck would have it, his men were posted farther than Leonidas' from the foe.

*Maybe I should order Ned of the Forest forward against the enemy*, Thraxton thought. But then he shook his head. *Not unless I find no other way.* For one thing, he reckoned Ned better at harassing the southrons than at actually hurting them. And, for another, Count Thraxton was not inclined to give the baseborn commander of unicorn-riders the chance to win real glory for himself.

Thraxton looked up through the ceiling of the home in Fa Layette where he made his headquarters. In his mind's eye, he saw the heavenly home of the gods. *Why have you chosen to afflict me with idiots?* he asked. If the gods had an answer, they did not choose to vouchsafe it to him.

He held out his hands and looked at them. They were large-palmed, with long, thin fingers: the hands of a mage—which he was—or a chirurgeon or a fiddler, not those of a general, not really. He contemplated his fingers. They quivered, ever so slightly, as he did so. Somehow, victories kept slipping through them.

"Not this time," he said. "No, by the gods, not this time."

Sometimes magecraft was not enough. He shook his head. Sometimes one needed magecraft of a sort different from that found in grimoires. Sometimes the direct personal presence and encouragement of the commanding general were all the magic necessary to get a laggard, sluggard subordinate moving.

"Encouragement," he murmured, and his thin lips skinned back from his yellow teeth in a smile that would have made anyone who saw it quail. His hands folded into fists again. By the time he got done ... encouraging Leonidas the Priest, the man would do what was required of him. Either that, or Thraxton would try out some of his choicer sorceries on a soldier at least nominally on his own side.

He muttered another curse. Some of the choicer sorceries he'd aimed at the southrons in battles past had unaccountably gone awry, coming down on the heads of his own troops. He'd managed not to talk about that in the reports he'd submitted to King Geoffrey. Most of the time, he managed not to think about it, too. Every so often, though, the memories would crawl out where he had to look at them.

"Not this time," he said. "Never again. May the gods cast me into the seventh hell if such a thing ever happens again." Even when it had happened, it hadn't been his fault. He was sure of that.

And he was sure he could linger in Fa Layette no more. He'd sent the army forward again, and he would have to ride south to be with it, to lead it in the triumph he hoped to create.

When he came bursting out of his study, his aides jumped in surprise. "Is something wrong, your Grace?" one of the young officers asked.

"My being here is wrong," Thraxton answered, "here in Fa Layette, I mean. I must go south to rejoin the brave soldiers who fight for King Geoffrey and our traditional way of life. I am confident that my presence at the fighting front will inspirit my men and make them more eager to fare forth against the southrons."

A couple of the aides suffered coughing fits. One of them turned quite red despite his swarthiness. He had so much trouble recovering, another captain passed him a flask. A long swig made him turn even redder, but he did stop coughing.

"Are you certain you are all right, Nicodemus?" Thraxton asked coldly.

"Uh, yes, sir. Sorry, sir," Captain Nicodemus answered. "I had something go down the wrong pipe, I'm afraid."

"I daresay." One of Count Thraxton's shaggy eyebrows twitched. "You would do better not to suffer another such misfortune any time soon, I assure you. For now, though, go make sure my unicorn is ready. We have the enemy where we want him. Now we needs must strike him before he can pull the parts of his army together to make a single whole once more."

"Yes, sir!" Nicodemus said. He hurried to obey. If he also hurried to escape Thraxton's presence . . . that did not altogether disappoint the general. Being loved had always proved elusive. Love failing, being feared would do well enough.

He grimaced. He hadn't made Ned of the Forest fear him. Ned hadn't conveniently got himself killed, either. Count Thraxton shrugged. Ned would have more chances.

When Count Thraxton walked across the street to the stables, the blond serfs who cared for the unicorns fawned on him. So did Captain Nicodemus. He suspected—no, he knew—the display of respect and affection from both aide and serfs was false, but he accepted it as no less than his due even so. Serfs who showed they thought themselves as good as Detinans deserved whatever happened to them, as far as he was concerned. Few estate-owning nobles in the northern provinces would have disagreed with him.

He swung himself up onto the unicorn Captain Nicodemus gave him and began riding south toward the army's encampments. He hadn't gone far before peevishly shaking his head. Had the fighting begun, had the officers who were supposed to obey actually carried out their orders, he could have stayed back here in Fa Layette and let them destroy Guildenstern and the southron invaders in detail. But would they heed him? Another peevish headshake. King Geoffrey had made him commander in the east, but his subordinates seemed unaware of it.

His aides came boiling out of the building he'd used as his headquarters since abandoning Rising Rock. "What about us, your Grace?" one of them called after him.

Thraxton reined in and answered over his shoulder: "Come along if you care to." If they came, well and good. If they didn't, he would commandeer junior officers from the staffs of his division commanders. Like serfs, like unicorns, junior officers were for all practical purposes interchangeable.

He didn't let the aides delay him long. He turned toward the south and booted his mount forward once more. *On toward the River of Death*, he thought, and then, *On toward Rising Rock again, once I give the stinking southrons what they deserve*.

His left hand folded into a fist. He slammed it down on his thigh. The story that refugee had told still burned within him. So Guildenstern had marched into Rising Rock with bands playing and banners waving, had he? *When I take Rising Rock back, when I free it from the gods-accursed southrons, I shall have my own parade, and everyone will cry out my name.*

With a nod, he spurred his unicorn up from a walk to a trot. What could be finer than streets lined with hundreds, with thousands, of cheering people, all of them shouting things like, "Huzzah for Thraxton!" "The gods bless the great Count Thraxton!" "Hurrah for Thraxton, savior of the realm!"? Nothing in the world could be finer than that, not to Count Thraxton.

*And let those envious sons of bitches call me Thraxton the Braggart after that,* he thought with a sour smile. *Let them try. I shall have done something worth bragging about, something none of those feeble little men could hope to match.*

In his mind, he saw himself bowing before King Geoffrey, heard the King acclaiming him Duke Thraxton of Rising Rock, imagined himself taking over broad new estates, earned by the swords—well, actually by the crossbows and pikes—of the men under his command. Maybe that was an even more splendid vision than the one he'd had a moment before.

He trotted past companies of footsoldiers trudging south toward what he hoped would be the battle. Reality differed from his visions, as reality had a way of doing. He heard one crossbowman say to another, "Who's that scrawny old bugger? He looks like a teamster, but he rides like he owns the road. Silly old fool, anyone wants to know what I think."

"Nobody gives a fart what you think, Carolus," another trooper answered. "Nobody ever has, and nobody ever will, not even that old geezer."

"Shut up, the both of you," a third man said. "That

was Thraxton the Braggart, and he'd just as soon turn you into a crayfish as look at you."

*Sooner*, Thraxton thought. He pointed a finger at the soldier who'd spoken scornfully of him. For good measure, he also pointed at the fellow who'd used the nickname he hated. Then he muttered the spell he'd tried to use against Ned of the Forest. It had failed against Ned. It didn't fail here. Both men doubled over, clutching their bellies. Then they both sprinted for the bushes off to the side of the road. With a harsh laugh, Count Thraxton urged his unicorn forward.

He reached the headquarters of Leonidas the Priest as the sun was sliding down the sky toward the western horizon. But, when he stuck his head into Leonidas' pavilion, he discovered the hierophant of the Lion God wasn't there.

"Er—how may I serve you, your Grace?" one of Leonidas' aides asked. He sounded nervous, probably because he hadn't expected Count Thraxton to come down toward the River of Death. He had more reason to be nervous than that. If he didn't realize as much, he was going to find himself in as much trouble as his principal.

"Where is Leonidas?" Thraxton demanded.

"Offering sacrifice, your Grace," the aide replied. "As always, he hopes to win the aid of the gods through his piety, and to enspirit the men he leads."

"To enspirit them to do what?" Thraxton asked, acid in his voice.

"Why, to drive back the accursed southrons, of course," the young officer said.

"They why won't he attack them when I order him forward?" Thraxton snapped. Before the aide could answer, he held up a warning hand. "I don't care to hear your response, sirrah. I care to hear Leonidas'. Fetch him here. Fetch him at once."

"Sir, as I say, he is at his devotions," the aide replied.

"Fetch him," Thraxton said for the third time. "Let the underpriests finish the sacrifice. If he doesn't care to come, tell him he would do better to cut his own throat than the lamb's."

That sent Leonidas' aide off at a run. Thraxton folded thin arms across his narrow chest and waited, none too patiently. Before his temper quite kindled, the young officer came back with Leonidas the Priest, who as usual wore the vestments of his holy office rather than uniform. He looked most unhappy, which suited Thraxton fine. "Why are you harassing me, your Excellency?" he asked.

"Why do you not obey my orders?" Thraxton roared in return. "We have the foe divided. If we can strike him thus, he is ours. But we must *strike*. Why do you not move on him when I command it?"

"Oh." Leonidas' eyebrows rose. "Considering how we've had to fall back and back lately, and considering how I think we ought to fall back more to defend Marthasville, I didn't imagine you could possibly have meant your order to go forward."

"*You shall obey me!*" Count Thraxton had only thought he was roaring before. That full-throated bellow made everyone within earshot whirl and stare at him. Even Leonidas, after blinking a couple of times, bowed his head in acquiescence. Thraxton hoped that acquiescence didn't come too late. Once upon a time, someone had written, *Against stupidity, the very gods themselves contend in vain.* Whoever that was, he'd probably known Leonidas the Priest.

❖     ❖     ❖

Doubting George scratched his head. Some things could no longer be doubted, even by him. He'd called his brigadiers together to see if they still found such matters doubtable.

But when he said, "Seems to me there may be more traitors around these parts than if they were hightailing for Marthasville fast as they can go," not a one of them argued. Instead, three heads bobbed up and down in solemn agreement and the fourth officer stood mute.

"I'd say you're likely right, sir." Brigadier Brannan might have been the handsomest man in King Avram's army. He had curly black hair and a curly black beard, elegant eyebrows, and a proud hooked nose. He was also a professional soldier and a connoisseur of catapults; he commanded Doubting George's dart- and stone-throwers. He went on, "Looks to me as if Thraxton's decided to hang around and fight."

"Can we lick him if he does?" George asked. He knew his own opinion, but wanted to hear what his brigadiers had to say.

But then Brigadier Negley said, "May it please you, sir, I'm not altogether convinced these aren't more holdouts making nuisances of themselves, like those dragoons a few days ago."

"Nonsense," Brannan said.

Negley glared at him. He was handsome, too, in a foppish way. He wore a bushy mustache and a neatly trimmed little tuft of hair under his lower lip. He hadn't been a soldier before the war—in fact, he'd got wealthy as a horticulturalist, of all unlikely things—but he'd raised a regiment of volunteers for King Avram and had fought it well enough to win promotion from colonel to brigadier.

"It isn't nonsense," he said, looking from Brannan

to George and back again. "Some people just think they know everything to know, that's all." He sniffed. Having dismissed the catapult enthusiast, he spoke to George again: "Why should the traitors fight here when everything they need to hold is so much farther north?"

George couldn't dismiss that argument out of hand, not when it was the same one General Guildenstern had made to justify splitting up his army. He said, "By all the signs I've seen, by all the reports the scouts are bringing in, there are more than holdouts in front of us. Suppose Thraxton the Braggart hits this column with everything he's got. Can we whip him?"

His brigadiers looked at one another. Absalom the Bear was first to answer, in rumbling tones that helped explain how he'd acquired his nickname: "I wouldn't care to bet on it, sir. He's got more men than we do here, and we're stretched out pretty stinking thin, too."

Brigadier Rinaldo nodded. "He could hurt us. But I don't think he's stayed in the south, either. What's the point of it?"

"Nice to know *someone* can see sense," Brigadier Negley murmured.

Brigadier Brannan set a hand on the hilt of his sword. "If you don't care for the way I think, sir, we can meet at a place of your choosing and you are welcome to try to make me change my views. Make sure you let someone know where you want your urn interred, though."

Negley returned a stiff bow. "I am altogether at your service, sir."

Doubting George decided it was a good time to lose his temper, or to seem to. He slammed the palm of his hand on the folding table behind which he sat. His brigadiers all jumped at the noise. "That will be quite enough of that," he growled. "What do you think you are, a pack of northern nobles? They've got the blue blood and the blue shirts, and as far as I'm concerned they're welcome to them. You both know perfectly well that dueling is forbidden in this army, and for good reason, too. We've got ourselves a job to do. By the gods, we're going to do it. Do I make myself plain?"

"Yes, sir," Brigadier Brannan said. Brigadier Negley nodded as stiffly as he'd bowed.

"Good." George hoped he could let it rest there. "If we have traitors in the neighborhood, what do we need to do?"

"We'd better let General Guildenstern know," Absalom the Bear declared.

"I've already done that," George said.

Absalom nodded. "Does he believe you?"

That was indeed the right question to ask. "I don't know yet," George replied. His smile was dry. "I have my doubts."

All four brigadiers chuckled. They took a certain amount of pride in serving under a man who had the sort of a reputation that had won him a nickname like Doubting George. George didn't want anyone serving under him who didn't take that sort of pride. He'd weeded out a few officers who didn't measure up. But he'd done it quietly, so as not to touch off doubts in anyone else.

Brigadier Brannan asked, "Have you checked with our mages, to see what they think?"

That was another good question. George thought so, at any rate. But before he could answer it, Negley snapped his fingers and said, "The mages will tell you they don't know. That's all they're good for."

"Well, not quite," George said, though he'd been disappointed in the quality of the sorcerers who served King Avram a good many times.

Brannan's smile showed sharp teeth as he nodded to Negley. "I presume the sorcerers aren't much use in the flower trade, eh?" he asked with exquisite, sardonic politeness. Beneath Negley's swarthy hide, he turned red.

Before he could snap back, before Brannan could take it any further, George said, "I've already told you once, that will be quite enough of that." He'd enjoyed Brigadier Brannan's gibe, too, but not enough to want to watch his subordinates quarrel among themselves. "We'd do better turning all our tempers against the traitors, don't you think?"

None of the brigadiers had the nerve to say no. Absalom the Bear said, "Mages are good for something every now and again. You never can tell."

"That's true—you never can." Doubting George raised his voice. "Colonel Andy!"

"Sir?" His aide-de-camp bustled into the meeting. All four brigadiers gave him matching fishy stares. He didn't have so much rank as any of them, but he had—or they thought he had—more influence with George, so they resented him.

"Fetch me Colonel Albertus, if you'd be so kind," George said. Colonel Andy nodded, saluted, and bustled away to get the mage. He was very good at looking busy, even when he wasn't.

"Albertus." Brigadier Negley sniffed. "Calls himself the Great, like a circus mountebank. Great compared to what, is what I want to know."

He kept on fuming and muttering insults till the

tent flap opened and Colonel Albertus strode into the pavilion. Then, most abruptly, Negley fell silent. Insulting a mage to his face was risky business.

But the brigadier had had a point. When Albertus the Great bowed to George and asked, "How may I serve you, your Excellency?" in deep, vibrant tones, he sounded like a circus mountebank. And he looked like one, too. He wore his gray beard very long, and trained it to a point. His eyes flashed. His posture was very erect. His hands twitched, as if he were about to pull a goldpiece from Doubting George's ear.

George didn't want a goldpiece. He was after something more precious still, and more elusive: the truth. "By your magecraft, Colonel, have you noted any signs that Count Thraxton's men are nearby in numbers greater than they ought to be? You and your fellow sorcerers, I mean."

"Yes, of course." Even Albertus' frown was theatrical. "Sir, I am able to give no certain answer, much as I should like to. The northerners have set so many masking spells on the landscape, my colleagues and I are hard pressed to see anything at all."

"Why would they do that, if they didn't have something to hide?" Brigadier Brannan asked.

"Why? I can think of several reasons," Albertus said. "One, obviously, is to conceal their forces. But another would be to conceal that which is not there, to use magic to deceive and slow us where warriors cannot."

"Are they such sneaky demons as that?" Brigadier Rinaldo asked.

"Do we dare think they aren't?" Absalom the Bear said before anyone else could answer. George had to give Rinaldo credit: he very visibly thought about that before at last shaking his head.

To Colonel Albertus, the so-called Great, George said, "Can you tell whether the enemy is masking emptiness or building up his forces behind all those screening spells?"

"Maybe," Albertus said—an answer Doubting George accepted as basically honest, if nothing else. The mage went on, "If the masking spells are laid on with enough skill and force, they will hide whatever lies behind them, whether that be nothing or a great deal. That is their function, after all."

"Well, so it is," George said. "But your function, Colonel, is to pierce that magic, no matter how skilfully and forcefully the traitors use it."

"In theory, no doubt, that is true," Albertus replied.

"If the theory's not worth anything, Colonel, why aren't you carrying a pike instead of your wand there?" Brigadier Absalom demanded. His manners were altogether unpolished, but he was the man George relied upon when the going got heavy.

Albertus the Great, however, looked at him as if he'd just found him on the sole of his boot. He stroked his splendid, gleaming beard and said, "I assure you, sir, we of the mystical profession are doing everything within our power to aid in King Avram's just fight to keep Detina a single kingdom."

That *within our power* was, of course, the rub. King Geoffrey's mages were on the whole better than the ones who'd stayed loyal to Avram, even if Albertus had a more impressive beard than any of them. George said, "Colonel, we urgently need to know what, if anything, is behind those masking spells. You and your fellow mages are to attempt to learn that. You are to do whatever becomes necessary in order to learn it. Do I make myself clear?"

"Yes, sir!" Albertus saluted as crisply as any soldier

could have—or perhaps as crisply as an actor imper- sonating a soldier might have done up on the stage. His about-face also held some of that theatrical qual- ity. He stalked out of Lieutenant General George's pavilion.

After he was gone, Brigadier Brannan said, "It would probably be a good idea to nab some north- ern prisoners, too, sir, to find out what they say. Anybody who counts on mages and nothing else dooms himself to disappointment."

"I'm already doing it, Brigadier," George said, and Brannan grinned at him. George went on, "If we could rely on our mages, we'd've long since won this war." He held up a hand before any of his fractious subordinates could speak. "I'm not done, gentlemen. If the traitors could rely on *their* mages, they'd've long since won the war."

The meeting with his division commanders broke up a few minutes later. The four brigadiers left the pavilion, Brannan and Negley ostentatiously not speaking to each other. Doubting George stepped out with them. Part of that was so they wouldn't go for their swords as soon as they were out from under his eye. Part of it was in the hope that the air would be cooler and a little less muggy. His two quarrel- ing officers left each other alone, so that was a success. But hoping for cool, dry air in summer anywhere in Peachtree Province . . . George shook his head. No chance. No chance at all.

He glanced toward the mages' tents. He couldn't see anything summoning the sorcerers, but one by one they left their own tents and strode into Colo- nel Albertus'. *Going to get crowded in there before long*, he thought, but more and more magicians went inside without the tent's bursting at the seams. Maybe there *was* something to this magecraft business, if magic could make tents bigger inside than out-.

Then George shrugged. He would have been happier with his mages if they'd shown better at the little skirmish by the stone fence. He would have been happier with them if they'd shown better at any number of fights in two and a half years of war.

*They are trying*, he thought. *Yes, they're very trying*. The sardonic second thought followed the charitable first as naturally as night followed day.

He could hear them chanting, there in Albertus' tent. They had fine, resonant voices. He wondered what, if anything, that had to do with the price of brandy. Maybe better music made for better magecraft. He could hope so, at any rate. He'd hoped for all sorts of things from mages, and been disappointed more often than he cared to recall.

All at once, the chanting stopped. The ground shook beneath Doubting George's feet, as if a troop of unicorns were trotting by not far away. Mages started spilling out of Albertus' tent. By the way they fled, by their cries of horror and expressions of dismay, the shaking had been worse, a great deal worse, in there. George hadn't thought there were so many synonyms for *earthquake*, or so many lewd adjectives that would cling to the term.

Colonel Albertus the Great was the last man out of the tent. George gave him some credit for that, as he would have given the captain of a sinking quinquereme some credit for being the last man off his stricken vessel. "What happened?" George called.

Colonel Albertus' eyes were wild. So was his beard; instead of doing as he wanted, it stuck out in all directions. He staggered over to Doubting George and managed a sort of a salute. "Sir," he said, "if you want to find out what's on the other side of those masking spells, you're just going to have to do it with soldiers. I'm sorry, but I must report myself . . . not quite fit for duty."

He swayed and toppled. As George caught him, the general reflected that he'd got information from the mage—if only he knew what to do with it.

"Well, where are the stinking sons of bitches?" Captain Ormerod demanded. "By the gods, I'm sick of tramping through these endless woods for southrons who might as well be down in New Eborac for all we've seen of them."

"Beats me," Colonel Florizel replied. The regimental commander didn't mind complaints, not when he was none too happy about tramping through these pine woods himself. "As far as I'm concerned, if they didn't know exactly where the enemy was, they should have used mages or bloodhounds to find him, not soldiers. We've got better things to do."

"Or Ned of the Forest's unicorn-riders," Ormerod said. "Ned's a serfcatcher, or he was. He ought to be able to find out where the southrons are skulking if anyone can."

"Everything started boiling after Count Thraxton paid a visit to Leonidas," Lieutenant Gremio said. "My guess is, Thraxton wanted Leonidas to do more, and so Leonidas started flailing around every which way."

"Leonidas the Priest is a very holy man," Florizel said reprovingly. "The gods love him."

"They must," Gremio said. "Otherwise, how could such a dunderhead have become a general in the first place?"

"Now, Lieutenant," Ormerod said, deliciously

scandalized. "Do have a care what you say. Isn't that libel?"

"Of course not," Gremio replied with a barrister's certainty. "Slander, yes. Libel, no. I wouldn't waste time libeling Leonidas, anyhow—except for hymn books, there's no proof he can read."

Something buggy bit Ormerod. He swatted at it. Whatever it was, Gremio had proved he owned a sharper tongue than it did.

Sergeant Tybalt came out from behind a tree. He was buttoning his fly, which gave more than a hint of why he'd gone back there in the first place. Seeing Ormerod, he asked, "Sir, even if we do find the stinking southrons in this miserable country, how in the names of all the gods are we supposed to fight them hereabouts?"

"As best we can, Sergeant," Ormerod answered. "As best we can."

Tybalt looked dissatisfied. Ormerod didn't blame him, but he had no better answer to give. Battles, proper battles, were usually fought in broad plains that gave both sides room to maneuver and to see farther than a few feet. But there were no broad plains here in this miserable country—Tybalt had had the right word for it—by the River of Death, only endless woods, mostly pine, some oak, punctuated by occasional farms and their mean little fields.

Colonel Florizel said, "Our ancestors beat back the blonds and broke them to scrvitude in country like this. If they could do it, we can do it, too."

Lieutenant Gremio looked about to say something, too. Before he could, Ormerod contrived to kick him in the ankle. Gremio let out an indignant yelp. Ormerod looked as innocent as he could, which wasn't very. Knowing Gremio, he had a pretty good idea of what the lieutenant would have said: something that exposed all the historical inaccuracies in Florizel's remark.

"There's a time and a place for everything, by the gods," Ormerod muttered. Maybe Gremio heard him, maybe he didn't. Ormerod wasn't going to worry either way. Gremio kept quiet, and Ormerod did worry about that. Contradicting Earl Florizel at a feast where the audience was nobles and wealthy commoners was one thing. Contradicting Colonel Florizel, the regimental commander, and disheartening the sergeant whom the colonel had been encouraging was something else again. Perhaps because he was an aggressive barrister, Gremio had trouble grasping the distinction.

Before Ormerod could explain it to the lieutenant—not that Gremio, who was convinced he knew it all, would have been likely to listen—a sharp challenge rang out ahead: "Who goes there?"

"Hold up!" Ormerod called to the rest of his company. Then he pitched his voice to carry: "Who are you?"

"Third company, twenty-sixth regiment from New Eborac," came the reply. "The sign is *Avram*. Give the countersign, or be known for a traitor and an enemy."

Rage ripped through Ormerod. "The countersign is, *Die you son of a bitch!*" he shouted, and yanked his sword from its scabbard. "Come on, boys!" he yelled to his own company. "We've found some of the southrons, anyway."

A crossbow quarrel hissed past his head and buried itself in a pine behind him. More than half its length had vanished. It would have done worse yet had it pierced him. His leg twinged. Yes, he knew what a bolt could do when it tore through flesh.

His men fought the way their ancestors had when

attacked by blonds: they scurried behind trees and started shooting from in back of them. In country like this, how else could anyone fight? Captain Ormerod would have loved to come up with a different answer, a better answer, but none occurred to him.

"Geoffrey!" he shouted as he hurried toward a tree, too. He might brandish that sword, but how much good did it do him with no foeman within reach of his steel? "Geoffrey and provincial prerogative!" That was the slogan the northern provinces used to deny that Avram had the authority to make them do anything they didn't care to do—such as freeing serfs from their ties to the land—unless their nobles consented.

"King Avram!" the southrons shouted back. "King Avram, and to the seven hells with provincial prerogative!" Other cries rose, too, wordless cries of pain as crossbow quarrels from both sides began finding targets.

A soldier near Ormerod went down. His feet drummed and thumped on the pine needles, but he wouldn't be getting up again, not with a bolt between the eyes. Ormerod looked again at the sword in his hand. If the enemy charged, it would do him some good. Meanwhile . . . Meanwhile, he scrambled over and scooped up the shot man's crossbow and pulled the sheaf of bolts off his belt. By the time he got back to his own tree, the soldier had realized he was dead and stopped kicking.

Ormerod set a quarrel in the crossbow's groove, yanked back on the bow to cock it, and steadied his finger on the trigger. Sticking some part of his head out to look for a target gave him a certain amount of pause—suppose one of the gray-clad southrons was waiting for him to do exactly that? He would kick mindlessly for a few heartbeats and then stop, too.

*This is your duty to King Geoffrey*, he told himself, and made himself do what was required. A quarrel slammed into the tree trunk a couple of inches from his head. He jerked back, cold sweat springing out on his brow. When he peered out again, it was from much lower down.

He shot at an enemy soldier. The fellow didn't shriek, so he supposed he missed. Cursing under his breath, he loaded and cocked the crossbow as fast as he could. He wished he were ambidextrous, so he could have put the bow to his left shoulder and pulled the trigger with his left hand. That would have let him look out from behind the tree on the side enemy sharpshooters didn't expect.

But no such luck. Like most men, he was doomed to predictability. "Forward!" he called to his men— at the same time as an officer on the other side was also shouting, "Forward!"

Ormerod's men had learned in a hard, bloody school. They knew how to advance through woods. Some of them shot at the enemy and made him keep his head down while others actually moved forward. Then the two groups traded roles, the ones who had been shooting now leapfrogging past the men who, in new cover of their own, kept the southrons busy.

Against raw enemy troops, such tactics were almost bound to succeed. But the third company of the Twenty-Sixth New Eborac proved to consist of veteran soldiers who fought the same way as the men from Palmetto Province whom Ormerod commanded. The southrons offered his soldiers few targets as they worked their way forward—only the occasional glimpse of a gray tunic or a dark head or, now and again, a blond one.

Blond heads . . . When Ormerod realized what that meant, he let out a great, full-throated bellow of rage. "They've got runaways fighting for 'em, the bastards!" he shouted when he finally found words. "Now we really have to make them pay!"

He wanted to throw aside the dead man's cross-bow and charge the enemy swinging his sword, as if he were a conqueror from the heroic days not long after the Detinans first crossed the Western Ocean and cast down the kingdoms the yellow-haired men had made hereabouts. But the blonds who fought for King Avram didn't lumber around in ass-drawn chari-ots and wield cumbersome bronze-headed axes. Their weapons were as good as his, and they had real Detinans alongside to help stiffen them if they fal-tered. The sword stayed in Ormerod's scabbard.

As he ran forward, he wondered if any of those blonds there on the other side had escaped from his estate. *Maybe we'd do better coming after them with whips, to make them remember they serve us*, he thought. Then another crossbow quarrel snarled past him. He shook his head. The blonds had been serfs, but some of them were soldiers now.

"Avram!" they shouted. He recognized their accent— not so very different from his own, not much like the clipped tones most proper southrons used. "King Avram! Avram and freedom!"

"Avram and ass piss!" Ormerod yelled back. *Free-dom*, he thought. *As if the serfs deserve it. Not likely. We made Detina what it is by conquering them. What would it be if we let them pretend they were as good as we are?* He didn't know what it would be. He did know it wouldn't be any place where he cared to live.

He grimaced. Without serfs to work his fields and harvest the indigo, it wouldn't even be any place where he could make a living.

"Forward!" the southron officer shouted again.

"Forward!" Captain Ormerod echoed. As if from far away, he heard other company commanders from Colonel Florizel's regiment shouting the same thing, and other southrons as well. He paid them only scant attention. They weren't directly affecting him, and so he didn't worry about them. He had plenty to worry about right here—in these woods, he couldn't tell what most of his own company was doing, let alone anyone else's.

He ran for a pine up ahead. Somebody else was running for it, too—somebody in a gray tunic and pantaloons. Out came the sword he'd resheathed not long before. He set the crossbow down on the ground. Once he settled with the foe, he would pick it up again.

Had the enemy soldier had a bolt in the groove of his own crossbow, Ormerod might not have had such a good time of it. But the fellow's crossbow was also empty. He threw it aside and yanked out his own shortsword to defend himself against Ormerod's onslaught.

Steel belled on steel. Sparks flew. Ormerod's lips skinned back from his teeth in a fierce grin. He had a proper blade, and knew what to do with it. The southron's sword was intended for use only after all else failed. By the way the fellow held it, he hadn't had to use it very often up till now.

"Ha!" Ormerod said. The slash would have split the southron's skull, but the enemy trooper jerked his head aside at the last instant. The blade hacked off most of his left ear. Howling, dripping blood, he turned and fled, throwing aside the shortsword so he could flee the faster.

Ormerod took two steps after him, then checked himself. Any farther and he risked running into the gods only knew how many southrons. He snatched up his crossbow again, slid a bolt into the groove, and cocked the piece.

"Forward!" the southron captain, or whatever he was, shouted again. His voice didn't sound as if it came from very far away. Ormerod froze into a hunter's crouch, as he might have done going after tiger or basilisk in the swampy near-jungle of the woods of Palmetto Province. The enemy officer went on, "We can lick these bastards—they aren't very tough."

"No, eh?" But Ormerod's lips shaped the words without the slightest betraying sound. Sure enough, there stood the southron, behind an oak not fifty yards away. Ormerod brought the crossbow to his shoulder. He pulled the trigger. The bowstring thrummed. The stock kicked against him.

And the enemy captain clutched at his ribcage and slowly crumpled to the ground. "Take that, you filthy, fornicating robber!" Ormerod yowled. "King Geoffrey and victory!"

The gray-clad soldiers cried out in dismay as their leader fell. But they had no quit in them. "Come on!" someone else—a lieutenant? a sergeant?—yelled. "We can still whip these bastards!" And, instead of falling back as Ormerod had hoped, the southrons surged forward more fiercely than before.

Some of them had their shortswords out, as did some of Ormerod's men. Usually, one side or the other gave way in a fight like this. That didn't happen here. Both Ormerod's troopers and the southrons wanted to get their hands on their foes, and both kept coming despite everything their foes could do to them. It wasn't an enormous fight, but it was as fierce as any Ormerod had seen.

A big blond fellow swinging his shortsword rushed straight at Ormerod, yelling, "King Avram and freedom!" at the top of his lungs. His slash would have taken off Ormerod's head had it connected.

It didn't. Ormerod parried and thrust. The blond—surely an escaped serf by his accent—beat the blade aside. "King Geoffrey!" Ormerod shouted. Then he stopped and stared—and almost got killed because of it. His next word was a startled bleat: "Rollant?"

"Baron Ormerod?" Rollant's astonishment almost got him killed. For a quarter of a heartbeat, he started to duck his head and bow, as he'd been trained to do since boyhood when the baron went by. Had he finished the motion, Ormerod would have spitted him as if he were to go over the fire.

He'd dreamt of facing his old liege lord in battle, dreamt of killing him in any number of slow and nasty ways. He'd been sure Ormerod would take service with false King Geoffrey, just as he'd taken service with Avram, who was not only the rightful king but also the righteous king.

Reality proved vastly different from his dreams, as it had a way of doing. He'd never dreamt Ormerod would swing a long sword, while he had only a short one. He'd known the baron could handle a blade. In his dreams, it hadn't mattered. Now . . . Now he backpedaled. However hateful his liege lord was to him, Ormerod was also a better swordsman with a better sword. And he looked as if he wanted to kill Rollant at least as much as Rollant wanted to kill him.

"Run away from me, will you, you son of a bitch!" he shouted, and thrust at Rollant's face. Rollant had no idea how he managed to beat the northern noble's blade aside, but he did. Then he sprang backwards, to put a tree between them.

Cheers from the north said more traitors were coming in. Rollant darted back to another tree. Ormerod was bellowing orders. Rollant couldn't make out the words, but he knew the tone. *I'd better*, he thought. *He's given me enough orders. He gave me one order too many, by the gods, and I'll never take another one from him again.*

While the baron—the enemy officer—directed his company, Rollant put more trees between them. No, the meeting hadn't gone as he'd dreamt. He counted himself lucky that it hadn't gone as Ormerod was likely to have dreamt.

"Back! We have to fall back!" That was Sergeant Joram. Captain Cephas was down—some traitor had put a crossbow bolt between his ribs. Rollant didn't know what had happened to the company's two lieutenants. He didn't care that much, either. As far as he was concerned, neither Benj nor Griff made much of an officer: Joram was worth both of them and then some.

And if Joram said they had to fall back, they did. Rollant looked over his shoulder. No, he didn't see any southrons coming up into this nasty little fight to give him a hand. If Geoffrey's men had reinforcements, they were going to win it.

"I thought the traitors were running away." That was Smitty, right at Rollant's elbow. Rollant almost slashed at him; he hadn't realized anybody was there. Smitty went on, "One more thing our generals got wrong. The list gets longer every day."

"Sure enough," Rollant said, and then, "You're bleeding."

Smitty looked astonished. "I am? Where?" Rollant pointed to his arm. His tunic sleeve was torn and bloody. Smitty stared down at it. "Wonder how that happened."

"However it happened, you ought to get it seen to," Rollant said.

"Yes, granny dear. When I have time, granny dear," Smitty said, which made Rollant want to give him a wound more severe than the one he already had. He went on, "Besides, the thing I really need to do is get myself seen to. And so do you. If the traitors catch up with us, a scratch on the arm is the least I've got to worry about."

He was inarguably right. He was, in fact, more right for Rollant than he was for himself. If the northerners caught him, he would just be a prisoner. If they caught Rollant, they were liable to send him back to Ormerod's estate to work in chains the rest of his days. Or they might just knock him over the head, figuring a serf who'd not only run away but raised his hand against them was more trouble than he was worth.

In wondering tones, Rollant said, "That was my liege lord I was fighting back there. I did my best to kill him, but I couldn't." He grimaced. "I think he came a good bit closer to killing me than the other way round."

"Your liege lord?" Smitty echoed. Rollant nodded. "The fellow who ran your estate, who told you what to do?" Smitty went on.

"That's what a liege lord is. That's what he does," Rollant said impatiently.

"Don't get all salty with me," Smitty said. "I come

from a province full of small freeholders, remember. We haven't had liege lords in New Eborac for a demon of a long time. Anybody tried to tell me or my neighbors what to do, he'd get himself a crossbow bolt in the belly for his trouble." He raised an eyebrow. "How come that didn't happen more up in the north?"

There *had* been serf uprisings, especially in the early days of the northern provinces. The Detinans had crushed them all, without mercy. Over the past few generations, the subjected blonds had been quieter. Down on Baron Ormerod's estate, Rollant hadn't thought much about that. It was just how things were. When he'd fled from Ormerod's lands to those where there were no serfs, though, it seemed more reprehensible.

He tramped on for perhaps half a minute without answering. At last, he said, "I suppose a lot of the ones who would've risen up went south instead."

To his relief, Smitty nodded and said, "That makes sense, I guess."

Sergeant Joram came over and slapped Rollant on the back. "I saw you tangling with the traitors' captain. That was bravely done, by the gods—shortsword against an officer's blade. Not many would have tried it."

"Thanks, Sergeant." Rollant knew he had to prove himself every time he went into a fight. A lot of Detinans—southrons included—had trouble believing blonds *could* be worth anything on the battlefield. If he'd run away, he wouldn't just have disgraced himself. He would have let down every man of his blood.

Smitty said, "That wasn't just the enemy captain, Sergeant. That traitor son of a bitch used to be

Rollant's very own liege lord before he ran off. His duke, or whatever in the seven hells he was."

Rollant laughed. "Ormerod was no duke, just a baron scrabbling to get by."

That made Smitty laugh, too. "If you had to be somebody's serf, didn't you ever wish you were tied to the land of someone really important?"

"I've known serfs who did put on airs because of who their liege lords were," Rollant said. "I always thought it was pretty stupid, myself. It doesn't change *you* any, and an important liege lord doesn't have to treat you better than any ordinary baron." He brought his mind back to more immediately important matters, asking Joram, "How's the captain doing?"

"Don't know if he's going to make it," the sergeant answered with a scowl. He put his hand to the right side of his chest to show where the bolt had struck. "It's a nasty wound."

"So Benj is in charge of us?" Rollant said.

Joram shook his head. "No, Griff. Benj took a quarrel that went like so" —he ran a finger along the right side of his head, just above the ear— "and he had to go to the rear; he was bleeding like a stuck hog. He'll be back, though, unless the wound mortifies. If the bolt had been a couple of inches over, they'd have thrown his body on the pyre and his spirit would be standing on the Scales of Justice right this minute."

Among the gods Rollant's people had worshiped was the Merciful One, who'd done everything he (or, some people said, she) could to give souls a happy afterlife. The Detinans talked much more about justice than about mercy. That, as far as Rollant was concerned, was one of the more frightening things about them.

He looked back over his shoulder. "I don't think the traitors are chasing us very hard any more," he said.

Smitty cupped a hand behind his ear. "Doesn't sound like it," he agreed. "But I'll tell you one thing: they haven't all run away to Marthasville, the way our fancy-pantaloons generals were saying."

"Anybody with an ounce of brains could have figured that out after Ned's riders smashed up the front end of Doubting George's column," Rollant said.

"Anybody with an ounce of brains?" Smitty said. "Well, if that doesn't leave out most of our generals, to the seven hells with me if I know what would."

"You'd better watch your big mouth, Smitty," Sergeant Joram said.

But Smitty shook his head. "I'll think what I want, and I'll say what I want, by the gods. I'm just as much a free Detinan as General Guildenstern is, and just as entitled to speak my mind."

He sounded angry. In fact, he sounded furious. And, while Joram shook his head, too, he said not another word. Not for the first time, Rollant marveled at the way the Detinans defended what they saw as their liberties. He also marveled at the way so many of them didn't think the serfs in the northern provinces deserved those same liberties.

After tramping on for a few more paces, he remarked, "You know, when I saw I was fighting my old baron back there, I wanted to kill him for trying to bind me to the land my whole life long."

"Don't blame you a bit," Sergeant Joram said, and Smitty nodded. Perhaps because he'd fought alongside them, they understood he craved liberty as much as they did.

He went on, "But the funny thing is, he wanted

to kill me just as much, because I'd had the nerve to run away from his estate."

"Not so funny if you're on the wrong end of the bastard's sword," Joram said.

"I found that out," Rollant answered. "If we ever get some time back in camp, Sergeant, will you teach me swordstrokes? I know we're supposed to be a crossbow company, but this is the second time in a couple of weeks that we've come to close quarters with the traitors."

"I'll show you what I can," Joram said, "but you'd better not think a few lessons will let you stand up against somebody who's been putting in an hour's practice every day since he got as tall as his sword."

"That sounds fair enough," Rollant said. "Still, the more I know, the better the chance I've got of going home to my wife after this miserable war's finally over."

Up ahead, Lieutenant Griff called, "Third company, rally to me!" His voice was high and thin. He couldn't have been more than nineteen. Rollant was convinced he'd bought his commission—he didn't see how Griff could have got it any other way. "To me!" the new company commander called again.

To him Rollant and Smitty and Sergeant Joram went. "Reporting as ordered, sir," Joram said. "I don't think the traitors are pursuing us any more."

"I believe you're right, Sergeant," Griff answered. "But what are they doing here? What are they doing here in such numbers? By the gods, they're supposed to be running, not sneaking back to bushwhack us. That's not what our officers said they'd do." He sounded furious. He sounded doubly furious, in fact: furious at the northerners for handling the company roughly, and as furious at them for turning up in an unexpected place.

Gently, Sergeant Joram said, "Sir, maybe you'll have noticed that things don't always turn out just the way the people with the fancy uniforms think they will." He might have been explaining the facts of life to a youngster who was at least as likely to find them appalling as interesting.

Lieutenant Griff certainly looked appalled. He said, "But they wouldn't be wearing those fancy uniforms if they didn't know what was going on."

"There's a pile of difference between *wouldn't* and *shouldn't*," Smitty said. "Sir."

Rollant added, "Besides, sir, there are plenty of fellows in fancy uniforms on the other side, too."

"Keep your mouth shut, soldier," Griff snapped. He hadn't complained when Joram tried to correct him, or even when Smitty did. Of course, they were both of Detinan blood, as he was. Rollant was only a blond.

*I'm good enough to die for my kingdom, but not to speak up for it*, he thought. The first few times such things had happened to him, he'd been both angry and humiliated. He still was, but only to a degree. All he could do to keep them from happening so often was to show, over and over if need be, that he knew what he was doing and knew what he was talking about. Lieutenant Griff hadn't seen that yet, but maybe he would one of these days.

Or maybe he never would. Some southron Detinans, like most of their northern counterparts, refused to believe blonds could be anything more than beasts of burden that chanced to walk on two legs.

"We'd better get back to the encampment," Griff said. Rollant couldn't argue with him about that.

At the encampment, Griff hurried off to report to his superiors. Rollant hoped the news would soon get

to someone with the wit to see what it meant. He had
his own opinions about which general officers in the
army owned such wit and which carried their headquarters in their hindquarters, as a wag had put it.

Hagen, the runaway serf he'd brought back to the
company, said, "Where are the rest of you?"

"Where in the seven hells do you think?" Rollant
answered irritably. "We ran into the traitors—more
of 'em than we expected—and some of us stopped
bolts. That's part of what war's about, worse luck."

"Where is Captain Cephas?" That was Corliss,
Hagen's wife.

"He got shot," Rollant said. As Joram had, he put
his hand to the right side of his chest. "I didn't see
it happen, but I hear it's not so good."

"Oh, no," Corliss said softly, turning pale. Then
she started to sob. Rollant stared at her. So did
Hagen. Cephas had let the two serfs and their children stay with the company as laborers. Was that
enough to set Corliss crying so? Maybe. But maybe
not, too. What else had Cephas done for—or with—
Corliss in particular?

Rollant didn't know. Hagen looked as if he didn't
know, either, and as if he was wondering the same
thing. It wasn't Rollant's worry. At the moment, he
was very glad it wasn't his worry, too.


"Gods damn it to the hells, maybe the stinking
traitors haven't all scurried north to Stamboul." General Guildenstern admitted even so much with the
greatest reluctance.

"I'm afraid you may be right, sir," Brigadier
Alexander agreed.

"Of course I'm right," Guildenstern snarled. He
rarely doubted himself, even, perhaps, when he

should have. "Bugger Thraxton the Braggart's arse with a red-hot poker, why isn't he behaving the way he's supposed to? Does the stinking son of a whore think he can beat *me*?" He paused in his tirade to pour more brandy down his throat, then resumed: "If he thinks he *can* beat me, I'll kick his scrawny backside so hard, he'll end up in Marthasville whether he wants to or not." He gulped from the flask again, only to discover he'd drunk it dry. That set off a fresh barrage of foul language.

His division commander said, "It certainly is surprising that he would dare to try conclusions with you."

"Surprising? It's bloody idiotic, that's what it is," Guildenstern thundered. "I've seen beers with better heads on 'em than Thraxton's got, if he's enough of a moron to want to join battle with us when our army outnumbers his close to two to one."

Brigadier Alexander coughed a couple of times, the coughs of a man who's just had an uncomfortable thought. "Our *whole* army outnumbers his close to two to one, yes, sir. But his is larger than any of our three separate forces. If he were to concentrate against one of them . . ."

"That's why I sent Doubting George out by his lonesome, you nincompoop," Guildenstern said. He shook his flask. It *was* empty, and he remained thirsty. That he couldn't do anything about his thirst at the moment only made him more irritable. Ignoring Alexander's wounded look, he went on, "I wanted to lure Thraxton into trying to hit him, so the rest of us could land on the traitors like a ton of bricks and get rid of them once for all."

"Yes, sir. I understand that, sir," the division commander said carefully. "But with Lieutenant General

George well east of us and with Brigadier Thom so far off to the west, Thraxton might be able to, to hurt one of our wings before the others could come to its rescue."

*Thraxton might be able to smash one of our wings.* That was what Alexander had intended to say. *You can't fool me*, Guildenstern thought. *I know what you meant, you mealy-mouthed son of a bitch.* Even with brandy (*not enough brandy, gods damn it*) coursing through him, Guildenstern had no trouble seeing through his subordinate's deceptions.

But had he somehow failed to see through one of Thraxton the Braggart's deceptions? The trouble was, Brigadier Alexander, however mealy-mouthed he might be, had a point. If Thraxton *was* lingering in southern Peachtree Province, he might indeed handle one of King Avram's isolated forces very roughly before the other divisions could get to it.

Guildenstern's mouth twisted into a thin, bitter line. As if every word tasted bad—and every word *did* taste bad, as far as he was concerned—he said, "Maybe—just maybe—there is something to what you say. Maybe we ought to bring the wings of the army closer together."

Brigadier Alexander's face lit up. "Sir, I think that would be a *wonderful* idea!" he exclaimed, as if he expected to see Ned of the Forest's unicorns rampaging through the division he commanded any minute now. "If we're all together, the Braggart would have to come up with reinforcements before he could even think about attacking us, and where can he find them?"

"He can't." General Guildenstern spoke with great certainty. "There aren't any in this part of the kingdom."

"I'm sure you're right, sir," Alexander said. "And

so—a united army for a united kingdom, eh?" He chuckled stagily. "King Avram would surely approve."

"Yes." Guildenstern had no trouble holding the enthusiasm from his voice. He didn't particularly love King Avram. But he thoroughly despised Grand Duke Geoffrey—false King Geoffrey, these days. And he even more thoroughly despised the northern nobles who backed Geoffrey. They had everything he wanted— rank, wealth, elegance. No . . . They had almost everything he wanted. He turned to Brigadier Alexander and coughed a significant cough. "By the gods, I'm thirsty."

"Here, sir." Alexander took the bottle off his belt and handed it to the general.

"Thanks." Guildenstern yanked out the stopper, took a long pull—and then spat in disgust. He all but threw the flask to the brigadier. "You've got your nerve, giving a thirsty man *water*."

Alexander blushed bright red, as if he were a blond. "I—I'm sorry, sir," he stammered. "I—I'm not fond of spirituous liquors myself, and so it never occurred to me that—"

"Dunderhead," Guildenstern growled. The commanding general turned his back on his luckless subordinate and stalked off toward the scryers' tent. Brigadier Alexander took a couple of steps after him, then broke off the pursuit, sure it would do no good. And in that, if in nothing else, Guildenstern thought, the brigadier was absolutely right.

*I wonder if the scryers will have anything worth drinking*, Guildenstern thought as he ducked through the tent flap. He doubted it. And even if they did, odds were they wouldn't share with him.

The bright young men sitting behind their crystal balls sprang to attention when the commanding general walked in. One of them sprang so enthusiastically, he knocked over his folding chair and then had to bend and fumble to pick it up. "What can we do for you, sir?" asked Major Carmoni, who headed the scryers' section.

"I need to send some messages," Guildenstern answered. "What did you think I came in for, roast pork?"

Several of the bright young men snickered. Major Carmoni said, "Yes, sir: I understand you need to send messages. To whom, sir, and what do you need to say?"

That was business. So Guildenstern took it, at any rate. He was too elevated by brandy to suppose it might be scorn. "Send one to Doubting George," he answered, "ordering him to move toward me. And send the other to Brigadier Thom, also ordering him to move toward me. We shall concentrate our forces." He spoke the long word in the last sentence with great care.

"Yes, sir." Carmoni turned to the scryers. "Esrom, your crystal ball's attuned to the ones in Lieutenant General George's wing. And you, Edoc, you can deliver the message to Brigadier Thom's wing."

Both scryers nodded. One of them (Esrom? Edoc? the commanding general neither knew nor cared) turned to Guildenstern and murmured, "By your leave, sir." He nodded. The scryers sat down and bent over their crystals. They muttered in low voices. First one crystal began to glow, then the other. The scryers passed on General Guildenstern's orders. He heard those orders acknowledged. As the scryers looked up from the crystals, the glass globes went dull and dark again.

"It is accomplished, sir," Major Carmoni said.

"It had bloody well better be," Guildenstern said. "I wouldn't put it past George to pretend he'd never got the order so he could go on after Thraxton the Braggart all by his lonesome. He's a glory-sniffer, if you ask me." Off he went, not quite realizing how much juicy gossip he'd just left in his wake.

He still remained imperfectly convinced that the northern traitors really were loitering here by the southern border of Peachtree Province. He wouldn't have done it himself, which made it harder for him to believe Count Thraxton would. And the column in which he advanced, the column led by Brigadier Alexander, hadn't been assailed the way Doubting George had—the way Doubting George said he had, at any rate. Oh, a few bushwhackers had shot crossbows at the men in gray from the underbrush, but that happened marching along any road in any northern province.

Musing this, he glumly tramped back to his own pavilion. His stride grew glummer still when he bethought himself that no one soft and young and round and friendly was waiting for him in the pavilion. He sighed and scowled and kicked at the dirt. *By all the gods, I should have brought that wench with me when we marched out of Rising Rock*, he thought. *I expected to be heading up toward Stamboul by now. Bound to be plenty of women once I get into settled country—plenty of serfs who want to be nice to King Avram's general. But there aren't any at all in this wilderness.*

If he couldn't have a woman, more brandy needs must do. He didn't know where to get his hands on a woman, but brandy—or something else just as potent, such as the amber spirits for which Franklin was famous—was never hard to come by, not in any army on either side of this civil war.

Just before General Guildenstern went into his

pavilion, shouts rose from the mages' tents not far away: "Sorcery! Magecraft! Wizardry!" The men started rushing about in the gray robes that always made them look—to Guildenstern, at least—as if they'd just come from the baths. They would run from one tent and then into another, calling out all the while.

Guildenstern's lip curled. Mages were always running around yelling about magic, whether it was there or not. Guildenstern couldn't sense it, which made him doubt it was there. He wanted to see mages running around yelling about cauliflowers. He rumbled laughter. With cauliflowers, at least, an ordinary human being would have some hope of telling whether or not the mages were flabbling over nothing.

Sentries saluted as Guildenstern came up to the pavilion. "Cauliflowers," he muttered. Their eyebrows rose. But they didn't ask questions. Asking questions wasn't their job. Into the pavilion he strode. Sure enough, he had no trouble coming up with a bottle of brandy from which he could restore his sadly depleted flask—and from which he could restore his sadly depleted self.

He was smacking his lips over the restorative when one of the sentries stuck his head inside and said, "General Guildenstern, sir, Colonel Phineas would like to talk to you."

"Ah, but would I like to talk to Colonel Phineas?" Guildenstern replied grandly. It wasn't altogether a rhetorical question; his chief mage had and persisted in the unfortunate habit of telling him things he didn't want to hear. He scowled. Phineas would also write a nasty report if he sent him away without listening to him. King Avram read reports like those. Scowling still, Guildenstern said what he had to say: "Very well. Send him in."

In came Phineas, a round, agreeable man who looked more like a patent-medicine seller or a carnival barker than anyone's usual idea of a mage. "Sir!" he said, clapping a dramatic hand to his forehead, "we have been probed!"

"Probed?" Guildenstern echoed. It didn't sound pleasant; he was willing to admit that. What it did sound like was something a physician might do, not a sorcerer. "What exactly do you mean, Colonel?"

"What I say, of course," Phineas answered. "We have been probed—quite thoroughly, too, I might add."

"If you can't explain yourself in plain Detinan so an ordinary human being can understand you, Colonel, perhaps you should find yourself another line of work," Guildenstern said acidly. "Footsoldier springs to mind."

As he'd thought it would, that got Phineas' attention. "What I mean, sir, is that the northern mages have done everything they could to learn everything they could about our dispositions through sorcerous means. Perhaps you will criticize my style there. I am not used to being judged on my literary technique."

"Never mind," Guildenstern said: he'd finally found out what he needed to hear. "All right—they probed us, if that's what you wizards call it. How much did they find out? I presume you fellows blocked them. That's what we pay you for, anyhow." He laughed at his own wit.

Colonel Phineas didn't laugh. Colonel Phineas, in fact, looked about as somber as Guildenstern had ever seen him. "We did the best we could, General," he said, his voice stiff and anxious. "We always do the best we can, as you must surely know. But, I have to admit, we were taken somewhat by surprise."

Guildenstern didn't like the way that sounded. By the miserable expression on his chief mage's face, he had good reason not to like it. "How much did they learn?" he demanded. "They must have learned something, or you wouldn't look as though a brewery wagon just ran over your favorite kitten."

"They learned . . . perhaps a good deal, sir," Phineas said, forcing the words out one by one. "We . . . might have detected the probe rather sooner than we did. We are still . . . not quite so good as we might wish at reacting when taken by surprise. Such things . . . don't happen quite so often in civilian life."

"You've gone and futtered things again, is what you're telling me," Guildenstern boomed, his rage fed both by brandy and by knowing such things had happened to southron armies far too often. "You're telling me Thraxton the Braggart knows where every louse is on every man I command. That bloody well *is* what you're telling me, isn't it?"

"I don't think it's quite *that* bad, sir," Colonel Phineas said. "But, considering how scattered our forces are . . ."

The commanding general took great pleasure in laughing in his face. "If that's all you're having puppies about, you can rest easy," he said. "I'm already pulling them together." Phineas blinked. That wasn't enough for Guildenstern, who went on, "No thanks to you, gods damn you to the hells. Now get out of my sight!" Phineas fled. Guildenstern nodded. That was better. He swigged from the brandy flask again.

# V

Ned of the Forest could not have been more disgusted if he'd been invited to King Avram's coronation. "Why have we even got an army?" he demanded of Colonel Biffle. "What good is it if we just sit around with it and don't use it?"

"Tell you what I heard," Biffle said.

"Well? Go on," Ned said. "How come General Thraxton's being an idiot this time out?" He was willing to assume Thraxton *was* being an idiot, for one reason or another.

But Colonel Biffle shook his head. "It's not Thraxton's fault this time, Ned." He held up a hasty hand. "I know the two of you don't see eye to eye. Everybody knows that, I expect. But what I hear is, Thraxton's flat-out ordered Leonidas the Priest to get up off his arse and go for the stinking southrons, and Leonidas just keeps sitting on his backside and won't move for anything."

"I wouldn't be surprised," Ned allowed. "Leonidas has got himself plenty of holy where you ought to have smart, you know what I mean? But the southrons are figuring out we didn't run for Stamboul or Marthasville. They're starting to pull their own army together. If we don't start taking bites out of their separate columns pretty soon, we lose the chance for good."

"I know that, sir," Biffle said. "But I can't make Leonidas move, either."

"Only thing that'd make Leonidas move is a good, swift kick in the backside," Ned said scornfully. He raised a bristling black eyebrow. "I will be cursed if I don't feel a little bit sorry for Thraxton, and that's nothing I reckoned I'd ever say."

"Won't be so good if Guildenstern does pull his whole army together before we get the chance to hit it," Colonel Biffle remarked. "He's almost done it already."

"Won't be good at all," Ned agreed. "Not at all, at all." He and his men occupied the extreme left wing of Count Thraxton's army, with Leonidas the Priest's force on his immediate right. A slow grin spread over his face. "We'll just have to make sure it doesn't happen, that's all. And I know how, too."

"Do you?" Biffle asked. "What do you know that Count Thraxton doesn't?"

"Oh, all sorts of things," Ned answered, and his grin got wider. "But one of the things I know—and the one that really matters here—is how to get Leonidas moving irregardless of whether he wants to or not."

"That'll be good—if you can do it." Biffle sounded dubious. He explained why: "I've seen you do things on the field that nobody'd believe if you just told the story. But how do you propose to make somebody else—somebody on your own side—move when he cursed well won't?"

Instead of answering directly, Ned filled his lungs and let out a one-word shout: "Runners!"

As always, the young men who fought under him hurried to obey. "Lord Ned, sir!" they cried in a ragged chorus.

He pointed to one of them. "Go to Count Thraxton and tell him I am moving out to meet the enemy. Tell him I hope to have Leonidas the Priest moving with me on my right, but I'm going to attack with him or without him. Have you got that?"

"Sure do, Lord Ned," the messenger said, and repeated it back.

"That's fine. That's right fine." Ned of the Forest waved to him, and he hurried off. Ned pointed to another runner. "Now, Mort, you're going to go to Leonidas the Priest. You tell him, I'm moving out to attack the southrons with him or without him. Tell him I hope he comes along for the ride, but I'm moving out whether he does or not. *And* tell him I've sent another runner to Count Thraxton, so Thraxton knows just exactly what I'm doing. Wouldn't want to take Count Thraxton by surprise, no indeed." For a moment, he sounded every bit as pious as Leonidas the Priest. "Have *you* got *that*?"

"I've got it, Lord Ned," Mort replied. When he started to repeat it for the commander of unicorn-riders, he stumbled a couple of times. Ned patiently led him through it till he had it straight, then sent him off.

After dismissing the rest of the runners, Ned turned back to Colonel Biffle. "Well, sir, if that doesn't shift Leonidas off his sacred behind, to the seven hells with me if I know what would." Biffle clapped his hands together, as if admiring a stage performance. In a way, Ned knew he'd just delivered a performance. "What does it say about a man when you've got to trick him into doing what he's supposed to do anyhow?" he asked, and answered his own question: "It says the bastard isn't worth the paper he's printed on, that's what."

"Yes, sir," Biffle agreed. "Now—are you really going to move forward before you find out whether Leonidas will come with you?"

"You bet I am," Ned replied without the least hesitation. Colonel Biffle looked worried. Ned set a hand on his shoulder. "Now don't you fret about a thing, Biff. The good part of riding unicorns is that we can get out of a fight as fast and easy as we can get into one. If we run into more southrons than we can handle, and if Leonidas still hasn't woken up, we'll pull back again, that's all."

Now Biffle's face showed relief. "That's better, sir. That's a hells of a lot better. We can't lick Guildenstern all by our lonesome."

"I wasn't finished," Ned said. "The other thing is, if the footsoldiers don't follow, the Lion God won't feast on the blood of the lamb. He'll taste Leonidas' blood, you see if he doesn't."

From any other man, that might have been a joke. Colonel Biffle didn't act as if he thought Ned were joking, which was just as well, for Ned meant every word. Biffle said, "Don't be hasty, sir. If the priesthood curses you, half your riders will desert."

"Ah, but what a fine bunch of devils the other half would be," Ned replied, now with a charming grin. "Besides, I'm hoping it won't come to that. Let's get mounted up, Colonel, and we'll find out, eh?"

At his command, the trumpeters blew *advance*. The unicorns rode south and east over a little wooden bridge, their hooves drumming on the timbers. Looking back over his shoulder at the troopers who followed him, Ned of the Forest nodded to himself. He already had a pretty fine bunch of devils. The southrons had found that out on a number of fields. Now he intended to teach them another lesson.

"We're going to find Guildenstern's men," he called to the unicorn-riders. "We're going to find 'em, we're going to smash through 'em, we're going to get between them and Rising Rock, and we're going to break their army all to flinders. How's that sound, boys?"

The unicorn-riders whooped. They growled like wolves and roared like lions. For a heady moment, Ned felt as if they could beat Guildenstern's army to flinders all by themselves. *Steady down*. He deliberately made the mental command stern. Thinking you could do more than you really could was as dangerous as not thinking you could do enough.

They hadn't gone much more than a mile when shouts of alarm and crossbow bolts hissing through the air announced they'd found the foe—and that the foe had found them. Ned grimaced. It wasn't an ideal place for a fight: the road ran through dense forest, in which a man couldn't see very far. But Ned didn't hesitate. If this was where King Avram's men were, this was where he'd hit them.

"Dismount!" he shouted, and the trumpeters echoed his commands. "Form line of battle and forward!"

Colonel Biffle said, "Leonidas had better come after us now." He cocked his head to one side. "Unless I'm plumb daft, we've run into a lot of southrons here."

"I'd say you're right," Ned agreed. "Well, this here is what we came for. Ride on up the road with me a ways, Colonel, why don't you? We'll just see what we've got." Without waiting to find out whether Biffle followed, he spurred his unicorn on.

Biffle didn't hesitate. No man under Ned's command hesitated when ordered to ride with him. On they went—and collided headlong with a squad of southron cavalry trotting north down the road to see what sort of force they'd just bumped into.

Ned's saber flew into his left hand before he was consciously aware of reaching for it. Where a more prudent man would have drawn back, he howled curses and galloped toward the enemy. Their startled cries became shouts of pain when he slashed two of them out of the saddle in quick succession. His unicorn, a well-trained beast, plunged its horn into the side of another southron's mount. The wounded animal let out a scream like a woman in torment and bucketed off, carrying its rider out of the fight.

Colonel Biffle traded swordstrokes with a southron, then slashed his shoulder to the bone. That was enough for the unicorn-riders in gray. They fled back up the road they had ridden down so confidently. But as they fled, one turned back and shot a crossbow over his shoulder.

The quarrel caught Ned of the Forest in the right upper arm. He cursed foully as blood began soaking his sleeve. It wasn't a bad wound; he could still open and close his right hand. But he felt dizzy and weak and more than a little sick. It might not have been a bad wound, but no wound was a good one.

"You all right, Lord Ned?" Colonel Biffle asked anxiously.

"Just a scratch," Ned answered. But his voice gave

him away—he sounded woozy, even to himself. It was
more than a scratch, even if the bolt had only torn
a gouge in his arm rather than piercing him through
and through. Angry at himself for showing weakness,
he tried to make light of it: "I'm fine."

Biffle shook his head. "You don't look fine, sir, and
you don't sound so fine, either. Let me bind that up
for you, and you take a drink of this here while I'm
doing it." Like a lot of officers, he carried a flask on
his belt. He handed it to Ned.

"I don't know. . . ." Ned was rarely irresolute, but
he hesitated here. He hardly ever drank spirits, and
despised drunkards with all his soul.

"It's medicine, sir," Colonel Biffle said firmly as
he got to work on Ned's arm. "It'll put the heart back
in you. You need it, by the gods. You're green around
the gills. Nothing to be ashamed of—any man who
gets wounded looks that way."

"All right." Ned yielded. "Here, you'll have to pull
the stopper out." Colonel Biffle briefly paused in his
work, took the flask from Ned, and then gave it back
to him. Still unhappy, Ned raised it to his lips and
took a long pull. He almost spat the mouthful out
into the dirt of the roadway. After he'd choked it
down, he wheezed, "Gods, that's foul! How can you
stand to drink it?"

Biffle looked affronted. "Them's prime Franklin
sipping spirits, Lord Ned. You won't find better anywhere in Detina. Take another slug. It'll do you
good."

"It tastes nasty enough—it must be strong medicine," Ned said, and forced himself to drink again.
Flames ran down his throat. They exploded like a
firepot in his belly, spreading heat all through him.
The wound still hurt, but Ned felt himself once more,

or at least better able to carry on. He gave the flask back to Biffle. "Thank you, Colonel. I reckon that did some good."

"Fine," Biffle said. "I've got you just about patched here, too."

"Thank you kindly," Ned of the Forest repeated. Thinking of firepots made him raise his voice to a battlefield shout: "Captain Watson! Come here—I want you!"

"Coming, sir!" The officer who headed Ned's field catapults was a fresh-faced boy who couldn't yet have twenty summers. When he'd reported to the unicorn-riders, Ned had thought some capricious fellow over in Nonesuch was playing a joke on him.

But Viscount Watson always got the dart- and stone-throwers up to the very front of the fight, and any officer who did that had little to complain of from Ned of the Forest.

Ned pointed toward the trees not all that far away, from which the southrons were still shooting at him. "I want your engines to pound those bastards. Pound them, do you hear me? They're here in numbers, and we've got to shift 'em."

"Yes, sir!" Excitement glowed on Watson's face. "I'll see to it, sir. You can count on me!" He went back at a gallop, shouting for his catapult crews to hustle their deadly machines forward. Ned grinned and shook his head. Like a lot of common soldiers, Watson was young enough to imagine himself immortal as a god. Ned wished he were still that young. He knew the southrons could kill him—unless he killed them first.

So did Colonel Biffle. "Sir, they're still pushing on us. We're going to stop more bolts if we don't pull back a bit."

"Right you are," Ned said. As he and Biffle rode back toward their own line, he saw Captain Watson and the catapult crews bringing their engines forward. In minutes, stones and darts and firepots started coming down on the southrons' heads. Ned whooped. "That's the way to give it to 'em!"

But the southrons had engines of their own, and punished his dismounted riders with them. And they had footsoldiers in great numbers. They kept on storming forward, ready to fight. A captain called out to Ned in some alarm: "Sir, I don't know how long we can hold 'em unless we get some more men here."

"Do your best, gods damn it," Ned answered. He slammed a fist—his left fist—down on his thigh. "Where in the seven hells is that low-down, no-good son of a bitch called Leonidas the Priest? If he really has turned coward on us, we're going to have to get out of here, and I'm cursed if I want to do it. We can lick the stinking southrons, if only we get to work and do it."

But General Guildenstern's men came on like a gray wave of the sea, always looking to lap around the edges of Ned's line and roll it up. At last, he couldn't bear it any more. He spurred his unicorn back toward the rear. *If I catch Leonidas back there praying when he ought to be fighting, I will sacrifice him to the Lion God*, he thought. *But to the seven hells with me if I think his lion would much care to gnaw on his scrawny old carcass.*

That thought—and maybe Colonel Biffle's spirits coursing through him, too—made him laugh out loud, his own spirits almost completely restored despite the wound. And then he took off his hat and waved it and whooped out loud: up the road marched a long column of crossbowmen in indigo tunics and pantaloons (some in gray pantaloons, taken from dead southrons). Leonidas might not have been quite so fast as Ned would have liked, but he'd got his soldiers on the move.

"Come on, boys!" Ned yelled, and pointed to the south. "We've got plenty of southrons up there for you to kill!" When Leonidas' troopers cheered, they sounded like roaring lions themselves. Ned rode forward with them. Going forward, going toward the fight, was what he did best.

A crossbow quarrel slashed the bushes behind which Rollant hid. He flattened himself even lower to the ground. He wished he could burrow his way down into it, like a mole or a gopher. Something— a shape in blue?—moved out there among the trees. He shot at it, then set another bolt in the groove to his crossbow and yanked back the bowstring as fast as he could. He had no idea whether he'd hit the enemy soldier. He wasn't altogether sure there had been an enemy soldier. The only thing he was sure of was that he dared not take a chance.

Smitty crouched behind an oak not far away. "How many traitors are there, anyway?" he asked, reloading his own crossbow.

"I don't know," Rollant answered. "All I know is, there are too many of them, and they all seem to be coming right at us."

This was different from the savage little skirmish his company had fought a few days before. Now all of Lieutenant General George's soldiers were in line together—and all of them, by the racket that came from both east and west of Rollant, were being pressed hard. The traitors roared like lions when they came forward, as if to say they were the true children of the Lion God.

The sound made the hair prickle up on the back of Rollant's neck. The Detinans had roared when they smashed the blond kingdoms of the north, too, back in the days not long after they crossed the Western Ocean and came to this land. Iron and unicorns and catapults and magic had had more to do with their triumphs than the roaring, but no blond to this day could hear it without wanting to flinch.

*They won't capture me*, Rollant thought. *I won't let them capture me*. If they let him live, they would haul him back to Ormerod's estate in chains. *I should have killed him. I had the chance*. He shook his head. He knew he was lucky his former liege lord hadn't killed him.

Somewhere not far away, the din rose to a peak—and then started coming from farther south than it had. Smitty and Rollant both cursed. "They've broken through, Thunderer blast them," Smitty said. Then he said a worse word: "Again."

"What do we do?" Rollant looked nervously in that direction.

"Hang on here till we're ordered back," Smitty answered. "What else can we do?"

Rollant shrugged. *Hang on here till the traitors flank us out and roll over us*, went through his mind. He couldn't say that. An ordinary Detinan trooper might have, but he couldn't. He didn't think Smitty would start going on about cowardly blonds, but he wasn't altogether sure. And he was altogether sure some of the other Detinans in the squad would go on about exactly that.

"Hold your places, men!" That was Lieutenant Griff, still in command of the company. His voice was high and anxious. Had Captain Cephas been there, the identical order from his lips would have heartened the men. After Griff gave it, plenty of Detinans started looking back toward the rear, to make sure their line of retreat remained open. Rollant wasn't ashamed to do the same.

Great stones and firepots started landing close by. A stone that hit a tree could knock it flat, and the soldier beside it, too. "Curse the traitors!" Smitty howled. "They've found a road to move their engines forward."

In country like this, engines could move forward only on roads. Hauling them through the woods was a nightmare Rollant didn't want to contemplate. He had other things he didn't want to contemplate, too. "Where are *our* engines hiding?" he asked.

"They're back there—somewhere." That was Sergeant Joram, pointing back toward the rear. "You wouldn't expect the fellows who run them to come up here and mix it with the traitors, would you? They might get their fancy uniforms soiled."

That was unfair: catapult crews fought hard. But none of them seemed close by right now, when the company needed them. And Joram's sarcasm did more to steady the men who heard it than Lieutenant Griff's worried command to stand fast. *Why isn't Joram an officer?* Rollant wondered.

Then he cheered like a man possessed, and so did the soldiers close by, for Doubting George's army *did* have some engines hidden up a tunic sleeve. Stones smashed down on the enemy soldiers pushing forward against Rollant's company. A bolt from a dart-thrower transfixed two men at once as they ran forward. A firepot landed on them a moment later, giving them a pyre before they were quite dead.

"See how you like it!" Rollant shouted. Another crossbow quarrel tore leaves from the bushes behind which he lay.

"Don't be stupid," Sergeant Joram said. "Just do your job. Everybody does his job, everything will turn out fine." He sounded calm and confident and certain. By sounding that way, he made Rollant feel guilty. Captain Cephas had had the same gift, but who could say when—or if—Cephas would return to the company?

No sooner had Rollant started reflecting on how calm he felt than a storm of crossbow bolts came, not from ahead of him, but from off to the left. The traitors gave forth with their roaring battle cry.

"Flanked!" Half a dozen men shouted the same thing at the same time. Rollant wasn't the least bit ashamed to be one of them. He scrambled away from the bushes, trying to find a couple of trees that would protect him from the left and from the front at the same time. It wasn't easy. It was, in fact, next to impossible—trees didn't grow so conveniently close together.

"Fall back!" Lieutenant Griff commanded. "They've broken through on this line. We'll have to try to hold them on the next one."

The men had hesitated to obey his order to stand. They didn't hesitate to retreat. Rollant wondered if they could hold Thraxton the Braggart's army on the next line. He wondered if they could hold it anywhere.

More arrows tore at them from the flank as they dropped back to look for a line they could hold. Lieutenant Griff did a good job of keeping them moving and fighting at the same time. Rollant admitted as much to himself later; while the retreat was going on, he just hoped to make it to some kind of safety before Thraxton's men overwhelmed not only the company but the whole regiment—and possibly the whole brigade.

He was part of the group Griff had ordered to keep shooting to the front no matter what happened. Having a clear sense of what to do helped him do it. He would shoot a bolt or two from whatever cover he could find, reload, and scurry back behind another tree or bush or rock to do the same thing over again. If an enemy quarrel slammed into him from the left . . . then the group commanded to hold off the traitors on the flank weren't doing their job. That was their worry, not his—except indirectly, of course.

"King Avram!" he shouted as he loosed a bolt at a fellow in an indigo tunic. The northerner went down, whether hit or merely alarmed Rollant didn't know. He hoped he'd put that bolt right between the northerner's eyes—and he hoped it was Baron Ormerod. He knew perfectly well that that was too much to hope for. He'd had one chance at his old liege lord. How likely were the gods to give him two?

"Avram and justice!" somebody else yelled, not far away. The traitors could roar as much as they liked, but they weren't the only soldiers on this part of the field.

When Rollant burst out of the woods and into a good-sized clearing, he blinked in surprise—and in no little alarm. How were he and his comrades supposed to take cover crossing open ground like that? Then he saw the engines lined up almost hub to hub in the clearing. They were—they had to be—the ones that had punished the northerners before things went wrong on the flank.

Rollant's company weren't the only men bursting into that clearing. The soldiers in northern blue didn't just roar when they burst into it. They howled and whooped with delight and rushed at the engines. Capturing catapults was every footsoldier's dream.

Chains clattered as they went ratcheting over five-sided gears. The dart-throwers that were like concentrated essence of crossbowmen sprayed streams of death into the men who called Grand Duke Geoffrey their king. The traitors went down as if scythed. But men among the catapult crews fell, too: and not only men, but also the unicorns that moved the engines. Some of the traitors had got close enough for their crossbows to reach their foes.

And then stones and firepots started landing among the siege engines in the clearing. Rollant cursed. Whoever was in charge of the traitors' catapults was doing a very smart job indeed of pushing them to the forefront of the fighting.

"We've got to pull out!" one of Avram's officers shouted as a stone smashed a dart-thrower flat. That made Rollant curse again, but he could see the sense of it. The engines were up against more than they could handle here. If they stayed, they would either be wrecked or overrun and lost.

Harnessing unicorns to the catapults was but the work of a moment. Off they went, those that could go. Soldiers pulling ropes hauled a couple of them away, doing the work of beasts already slain. And the crews set fire to a couple of machines too badly damaged to take away but not so wrecked that Geoffrey's men couldn't get some use from them.

"Form skirmish line!" Lieutenant Griff shouted. "We have to give them time to get away!"

Militarily, the order made perfect sense. In the red balance sheet of war, catapults counted for more than a battered company's worth of footsoldiers. That made standing— actually, dropping to one knee—out in the open no less lonely for Rollant.

He muttered prayers to the Lion God and the

Thunderer. And, although he didn't pray to them, he hoped the old gods of his people were keeping an eye on him, too. Those old gods weren't very strong, not when measured against the ones the Detinans worshiped. The blonds had seen that, again and again. But the Detinans' gods didn't seem to be paying much attention to Rollant right now. Maybe the deities his people had known in days gone by would remember him when the strong gods forgot.

Here came more northerners, out into the clearing. "Give them a volley!" Griff said. "Don't shoot till you hear my orders. Load your crossbows . . . Aim . . . Shoot!"

Rollant squeezed the trigger. His crossbow bucked against his shoulder. All around him, bowstrings twanged. Quarrels hissed through the air. Several blue-clad soldiers fell. "Die, traitors!" Rollant shouted, reloading as fast as he could.

"Steady, men," Lieutenant Griff called. He was steadier himself than Rollant had thought he could be—certainly steadier than he had been when the battle erupted. "Make every shot count," he urged. "We can lick them."

Did he really believe that? Rollant didn't, not for an instant, not while the company was standing out here in the open, trying to hold back the gods only knew how many of Thraxton's men. But Griff sounded as if he believed it, whether he did or not. And that by itself got more from the men than they would have given to a man with panic in his voice.

A couple of soldiers not far from Rollant went down, one with a bolt in the leg, the other shrieking and clutching at his belly. But then, although quarrels kept whizzing past the men in the company and digging into the dirt not far from their feet, none struck home for a startlingly long time. That was more than luck. That was . . . Behind Rollant, somebody said, "A mage!"

Rollant turned his head. Sure enough, a fellow in a gray robe stood busily incanting perhaps fifty yards behind the company's skirmish line. "I'll be a son of a bitch," Smitty said. "A wizard who's really good for something. Who would've thunk it?"

"As long as he can keep the bolts from biting, he's worth his weight in gold," Rollant answered. "And as long as he can keep us safe like this, *we're* worth a brigade."

"That's the truth," Smitty said. "Do you suppose he can keep mosquitoes from biting, too? If he could do that, he'd be worth twice his weight in gold, easy."

Before Rollant could come up with a response to that bit of absurdity, the mage let out a harsh cry, loud even through the din of battle. Rollant looked back over his shoulder again. The wizard was staggering, as if pummeled by invisible fists. He rallied, straightened, but then grabbed at his throat. Someone might have been strangling him, except that nobody stood anywhere close by. The northern wizards had found the mage. With another groan, he fell. His feet drummed against the ground. He did not rise.

An instant later, a crossbow bolt struck home with a meaty slap. A man only a few paces from Rollant howled. Whatever immunity the company had enjoyed died with the sorcerer in gray.

A runner dashed up to Lieutenant Griff through the hail of quarrels. Griff listened and nodded. The runner pelted away. Griff called, "Fall back, men! We've done our duty here. The gods-damned traitors won't take those engines. And George's whole wing is falling back on Merkle's Hill. We'll make our stand on the high ground there."

"Where's Merkle's Hill?" Rollant asked. Smitty only shrugged. So did Sergeant Joram. Rollant hoped Griff knew where he was going. The lieutenant was right about one thing: the catapults had escaped Thraxton's men. *Now I have to get away from them myself*, Rollant thought. He didn't run to the far edge of the clearing, but his quickstep was fine, free, and fancy. And he didn't get there first, or anything close to it.

His company—indeed, his regiment—were not the only men retreating toward Merkle's Hill. The traitors had treated Doubting George's wing of General Guildenstern's army very roughly indeed. Thraxton's soldiers kept pushing forward, too, roaring like lions all the while.

"We have to hold them, men." Rollant looked around, and there stood Lieutenant General George. The wing commander had his sword out; blood stained the blade. "We have to hold them," Doubting George repeated. "If they get through us or past us, we haven't just lost the battle. We've lost this whole army, because they'll be sitting on the road back to Rising Rock. So hold fast and fight hard."

George had a habit of telling the truth. This once, Rollant could have done without it.

"Hold fast, men!" Lieutenant General George was getting tired of saying it. He hoped his soldiers weren't getting tired of hearing it. If they stopped holding, if they lost heart and ran, the army was ruined. He hadn't been lying when he warned them of that. He wished he had.

Colonel Andy appeared at Doubting George's

elbow. George almost wheeled and slashed at him, but realized who he was just in time. The aide-de-camp's gray tunic was splashed with blood; by the way Andy moved and spoke, it wasn't his. "Well, sir," he said now, surprisingly cheerful in view of the situation, "I think we can be pretty sure Thraxton the Braggart's not back at Stamboul."

"Seems a fair bet," George agreed, dryly enough to draw a chuckle from Colonel Andy. "What we have to do now is make sure the traitors don't get to Rising Rock."

"Don't you think we can lick them, sir?" Andy asked.

"I doubt it," George said, and Andy chuckled again. George went on, "They've got the bit between their teeth, the way a unicorn will sometimes. My guess is, we'll just have to ride it out and see what's left of us at the end of the fight. The only consolation I take is, it could be worse."

His aide-de-camp's eyes widened. "How?"

"They could have hit us a few days ago, when we were scattered all over the gods-damned map," George answered. "Thraxton's pulled extra men from somewhere—for all I know, he magicked them up. He's got more than I ever thought he could, anyway. If he'd smashed our columns one at a time instead of letting us regroup, he could have bagged us one after another. Now, at least, we've got a fighting chance."

A runner, also bloodied, came panting up and waited for Doubting George to notice him. When George did, the fellow saluted and said, "Brigadier Brannan's compliments, sir, and he wants you to know he's massing his engines at the crest of Merkle's Hill, just behind our last line. If the traitors come up the hill, a demon of a lot of 'em won't go down again. That's what Brannan says, anyhow."

"Good." George slapped the runner on the back. "You hustle up to Brigadier Brannan and tell him he's doing just the right thing. Just exactly the right thing—have you got that?"

"Yes, sir." With another salute, the youngster hurried away.

"We're doing as well as we can, sir," Andy said.

"Of course we are," George said. "We're doing as well as any army could that gets hit from the front and the flank when it doesn't really believe there's any trouble around at all." He wanted to say something a good deal harsher than that about the way General Guildenstern had handled the advance from Rising Rock, but held back.

His aide-de-camp had no trouble hearing what he didn't say. "King Avram won't be happy once the scryers get word of what's happened back here to the Black Palace in Georgetown."

"Let's hope that still matters to us after the battle's over," George replied.

Colonel Andy's eyes widened. "Do you think the traitors are going to surround us and slay us all, the way we Detinans did to the blonds at the Battle of the Three Rivers back in the early days?"

"That had better not happen," Doubting George said severely, and managed to jerk a startled laugh from Andy. George went on, "No, what I had in mind was what the king is liable to do to us once he hears how things have gone wrong. Do you think our commander will keep on commanding after this?"

"The men like General Guildenstern," Andy answered. "He takes good care of them, and" —he lowered his voice a little— "he has all their vices, though on a grand scale."

"He takes good care of them on the march. He takes good care of them in camp," George said. "If he took good care of them in battle, we wouldn't be where we are right this minute." Where they were, right this minute, was halfway up the slope of Merkle's Hill, and falling back toward the line near the crest. Thraxton's men kept up their roaring, and they kept coming as if someone had lit a fire behind them. George kicked at the dirt as he trudged up the long, low slope of the hill. "This is partly my fault. I told General Guildenstern I didn't think Thraxton had headed north, but I couldn't make him believe me."

"If Guildenstern wouldn't believe you, sir, why is that *your* fault?" Andy asked.

"I should have *made* him believe me, gods damn it," George answered. His aide-de-camp raised an eyebrow, but didn't say anything. After a moment, George nodded. Nobody, up to and possibly including the Lion God and the Thunderer, could make General Guildenstern do what he didn't feel like doing.

"Lieutenant General George! Lieutenant General George!" somebody shouted from not far away. A heartbeat later, the shouter went on, to himself this time, "Where *is* the miserable old son of a bitch, anyways?"

"Here!" Doubting George yelled. A runner trotted up to him. He fixed the fellow with a mild and speculative stare. "And what do you want from the miserable old son of a bitch, anyways?" The runner flushed and stammered. "Never mind, son. I've been called worse," George told him. "Just speak your piece."

"Uh, yes, sir." The runner kept on stammering, but finally said, "Uh, sir, Brigadier Negley, uh, says to tell you he's hard pressed, sir, and he doesn't know how much longer he can hold on. Thraxton's men are all over the place, sir, like syrup on pancakes." He flushed again. "That last bit, that's, uh, mine, sir, not Brigadier Negley's."

"It's not the worst figure I've ever heard," George said, which didn't keep him from scowling. Brigadier Negley's men held the left end of his line, the end that connected the wing he commanded to the rest of General Guildenstern's army. "You tell Negley that he's got to hold, that if he doesn't hold we're all in a lot of trouble, and him in particular. Use just those words."

"Yes, sir." The runner repeated them back. He saluted—much more smartly than he would have if he weren't embarrassed; Doubting George was sure of that—and then hurried back toward the left.

"Where in the seven hells *did* Thraxton the Braggart come up with enough men to make an attack like this?" Colonel Andy demanded as he and George accompanied their retreating men up toward the crest of the hill.

George had more immediate worries—not least among them whether he could get the men to stop retreating once they neared the crest. But he answered, "I don't think he pulled them out of *there*, Colonel. He'd have got some when the traitors' garrison pulled out of Wesleyton before Whiskery Ambrose took it. The rest? I don't know. Maybe Geoffrey sent soldiers from Parthenia. He's never done that before, but maybe he did. I don't know. Thraxton's got 'em. I know that."

"Yes, sir. So do I," Colonel Andy said.

"What we really need to do," Doubting George said, "is stop worrying about where they're from and start worrying about how we're going to drive them back." He'd said that before. He'd had trouble getting anybody to listen to him. There were times when he had trouble getting himself to listen to him.

Andy asked, "If the king does sack General Guildenstern over this, who do you suppose will replace him?" Avid curiosity filled his voice.

"I'm not going to play that game," George insisted. "Let's worry about getting through this battle first. If we don't do that, nothing else matters."

Directly rebuked, his aide-de-camp had no choice but to nod. But the question, once posed, kept echoing in George's mind. If Geoffrey had sent soldiers from the west, King Avram might pluck a general out of Parthenia to take command here in the east. Or he might promote another of the eastern generals.

Colonel Andy refused to stay squelched. He said, "Sir, it could be you."

"Yes. It could." Try as he would to avoid it, George found himself drawn into the quicksand of speculation. "It could, but I wouldn't bet on it. For one thing, I'm a Parthenian, and people still wonder how loyal I am. For another, if we lose this fight, my reputation suffers along with General Guildenstern's."

"That's not fair, sir," Andy said.

"Life isn't fair," George answered. "If I had to put my money on any one man, I'd bet on General Bart."

"Why?" Andy asked.

"Why? Because Bart seems to be the one man who wants to start pounding on the traitors and keep pounding till they fall over or we do," George said. "And because King Avram thinks the world of him for taking Camphorville on the Great River earlier this summer and cutting the traitors' realm in half."

"He's a man of no breeding," Andy said. "A tanner's son. And he drinks."

"And General Guildenstern doesn't?" Doubting George said. His aide-de-camp spluttered, but didn't say anything. Andy couldn't very well say anything, not to that. George went on, "Bart's a solid soldier. You know it, I know it, King Avram knows it, and the northerners know it, too—to their cost. And if we can make serfs into soldiers, we can make a tanner's son a general. We already have, as a matter of fact."

"The northerners don't," Colonel Andy said.

"No?" George chuckled. "They talk about nobility, but look what they do." He pointed to the right of his line. "Those are Ned of the Forest's troopers taking bites out of us over there. Do you think Ned got his command on account of his blue blood?"

"Ned got his command on account of he's a son of a bitch," Andy answered.

"Well, that's true enough," George said. "But he's a gods-damned good fighting man, too, no matter what else he is. And so is General Bart. The difference is, General Bart's *our* son of a bitch."

He broke off to look around again and see how his men were doing. The short answer was, *not very well*. The traitors had bent their line back into what looked like a unicornshoe on the slopes of Merkle's Hill. If they could bend the line back on itself, if they could get around it or break through it . . . If they could do any of those things, then talk about who might take over command of this army would prove meaningless, for there would be no army left to command.

General George peered west. He wished he knew how the fight was going for the rest of Guildenstern's army. Odds were it wasn't going any too well, or the commanding general would have sent him reinforcements. He could use them, but maybe Guildenstern couldn't afford to send anyone his way. That didn't seem good.

And then George stopped worrying about the bigger picture and started using the sword that was supposed to be a ceremonial weapon. As had happened farther northwest, Thraxton's troopers broke through the line in front of him. The men he commanded had to fall back or die. And he had to fight or die or end up ignominiously captured.

The thought of living off Thraxton the Braggart's hospitality, of enduring the traitor lord's society, was plenty to make Doubting George fight like a madman. Crossbow quarrels whistled past him. He didn't worry about those; he couldn't do anything about them, anyhow. The roaring northerner in front of him was a different matter. The fellow swung his shortsword as if he were carving meat. "Geoffrey!" he shouted. "Geoffrey and freedom!"

"King Avram!" George yelled back, as if his gray tunic and pantaloons weren't enough to announce which king he served. "King Avram and one Detina!"

"To the seven hells with King Avram!" the northerner bawled. He slashed again. He was strong as a bull; George felt the blow all the way up his arm and into his shoulder. But strength was all he had going for him. He would never make a real swordsman, not without long training. And he would never get the chance to have such training. Doubting George, like most nobles, had begun swordplay while still a boy. Unlike most nobles, he'd had his skills refined by the tough, unforgiving swordmasters at Annasville while training to become an officer in Detinan service.

He sidestepped a third slash and thrust for the northerner's throat. The force of the fellow's own stroke had bent him half double; he had no chance of getting his own blade up in time. Blood spurted when George's point punched through the soft, vulnerable flesh under his neck. The northerner gobbled something, but blood filled his mouth, too, and made the words meaningless. He stumbled, staggered, fell. He wouldn't get up again.

Another one of Thraxton's men, though, had Colonel Andy in trouble, attacking so furiously that the aide-de-camp couldn't do much against him. George drove his own sword into the blue-clad man's back. The fellow shrieked and threw up his hands, whereupon Andy ran him through.

"That wasn't even slightly sporting, sir," Andy said as the two of them went up the slope of Merkle's Hill.

"You're right. It wasn't," George replied. "Now ask me if I care. I meant to kill the son of a bitch, and I cursed well did."

They fell in with more of their own men, and then got behind a hasty breastwork of felled trees. Crossbowmen worked a slaughter on Geoffrey's soldiers trying to drive them back. Soldiers who could shoot from cover always had an edge on those who fought in the open. And Brigadier Brannan's engines pounded the northerners, too.

"Hold 'em, boys!" Doubting George shouted. "The River of Death isn't far from here. Up to us to be the rock in it, not to let the traitors by."

The men in gray cheered. Colonel Andy set a hand

on George's arm. "Sir, *you're* the rock in the River of Death."

"Me? Nonsense," George said. "Can't do a thing without good soldiers." The men cheered again. He waved his hat. "Let's beat 'em back!" he yelled. "We *can* do it!"

Ned of the Forest scowled at the slopes of Merkle's Hill. "Damn me to the seven hells if they're making it easy for us," he said.

"It'd be nice if they would, eh?" Colonel Biffle said. "How's your arm, Lord Ned?"

"Not too bad," Ned answered. After gulping Biffle's spirits, he'd hardly thought about the wound, so he supposed they'd done their job. "We could use some magecraft to help finish off those southron bastards."

"Don't look at me, sir," Biffle said. "Only magic I know is how to make some of the gals friendly, and I don't think that'll do us much good here. In fact, if you want to get right down to it, it's not even magic, not rightly, anyhow." He looked smug.

"I wasn't expecting it from *you*, Biff," Ned said. "But where's Thraxton the Braggart? Back when we were still in Rising Rock, he bragged me as big a brag as you'd ever want to hear about how he would lick Guildenstern's army, lick him out of Rising Rock, lick him clean out of Franklin. He's supposed to be such an all-fired wonderful he-witch, why isn't he *doing* anything?"

Colonel Biffle shrugged. "I expect he'll get to it in his own time."

"I expect you're right." Ned of the Forest growled something under his breath. "That's how Thraxton goes about things—in his own sweet time, I mean.

He'd better get around to doing 'em when they need doing. We'll all be better off."

"I don't know how you can make a man move when he's not inclined to," Biffle said.

"*I* do, by the gods. You build such a hot fire underneath his backside, he can't do anything *but* move." Ned kicked at the dirt in frustration. "I did it with Leonidas. But he's the high and mighty Count Thraxton, don't you know." He did his best to affect an aristocratic accent, but couldn't get rid of his backcountry rasp. "So we'll just have to do our best, on account of Thraxton's backside's so far away, it's godsdamned near fireproof. But he'd better do something, or he'll answer to me." He held his saber in his left hand. The blade twitched hungrily. He pointed ahead with it. "What's the name of the high ground the southrons are holding?"

"That's Merkle's Hill, Lord Ned," Colonel Biffle answered.

"We've got to get through it or around it some kind of way," Ned said. "You reckon we can put enough of a scare on their general to make him turn around and skedaddle?" His grin was impudent. "You put a scare on the general, you've got your fight won, and it don't hardly matter what his soldiers do."

But Biffle said, "Those are Doubting George's troopers."

Ned of the Forest cursed, the heat of battle still in him. "We can lick him. We can fool him, the way we did when he was coming up from Rising Rock toward the River of Death. But I don't reckon we can frighten him out of his pantaloons."

"Do you want me to send the men forward again, sir?" Colonel Biffle asked. "They'll go—I know they will—but they've already taken some hard licks."

"I know they have," Ned said. "Curse it, unicorn-riders aren't made for big stand-up fights. We can be dragoons. We're cursed good dragoons, by the gods. But only half the point to dragoons is the fight. The other half is getting somewheres fast so you can fight where the other bastards don't want you to."

"Can't do that on Merkle's Hill," Colonel Biffle said positively.

He was right. Ned of the Forest wished he were wrong. But then Ned pointed with his saber again, this time toward the southeast. "We'll just have to see if we can't slide around behind 'em, then. If we can get a decent-sized band of soldiers on the road between them and Rising Rock, they'll have to fall back, on account of if they don't, they'll never get another chance."

"Can we do it?" Biffle asked.

"Don't know," Ned answered. "But I'll tell you what I do know—I do know I'd sooner try something my own self than wait for Thraxton the gods-damned Braggart to huff and puff and blow their house down." He raised his voice to a bellow: "Captain Watson!"

"Yes, Lord Ned?" Watson had a way of appearing wherever he was needed.

"If we try and slide some men around to the south side of this here Merkle's Hill, can you bring some engines along?" Ned asked.

Captain Watson said, "I'll give it my best shot, sir. Don't quite know what kind of ground we'll run into, but I'll give it my best shot."

Ned of the Forest slapped him on the back. "That's good enough for me." He had to bite his tongue to keep from adding, *sonny boy*. He was young as generals went himself, but Watson could easily have been his son. When the youngster was first assigned to him, he'd thought Watson might be somebody's nasty joke. But the boyish captain had proved able to handle catapults—to get them where they needed to be and to fight them once they got there—better than most men Ned's age and older.

"Let me gather up some dart-throwers and a couple of engines that will fling stones or firepots," he said now. "I'll be with you in half an hour." He went off at a dead run. He almost always did. Ned, a man of prodigious energy in his own right, envied Watson his.

He turned to Biffle. "We'll take your regiment, Colonel. Get them on their unicorns and ready to ride inside an hour." Colonel Biffle saluted and hurried away, not quite at Watson's headlong speed but plenty fast enough.

And Ned shouted for a runner. When he got one, he said, "Go back to the unicorn-holders. Tell all of them—no, tell all of them who aren't in Biffle's regiment—to tie the gods-damned beasts to whatever trees or bushes they choose, to grab their crossbows, and to get their arses forward into the fight."

"Yes, sir," the runner said, and *he* hurried off. Ned grinned after him. That was what a general was good for: to set a whole lot of men running every which way. Putting the unicorn-holders into the fight wouldn't replace as many men as he was pulling out with Biffle's regiment, but it would be better than nothing. And, if things went as Ned hoped, he would soon set an army's worth of southrons running every which way.

He yelled for a scryer. At his command, the mage relayed what he aimed to do to Count Thraxton's headquarters. Unlike Watson and Biffle and the runner, the scryer could stay where he was. Once he'd sent Ned's message, he asked, "Shall I wait for a reply from the count, sir?"

"By the gods, no!" Ned exclaimed. "Matter of fact, put your crystal ball away and don't look at it for a while. He can't say I didn't tell him what I have in mind, but I don't want him to go telling me he won't let me do it. He can't very well do that if you aren't listening for him, now can he?"

"No, sir," the scryer answered with a grin. He wasn't one of the northeastern yeomen who made up the bulk of Ned's force—men much like Ned himself, with more grit than blue blood and more stubbornness than learning from a codex. He'd had to have some book learning, or he wouldn't have known what to do with that crystal ball of his. But by now he was just as ornery as any of the unicorn-riders with whom he served.

A little more than an hour after Ned gave his orders, he led Colonel Biffle's regiment and half a dozen engines south and east in a long loop around Merkle's Hill. The battle there had lost none of its ferocity. If his men, or Leonidas the Priest's, could dislodge Doubting George's soldiers, Count Thraxton would have the smashing victory he hoped for. *Well, if that happens, we'll make it a bigger one, on account of we'll ruin the southrons' retreat*, Ned thought.

If Thraxton got the victory, he would surely take all the credit for it. People didn't style him the Braggart for nothing. And he had King Geoffrey's ear. *If he didn't have Geoffrey's ear, he wouldn't still be in charge of an army after all the fights he's bungled.* Ned was sure that thought had crossed other men's minds, too. But, since Thraxton *did* have the king's ear, he couldn't do much about it, and neither could anyone else.

The path the regiment followed wound through thick woods—perfect for keeping the southrons from spying them. "If we get in their rear, we'll give them a hells of a surprise," Ned said, anticipation in his voice.

"Yes, sir." Colonel Biffle nodded. "Of course, that's what the hierophant told the actress, too." He laughed. Ned of the Forest chuckled. Young Captain Watson howled with mirth, and almost fell off his unicorn. That made Ned chuckle again. When he was Watson's age, he would have laughed himself silly at such bits of dirt, too.

The forest opened out onto a broad clearing. There on the far side of the clearing was the road leading north toward the River of Death—and there, marching along the road, was a long column of King Avram's gray-clad soldiers heading toward the fight. They shouted when they caught sight of Ned and the first of his troopers.

Ned shouted, too: he shouted curses. Such a splendid idea, ruined by brute fact. Or was it ruined? If he could make the southrons run away, he'd have the road and he'd have their whole army by the throat.

"Forward!" he shouted, and spurred his own unicorn toward the southron soldiers. Roaring as if the Lion God spoke through them, the riders of Colonel Biffle's regiment followed him.

Avram's soldiers were marching in blocks of pikemen and crossbowmen. They wouldn't have anywhere near the time they needed to put up a proper line in front of the archers. If Ned's men could get in among them, they would work a fearful slaughter.

If. The southrons were veterans. Ned could see as much by the way they turned from column into line, by the way their first rank dropped to their bellies and their second to one knee so the third, standing, rank could shoot over both of them. And he could see as much by the volley of bolts that tore into his men.

Unicorns fell. Men crumpled in the saddle and crashed to the ground. And the first three ranks of enemy footsoldiers moved back to the rear of the line while the next three stepped forward. They poured in a volley as devastating as the first—if anything, more devastating, because the unicorn-riders were closer and easier to hit.

Easier to hit, yes, but they couldn't hit back. Ned cursed again. This time, though, he cursed himself, for folly. He'd been annoyed at having his ploy thwarted, and he'd gambled on putting a scare on King Avram's men. It wasn't the worst of gambles. Charging unicorns, their iron-shod horns and their riders' sabers gleaming in the sun, were among the most terrifying things in the world. But King Avram sometimes led brave men, too.

*How many men will I have left if they take another volley? Enough to drive the southrons off the road? Enough to hold it if I do?* Neither seemed a good bet to Ned. And so he shouted, "Back! Back, gods damn it! We aren't going to do what we came for, and there's no point to doing anything less." He wheeled his own unicorn back toward the forest without a qualm. Unlike some of King Geoffrey's officers, he didn't fight for the sake of fighting. If he couldn't win, he saw no point to it.

As the unicorn turned, a crossbow quarrel caught it in the throat. Blood gushed, spurted, fountained—

a big artery must have been cut. Ned leaned forward
and thrust a finger into the wound. With it plugged,
the unicorn galloped on. It even had the spirit and
strength to leap over another unicorn that lay dead
on the grass of the meadow.

Back under the trees, Ned pulled his finger out
again. The unicorn took a couple of steps forward,
then sank to the ground and finished its interrupted
job of dying. Ned scrambled off. He looked around
for another mount. He didn't have to look long. More
than a few unicorns had been led back to the forest without their riders.

"If we can't do it here, we'll have to do it at the
real fight," he told Colonel Biffle. Then he shouted,
"We're going back!" to Captain Watson.

Watson was busy bombarding the southrons with
firepots and hosing them down with darts. "Do we
have to leave?" he shouted back.

"Yes, gods damn it, we do have to leave," Ned
answered. "We can't do what we came to do—fool
bad luck, but no help for that. So we'll go back
and give the rest of King Avram's bastards a hard
time."

His men rode hard. More often than not, they
didn't take their unicorns straight into battle, but
fought dismounted. That let them push the pace
when they were on the move. They tied their mounts
beside those of the rest of Ned's riders and hurried
back to the fight on Merkle's Hill.

"General Ned!" someone called in a battlefield
bellow. "General Ned!"

"I'm here," Ned shouted back. He advanced toward
the call, sword in hand. If any southron wanted to
meet him man to man, he was more than ready to
oblige. The gods would judge one of them after the

fight was done, and Ned didn't intend that they should judge him for a good many years to come.

But it wasn't a southron. It was Baron Dan of Rabbit Hill. Ned hadn't had much to do with him since his quarrel with Count Thraxton back in Rising Rock. Dan thrust out his hand. As Ned took it, the other general saw the bandage on his right arm and exclaimed, "You're wounded?"

"Just a scratch, and I'm a lefty anyways," Ned replied. "What can I do for you?"

"Not so long ago, Doubting George's men made a counterattack here, and they had some numbers while they were doing it," Baron Dan said. "I saw some of our men most bravely holding them back, and I asked whose footsoldiers they were. The answer I got was, 'We're Ned of the Forest's unicorn-riders.' I salute you, sir, for their magnificent behavior." He suited action to word.

"Thank you kindly." Ned returned the salute. "Thank you very kindly indeed. You're a gentleman, sir." He did not use the word lightly, or often. Perhaps sensing as much, Dan of Rabbit Hill bowed. Ned returned that compliment, too, and said, "Now let's whip these southron sons of bitches clean out of their boots."

"Right you are, Lord Ned," Dan said with a laugh. They went up the hill toward the fighting together.

"Come on, boys!" Captain Ormerod shouted. "One more good lick and those stinking southrons'll run like rabbits."

At his side, Lieutenant Gremio said, "In the courts back in Karlsburg, sir, I would object to a statement such as that on the grounds of insufficient evidence to support it. The southrons not having run up to this point in time, why should they commence now?"

"Because we're going to hit them that one good lick, that's why," Ormerod answered in a voice everyone around him could hear. For Gremio's ear alone, he went on in quieter tones: "And because I want the men to fight like mad bastards, and I don't care a fart about evidence. Have you got that?"

"Yes, sir," the lieutenant said. In thoughtful tones, he said, "This does make a certain amount of practical sense, I admit."

"And to the seven hells with practical sense, too." Ormerod started toward the west, where the sun was sinking. "By the gods, we'd better drive King Avram's men off this hill before nightfall. Otherwise, they'll have time to get their reinforcements into place tonight, and the battle will be that much harder tomorrow."

"True enough." But Gremio neither sounded nor looked worried. If anything, he looked sly. "I hear tell we have reinforcements coming, too."

"Where from?" Ormerod demanded. "And what's the evidence for that, Master Barrister, sir?"

"Oh, it's hearsay," Gremio said. "No doubt about it, it's hearsay: I heard Colonel Florizel talking about it with another officer in the brigade."

That was hearsay, sure enough. But it was hearsay at a high level, which made it seem promising to Ormerod. One obvious problem still bothered him, though. "Where in the seven hells would these reinforcements come from?" he repeated. He paused a moment to turn out the pockets of his pantaloons. "I haven't got any on me, that's sure."

Gremio smiled the dutiful smile of a junior officer who had to acknowledge a senior officer's joke. Then he said, "I heard—I can't prove it, mind—they'd be coming from Parthenia Province."

"By the gods, that'd be fine if it was so," Ormerod said. "About time King Geoffrey figured out that what happens over here in the east is important, too. The war's bigger than just the fight to keep the southrons away from Nonesuch."

Before the war, he'd cared little about the east. Karlsburg lay on the Western Ocean, and his estate was just a few miles outside the oldest city in Palmetto Province. Had Colonel Florizel's regiment gone into the Army of Southern Parthenia rather than the Army of Franklin, he probably still wouldn't care very much about the east. But his horizons had broadened since.

"King Avram!" shouted the southron soldiers in front of Florizel's regiment. "King Avram and justice!"

"King Avram and thievery," Ormerod muttered under his breath. He turned to Gremio. "Where in the seven hells is the justice if that scrawny little toad who calls himself king in Georgetown wants to take my serfs away from me without my leave? Answer me that."

"Can't do it," Gremio said solemnly.

"Of course you can't," Ormerod said. "Those serfs have been on that land ever since we conquered it. He's got no business interfering with me, none at all." He raised his voice to a battlefield roar: "Come on! Let's give those southrons some of their justice!"

Crossbow quarrels whistled past him as he led his company forward. But his men were shooting, too. Cries from ahead said they'd hit some of the enemy soldiers. And then, sooner than he'd expected, his men were in among the southrons. The whole fight in these woods had been like that. The trees and bushes were so thick, they hid things till too late, and made the battle more a series of bushwhackings and ambushes than a proper standup fight.

The men in gray cried out in dismay and surprise—they hadn't thought the northerners could bring so many men to bear on them so quickly. Some of them threw down their crossbows and shortswords and threw up their hands. Some retreated up the slope of Merkle's Hill. And some, even taken at a disadvantage, stood and fought.

Some of the men who wouldn't retreat and wouldn't surrender had yellow beards and golden hair under their hats. "King Avram!" one of them shouted, hurling himself at Captain Ormerod.

For a moment, Ormerod wondered if he'd run into Rollant again. But no—he'd never seen this blond before. "You'll get what you deserve, runaway," he snarled, and thrust at the enemy soldier's chest.

The blond was no swordsman: he almost spitted himself on Ormerod's blade. Only at the last instant did he beat it aside with his own. His answering slash was fierce but unskilled. Ormerod parried, thrust again. This time, he felt the yielding resistance of flesh as the sword slid into the blond's belly. He twisted the blade as he drew it out, to make sure the wound would kill. The serf shrieked like a lost soul. Captain Ormerod hoped he was.

"May the gods give you what you deserve," Ormerod panted as the runaway sagged to the ground. He raised his voice again: "Push them!"

But as the men in blue tried to advance, a barrage of flying boulders and firepots smashed into the ground. And the southrons had a couple of their accursed repeating crossbows stationed among the trees where they could rake the more open ground in front of them. Some of Ormerod's men shot back at the engines, but they were out of range for hand-held weapons. The advance faltered.

"I don't think we can do it, Captain," Lieutenant Gremio said.

Baron Ormerod wondered whether they could do it, too. Enough engines in front of footsoldiers would simply shred them before they could close. But he said, "I'm going forward. Stay behind if you haven't got the nerve to come with me." He brandished his sword and trotted toward the catapults.

His men followed. Gremio came with the rest. He was cursing under his breath, but Ormerod didn't mind that. As long as he followed, he was welcome to think whatever he liked.

Soldiers in blue fell, one after another. Some lay unmoving. Some thrashed and writhed and shrieked. A few tried to crawl back in the direction from which they'd come. The rest of the company slogged on.

Every so often, a soldier would pause to shoot and reload: bolts hissed past Ormerod from behind as the bigger, heavier ones from the repeating crossbows hummed by him—some much too close—from the front. He'd heard of officers shot in the back during charges like this. A man would take out his hatred and say it was an accident—if it ever came to light, which it probably wouldn't.

Gray-clad troopers around the siege engines began falling. Ormerod's soldiers had finally fought their way into range. As more quarrels reached the engines, they shot less often and less effectively. At last, their crew-men scurried back into the woods to keep from get-ting killed.

Roaring with fierce glee, Ormerod's men swarmed over the engines, smashing and slashing them with spades and shortswords. "Let's see Avram's sons of bitches pound us with these now!" Ormerod shouted.

"I think we would have done better to save them, so our own artificers could turn them against the southrons," Lieutenant Gremio said.

In a narrow sense, he was probably right. Ormerod cared nothing about narrow senses. He said, "Let the boys have their fun, Lieutenant. Look at the price they paid to earn it." The ground in front of the engines was covered with fallen soldiers.

The southrons did not give the survivors long to enjoy their little triumph. The men who'd served the engines weren't the only soldiers in gray on that part of Merkle's Hill. Pikemen and crossbowmen assailed Captain Ormerod's company in such numbers, he had to order them to fall back.

They lost more men retreating to about the place from which they'd begun the attack on the engines. Ormerod wondered if the assault had been worth it. He shrugged and made the best of it: "We hurt them."

"And they hurt us, too," Gremio said.

Ormerod would have bet that his lieutenant would say something like that. "We can't do these little tricks without losses," he replied.

Gremio was ready to argue. He always was—what barrister wasn't? "But does what we gained justify the losses?" he asked.

"I don't know how to weigh that." Ormerod looked at the sky again. The sun was low, very low. He cursed. "I do know we're not going to run the miserable southrons off this hill today. I know that's not good, too."

"No, it isn't." Gremio didn't argue that. Ormerod wished he would have. Instead, the lieutenant went on, "You can bet they'll have more men in their lines tomorrow than they have today. You can't bet on it with us. You can only hope."

"I do hope," Ormerod said. "Parthenia Province, you tell me?" He waited for Gremio to nod, then twisted his fingers into a gesture invoking the Lion God. "That'd be very fine indeed. So it would. So it would. Here's hoping it's true."

"Colonel Florizel thought so," Gremio observed.

"Maybe he knows more now than when you heard from him." Ormerod looked around. "Have you seen him lately? I haven't."

A trooper said, "Captain, he's wounded. He went down with a bolt in the leg a couple of hours ago."

"No wonder I haven't seen him," Ormerod said. "Is it a bad wound?" A bolt in the leg could prove anything from a little gash to a killer. At Pottstown Pier, General Sidney, one of King Geoffrey's best officers, had tried to stay in the saddle with a crossbow quarrel in the thigh and had quietly bled to death before anybody, including himself, realized how badly he was hurt. But the trooper only shrugged—he didn't know. Ormerod muttered a curse.

Gremio said, "That means Major Thersites is in charge of the regiment. I don't much care for him."

"Don't let him hear that," Ormerod warned. Truth was, he didn't care much for Major Thersites, either. Thersites grew indigo on an estate deep in the swamps outside Karlsburg. He was liege lord over a good many serfs and called himself a baron, though neither Ormerod nor anyone else in the neighborhood was sure he truly had noble blood in his veins. But he'd killed the one man who said as much out loud, and being good at killing wasn't the worst claim to nobility in the northern provinces of Detina in and of itself.

Lieutenant Gremio said, "I know." With fairly obvious relief, he changed the subject: "You're not going to order us forward again before sundown?"

Ormerod shook his head. "Not me. I don't think we can break the southrons, and I don't see much point to anything less. Of course, if Thersites tells us to advance, then we will."

"Oh, yes, I understand that," Gremio said. "But I agree with you, sir. We've done everything we can do today, I think. We've driven the southrons a long way. We might have done even better if Leonidas the Priest had started his attacks when Count Thraxton first ordered him to, but we'll never know about that, will we?"

"Leonidas is a very holy man," Ormerod said. "Surely the Lion God favors him."

"Surely." But Gremio's agreement dripped irony. "And surely the Lion God favors a good many hierophants back in Palmetto Province, too. Does that suit them to command a wing of Count Thraxton's army?"

The answer was obvious. It was so obvious, Ormerod didn't care to think about it. To make sure he didn't have to think about it, he ordered pickets forward. "I don't expect Doubting George to try anything nasty during the night, but I don't want to get caught with my pantaloons around my ankles, either," he said.

"Sensible, Captain." This time, Gremio sounded as if he meant it.

Here and there, northern soldiers started campfires on the lower slopes of Merkle's Hill. The fighting hadn't stopped everywhere, either there or farther west: shouts and curses and the occasional clash of steel on steel still sounded in the distance. And everywhere, near and far, wounded men moaned. Ormerod said, "I hate that sound. It reminds me of everything that can go wrong."

Gremio gave him an odd look, or so he thought in the fading light. "I didn't think you worried about such things."

"Well, I do," Ormerod answered.

A voice came from out of the gloom: "You do what, Captain?" Major Thersites strode up. He wasn't a handsome man; one of his shoulders stood higher than the other, and a sword scar on his cheek pulled his mouth into a permanent sneer. Some said he'd got the scar in a duel. According to others, he'd got it from an outraged husband. Ormerod knew which version he believed.

But Thersites had somehow ended up with a higher rank than his own, and was at the moment commanding the regiment. It behooved Ormerod to speak softly, and he did: "I do worry about the cries the wounded make, sir. If I'm not lucky, I might be making them myself one day."

"That's true, but a soldier shouldn't fret about it," Thersites said. His voice had a permanent sneer in it, too. *Or maybe I'm just touchy*, Ormerod thought. Then Thersites added, "You can't be ready to run away from a little pain," and Ormerod knew he wasn't the one who had the problem.

Stiffly, he said, "Command me, sir, and I shall advance."

"Tomorrow," Thersites replied. Ormerod's nod was stiff, too. *I'll show you*, he thought.

# VI

Count Thraxton sat in a rickety chair in an abandoned farmhouse not far from the River of Death, staring into the fire. Baron Dan of Rabbit Hill and Leonidas the Priest perched on stools to either side of him; Ned of the Forest, too active to sit, paced back and forth through the bare little room.

"We hit them a mighty blow today," Thraxton said.

"By the Lion God, we did," Leonidas agreed. "We've driven them back over a mile, and bent their army nearly double. One more strong stroke tomorrow, and they fall into our hands."

*If you'd struck them a few days ago, when I ordered you to attack, they would have already fallen into our hands*, Thraxton thought resentfully. But Leonidas wasn't wrong even now. "Strike that blow we shall," Thraxton said.

"Almost had 'em today," Ned of the Forest said. "I got a regiment of riders all the way around behind 'em, but they were bringing up reinforcements right where we came out, and so I couldn't quite pull off what I had in mind." He snapped his fingers. "Came *that* close, though."

"So you said earlier this evening," Thraxton answered. "It sounds very pretty, but it would be all the better for proof."

That made Ned stop his pacing. The firelight flashed in his eyes as he growled, "If you're calling me a liar, Count—"

"I said nothing of the sort," Thraxton replied smoothly.

"You better not have," Ned said. Thraxton ignored him. The count's lean, somber face showed nothing. Inside, he jeered, *You stupid bumpkin, do you think I'm foolish enough to do anything so overt?*

"Ned's men fought very well today on Merkle's Hill," Baron Dan said. "They put up such a stand against a swarm of southrons that I took them for footsoldiers, not unicorn-riders."

"Good," Thraxton said, but not in a tone of voice to make either Dan of Rabbit Hill or Ned think he approved. They both glowered. He looked back at them as innocently as he could. The more they squabbled, the happier he was.

Leonidas the Priest said, "I am sure the Lion God will give our just cause victory when the fight resumes tomorrow."

Before Count Thraxton could come up with a snide comeback to that, a commotion outside distracted him. His long, pale hand paused in midair, uncertain whether to reach for the sword on his belt or the sorcerer's staff leaning against the wall behind him.

Then one of the sentries exclaimed, "Earl James!" and Thraxton's hand fell back into his lap.

"So he got here in time for the dance after all," Ned of the Forest said. "Next question is, did he bring his friends along?"

"Surely he would not have come alone," Leonidas the Priest said. One of Ned's eyebrows rose. So did one of Count Thraxton's. *Leonidas is a trusting soul,* he thought. A moment later, he amended that: *Leonidas is a trusting fool.*

Earl James of Broadpath strode into the farmhouse. He was a bear of a man, bigger and more imposing than Thraxton had expected, burly and shaggy and, at the moment, in something of a temper. Giving what struck Thraxton as a perfunctory nod, he said, "By the gods, your Grace, I've been wandering over some of the wretchedest landscape I've ever seen, trying to find out where in the eternal damnation you'd hidden your headquarters."

"I am glad you did at last," Thraxton said, his bloodless tone suggesting he was anything but glad. "Allow me to introduce my subordinates to you, General—though I expect you will already know Dan of Rabbit Hill."

James rumbled laughter. Baron Dan smiled, too. "I expect I will," James agreed. "We're both out of Palmetto Province, we both graduated from the officers' collegium at Annasville the same year, and Dan's out of the Army of Southern Parthenia, too. Good to see you again, by the Thunderer." He clasped Dan's hand in his own big paw.

"Touching," Count Thraxton murmured. "Here is my other wing commander, Leonidas the Priest, and the commander of my unicorn-riders, Ned of the Forest."

Leonidas rose and bowed. Ned was already standing. He bowed, too. James returned both bows, bending as much as a man of his physique could. He and Ned of the Forest sized each other up—*like two beasts of prey meeting in the woods*, Thraxton thought with distaste. Earl James said, "I've heard of you. By all accounts, you do good work."

That made Ned bow again, just as if he were a real gentleman. "Thank you kindly," he answered. "Everybody knows the Army of Southern Parthenia does good work."

Count Thraxton fumed. Ned had just given him the back of his hand, and more smoothly than he would have expected from such a lout. Thraxton wondered if James of Broadpath had noticed. He couldn't tell: that thicket of beard kept James' face from showing much.

With a small sigh, Thraxton returned to business: "How many of your men have come here with you, Earl James?"

"Rather more than half, your Grace," James replied. "Brigadier Bell is bringing the rest forward as fast as the accursed glideways in Peachtree Province will let him. The southrons don't have to go through this sort of nonsense when they move their troops from hither to yon, believe you me they don't."

"That, unfortunately, is true," Thraxton said. "Nonetheless, the men you do have will greatly augment our strength. You are senior to Baron Dan, I believe?"

"I may be," James said quickly, "but you don't need to do anything on my account. Dan knows what's going on hereabouts hells of a lot better than I do."

"Rank must be served," Thraxton declared. "Were it not for matters pertaining to rank, would we have a quarrel with King Avram's so-called justice?" He turned the last word into a sneer. "By your rank, your Excellency, you deserve to command the wing Leonidas the Priest does not."

Dan of Rabbit Hill said, "It's all right, James. I don't mind—I know things will be in good hands with you."

Earl James bowed to him. "Thank you very much, your Excellency. That's gracious of you." He nodded to Thraxton. "If you're going to give me this, your Grace, I'll do my best with it. Baron Dan's men are your right wing—have I got that much straight?"

"Not just the right wing—the whole right side of my army," Count Thraxton replied. "I look forward to seeing what a man from the famous Army of Southern Parthenia can do here among us easterners." In another tone of voice, that would have been a graceful compliment. As things were, he implied he didn't expect much at all from James of Broadpath.

"I'll do my best," was all James said. No matter how well his beard concealed his expression from the outside world, he didn't sound very happy. That suited Thraxton fine. He reckoned happiness overrated. Since he was rarely happy himself, he found little reason for anyone else to be.

"Let us examine the map," he said. Happy or not, he had every intention of hurling his army at the southrons again as soon as it grew light.

But Ned of the Forest said, "Hold on. You just hold on there, by all the gods. You're supposed to be a mage along with being a general. Isn't that so, Count Thraxton, sir?"

"I *am* a mage," Thraxton said coldly. "And your point is . . . ?"

"I'm coming to that, never you fear," Ned said. "My point is, when we were up in Rising Rock you bragged this enormous brag about what all we were going to do—what all *you* were going to do—to the stinking southrons. What I want to know is, what's General Thraxton's brag worth? Can you do what you said you'd do, or is it all just wind and air?" He stared a challenge at Count Thraxton.

Thraxton stared back. He heartily wished Ned of the Forest dead. But wishes had nothing to do with magecraft, no matter what benighted serfs might think. Picking his words with care, Thraxton said, "I have been incanting all through the battle. Without my cantrips, we should be in far worse state today than we are."

"So you say," Ned jeered. "So you say. It'd be all the better for proof, that's all I've got to tell you."

Leonidas the Priest said, "You must remember, the southrons have mages in their service, too, mages who wickedly seek to thwart Count Thraxton in everything he undertakes."

"Isn't he better than any of those fellows?" Ned rounded on Thraxton. "Aren't you better than any of those fellows? You *say* you are. Can you prove it?"

"I can prove it. I *will* prove it," Thraxton replied. "By this time tomorrow, neither you nor Earl James nor anyone else will be able to doubt what I can do." He folded his arms across his chest. "Are you answered?"

"Ask me tomorrow this time," Ned of the Forest said. "I'll be able to tell you then. Meanwhile, I'm going back to my men." With a mocking bow, he swept out of the farmhouse.

"Never a dull moment here, is there?" James of Broadpath remarked.

"Not hardly," Baron Dan said, a remark almost uncouth enough to have come from Ned.

"Perhaps we should rest now, and beseech the Lion God to show us the way to victory come the morning," Leonidas the Priest said. "If he is gracious, he will send us dreams to show the direction in which we should go."

"I know the direction in which we should go," Thraxton said. "I intend to take us there." He pointed toward the southeast. "The direction in which we should go is straight toward Rising Rock."

"Well said." Dan of Rabbit Hill nodded. Leonidas looked aggrieved because Thraxton wasn't giving the Lion God enough reverence, but Thraxton cared very little how Leonidas looked.

"Let me have a look at the map," James of Broadpath said. "Dan, if you'd be so kind as to walk over here with me and tell me what the southrons might be up to that doesn't show up on the sheet here, I'd be in your debt."

"I'd be glad to do that, sir," Baron Dan replied.

Leonidas the Priest got to his feet. He didn't go over to the map. Instead, he said, "I shall pray for the success of our arms," and left the farmhouse. That struck Count Thraxton as being very much in character for him.

Then another thought crossed his mind: *and what of me?* He shrugged. He was what he was, and he didn't intend to change. And one of the things he was, was a mage. He had done a good deal of incanting this first day of the fight, but it had been incanting of a general sort, incanting almost any mage, even a bungling southron, might have tried. *A bungling southron would not have done it so well*, he thought. He knew his own worth. No one else gave him proper credit—to his way of thinking, no one else had ever given him proper credit, not even King Geoffrey—but he knew his own worth.

And he realized he'd not been using his own worth as he should. He was a master mage, not a journeyman, and he'd been wasting his energy, wasting his talent, on tasks a journeyman could do. Any mage could torment the other army's soldiers. What he needed to do—and it struck him with the force of a levinbolt from the Thunderer—was torment the other army's commander.

General Guildenstern would be warded, of course. The southrons would have wizards protecting him from just such an assault. *But if I cannot overcome those little wretches, if I cannot either beat them or deceive them, what good am I?* Thraxton asked himself.

Decision crystallized. "Gentlemen, you must excuse me," he told Dan of Rabbit Hill and Earl James. "I have plans of my own to shape."

The two officers looked up from the map in surprise. Whatever they saw on Count Thraxton's face must have convinced them, for they saluted and left the farmhouse. Thraxton pulled out first one grimoire, then another, and then yet another. He sat by the hearth and pondered, pausing only to put more wood on the fire every so often to keep the flames bright enough to read by.

What made him realize dawn had come was having to feed the fire less often. As the light grew, so did the sounds of battle from the south. He put down the grimoires and began to cast his spell. A runner came in with a message. Without missing a single pass, without missing a word of his chant, Thraxton seared the fellow with a glance. The runner gulped and fled. Whoever had sent him would just have to solve his own problems.

Thraxton's spell reached out for his opposite number in King Avram's army. *Strike for the head, and the body dies*, he thought. But General Guildenstern was well defended, better even than Thraxton had expected. One after another, counterspells grappled with his cantrip, like so many children's arms trying to push aside the arm of one strong man.

Driving on despite them took all the power Thraxton had. A lesser man, a less stubborn man, would have given up, thinking the spell beyond his power. But Count Thraxton persevered. *This time*, he thought, *this time, by all the gods, I shall drive it home to the hilt*.

And he did. For once, the spell did not go awry, as had happened before. For once, it did not rebound to smite his own soldiers, as had happened before. For once, Count Thraxton lived up to a brag as fully as any man might ever hope to do. He cried out in something as close to delight as his sour spirit could hold, and in full and altogether unalloyed triumph.

As Count Thraxton and his generals hashed over the first day's battle that evening in a farmhouse close by the River of Death, so General Guildenstern and his generals spent that same night doing the same thing in another farmhouse, a widow's miserable little hut made of logs, only a very few miles to the south.

"Well, boys, we're in a scrap, no two ways about it," Guildenstern said. He swigged from a bottle of brandy. "Ahhh! That's good, by the gods. We're in a scrap," he repeated, hardly noticing he'd already said it once. "We are, we are. But we can still lick 'em, and we will."

He clenched the hilt of his sword as if it were a traitor's neck. When Thraxton's attack went in, he'd had to do some real fighting himself. He knew there were men who questioned his generalship—he had plenty of them right here in the farmhouse with him. But no man ever born could have questioned his courage.

He looked around at the assembled military wisdom—he hoped it was wisdom, at any rate. "All right. Here we are, not quite where we wanted to be when we set out from Rising Rock. But we aren't lost yet. Anybody who says we are is a gods-damned quitter, and welcome to go home. Question is, what will that Thraxton son of a bitch try and do to us when the fighting picks up in the morning?"

Lieutenant General George shook his head. "No, sir. That's only part of the question."

Guildenstern glared at him. *Gods damn you, too, Doubting George*, he thought. George had warned him Thraxton wasn't retreating so fast as he'd thought himself. And George had had the nerve to be right, too. General Guildenstern did his best not to remember that as he growled, "What's the other part?"

"Why, what we can try to do to him, of course," George answered.

George's Parthenian accent made it seem as if Thraxton the Braggart had an officer of his own at this council of war. But no one, not even Guildenstern, could challenge his loyalty to King Avram. And he wasn't wrong here, either. "Fair enough," Guildenstern said. "What *can* we do to that Thraxton bastard?"

"I would strengthen the right," George answered around an enormous yawn. That yawn made Guildenstern yawn in turn, and went in progression from one officer to the next till they'd all shown how weary they were. Guildenstern had a cot to call his own. Doubting George—who yawned again—was perched on a three-legged milking stool. The rest of the generals either stood up or sat cross-legged on the rammed-earth floor.

"Of course you would strengthen the right, sir," Brigadier Alexander said. "You *are* the right."

"And if the traitors get through me or around me, everything goes straight to the seven hells," Doubting George replied. "Ned of the Forest took a whack at it this afternoon, and the bastard almost ended up sitting on our route back to Rising Rock. If he hadn't bumped into some of our boys coming forward, that would have been a lot worse than it was."

"If you think the fighting wasn't heavy in the center, too, you can think again, sir," Brigadier Thom said.

Doubting George yawned once more. "I would strengthen the right," he repeated. His eyes slid shut. Guildenstern wondered why he didn't fall off his stool.

A couple of brigadiers started to snore, one lying on the ground, the other leaning up against the log wall of the widow's hut. General Guildenstern took another pull at the brandy. It might not have made him think better, but it made him feel better. Right now, that would do.

It also made him sleepy. He yawned and stretched out on the cot. Some of his subordinates had higher social rank than he did, but he held the highest military rank. In wartime, that was what counted, not who was a count. The commander got the cot.

Before General Guildenstern could fall asleep, Doubting George stirred from his restless doze. "I would strengthen the right," he said for the third time. He wasn't looking for an answer. Guildenstern doubted he was even fully awake. But he said what was on his mind, awake or not.

*He's probably not even wrong*, Guildenstern thought—no small mark of approval when contemplating the views of his second-in-command. *If he needs help, or if I see the chance, I* will *strengthen the right.*

He yawned again, rolled over, and fell asleep. The next thing he knew, morning was leaking through the narrow windows in the log hut. He muttered a prayer of greeting to the sun god, then noticed he had a headache. His hand reached out and unerringly found the brandy flask. He took a swig. "Ahh!" he said—not quite a prayer of greeting, but close enough.

With a little restorative in him, he noticed the delicious smell filling the little farmhouse. A blond steward was frying ham and eggs in a well-buttered pan over the fire in the fireplace. A couple of brigadiers already had their tin plates out, waiting for the bounty that was to come. Guildenstern wasted no time in grabbing his own. As he'd got the cot, so he would get the first helping.

"Where's Doubting George?" he asked, noticing Brigadier Thom perched on the milking stool. "He'll miss breakfast."

"He went back to his wing, sir," Thom answered. "A runner came in right at first light and said the fighting over there had started up again."

"Curse the traitors," Guildenstern said as the steward ladled ham and eggs onto his plate. "They're an iron-arsed bunch of bastards indeed, if they won't even let a man get a little food inside him before he goes back into battle." He started shoveling food into his own face. "By the gods, that's good. Poor old George doesn't know what he's missing."

Another runner came in just as Guildenstern was finishing. "Sir, there's fighting all along the line," he said. "And Thraxton the Braggart's got men from the

Army of Southern Parthenia fighting alongside his own, sir. We've captured some."

That produced exclamations from every officer still inside the log hut. Guildenstern's was loudest and most profane. "No wonder the gods-damned son of a bitch had the bastards to hit us with," he said once the stream of curses had died to a trickle. "Well, we'll whip 'em any which way."

He got up, jammed his hat down low on his head so the wide brim helped shield his eyes from the light—which seemed uncommonly bright and fierce this morning—and went outside. Sure enough, the din of combat had begun again, not far to the north of the widow's house. His own men were yelling King Avram's name and cheering, while the traitors roared like lions.

Colonel Phineas hurried up to him. "Sir, the northerners are seeking to work some large and desperate sorcery," the mage said.

"Are they?" Guildenstern said, and the wizard nodded. With a shrug, Guildenstern went on, "Well, it's your job to see they don't do it. Why else are you here, by the gods, if not for that?"

Phineas saluted. "We shall do everything in our power, sir."

Guildenstern shook his head. That reminded him he had a headache. He couldn't figure out why. *Maybe a slug of brandy will help*, he thought, and tried one. He wasn't so sure about the headache, but the brandy made *him* feel better. He shook his head again. It still hurt, but not so much. "Ahh. No, Colonel. I don't want you to do everything in your power." He put a mocking whine in the last four words. "I want you to bloody well stop them. Have you got that?"

"Yes, sir." The unhappy-looking mage saluted again.

"We'll do our best, sir. But the northerners seem to be pressing this with all their strength."

"All the more reason for you to stop them, wouldn't you say?" Guildenstern demanded. "What are they up to, anyway? Are they *probing* us again?" He spoke the word with heavy-handed irony.

Phineas' jowls wobbled as he shook his head. "I don't think so, sir. I think this is something else. It is something unusual, whatever it is. And it has the stamp of Count Thraxton all over it."

"All the more reason to stop it, then, wouldn't you say?" Guildenstern asked.

"All the more reason to, yes, sir," Colonel Phineas agreed. "But stopping Thraxton the Braggart is not so easy as stopping an ordinary man."

"Oh, foof!" Guildenstern said. "Half the time, Thraxton's spells come down on the heads of his own men, not on ours."

"Yes, sir, that is true." Phineas still looked thoroughly grim. "But Thraxton's failures have come through his own errors, not because we thwarted him. He is not very careful, he is not very lucky—but he is very strong."

"I don't care what he is," Guildenstern rasped. He poked Colonel Phineas' protruding belly with his forefinger. The finger sank unpleasantly far into flesh; Guildenstern jerked it away. "What I care about, sirrah, is that we have more mages than the traitors do. If you aren't so strong as the Braggart, then you had better work together. A dozen little men can drag down one big one."

"We *are* doing our best," Phineas repeated.

"Go on, little man," General Guildenstern said contemptuously. "Go on. Go away. I have a battle to fight."

Clucking like a mother hen with a missing chick, the mage hurried away. Guildenstern resisted the urge to apply his boot to Phineas' backside. It probably would have sunk in even farther than his finger had.

And he was right when he told the wizard he had a battle to fight. Colonel Phineas hadn't been the only man waiting for him, just the first of an endless stream. Runners dashed up to report northern attacks on the right against Doubting George on Merkle's Hill, against Brigadier Thom's soldiers on the far left, and against the center, where Guildenstern and Brigadier Alexander still held sway.

Guildenstern didn't need to be told about enemy assaults on the center. He was there, and could see them for himself. The traitors flung great stones and firepots at the loyal soldiers in front. His own engines responded in kind, and he had more of them than Thraxton the Braggart did. Thraxton might have got soldiers from the Army of Southern Parthenia, but he hadn't got any engines to go with them. Had he got some engines, life would have been even more difficult for Guildenstern's soldiers.

Every so often, Phineas would send a messenger. All the mage's messengers said the same thing: "We're still grappling with Count Thraxton."

After a while, Guildenstern got sick of hearing them. "I'm still trying to fight my battle here," he growled.

As morning wore along toward noon, his sense of confidence began to grow. "By the gods, we *are* going to throw the cursed traitors back," he said to Brigadier Alexander. "They can't lick us. No way in the seven hells can they lick us."

"I hope you're right, sir," Alexander replied. "I think you may be right. We're holding pretty well, aren't we?"

"Bet your arse we are," Guildenstern said. But then he glanced nervously toward the right. "I wonder how Doubting George is doing over there." When he thought of the right, he somehow couldn't stay confident no matter how hard he tried. He swigged more spirits, to bolster his courage.

Brigadier Alexander said, "Sir, if he needed help over there, don't you think he'd ask for it?"

"You never can tell with George," Guildenstern insisted. No matter how hard he tried to keep his mind on other things, his eyes kept drifting back toward Merkle's Hill. Something was going to go wrong there. Something *was*. He couldn't tell how he'd grown so sure, but he had. The knowledge, the certainty, built in him, seeping up from below. It didn't feel like conscious knowledge: more like the faith he had in the Lion God and the rest of the Detinan pantheon.

"I know you and Lieutenant General George don't get along perfectly, sir," Alexander said, "but he's a solid soldier. If he needs help, I'm sure he won't risk the battle by going without. After all, he was saying just last night that he *was* worried. If the worries come true, he'll let us know."

That made good logical sense. Somehow, though, good logical sense seemed to matter less to General Guildenstern than it might have. Trouble was brewing on the right. He felt it in his bones.

Before Guildenstern could explain as much to Alexander, Colonel Phineas came rushing up to him at a turn of speed astonishing for one so roly-poly. "General!" he cried. "Woe to us, General! Count Thraxton's magic has defeated our best efforts to withstand it, and now runs loose in our army!"

"Ha!" Guildenstern cried. "I knew it. The Braggart's

trying to deceive me. But he won't! No, by the gods, he won't! I *knew* the right was threatened. Brigadier Alexander!"

"Yes, sir!" Alexander said smartly.

"Take Brigadier Wood's two brigades out of the line here and send them to the aid of Doubting George on the right at once," Guildenstern said. "At once, do you hear me?"

"That will leave us very thin on the ground here, sir, especially while we're making the move," Alexander said.

"Do it!" General Guildenstern thundered. "It is my direct order to you, sirrah! Do it, or find yourself relieved." Brigadier Alexander saluted stiffly and went off to obey. Guildenstern nodded in satisfaction. And, somewhere far inside Guildenstern—or somewhere far across the battlefield—a scrawny, sour-spirited soul cried out in delight and in altogether unalloyed triumph.

James of Broadpath was sipping his early morning tea after the nighttime meeting with Count Thraxton when a man on a unicorn galloped into his encampment. Pulling the unicorn to a halt, the rider slid off it and hurried toward James. He saluted smartly. "Reporting, sir," he said with a grin, "as not quite ordered."

"Brigadier Bell!" James said. "What in the seven hells are you doing here? I left you behind with the part of my army the stinking glideway couldn't carry. Where are they now?"

"Heading up from Marthasville real soon, sir," Bell replied. "But when the scryers said the fighting here had already started, I couldn't wait. I hopped on a unicorn and rode south as fast as I could go." He pointed to the blowing animal from which he'd just dismounted. "This isn't the one I started with. That one fell over dead. I'm sorry I rode it into the ground, but I'm glad I'm here."

"You disobeyed orders," Earl James rumbled. Bell nodded, quite unabashed. James grinned and pounded him on the back—on the right side, careful not to trouble his useless left arm. "Well, I'm cursed glad you're here, too," he said. "I needed somebody to lead the big attack when it goes in, and you're one of the best in the business."

"Thank you, sir." One of Bell's leonine eyebrows rose. "Why hasn't the big attack gone in already?"

"Because I've got orders from Count Thraxton to hold it till he gives the word, that's why," James answered. "He's working some sort of fancy magic against the southrons, and he wants me to wait till he gives the command."

Bell frowned, looking very much like a dubious lion. "Remember, sir, this is Thraxton the Braggart we're talking about. What are the odds this fancy magic will end up being worth anything at all?"

"I don't know the answer to that," James of Broadpath admitted. "But I can't disobey a direct order just because I'm not quite sure about the general who gave it, if you know what I mean."

"Why in the seven hells not?" Bell demanded. "Are you afraid he'll turn you into a rooster, or something like that?"

"No." James shook his big head. Where Brigadier Bell had seemed—and often did seem—leonine, James gave the impression of a bear bedeviled by bees. "No, I'm not afraid of that. But you haven't seen him. I have. He really thinks he can do this, and he makes me think he can do it, too."

"Does he?" Bell shook his head, too. "Why? If he'd done everything he said he could do, we would have won the war by now. You know that as well as I do. Why are you listening to him now?"

"Why?" James of Broadpath shrugged. "I'll tell you why. Because when he told me what to do, he looked like the pictures you see of the conqueror priests from the old days, the ones who led the armies that smashed up the blonds' kingdoms here in the north. You could almost hear the gods talking through him."

Brigadier Bell made a sign with the fingers of his right hand. Most Detinans would have used the left, but his left arm hung limp and useless. "Here's hoping you're right, sir," he said, which was what the gesture meant in words.

To the south of them, the racket of battle picked up as the sun climbed a little higher above the horizon. James said, "I am still allowed to fight, you see: along with our men from Parthenia, I've taken command of the ones Baron Dan of Rabbit Hill was leading."

"Dan's a good man," Bell said.

"I know he is. I feel bad about horning in on him like this. But—" James' broad shoulders slid up and down again. "Thraxton wanted me in charge of one of his wings, and this was how he went about it when I got here. So I've got his men fighting, and most of the soldiers from the Army of Southern Parthenia waiting in reserve for when Thraxton gives me the word. I'm going to put you in charge of them now that you're here."

"What if the word never comes?" Brigadier Bell demanded.

"Sooner or later, I'll throw you in without it," James allowed. "But I'm not going to do that right away.

Thraxton's incanting for all he's worth, and he's my superior. I've got to give him his chance."

"All right, sir," Bell said stiffly. By his tone, it wasn't all right, or even close to all right. By his tone, in fact, King Geoffrey would hear about it if things went wrong. Brigadier Bell was in good odor down in Nonesuch, probably in better odor than Earl James was himself: Geoffrey thought well of straightforward, hard-charging officers, no doubt because he'd been one himself.

"Just remember," James murmured, "that his Majesty thinks the world of Count Thraxton."

"I understand that." Surprise sparked in Bell's eyes. "How did you know what was in my mind, sir?"

"I didn't need to read the entrails of a sacrifice to figure it out," James of Broadpath answered. Brigadier Bell shook his leonine head, plainly still bewildered. James had all he could do not to laugh in Bell's face. He was no straightforward hard charger; he had a nasty, devious mind, and enjoyed using it. He sometimes thought that in itself went a long way toward explaining why King Geoffrey preferred certain other soldiers to him.

He shrugged. He couldn't help that. He was as the gods had made him. If King Geoffrey didn't fully appreciate him, then he didn't, that was all.

No complications, no deviousness in Brigadier Bell. There he stood in front of James, every inch of him but his dead left arm quivering with eagerness to get into the fight. "Why did we come here from Parthenia, if we're just going to wait in the wings?" he demanded.

"Our time will come," James said.

"When?" It wasn't a word—it was a howl of frustration from Bell.

"When Count Thraxton gives the order," James

repeated. "If you don't care for that, I suggest you take it up with the count. He can do something about it, and I can't."

He watched Brigadier Bell weigh that. Bell was a man of impetuous, headlong courage, but even he hesitated to break in on Count Thraxton while Thraxton was at his magics. That was one of the few bits of wisdom James had ever seen him show.

James said, "Perhaps you should—" but a messenger came trotting up before he could finish telling Bell to go soak his head. He nodded to the messenger. "Yes? What is it?"

Saluting, the messenger said, "Count Thraxton's compliments, sir, and you are to strike the center with all your strength as soon as may be. The time, he says, is now."

"There, you see?" James said to Bell. Returning the messenger's salute, he replied, "You may tell Count Thraxton we shall obey him in every particular." The messenger hurried away. James gave his attention back to Bell. " 'As soon as may be,' he said. He's had some trouble getting his own officers to move fast. Let's show him how the Army of Southern Parthenia executes orders."

"Right you are, sir. And now, if you will excuse me . . ." Bell didn't wait for an answer. He dashed off, shouting to the men he would lead into the fray. He didn't know what lay in front of him, and he didn't much worry about it, either. Whatever it was, he would hit it hard and hope it fell over.

Division commanders could have worse traits. A great many division commanders did have worse traits. Once pointed in the right direction, Brigadier Bell got the most from the men he led.

Unlike Count Thraxton's commanders, Bell wasted

no time. Not a quarter of an hour after he got the order, he had his men moving forward, all of them roaring with eagerness to close with the southrons at last.

And, not a quarter of an hour after Brigadier Bell sent his men into the battle, a messenger sprinted back to James of Broadpath. The young soldier in blue was almost bursting with excitement. "General James, sir!" he shouted. "There's nobody in front of us, nobody at all. We're rolling up the stinking southrons like a bolt of cheap cloth."

"By the gods," Earl James said softly. He turned away from the runner.

"What are you doing, sir?" the youngster asked.

"I am saluting Count Thraxton," James answered. He meant it literally, and gave a salute as crisp as he ever had at the military collegium in Annasville. He'd almost called the commander of the Army of Franklin *Thraxton the Braggart*. He shook his head. That wasn't right, not this time. If Thraxton had managed to magic away a big chunk of Guildenstern's army, to get it out of the way so this attack could go in unhindered, he'd earned the right to brag.

"Orders, sir?" the runner asked.

"Turn in on the southrons once you've accomplished the breakthrough," James said. "Don't let them rally. We want General Guildenstern's army *ruined*. Make sure you use that word to Brigadier Bell."

"Yes, sir," the runner said. "Ruined. Sir, I really think they are." He saluted, too—not Count Thraxton, but James—and hurried away.

"Ruined," James repeated, liking the sound of the word. He strode toward Count Thraxton's headquarters. He'd heard any number of uncomplimentary things about Thraxton before coming east. His meeting with Thraxton the night before hadn't left a good taste in his mouth. But if Thraxton's magecraft had done this, the officer's less than sterling personality didn't matter. In battle, victory mattered, nothing else.

When he reached the farmhouse, he was shocked to see Thraxton. The commander of the Army of Franklin might have aged five years since the previous night. He looked stooped and exhausted and so thin that a strong breeze could have blown him away. But the air was calm, and Thraxton had created the breeze that would blow the southrons away from the River of Death.

"Your Grace, we've broken them," James of Broadpath said, and saluted again. "The men are swarming into the gap your sorcery made for them."

No matter how worn Count Thraxton was, triumph blazed in his deep-set eyes. "Good," he rasped in a voice that seemed a ragged parody of the one he'd used only the day before. "We shall drive them out of Peachtree Province. We shall drive them out of Rising Rock. We shall drive them out of Franklin altogether." He muttered something under his breath that James didn't quite catch. It sounded like, *I shall have my parade*, but what was that supposed to mean?

"Give me your orders, sir, and I'll obey them," James said.

Thraxton yawned enormously. "For now, I am fordone. Your men cannot do wrong if they press the enemy hard."

"Yes, *sir*!" James said enthusiastically. "That's the sort of order Duke Edward of Arlington might give."

"Is it?" Thraxton's voice was cool, uninterested, distant. If being compared to King Geoffrey's best general pleased him, he concealed it very well. "How nice."

*Cold fish*, Earl James thought. *Fish on ice, in fact.* He shrugged. It still didn't matter, not after what Thraxton had done. With another salute, James said, "I'll be getting back to my own headquarters, sir."

Thraxton's nod said he would be just as happy not to see James again any time soon. Fighting to hold on to his temper, James left the farmhouse. He'd just returned to his own place when a runner dashed up and cried, "Brigadier Bell is wounded, sir!"

"Oh, gods damn it to the hells!" James of Broadpath exclaimed. "Is he badly hurt?"

To his further dismay, the runner nodded. "A stone from an engine smashed his leg, sir. The chirurgeons say they're going to have to take it off if he's to live. He was leading the men forward, sir, when he was hit."

"I believe that," James said somberly. "It's always been Bell's way—he never did know how to hang back and command from the rear. But oh, by the Thunderer's lightning bolt, the price he's paid." He shook his head. Bell had had that arm ruined earlier in the summer in Duke Edward's failed invasion of the south, and now a leg lost. . . . He wouldn't be leading attacks from the front, not any more. Trying to see if anything could be salvaged from misfortune, James asked, "Is the wound below the knee?" A peg leg might let Bell move around fairly well.

But the runner shook his head. "No, sir, it's up here." He touched his thigh. "I saw it myself." James winced and grimaced. That was about as bad as it could be.

Earl James gathered himself. Even if Bell was wounded, the fight had to go on. The southrons had to be whipped. "Is Dan of Rabbit Hill in command up there now?" he asked.

"Yes, sir," the runner said. "He sent me back for your orders."

"Tell him to keep on pressing the enemy hard," James of Broadpath replied. "That's also Count Thraxton's command: I've just spoken with him." The runner nodded. James went on, "Tell him to swing in and finish rolling up Alexander's wing, and Thom's. Once we've settled them, we'll deal with Doubting George, and that will be the end of General Guildenstern's whole army."

"Yes, sir," the runner said, and repeated his words back to him. When James nodded, the young man saluted and trotted away.

"Ah, Brigadier Bell," James said, and kicked at the dirt. Bell was fierce, Bell was bold, Bell was recklessly brave—and Bell was hurt, Bell was ruined, Bell was broken. And the war ground on without him. And, James thought with grim certainty, more than Bell would be ruined by the time it finally ended.

General Guildenstern had been so very sure of himself when he ordered Brigadier Wood's men out of their place in the line and over to the right to aid Lieutenant General George. The move had seemed so obvious, so necessary, so *right*, that the Lion God might have put it into his mind.

And, not a quarter of an hour after Wood's men left the line, before any replacements could fill the gap, what seemed like every traitor in the world swarmed into it, and now the battle was ruined for fair. "How in the seven hells did they do that?" Guildenstern groaned to anyone who would listen. "They might have known the cursed hole would open up!"

"General, I think they did." That was Colonel Phineas, so worn and wan as to look like a shadow— a fat shadow, but a shadow nonetheless—of his former self.

Guildenstern rounded on the mage. "What nonsense is that?"

"I told you the northerners had us under sorcerous assault," Phineas answered. "I told you Thraxton's wizardry was loose in our army. I think that wizardry was aimed at *you*, sir, to make you go wrong at just the right time—the right time for the traitors, I mean."

"You useless, blundering son of a bitch," Guildenstern growled. "I ought to cut your heart out and put it on the altar for the Lion God to eat. How are we supposed to set this fornicating mess to rights now?"

"I'm sorry, sir, but I really have no answer for that," Phineas said sadly. "I wish I did."

At the moment, Guildenstern had no answer for it, either. All he could do was watch his army fall to pieces before his eyes. And it was doing exactly that. Crossbowmen and pikemen turned their backs on the foe to flee the faster.

Siege-engine crews harnessed their unicorns to the catapults they served and hauled them away from danger. A few didn't bother with their engines, but clambered aboard the unicorns themselves so they could get away.

"Brigadier Alexander!" he shouted. "Where in the damnation are you, Brigadier Alexander?"

"Here, sir." Alexander looked as harried as Guildenstern felt. "Sir, they've knifed us right in the belly. A whole division of northerners has broken through here, maybe more. We can't stop 'em. What in the hells do we do?"

Before Guildenstern could answer, a breathless runner gasped, "Sir, Brigadier Thom says the left is falling to pieces. The traitors are turning in and flanking out his men one brigade after another. He can't hold, sir, not unless you've got reserves to give him. Even then it won't be easy."

"I have no reserves," Guildenstern groaned. "I've sent everything I could spare to the right. I was hoping Thom would have men to give me."

"What shall he do, sir?" the messenger asked.

"Tell him to fight as hard as he can and do his best to stem the tide with what he has," Guildenstern answered. "That's what I'm doing here. It's all I can do." The runner saluted and ran back toward the west.

No sooner had he gone than another runner hurried up to General Guildenstern and said, "Lieutenant General George's compliments, sir. He thanks you for Brigadier Wood's men and asks if you can spare him any more. He's hard pressed on the right."

Guildenstern groaned again, groaned and shook his head. "I wish I hadn't sent him those. Thraxton's magic made me do it—and now the traitors are pouring through the hole in my line here. I have nothing more to give him."

"That's . . . bad, sir," the runner said. "I'll give him your words. We'll try to hold on there, but I don't know how long we can do it." As the other messenger had only moments before, he hurried away.

"Ruined," Guildenstern muttered. It was the word he'd thought to fit to Thraxton the Braggart like a glove. He looked at his own hand. He wore that word now.

He took a swig from his brandy flask, then looked up, escaping his private world of pain for the real disaster building on the battlefield. Roaring northerners in blue were almost in crossbow range of where he stood, though he'd been well back of the line not long before.

Brigadier Alexander saw the same thing. "Sir, we can't stay here," he said. "If we do, they'll overrun us."

"And so?" Guildenstern said bitterly. Dying on the field was tempting—that way, he wouldn't have to face the blame bound to come after word of this disaster reached the Black Palace in Georgetown. But he might still be able to salvage something from the defeat, and so he nodded. "Very well, Brigadier. I fear you're right—it's the traitors' day today, and not ours. Where are our unicorns?"

Alexander was already waving to the men holding them. As they came up, the wing commander said, "Maybe we can do something to stop the retreat."

"Yes. Maybe." Guildenstern wondered if it would stop this side of Rising Rock. He shrugged as he mounted. Alexander was right. They had to try.

But the farther he went, the more he wondered if anyone or anything could save the army. Oh, here and there men and groups of men still battled bravely to hold back the onrushing northerners. But the army, as an army, had fallen to pieces. In the center and on the left, every regiment fought—or ran away and didn't fight—on its own. No one was controlling brigades, let alone divisions or wings.

General Guildenstern shouted and cursed and waved his sword. "Rally, boys!" he cried, again and again. "Rally! We can lick these sons of bitches!"

Men around him cheered and waved their gray hats. Here and there, a few of them would rally, for a little while. As soon as he rode out of earshot and tried to encourage other soldiers, they would resume their retreat. He might as well have been trying to hold back the waters of the Franklin River. The army kept slipping through his fingers.

"We are ruined," he said to General Alexander. "Ruined, I tell you. Do you hear me? Ruined!"

Had Alexander been a proper courtier, he would have reassured Guildenstern and tried to make him believe everything would turn out all right. In the midst of the present disaster, that would have taken some doing, but he would have tried. He was just a soldier, though, and all he said was, "Yes, sir."

Baron Guildenstern? Count Guildenstern? Duke Guildenstern, who'd ended the traitors' rebellion? All that had seemed possible. Now he had to hope he wouldn't end up Colonel Guildenstern, or perhaps even Sergeant Guildenstern.

Brigadier Alexander pointed over to the west. "Look, sir," he said. "There's Brigadier Thom."

"Wonderful," Guildenstern said sourly. "Now I know everything's gone to the devils."

Alexander waved. The first thing Brigadier Thom did on seeing him was grab for his sword. Then he must have realized Alexander and Guildenstern weren't enemies, for he waved back and rode his unicorn toward them. A look of stunned astonishment was on his face. "By the Lion God's claws, what happened, sir?" he asked Guildenstern.

While the general commanding wrestled with that question, Brigadier Alexander answered, "Thraxton the Braggart's magecraft broke through our sorcerers' screen and fuddled General Guildenstern's wits for a moment. He pulled some men out of the line to send them on to Doubting George, and the gods-cursed traitors swarmed into the gap."

"Didn't they just!" Thom exclaimed.

Guildenstern wondered how well that explanation would sit with King Avram. It was, as best he could piece things together, the absolute truth. Colonel Phineas would testify to it. The failure hadn't been his fault; Thraxton's spell had left him less than himself, ripe to make a mistake at the worst possible time.

All true. *So what?* Guildenstern wondered. In the war against King Geoffrey and the northerners who followed him, the only thing that really mattered to Avram was whether the battle was won or lost. This one was lost, lost beyond hope of repair. And who had been in command when it was lost? Guildenstern knew the answer to that. King Avram would know it, too.

"What do we do now, sir?" Thom asked.

"Pull the pieces together as best we can," Guildenstern replied. "Then we either find somewhere hereabouts to make a stand against the traitors or, that failing, we fall back on Rising Rock. I don't see what other choices we've got. If you have a better notion, I'd be glad to hear it."

"No, sir. Sorry, sir. Wish I did, sir." Thom pointed east. "What's happening over at Doubting George's end of the line?"

"Nothing good," Guildenstern said. "I got a request for more men from him just as things were going to the seven hells around here."

"If he gives way, too, I don't know how this army is going to make it back to Rising Rock," Thom said.

"We will," Guildenstern said. "We have to." But he didn't know how they would do it, either. He shouted, "Rally!" to the soldiers all around him. They gave him a cheer, those who still wore hats waved them—and they went right on retreating.

"They've given everything they have to give, these past couple of days," Brigadier Thom said. "I don't think we'll get any more, not today, not when—" He broke off, not quite soon enough.

*Not when you made a hash of the battle.* That was what he'd started to say, that or something close enough to it to make no difference. He didn't care that Thraxton the Braggart's sorcery had made Guildenstern blunder. All he cared about was what had happened. If that was an omen for Guildenstern's career, it wasn't a good one.

Behind Guildenstern, the northerners kept roaring out their triumph. Around him and ahead of him, the men from his own army tramped back toward the southeast. They might fight to try to save their own lives. They weren't going to fight to try to save the army.

"My gods!" Guildenstern exclaimed when he and Alexander and Thom rode into a little town. "This is Rossburgh! They've driven us back a good five miles."

Some few of his men had formed a line in front of Rossburgh, but General Guildenstern didn't think it would hold, not if Thraxton's army hit it hard— and they would, before long. He was only too glumly certain of that.

"General Guildenstern!" somebody called.

Automatically, Guildenstern waved. "Here I am."

As the officer who'd recognized him rode toward him on the crowded, narrow, dusty streets of Rossburgh, Brigadier Thom and Brigadier Alexander let out soft exclamations of dismay. "By the Lion God, that's Brigadier Negley," Thom said.

And so it was. "What's he doing here?" Guildenstern demanded, as if either Thom or Alexander could have told him that. Guildenstern pointed to Negley. "Why aren't you with Lieutenant General George?"

"I wish I were, sir, but my soldiers got swept away, along with what looks like everything else farther west," Negley answered, which held an unpleasant amount of truth. He went on, "I could have retreated up onto Merkle's Hill, but I went with them instead, to try to get them to rally." He grimaced and waved his hand. "You see how much luck I had."

"What of Doubting George?" Guildenstern asked. "You say he was still making a stand on Merkle's Hill? Do you think he can hold?" He found himself tensing as he waited for Negley's reply.

The brigadier of volunteers—the ex-horticulturalist— shrugged. "Sir, I hope he can, but I have no great faith in it. With the rest of the army broken, the traitors will surely rain their hardest blows on him now."

He made altogether too much sense. Guildenstern sighed. "The gods damn Thraxton the Braggart to the seven hells for what he's done to this kingdom today. What can we do now?"

"I see only one thing, sir," Brigadier Negley said. "We have to do all we can to hold Rising Rock. Without it, Thraxton cannot be said to have truly gained anything from this campaign, despite our piteous overthrow."

Guildenstern looked from one of his brigadiers to the next. "Does anyone think we can hold this side of Rising Rock?" They eyed one another and then, one by one, shook their heads. Guildenstern didn't think so, either. He'd hoped his brigadiers would convince him he was wrong. No such luck. He sighed and scowled and cursed. None of that did any good at all. Having done it, he said, "Do you think we have any choice, then, but retreating to Rising Rock and doing our best to hold off the traitors there?"

Again, the three brigadiers looked at one another. Again, they shook their heads. Brigadier Negley said, "Getting our hands on Rising Rock was the main reason we took on this campaign. If we can hold it, we've still accomplished a good deal."

"That's true, by the gods," Guildenstern said. It made him feel, if not good, then better than he had. He shouted for a trumpeter. After a while, one came up and saluted. "Sound *retreat*," Guildenstern told him. "We're going back to Rising Rock." As the mournful notes rang out, he and Brigadiers Negley, Alexander, and Thom turned their unicorns to the southeast and rode off, leaving the field in the hands of Thraxton the Braggart and the northerners.

"Can we hold on, sir?" Colonel Andy asked Doubting George. George's aide-de-camp was not a man to give in to panic, but, with the way things looked on Merkle's Hill, George could hardly blame him for worrying.

George was worried himself, though doing his best not to show it. "We've got to hold on, Colonel," he answered. "If we don't, where in the seven hells are we going to run to?"

Andy gave him a reproachful look. "That's not funny, sir."

"No, I don't think so, either," Lieutenant General George said. "I wish I did, but I bloody well don't." He peered west, toward the disaster that had engulfed the rest of General Guildenstern's army. "If we fold up now, I don't think any of this force will survive."

"What *happened* over there, sir?" his aide-de-camp asked.

"Nothing good," Doubting George answered. "All I know is, Albertus the so-called Great and the rest of my so-called mages all started bawling like branded unicorn colts a couple of hours ago, and then the traitors started pouring men through a great big fat hole in our line. It would almost make a suspicious man wonder if there was a connection."

"Thraxton the Braggart's magic did us in again," Colonel Andy said mournfully.

"Yes, I think Thraxton's magic did us in, too," George agreed. "I wouldn't say 'again,' though. This is the first time that sad-faced bastard managed to aim it at us and not at his own men."

"An honor I could do without," Andy said, which made George smile in spite of the lost battle from which he could only try to save what he might.

Before he could say anything, a runner came up from the west. "Sir, I'm sorry, but I couldn't deliver your message to Brigadier Negley," the fellow said. "Most of his division joined the retreat to the south, and he went with it."

"Too bad," Doubting George said. "Oh, too bad! We needed him in place. There's nothing left linking us to the rest of the army now."

"Sir, from what I could see, the rest of the army is scooting back toward Rising Rock as fast as it can go," the runner said. By the way he kept shifting from foot to foot, he either needed to squat behind a tree or else he too wanted to scoot back toward Rising Rock as fast as he could go.

"We can't scoot yet, son," Lieutenant General George said. "As long as we hold on here, we shield the retreat for the rest of the army. And the traitors haven't licked *us* yet, have they?"

"N-no, sir," the runner answered, though he

sounded anything but convinced. George was also anything but convinced, but not about to admit that to anyone, even himself.

He said, "Go on up to Brigadier Brannan, there at the crest of the hill, and tell him what you just told me about Negley. Tell him he may need to swing some of his engines around to the west, because we're liable to get attacked from that direction."

"Yes, sir." The runner gathered himself and hurried away.

"Miserable civilian," Colonel Andy growled, meaning not the runner but the departed Brigadier Negley. "This is what comes of making the bastards who recruit the troops into officers with fancy uniforms. The trouble is, people who really know what they're doing have to pay for their mistakes."

"There's some truth to that, but only some," Doubting George replied.

"There's a demon of a lot of it, if anyone wants to know what I think," Andy said. George's aide-de-camp had chubby cheeks that swelled now with indignation, making him look like nothing so much as an irate chipmunk.

But George repeated, "Some. It wasn't the amateur soldiers who made this battle into a botch. It was the professional warriors, the folks who learned their trade at the Annasville military collegium, the folks just like you and me."

"May I spend my time going between freezing and roasting in the seven hells if I think General Guildenstern's one bit like me," Andy said, still very much in the fashion of a chipmunk trying to pick a fight.

Before George had the chance to respond to that, another runner dashed up, this one with alarm all over his face. "Lieutenant General George!" he cried. "Lieutenant General George! Come quick, sir! The traitors have got a couple of regiments around our right flank, and they're doing their gods-damnedest to cornhole us."

"Oh, a pox!" Doubting George exclaimed. "Take me there this very minute." He followed the messenger along the side of Merkle's Hill. He'd been worried about the left, with Brigadier Negley pulling out, and hadn't dwelt so much on the right. True, Ned of the Forest had tried sliding around that way the day before, but the northerners had left that end of the line alone after their thrust didn't work . . . till now.

The shouts coming from the east would have warned him something had gone wrong if the runner hadn't found him. Brigadier Absalom greeted him with a salute. "Things are getting lively in these parts," he said.

"That's one word," George said. "What's going on?" As he had all through the fight by the River of Death, he felt like a man on the ragged edge of disaster. The least little thing might pitch him over the edge, too, and the whole army with him. *A lot of it's already gone*, he thought.

"They were coming from that way." Absalom the Bear pointed back over his shoulder. Doubting George was glad he had the big, burly brigadier commanding here. Nothing fazed him. Absalom went on, "I got a skirmish line of crossbowmen facing the wrong way and beat 'em back."

Doubting George set a hand on his shoulder and told him, "That's the way to do it." But at that moment, fresh roars broke out from behind them. Here came the northerners again, attacking the end of the line from both front and rear. If they rolled it up, they'd finish off George's whole wing. He said, "I don't think skirmishers will hold them this time."

"I'm afraid you're right," Absalom agreed.

Looking around, George saw a regimental commander standing only a few feet away. "Colonel Nahath!" he called.

"Sir?" Formal as if on parade, the officer from New Eborac came to attention.

"Colonel, I desire that you face your regiment to the rear and aid our skirmishers in repelling the traitors coming from that direction," George said.

Colonel Nahath saluted. "Yes, sir!" he said, and began shouting orders to his men.

Doubting George shouted orders, too: for another regiment to join Nahath's in repelling the enemy, and for men to come forward to fill their places in the line. "That's good, sir," Absalom the Bear said. "Don't want to leave a hole open, the way General Guildenstern did."

"No, I don't suppose I do," George agreed. "Now that I've seen what happens with a mistake like that, I don't much care to imitate it." He and Absalom both laughed. It wasn't much of a joke, but better than tearing their hair and howling curses, which looked to be their other choice.

"You chose your regiments shrewdly," Absalom observed as the southrons George had told off collided with Thraxton's troopers. "A good many blonds in both of them. They won't let the northerners through, not while they're still standing they won't."

"True," Doubting George said, and so it was. But his brigadier was giving him credit for being smarter than he was. He'd grabbed those two regiments because they were closest to hand, not because they were full of men with especially good cause to hate the soldiers who followed false King Geoffrey.

George chuckled. He was willing to have his subordinates think him smarter than he really was, so long as he didn't start thinking that himself. General Guildenstern had walked down that road—oh, surely, abetted by Thraxton the Braggart's magic, but Guildenstern had already seen a good many things that weren't there by then—and the results hadn't been pretty.

Brigadier Absalom saluted. "If you'll excuse me, sir, I think they can use another fighting man back there." Instead of drawing his sword, he bent down and picked up an enormous axe lying on the ground by his boot. George had assumed some engineer dropped it after making breastworks. But Absalom the Bear swung it as lightly as if it were a saber. "King Avram!" he bellowed, and rushed toward the traitors, looking for all the world like one of the berserk sea rovers who'd terrorized the Detinans' ancestors long before they crossed the Western Ocean.

George eyed the two battle lines. He'd never expected to have to fight back to back like this, but things in front of him still seemed to be holding pretty well in spite of the two regiments he'd pulled out of the line. The fight in the rear, on the other hand . . . Brigadier Absalom was right. They were going to need every man they could find to throw back the traitors.

"King Avram!" Doubting George yelled as his own blade came out of the scabbard. He didn't look like an axe-wielding barbarian, as Absalom the Bear did, and he probably wasn't a figure to frighten the northerners, but he did know what to do with a blade.

Were that not true, he would already have died here by the River of Death.

A crossbow quarrel hissed past his head. Soldiers with crossbows didn't care how good a swordsman he was. If they got their way, he would perish before he had the chance to use his sword. Colonel Andy would have called him a gods-damned fool for this. But Andy was near the top of Merkle's Hill, and Doubting George was here.

"King Avram!" he shouted again, and he rushed at the closest northerner he saw. The fellow had just shot his crossbow. He started to reach for another bolt, but realized Doubting George would be upon him before he could slide it into the groove and yank back the string. A lot of crossbowmen, in King Avram's army and King Geoffrey's, would have run away from a fellow with a sword who pretty obviously knew how to handle it.

Not this northerner, though. The traitors would have been easier to beat were they cowards. That thought had gone through George's mind before. Of course, since he was from Parthenia himself, he knew the mettle of the men who fought against King Avram. This fellow, now, set down his crossbow—carefully, as if he expected to use it again very soon—yanked out his shortsword, and, with a cry of, "King Geoffrey and freedom!" rushed at George as George ran toward him.

Courage the northerner had. Anything resembling sense was another matter. He wasn't so ignorant of swordplay as a lot of southrons from the cities were, but he hadn't learned in the hard, remorseless school that had trained Doubting George. Maybe he'd thought to overpower his foe with sheer ferocity. Whatever he'd thought, he'd made a mistake. George parried, sidestepped, thrust. The blue-clad northerner managed to beat his blade aside, but sudden doubt showed on his face. George thrust again, at his knee. The northerner sprang back. Now he looked alarmed. *Bit off more than you could chew, eh?* George thought. His blade flickered in front of him like a viper's tongue.

And then, before he could finish the traitor, a crossbow quarrel slammed into the fellow's side. The northerner shrieked and clutched at himself. George drove his sword home to finish the man. That wasn't sporting, but he didn't care. If his soldiers couldn't stop the northerners here, everything would unravel.

Not far ahead of him, Absalom the Bear's axe rose and fell, rose and fell. Somewhere or other, the broad-shouldered brigadier had actually learned to fight with the unusual weapon. He beat down enemy soldiers' defenses and felled them as if felling trees. Before long, nobody tried to stand against him.

Nor could the northerners in Doubting George's rear stand against his hastily improvised counterattack. He'd sent only a couple of regiments against them, but their own force was none too large. Instead of breaking through and rolling up his line, they had to draw back toward their own comrades, leaving many dead and wounded on the field and carrying off other men too badly hurt to retreat on their own.

Lieutenant General George caught up with Brigadier Absalom as the traitors sullenly fell back. Absalom plunged his axe blade into the soft ground again and again to clean it. He nodded to George. "That was a gods-damned near-run thing, sir," he said.

"Don't I know it!" George said fervently. "And it's not over yet. We just stopped them here."

"If we hadn't stopped them here, it would be over," Absalom the Bear observed.

That was also true. Doubting George surveyed the field. He couldn't see so much of it from here at the bottom of Merkle's Hill as he would have liked. After pausing to catch his breath, he asked, "Where did you learn to fight with an axe?"

"I read about it in that fellow Graustark's historical romances," Absalom answered, a little sheepishly. "It sounded interesting, so I found a smith who was also an antiquarian, and he trained me as well as he knew himself."

"I'd say he knew quite a bit." George kicked at the bloody dirt. "I wish *I* knew what was happening farther west. Nothing good, gods damn it." He kicked at the dirt again.

# VII

Rollant had never been so weary in all the days of his life. Now, he was yet a young man, so those days were not so many, but he had spent a lot of them laboring in the swampy indigo fields of Baron Ormerod's estate. Ormerod was not the worst liege lord to have, and never would be as long as Thersites remained alive, but he was far from the softest, and demanded a full day's labor from all his serfs every day. Rollant would not have cared to try to reckon up how many times he'd stumbled back to his hut at or after sundown and collapsed down onto his cot, sodden with exhaustion.

However many times it might have been, though, none of those days in the fields came close to matching this one. He'd been fighting for his life by the

River of Death for two days straight. By all accounts, a good part of General Guildenstern's army was already wrecked. He knew how close Doubting George's wing had come to utter ruin. George had pulled his regiment and the one beside it out of the line and sent it to the rear to face a couple of northern regiments that had got round behind them. If they hadn't driven back the traitors, he didn't see how George's wing could have survived, either.

But they had. And now, as the sun sank low in the direction of the Western Ocean, Rollant wiped sweat and a little blood off his forehead with the sleeve of his tunic. "That last traitor almost did for me," he told Smitty.

The youngster from the farm outside New Eborac nodded. "But he's dead now, and you're not, and I expect that's the way you want it to be," he said. He was surely as worn as Rollant, but could still put things in a way that made everybody around him smile.

"Sure enough," Rollant agreed. "Some of them don't have a much better notion of what to do with a shortsword than I do—and a gods-damned good thing, too, if anybody wants to know what I think."

Sergeant Joram said, "Don't fall down and go to sleep yet, you two. Nobody knows for sure they won't try and hit us one more lick." Rollant and Smitty exchanged appalled glances. If the traitors still had fight left in them after the two days both sides had been through . . .

Maybe they did. Way off to Rollant's left and rear, Thraxton the Braggart's men began their roaring battle cry. It was taken up successively by one regiment after another, passing round to Doubting George's front and finally to the right where Rollant stood and even beyond him to the remnants of the two regiments he and his comrades had broken, till it seemed to have got back to the point whence it started.

"Isn't that the ugliest sound you ever heard?" Smitty said.

"Yes!" Rollant agreed fervently. As the roars from the traitors went on and on, he stood there almost shuddering, feeling to the fullest those two days of desperate battle, without sleep, without rest, without food, almost without hope.

Almost. There was, however, a space somewhere to the back of George's battered host across which those horrible roars did not prolong themselves—a space to the southeast, leading back in the direction of Rising Rock. At last, just before the sun touched the horizon, orders came that the men were to retreat back through that space.

In profound silence and dejection, Rollant began to march. No one, not even the irrepressible Smitty, had much to say during the retreat. The only sounds were those of marching feet and the occasional groans of the wounded. Rollant clutched his shortsword—his crossbow remained slung on his back, for he'd shot his last bolt—and wondered if Thraxton's men would try to strike them as they fell back.

But the northerners let them go unmolested. As he stumbled along through the deepening twilight, Rollant wondered if Thraxton's army was as badly battered as Guildenstern's. For his own sake, for the sake of the army of which he was one weary part, he hoped so.

"We held them." That was Lieutenant Griff. He sounded as tired as any of the men in his company. He'd led them well enough—better than Rollant had expected him to—and he hadn't shrunk from the worst of the fighting. If his voice broke occasionally, well, so what? He went on, "The rest of Guildenstern's army ran away, but we held the traitors and we're going off in good order."

"That's right." Somebody else spoke in a rumbling bass. Rollant knew who that was: Major Reuel, who'd been in charge of the regiment since Colonel Nahath went down with a bolt through his thigh. "And Lieutenant General George chose *us* to throw back Thraxton's men when things looked worst. *Us. Our* regiment. And we did it, by the gods."

Rollant suspected Doubting George had chosen them more because they were handy than for any virtue inherent in them, but that was beside the point. Where so many men deserved to be embarrassed, he and his comrades could walk tall. They'd done their best.

Smitty said, "Doubting George was the rock in the River of Death, and the traitors couldn't get past him."

"Let's give him a cheer," Rollant said, and a few men called out, "Huzzah for Doubting George!"

A few more men shouted out George's name the next time, and more the next, and more still the time after that, so that soon the whole company, the whole regiment, and the whole long winding column of men were crying his name. That made Rollant walk taller, too. It made him feel much less like a soldier in a beaten army and more like one who'd done everything he possibly could.

And then he heard a unicorn's hooves on the dirt of the roadway. He peered through the deepening gloom, then whooped. That *was* Lieutenant General George on the white beast. "Huzzah!" Rollant shouted, louder than ever.

Doubting George waved his hat. "Thanks, boys," he said. "I don't know what in the seven hells you're cheering me for. You're the ones who did the work." He touched spurs to the unicorn and rode on.

Rollant felt ten feet tall after that, and ready to whip Thraxton the Braggart's whole army by himself, and Duke Edward of Arlington's, too. He even forgot how tired he was—till the regiment finally halted in a clearing through which the road to Rising Rock ran. When Lieutenant Griff didn't choose him as one of the pickets to watch for the northerners and try to hold them back if they attacked, he unrolled his blanket, lay down on the grass, and fell asleep at once.

Smitty had to shake him awake the next morning. Even then, Rollant felt more like his own grandfather than himself. He ached in every bone, in every muscle. He felt as if he ached in every hair on his head. Only seeing how Smitty moved like an old man, too, made him feel a little better.

Cookfires smoked off at one side of the clearing. Rollant dug out his mess kit and lined up with other soldiers who all looked as if they could have used more sleep. A cook who looked even tireder than the men he served spooned slop onto Rollant's tin plate. "Thanks," Rollant said. He ate like a wolf.

He was chasing scraps with his spoon when the pickets came back from the north. "Thraxton's men aren't chasing us," they reported. "We must've hurt them as bad as they hurt us."

"Then how come we're going back toward Rising Rock?" Smitty wondered aloud.

That was such a good question, Rollant wished Smitty hadn't asked it. He did his best to answer: "They hurt us more on most of the field, but we hurt them more on Merkle's Hill. That was too late to do the rest of the army any good, though, because it was already heading south."

"I suppose so," Smitty said. "And what Doubting George had with him couldn't lick the traitors' whole army by itself."

"If he'd been in charge of our whole army . . ." Rollant said.

"If unicorns had wings, we'd all carry umbrellas," Smitty said, which made Rollant look at a courier going by on a trotting unicorn in a whole different way. In spite of everything he'd been through, his laugh was close to a giggle.

Before long, the regiment started marching again. Easy enough to see it followed in the wake of a defeated army: it passed the wreckage war left behind. Here lay a crossbow someone had thrown away so he could flee faster, there a couple of pikes probably discarded for the same reason. Soldiers who'd already come this way had shoved a wagon with a broken axle over to the side of the road. Dead unicorns were already starting to bloat in the sun. So were the corpses of a couple of men in gray who'd died on the way south.

Rollant heaved a rock at a raven hopping around a dead man. The big black bird let out an angry croaking caw and sprang away from the body, but not far. It would, he feared, go back all too soon.

By the time his regiment got into Rising Rock, it was already full of soldiers. Some of them still had the panicked look of men who'd seen too much, done too much, and weren't likely to be able to do anything more for some time. But others were busy building breastworks that faced north. Those breastworks had men behind them, men who looked ready to fight.

"Well, Thraxton's not going to walk right on into Rising Rock behind us," Rollant said. "That's something, anyhow. If he wants it, he'll have to take it away from us."

"That really *is* something," Smitty agreed. "I was wondered if we'd stop here at all or just keep on marching back toward Ramblerton."

"That's a long way from here." Rollant knew just how far it was, too, having marched all the way from the capital of Franklin north and west to Rising Rock.

"Not a lot of good stopping places on the way, though," Smitty said, which was also true.

And there, up near those breastworks, stood General Guildenstern. The black-bearded soldier in gray tipped back his head and swigged from a flask. "Come on, you bastards! Dig!" he shouted. "Those traitor sons of bitches whipped us once, but dip me in dung if they're going to whip us twice. Isn't that right, boys?"

Heads bobbed up and down as the soldiers digging paused in the labor for a moment. Then they went back to it, harder than ever. Dirt flew. Rollant said, "He's not the worst general in the world, not even close. He takes pretty good care of his men."

"No, he's not the worst, but he's not the best, either," Smitty said. "And I wonder how much longer he'll have the chance to go on taking care of us. King Avram's not going to like the way this battle turned out. For all you know, Guildenstern had his beaky old nose in the brandy flask when he should have been thinking straight."

"That's so," Rollant admitted. "Getting drunk isn't taking care of your men, if that's what happened. But I don't know that it is, and neither do you. People are talking about Thraxton's magic."

"People say all sorts of stupid things," Smitty observed. "Just because they say them doesn't make them true, though Thraxton might have magicked Guildenstern."

"I'm ready to believe anything when it comes to the northern nobles' magecraft," Rollant said. "You never lived up there. I did." He shivered at the memory. "By the gods, I'm glad I don't live there any more."

Smitty started to answer, then checked himself and stared in delight. Rollant followed his gaze. "Captain Cephas!" they both exclaimed at the same time.

"Hello, boys." The company commander was thin and pale, but he was on his feet. "It's good to be up and moving—a bit, anyhow. I hear I missed a little something."

"Yes, sir," Rollant said. "Awfully good to see you again, sir. From what they were saying about your wound . . ." His voice trailed off.

Cephas' hand went to the right side of his ribcage. "I've still got bandages under my tunic," he said. "But I can walk, and I think I'll be able to fight before too long." He sounded as if he was trying to convince himself. "I was lucky. The wound didn't fester at all. And they threw me off my cot because so many soldiers hurt worse than I am started coming in."

"How's Lieutenant Benj?" Smitty asked. Benj had been wounded in the same skirmish as Captain Cephas.

Cephas' face clouded. "He didn't seem so bad when we first got hurt, but the fever took him." He shrugged, then winced. He didn't seem ready to swing a sword any time soon. "It's as the gods will. That's all I can say about it."

"Don't you worry about a thing, Captain," Smitty said with a sly smile. "I expect Corliss will take good care of you now that you're back."

Rollant wanted to stick an elbow in Smitty's ribs, but didn't quite dare, not where Cephas could see him do it. He hadn't brought Hagen and Corliss and their children back to the camp so the escaped serf's wife could become the captain's leman. On the other hand, Cephas hadn't forced her, as northern nobles were in the habit of doing when blond girls took their fancy. That also made Rollant stay his hand, or rather, his elbow.

Cephas smiled, too. "I'm glad she and Hagen came back safe from the fight. I'll be glad to see her; I wouldn't say any different."

*I'll bet you wouldn't*, Rollant thought. Other soldiers crowded forward to greet Captain Cephas. Even Lieutenant Griff had a grin on his face, though he would lose command of the company when Cephas was well enough to take it back. Rollant looked around for Hagen and Corliss. He didn't see either one of them. *Just as well, probably*, went through his mind. Corliss might be glad to see Cephas again. He didn't think Hagen would.

Count Thraxton had never felt so tired in his life. He wasn't a young man any more, and the struggle against the southrons' wizards to reach the mind, such as it was, of General Guildenstern had taken more out of him than he'd dreamt it could. But he'd done it, and Guildenstern's army had streamed back out of Peachtree Province in headlong retreat.

And now, after Thraxton had won the greatest victory of his career, his own junior commanders were nagging him. "Sir, we have to pursue harder," Baron Dan of Rabbit Hill said the morning after the fight by the River of Death. "The sooner we can throw a line around Rising Rock, the sooner we can drive the southrons out of the city or force them to surrender to us."

"Baron, I think you are worrying overmuch," Thraxton answered. "After the beating we gave them, with their army in such disarray, how can they possibly hope to stay in Rising Rock?"

"I don't know how, sir," Dan of Rabbit Hill answered. "I do know I don't want to give them any possible excuse."

"Any possible excuse to do what?" That was Earl James of Broadpath, whose blocky form kept almost as much light from Thraxton's farmhouse headquarters when he stood in the doorway as the door itself would have done.

"Any possible excuse for the southrons to stay in Rising Rock," Dan replied before Count Thraxton could speak.

"Oh." James of Broadpath nodded. "Well, I should hope not, by the gods. We ought to run those sons of bitches out of there—eh, my lord Count?"

"My opinion," Thraxton said coldly, "as I was explaining to Baron Dan here, is that Avram's ragtag and bobtail will abandon Rising Rock of their own accord, and thus there is no reason for us to stage a hard pursuit."

James frowned. "In the Army of Southern Parthenia, there's always a reason to stage a hard pursuit. Duke Edward says—"

"I don't care what the hallowed Duke Edward says," Thraxton broke in—nothing could have been more surely calculated to infuriate him. "What I know is the present state of this army. Are you aware, your Excellency, that in the fighting of the past two days we have had one man in four killed or wounded? One man in four, your Excellency! How can I pursue after that?"

He thought he'd startled James of Broadpath with his vehemence, for James took a step back: away from the doorway, which made the inside of the farmhouse much less gloomy. But James wasn't giving way to him, as he thought James should have done—James was stepping aside so someone else could come into the farmhouse.

When Count Thraxton saw Leonidas the Priest, he snapped, "And what in the seven hells do *you* want?"

In wounded tones, the hierophant replied, "I just came to ask, sir, when to order my troopers forward for the pursuit."

"Why the demon should that make any difference to you?" Thraxton demanded. "When I told you to order them forward for the battle, you paid me no heed. Will it be different now?"

Leonidas drew himself up to his full height, which was still several inches less than Count Thraxton's. "Your Grace, I am affronted," he said.

"Bloody idiot," Thraxton muttered, not quite far enough under his breath. Leonidas stiffened even further. Thraxton hadn't thought he could.

"Sir, I didn't come to Peachtree Province to quarrel with you," James of Broadpath said, trying—too late— to sound like the voice of sweet reason. "I came here to whip the southrons. We're off to a good start. Now we've got to finish the job."

"That's right," Baron Dan agreed. He'd fought in the Army of Southern Parthenia, too. *Of course he and James will take each other's side*, Thraxton thought resentfully.

Aloud, he said, "The job shall be finished. We shall,

in due course, advance upon and make a demonstration against Rising Rock, and the southrons will abandon the city to us." *And I shall have my parade through the town. The people will cheer me. The people will love me. They should have all along, but they* will *now*.

Sadly, Earl James of Broadpath shook his head. "Your Grace, you started this campaign to drive General Guildenstern out of Rising Rock, and all you managed to do was drive him back into it. Is that worth losing one man in four from your army—and from my division, too, I might add? And the chirurgeons still don't know whether Brigadier Bell is going to pull through after they cut the leg off him."

From under his bushy brows, Count Thraxton glared at James. "Who is in command here, your Excellency?" he asked, his voice as frigid as a southron blizzard. "Whose magics won this victory?"

"You are, sir," James said. "I've never denied it. And your magics won the day. Without them, Guildenstern wouldn't have torn a hole in his ranks. But I tell you this, sir: a good general can win a victory. It takes a great general to know what to do with it once he's got it."

That only made Thraxton more coldly furious. Before he could say anything more, though, a courier came in. "What do *you* want?" Thraxton snapped, aiming his wrath at the luckless fellow instead of at James of Broadpath.

"Sir, I've got a message here from Ned of the Forest for Leonidas the Priest," the courier answered.

"Let me see that," Leonidas said, and took it from him. The hierophant of the Lion God perched gold-framed spectacles on his nose before reading the despatch. When he did, he read it aloud: " 'Sir: Have been on the point of Proselytizers' Rise. Can see Rising Rock and everything around. The enemy's glideway carpets are leaving, going around the point of Sentry Peak. The prisoners captured report two pontoons thrown across for the purpose of retreating. I think they are evacuating as hard as they can go. They are cutting down timber to obstruct our passing. I think we ought to press forward as rapidly as possible. Respectfully &c., Ned of the Forest. Please forward to Count Thraxton.' " He looked up from the paper. "There you are, your Grace. You may consider it forwarded." He chuckled wheezily at what he reckoned his wit.

And Count Thraxton chuckled, too, though he was not a man who often gave way to mirth. He aimed a long, pale finger at James of Broadpath. "Do you see, Earl? Do you see? By Ned of the Forest's report, the southrons are indeed abandoning Rising Rock of their own accord."

James said nothing. He merely plucked at his vast beard and looked grave. But Baron Dan of Rabbit Hill spoke up: "Sir, I think you ought to note Ned's last sentence there. He urges you to press forward as rapidly as possible, and that strikes me as excellent advice."

"It strikes me as unnecessary advice. It strikes me as meddlesome advice," Thraxton said. He wasn't inclined to take Ned of the Forest's advice on anything. In fact, if Ned of the Forest advised something, he was inclined to take the opposite tack—especially when, as here, Ned's words also lent support to his doing what he'd already planned on doing.

"Sir," James said stubbornly, "if you move fast and swing us east of Rising Rock, we can get between the southrons and their supply bases. If we do that, they fall into our hands come what may." Dan of Rabbit Hill nodded.

But Thraxton shook his head. "It is, I repeat, unnecessary."

"Perhaps we should pray for guidance," Leonidas the Priest said, "beseeching the Lion God to show us his will."

Count Thraxton looked at the hierophant as if he'd taken leave of his sense. So did James and Dan. There, if nowhere else, Thraxton and his fractious generals agreed.

It soon became clear they agreed nowhere else. Earl James and Baron Dan, quite forgetting Thraxton's higher rank and bluer blood, went right on arguing with him. His own replies grew ever shorter and testier. Around noon, another courier from Ned of the Forest came into the farmhouse. Like the one before, this message was addressed to Leonidas the Priest. Again, the hierophant read it aloud: " 'My force has now come up quite close to Rising Rock. Previous report was in error. The southrons seem to be fortifying, as I can distinctly hear the sound of axes in great numbers. They can be driven from thence, but you will have to drive them.' " Spectacles glistening, Leonidas looked up from the paper. "The signature and the request to forward are as they were in the previous despatch."

"You see, your Grace?" James of Broadpath said with what Thraxton reckoned altogether too much pleasure. "Not even Ned of the Forest supports your view that delay will serve here."

"Whether Ned of the Forest approves of what I do is, I assure you, your Excellency, not of the least importance to me," Thraxton said. "In my view, the man is ignorant, and does not know anything of cooperation. He is nothing more than a good raider."

"Sir, whether you fancy Ned or not, he's quite a bit more than a raider," Dan of Rabbit Hill said. "You weren't up on Merkle's Hill with me, the first day of the fight. His riders were holding back Doubting George's southrons as well as any footsoldiers could have done. I told him so, in plain Detinan, because I've not seen many cavalry outfits that could have done the same."

Count Thraxton folded thin arms across his narrow chest and fixed Dan with his most forbidding stare. "I have never questioned his courage, your Excellency. I have questioned, and do continue to question, his wisdom and his military judgment. Merely because he believes something is no reason to proclaim that the Thunderer's lightning bolt has carved his opinion deep into stone."

Leonidas the Priest cleared his throat. "It would appear to me, your Grace, that you were willing enough to use Ned of the Forest's opinion as a touchstone when it marched with your own."

"When I want *your* opinion, you may rest assured that I shall ask for it," Thraxton growled. His own opinion was that the hierophant was a dawdling, prayer-mumbling blockhead. He didn't try very hard to keep Leonidas from seeing that that was his opinion, either.

Earl James said, "How does it harm you, how does it harm the army, to order a proper pursuit?"

"I *have* ordered a proper pursuit," Thraxton said. "We shall follow on General Guildenstern's heels as soon as the army recovers to the point where it may safely do so. And I remain convinced that, when we approach Rising Rock, the southrons shall be compelled to evacuate it and ignominiously retreat."

"Your Grace, I don't want those sons of bitches to retreat," James said. "Even if they do, they'll just come back and hit us again some other day. I want to kill them or take them prisoner. Then we won't have to worry about them any more. We need to get between them and Ramblerton and drive them to destruction. That's my view, and I still hold it."

"I am pleased to hear your view." Thraxton's tone suggested he was about as pleased as he would have been at an outbreak of cholera. "I must remind you, however, that King Geoffrey has entrusted command of this army to me. I needs must lead it as I reckon best."

"Even when your view is dead against that of every general serving under you?" James of Broadpath persisted.

"Even then. Especially then. I do not command this army for the sake of being loved," Thraxton said.

"I believe it, by the gods!" Baron Dan muttered.

Thraxton filed that away for future vengeance. Aloud, though, he said only, "What I command for is victory. And I have won a victory."

"So you have," Earl James said. "You could win a greater one. You could win a victory that would restore King Geoffrey's hopes here in the east, a victory that would give us a good chance to take Franklin away from the southrons and might even let us get back down into Cloviston. You *could* do that, your Grace, or you could fritter away what you've already won. The choice is yours."

"I have already made the choice," Count Thraxton said. "I have made it, and all of you seem intent on evading it. But *you* shall obey me, or you shall be dismissed from your commands. It is as simple as that, gentlemen."

James of Broadpath threw his hands in the air. "Now that I'm here, I begin to see how the armies of the east came to be in the straits in which they find themselves. Have it your own way, Count Thraxton. By all the signs, that matters more to you than anything else."

Thraxton started to tell James just what he thought of him, but the burly officer from the Army of Southern Parthenia paid no attention. He turned on his heel, all but trampling Leonidas the Priest, and stormed out of the headquarters. Baron Dan of Rabbit Hill followed. Leonidas held his place, but his expression was mournful. He said, "I believe you would be wiser to think again on the choice you have made."

"And I believe you're a gods-damned old idiot!" Thraxton shrieked, his voice and his temper breaking at the same time. Leonidas bowed stiffly and followed after James and Dan, his red vestments flapping around his ankles. Thraxton shouted again, this time for runners, and began giving the orders he thought right.

As Baron Ormerod trudged south, he could tell that the company he commanded was following in the wake of a beaten army. The wreckage and the stinking, bloated bodies of men and beasts by the sides of the road showed that Guildenstern's men had worried about nothing but escape as they retreated from the River of Death to Rising Rock. Seeing the southrons in disarray should have left him happier than it did.

He wondered why he was so glum. When he spoke

aloud of his worries, Lieutenant Gremio said, "I don't think that's very hard to figure out, sir."

"No, eh?" Ormerod raised an eyebrow. "Suppose you enlighten me, then."

He'd intended it for sarcasm, but Gremio took him seriously. *Trust a barrister*, Ormerod thought. But then Gremio said, "You're unhappy for the same reason I'm unhappy. You're unhappy for the same reason half the army's unhappy: you think we ought to be sliding in east of Rising Rock, too."

And Ormerod, in the face of such obvious, manifest truth, could do nothing but nod. "That's right, by the gods!" he burst out. "If we can all see it, why in the seven hells can't Count Thraxton?"

"What Thraxton sees are the holes in our ranks," Gremio said, and Ormerod nodded again. Major Thersites remained in command of the regiment for the wounded Count Florizel, and, after two days of hard fighting on the slopes of Merkle's Hill, a much-depleted regiment it was, too. Gremio added, "And, by what I've heard, Thraxton thinks the southrons will run right out of Rising Rock if we poke them a little."

"Gods grant he's right," Ormerod said. But, after marching on for a couple of paces, he added, "The southrons don't much like running. Things'd be a lot easier if they did."

"I am aware of this," Gremio said. "I am also aware that we did hurt them badly. I hope that will outweigh the other."

"It had better." Ormerod tramped on. "After all we did, after all we went through . . ."

"I don't know what we can do *but* hope," Gremio said. He trudged along for a while without saying anything more. Ormerod thought he had no more to say. But then he did continue: "It shouldn't have been like this."

Ormerod just grunted and kept on going. He'd figured that out for himself. They marched through Rossburgh, which the southrons had abandoned not long before. Some of the people in the little town cheered them. Others jeered: "Why aren't you getting out ahead of the southrons instead of just following along in back of them like a pack of hounds?"

"You see?" Gremio said. "Even the villagers can see what Count Thraxton can't." He shrugged a melodramatic shrug. "Who would do better, though? Not Leonidas the Priest, not unless I miss my guess."

"No. He's holy, but . . ." Ormerod said no more than that. He needed to say no more than that. After a few steps and a longing look at a tavern, he added, "Ned of the Forest might be up to the job."

"He might be up to it, but he'd never get it," Gremio said. "He has no birth to speak of. How many noble officers would obey a jumped-up serfcatcher?"

"Any noble who tried disobeying Ned would be sorry afterwards," Ormerod said, which didn't mean he thought Gremio was wrong. Though only a minor noble himself, he didn't like the idea of obeying a jumped-up serfcatcher, either. But thinking of serfcatching made him notice Rossburgh in a way he hadn't before. He was just about out of the place by then, but that didn't matter. Turning to Gremio, he asked, "You notice anything funny about this town?"

"Aside from its being the place they made the woodcut of when they wrote the lexicon entry for 'the middle of nowhere,' no," the barrister answered.

"Not enough blonds," Ormerod said. "Hardly any

blonds at all, in fact. They must have run away with the southrons."

"Nothing we haven't seen before," Gremio said, though that wasn't strictly true. Thraxton's men hadn't often been lucky enough to recapture land from which the southrons forced them. The serfs had shown their opinion of living under King Geoffrey— they'd shown it with their feet. Ormerod didn't much care to see that opinion expressed.

The regiment encamped a few miles south of Rossburgh as the sun slid below the horizon. Major Thersites prowled from one fire to another. When he came to the one beside which Ormerod and Gremio sat, he said, "Well, even if the general doesn't know what in the seven hells he's doing, maybe things will turn out all right. Maybe." Thersites didn't sound as if he believed it.

Even though Gremio and Ormerod had been saying very much the same thing, it sounded different in Thersites' mouth. They'd said it with regret. Thersites spoke with relish, as if he'd expected nothing better from Thraxton and the other nobles set over the army. Ormerod said, "We have to think they're doing the best job they can."

"If they are, gods help us all," Thersites said. "If I wanted a rock garden outside my house, I know whose heads I'd start with. If these are the best we can do, I reckon we deserve to lose the war."

"Why go to war, then, sir, if you feel like that?" Ormerod asked. He was too weary to want a quarrel with his bad-tempered neighbor.

"Why? I'll tell you why. On account of the southrons are worse, that's why," Thersites replied. "But that doesn't make what we've got in charge of us any too bloody good. I hate having to choose between thieves and fools, I purely do, but we've got more fools in fancy uniforms than you can shake a stick at. I'd like to shake a stick at some of 'em, and break it over their heads, too."

Contempt blazed from him. Part of it was contempt for the southrons, part for the army's higher officers. And part of it, Ormerod realized, was contempt for him and people like him. He fit into the neat hierarchy of life in the north. Thersites didn't, even if he called himself a noble and lived like a noble. He was one who'd forcibly kicked his way into the picture from the outside, and still felt on the outside looking in.

Before Ormerod had the chance to think about what he was saying, he blurted, "You remind me of Ned of the Forest."

Lieutenant Gremio stirred beside him, plainly unsure how Major Thersites would respond to that. And Thersites in a temper was nothing any man in his right mind took lightly. But the new regimental commander only nodded. "Thank you kindly," he said, and bowed to Ormerod. "Ned's a *man*, by the gods. He doesn't need any blue blood to make him a man, either. He just is." He bowed again, then went off toward another campfire.

"Well, you got away with that," Gremio said once he was out of earshot. "I wasn't sure you would."

"Neither was I," Ormerod answered. "Thersites is . . . touchy."

"Touchy!" Lieutenant Gremio rolled his eyes. "Thersites is a fellow who hates everybody that's better than he is: everybody who's handsomer, or who has more silver, or who has bluer blood. And since there are a lot of people like that, Thersites has a lot of people to hate."

"He doesn't hate Ned," Ormerod pointed out.

"No, I see he doesn't." Gremio spoke with exaggerated patience. "You got lucky—Ned's everything he wants to be."

"But Ned hasn't got any noble blood at all." Ormerod didn't *think* Thersites did either, not really, but nobody liked to say anything about that, not out loud. Thersites' temper was *most* uncertain.

"And he's a brigadier without it," Gremio said. "And he got the chance to tell Count Thraxton off right to his face, if what they say is true. All Thersites can do is grumble behind Thraxton's back. He'd probably give his left ballock to be Ned of the Forest."

"I'd give *my* left ballock to be back on my own estate, with no more worries than a serf running off every now and then." Ormerod sighed for long-gone days. "I didn't know when I was well off, and that's the truth."

"Gods curse King Avram for overturning what was right and natural," Gremio said. "We couldn't let him get away with it."

"Of course not," Ormerod agreed around a yawn. "Not if we wanted to stay men." He lay down, rolled himself in his blanket, and went to sleep.

Breakfast the next morning was hasty bites of whatever he had in his knapsack. Count Thraxton might not have pursued the southrons so swiftly as Ormerod would have liked, or down the path he reckoned proper, but Major Thersites pushed the regiment hard. It was almost as if Thersites intended to drive General Guildenstern's army out of Rising Rock all by himself.

That wasn't going to happen, no matter how much Thersites and Ormerod might want it. Guildenstern had too many men in the town, and they sheltered behind formidable field fortifications. But those works to the north and west of the town weren't quite so formidable as they might have been.

"Look, boys!" Thersites called, pointing ahead. "I don't think those sons of bitches have a single man up on Sentry Peak."

"If they don't, we ought to get up there and take it away from them," Ormerod said, excitement in his voice no matter how tired he was.

Major Thersites needed nothing more to spur him into action. Maybe he wouldn't even have needed Ormerod's push, though Ormerod had his own strong opinion about that. But now Thersites' nod was as sharp and fierce a motion as a tiger turning toward prey. "Yes, by the gods," he said softly, and then raised his voice to a full-throated battlefield shout: "My regiment—to the left flank, *march!*"

Some of his men let out startled exclamations. They didn't obey quite so fast as they would have moved for Colonel Florizel. But move they did, scrambling up the steep slopes of Sentry Peak toward the rock knob's summit a couple of thousand feet above the town of Rising Rock. And not a single southron soldier shot at them or even tried to roll a rock down on their heads.

Ormerod enjoyed himself, scampering like a mountain antelope and leaping from one boulder to another with a childlike zest he hadn't known he could still muster. If he fell during one of those leaps, he would be very sorry. *All the more reason not to fall*, he told himself, and leaped again.

He wasn't the only one whooping like a little boy, either. Half the company, half the regiment, squealed with glee as they climbed. And, once Thersites had shown the way, the regiment wasn't the only force scaling Sentry Peak. No one above the rank of colonel had ordered the ascent, but it made obvious good sense to everyone near the foot of the mountain.

Panting more than a little, Lieutenant Gremio said, "I do believe I would have fallen over dead if I'd tried to make this climb back before I took service with King Geoffrey's host. It's made a man of me. I spent too many years peering at law books. No more."

"No, no more." Ormerod hadn't wasted his time with books before Geoffrey raised his banner in the north. He'd worked on his estate, worked almost as hard as the serfs whose liege lord he was. But he was a fitter, harder man after two and a half years of war, too.

When he reached the top of Sentry Peak, the first thing he felt was surprised disappointment: he wanted to keep going up and up and up. But then, as he looked around, that disappointment drained away, to be replaced by awe. He murmured, "You can see *forever*."

For the first time, he grasped one of the reasons the Detinan gods lived atop Mount Panamgam: the view. There below Sentry Peak lay Rising Rock, with a loop of the Franklin River thrown around it like a serpent's coil. Beyond Rising Rock, the flatlands of the province of Franklin stretched out endlessly, green of farm and forest gradually fading toward blue. He wondered if he could see all the way across Franklin and into Cloviston to the south.

If he turned around and looked back the way he'd come, there lay Peachtree Province. If he looked straight west, those distant mountains beyond Proselytizers' Rise had to belong to Croatoan. And there to the northeast lay Dothan, where the blonds had

had one of their strongest kingdoms before the Detinans arrived, and where, as was true in his own Palmetto Province, they still outnumbered folk of Detinan blood.

But his eye did not linger long on the distant provinces. Instead, it fell once more to Rising Rock. "If we can get engines onto the south slope of Sentry Peak here," he said, "we can almost reach the town itself, and we can surely reach the southron soldiers in those field works down there." He pointed to the trenches and breastworks near the base of the mountain.

"General Guildenstern was a fool for not letting this place anchor his line north of the town," Gremio said.

"You're right," Ormerod agreed—he could hardly say Gremio was wrong, not when he'd just come out with such an obvious truth. "But that doesn't mean we can't take advantage of him for being a fool."

"No, and we'd better," Lieutenant Gremio said. "If we didn't have a fool commanding our own army, we'd be over there" —he pointed east— "astride the southrons' supply line instead of here just outside of Rising Rock."

"Maybe Count Thraxton had some reason for doing things the way he did." Ormerod tried to make himself believe it. It wasn't easy.

Gremio killed his effort dead: "Of course Thraxton had a reason: he's a chucklehead."

Ormerod looked down at Rising Rock, tiny and perfect and almost close enough for him to reach out and touch it. "Maybe we can starve the bastards out anyway. Here's hoping." Gremio's look said he would sooner have had something more solid than hope. So would Ormerod, but he made the most of what he had.

❖   ❖   ❖

Even though Earl James of Broadpath could heave his bulk up to the top of Sentry Peak and peer down into Rising Rock, even though Count Thraxton's men also held the peak line of Proselytizers' Rise, he was furious, and he made no effort to hide it. "Idiocy!" he boomed at whoever would listen. "Nothing but idiocy!"

Some of Count Thraxton's officers did their best to shush him. "Your Excellency, nothing good can come of these constant complaints," one of them said.

Another was blunter: "Thraxton is liable to turn his magecraft your way, your Excellency, if you don't restrain yourself."

"Let him try, by the gods," James rumbled. "I'm warded by Duke Edward of Arlington's personal mage. I think Duke Edward's mage should be a match for just about anyone, don't you?" The colonel who'd warned him only shrugged and went away. James of Broadpath also shrugged. Thraxton *was* a mighty sorcerer—when everything went right. Had things gone right for him more often, James wouldn't have needed to come east with his division from the Army of Southern Parthenia.

And most of Thraxton's officers agreed with James, regardless of what their commander thought. Dan of Rabbit Hill and Leonidas the Priest had both backed him when he pushed Thraxton to make a proper pursuit. He had no doubt Ned of the Forest agreed with him, too, though Ned was fighting southwest of Rising Rock right now, holding off Whiskery Ambrose's effort to come to General Guildenstern's rescue from the direction of Wesleyton. And a good many lower-ranking officers had sidled up to him to say they regretted how things had turned out after the victory near the River of Death.

None of which, of course, mattered a counterfeit copper's worth. Thraxton the Braggart commanded the Army of Franklin, and what he said went. King Geoffrey had his victory in the east. Whether he would have more than that one victory, whether he would have everything it should have brought, remained very much up in the air.

"I don't care how fancy a mage Thraxton is," James complained to Brigadier Bell. "He has all the vision of a blind man in a coal cellar at midnight."

Bell looked up from the cot on which he lay. His usually fierce expression was dulled by heroic doses of laudanum. Even so, pain scored harsh lines down his cheeks and furrowed his forehead. Under the blanket that covered him, his body's shape was wrong, unnatural, asymmetrical. *I believe I would sooner have died than suffered the wounds he's taken*, James thought.

The laudanum dulled thought as well as pain. Bell's words came slowly: "We should be on our way to . . ." He groped for the name of the town. "To Ramblerton. To the provincial capital. We shouldn't be stuck here outside of . . . of Rising Rock." Even drugged and mutilated, he too could see what James of Broadpath saw.

"There's no help for it, Bell," James said sadly. "He is the commander of this army. He gives the orders. Even if they're stupid orders, he has the right to give them. I've argued till I'm blue in the face, and I had no luck getting him to change his mind. If you've got any notion of how to get him to do what plainly needs doing, I'm all ears."

He was just talking; he didn't expect Bell to come up with anything. What with the horrible wound— gods, Bell couldn't even have fully recovered from the mangled arm he'd got down in the south less than three months before—and the potent drug, that Bell could talk at all was a minor miracle. The other officer looked up at him from the cot and spoke with terrible urgency: "Let the king know, your Excellency. If the king knows, he'll do what needs doing."

Gently, James shook his head. "Remember, Count Thraxton is Geoffrey's dark-haired boy. If it weren't for Geoffrey, Thraxton wouldn't have held his command out here even as long as he has."

He wondered if Bell even heard him. "Let the king know, James," the wounded man repeated. "The king has to know."

"All right," James of Broadpath said. "I'll let him know." He didn't mean it, but he didn't want to upset poor Bell. The wound might still kill him, or fever might carry him off. No point tormenting him with refusals at a time like this.

But then, as James left the tent where Bell lay, he plucked at his beard in thought. Coming right out and speaking to King Geoffrey would surely fail; he remained convinced of that. Even so . . .

"How could I be worse off? How could *we* be worse off?" he murmured, and hurried away to the pavilion the scryers called their own.

One of the bright young men looked up from his crystal ball. "Sir?"

"I want you to send a message to Marquis James of Seddon Dun, over in Nonesuch," James of Broadpath said.

"To the minister of war? Yes, sir," the scryer said. "You will, of course, have cleared this message with Count Thraxton?"

"I don't need to do any such thing, sirrah," James

rumbled ominously, and tapped his epaulet to remind the scryer of his own rank.

"Yes, sir," the fellow said—he was just a first lieutenant, an officer by courtesy of his skill at magecraft rather than by blood or courage. Technically, he was in the right, but a lieutenant technically in the right in a dispute with a lieutenant general would often have done better to be wrong. The youngster had the sense to know it. Licking his lips, he bent low over the crystal ball. "Go ahead, sir."

"To the most honorable Marquis James of Seddon Dun, Minister of War to his Majesty King Geoffrey, legitimate King of Detina: greetings," James said, declaiming as if speaking to the minister of war face to face. "May I take the liberty to advise you of our conditions and wants. After a very severe battle, we gained a complete and glorious victory—the most complete of the war, perhaps, except the first at Cow Jog. To express my convictions in a few words, our chief has done but one thing he ought to have done since I joined his army. That was to order the attack. All other things that he has done he ought not to have done. I am convinced that nothing but the hand of the gods can help us as long as we have our present commander.

"Now to our wants. Can you send us Duke Edward? In an ordinary war I could serve without complaints under anyone whom the king might place in authority, but we have too much at stake in this to remain quiet now. Thraxton cannot adopt and adhere to any plan or course, whether of his own or of someone else. I pray you to help us, and speedily. I remain, with the greatest respect, your most obedient servant, James of Broadpath."

"Is that . . . all, sir?" the scryer asked. James of

Broadpath nodded brusquely. The scryer had another question: "Are you . . . sure you want me to send it?" James nodded again. The scryer didn't; he shook his head. But he murmured over the crystal ball, then looked up. "All right, sir. It's on its way." By his tone, he thought James had just asked him to send an earthquake to Nonesuch.

James hoped the scryer was right. As far as he was concerned, an earthquake was exactly what this army needed. But all he said was, "The minister of war should hear my views." He strode out of the scryers' tent.

In striding out, he almost collided with Baron Dan of Rabbit Hill and Leonidas the Priest, both of whom were striding in, grim, intent looks on their faces. "Oh, by the gods!" Dan exclaimed. "Don't tell me he's got you, too?"

"Don't tell me who's got me for what?" James asked.

Dan and Leonidas both started talking at once. Leonidas used language James would not have expected to hear from a hierophant. But he was the one who calmed down enough to give a straight answer: "Count Thraxton has ordered us removed from our commands, may he suffer in the seven hells for seven times seven eternities."

"He's done what?" James of Broadpath's jaw dropped. "He won't move against Guildenstern, but he will against his own generals?"

"That's the size of it, your Excellency," Dan said bitterly. "That's just exactly the size of it. And if he thinks I'm going to take it lying down, he can bloody well think again. King Geoffrey *will* hear of this."

"He certainly will," Leonidas the Priest agreed. "And so will the Pontifex Maximus back in

Nonesuch. Thraxton needs to be placed under full godly interdict."

"What on earth made him sack both his wing commanders?" James asked, still more than a little stunned.

"We have the sense to see that this army should be doing more than it is, and we have had what the Braggart reckons the infernal gall to stand up on our hind legs and say so out loud," Dan of Rabbit Hill replied. "As far as Thraxton is concerned, that amounts to insubordination, and so he sacked us."

"Which is why, when we saw you here, we wondered whether you had suffered the same fate," Leonidas said. "You have also seen that Count Thraxton's conduct of this campaign leaves everything to be desired."

"He hasn't got round to me yet." James felt almost ashamed that Thraxton hadn't got round to him—or was the Braggart holding off because he properly belonged to the Army of Southern Parthenia, not the Army of Franklin? "But I just sent a message to the minister of war expressing my lack of confidence in Thraxton as a leader of this host."

"Huzzah!" Baron Dan slapped him on the back. "Here's hoping it does some good. Here's hoping someone back in Nonesuch starts paying attention to the east. Someone had better. Without it, King Geoffrey has no kingdom."

"Well said," James told him. "That's just why Duke Edward prevailed on Geoffrey to send me hither. The victory a few days ago opened the door for us. But we still have to go through it, and Rising Rock stands in the way."

"It shouldn't," Leonidas the Priest said. Even he could see that, and he was hardly a soldier at all. "We should have pursued the southrons harder, and we should have flanked them out of it. Why didn't we?"

"Because Thraxton's an imbecile, that's why," Dan of Rabbit Hill snapped.

James was inclined to agree with him; no other explanation fit half so well. He said, "This army *can* still win, with a proper general at its head. I asked the minister of war for Duke Edward."

Dan whistled softly. "Do you think we'll get him?"

"Not likely," James answered with genuine regret. "King Geoffrey wants to keep him between Nonesuch and the southrons. He figures his capital is safe as long as Duke Edward's there, and he's probably right."

"Still, it is a telling cry of distress," Leonidas the Priest observed.

Now James nodded. "Just so. That's why I sent the message. If it doesn't draw King Geoffrey's eye to this part of the front, I don't know what will. If it doesn't draw his eye hither, I fear nothing will."

"That must not be," Leonidas said. "True, we can lose the war if Nonesuch falls, and Nonesuch is not far north of the border with the southrons. But we can also lose the war in these eastern parts, and Count Thraxton in his arrogant idiocy is doing everything he can to make that unhappy result come to pass."

"We aren't the only ones muttering, I'll have you know," Dan of Rabbit Hill told James. "Some few— some more than a few—of the brigadiers under us are circulating a petition amongst themselves, expressing their lack of confidence in the Braggart."

"Are they?" James said, and Dan and Leonidas both solemnly nodded. James shook his head in slow wonder. "We are spending as much of our substance fighting amongst ourselves as we are against the gods-damned southrons, and we have less to spare than they do."

"True. Every word of it true—and every bit of it Thraxton the Braggart's fault," Baron Dan said. "And yet we beat the foe at the River of Death. We could have won a bigger victory, and we could have won another victory afterwards. But did we?" His dismissive wave proclaimed what Thraxton's Army of Franklin had done—and what it had failed to do.

"We didn't." Leonidas the Priest stated the obvious. "I shall pray once more to the Lion God to look more kindly upon us—after I protest my dismissal. If you will excuse me, your Excellency . . ." He pushed past James of Broadpath and into the scryers' tent.

"I still have that to attend to myself." Dan of Rabbit Hill also bowed to James. "I hope to have the chance to discuss these things with you at greater length when we both have more leisure and when we both find ourselves in a better temper . . . if such happy days should ever come."

"May it be so," James said. "We shall have a great deal to discuss in those happy days—of that I am certain."

"Indeed." Ducking past him, Dan followed Leonidas into the tent.

"A great deal to discuss," James repeated, this time to himself. Everything had gone just as he'd hoped it would. His men had let Thraxton win a smashing victory against General Guildenstern, a smashing victory that turned out not to be quite smashing enough.

He looked south and east toward Rising Rock. Driving the southrons out of the city now wouldn't be easy, wouldn't be cheap, and might well prove beyond the power of Thraxton's army. Besieging them would have been easier had Thraxton thrown a proper line around the place when he had the chance. Which left . . . James cursed. He had no idea what it left.

❖　　　❖　　　❖

Riding for all they were worth, the southrons hurried off toward the southwest, where Whiskery Ambrose still held Wesleyton. Had they been on dogs instead of unicorns, their mounts would have had their tails between their legs. Ned of the Forest whooped to see them flee before him. If he'd had even a few regiments of footsoldiers to go with his riders, he might have taken Wesleyton back from the southrons.

Captain Watson's little collection of siege engines had, as usual, kept right up with the rest of Ned's riders. Watson sent a last couple of firepots after the retreating southron riders. One burst between a couple of unicorns and drenched both them and the men aboard them with flames. Ned whooped again. "Good shooting, by the gods!" he shouted. "Real good shooting."

Watson waved to him. "Thank you, Lord Ned."

"Thank *you*, Captain." Ned was ready, even eager, to give praise where it was due. And Watson, even though he couldn't raise a proper crop of whiskers yet, was as praiseworthy a soldier as Ned had found. "Those fellows won't be bothering us again any time soon."

A scryer rode toward him, calling, "Lord Ned! We've got orders from Count Thraxton, sir!"

"Do we?" Ned rumbled; orders from Thraxton the Braggart were the last thing he wanted right this minute. But, with the scryer's having made that public, he couldn't very well ignore them—*not unless they're really stupid*, he thought. With a sigh, he said, "And what does the count want with us?"

"Sir, we're ordered back to the rest of the army, north and west of Rising Rock," the scryer told him. That wasn't so bad; he'd been intending to rejoin the main force soon anyhow. Then the scryer lowered his voice and went on, "Some powerful strange things are going on back there right now, if half of what the fellow who sent the order to me said alongside of it is true."

"Is that a fact?" Ned said, and the scryer solemnly nodded. The cavalry commander asked the next question: "What kind of strange things?"

"Well, he didn't exactly know, sir—not exactly," the scryer said. Ned glared. When he asked a question like that, he expected a proper answer. Flushing under swarthy skin, the scryer did his best: "From what he says, everybody who's in command of anything is screaming bloody murder at everybody else."

"Is that a fact?" Ned of the Forest repeated. The scryer gave him a nervous nod. Ned forgot the man in front of him. He plucked at his chin beard, thinking hard. At last, he said, "So I'm not the only one who reckons we should ought to have done more to get the southrons out of Rising Rock, eh?"

"I don't know anything about that, sir, not for sure I don't," the scryer said. "I'm just telling you what I heard from the fellow back there."

"All right." Ned let him off the hook. Turning to the trumpeters who always accompanied him, he said, "Blow *recall*."

The unicorn-riders reined in in some surprise; Ned of the Forest wasn't in the habit of breaking off pursuit so soon. They'd whipped Whiskery Ambrose's men, but they hadn't crushed them. Colonel Biffle asked, "What's up, sir?"

"Thraxton wants us back close to home," Ned told him. "And, from what the scryer says, there's some kind of foofaraw back at the camp. Maybe it's just as well he ordered us back. I want to find out what's going on."

"He'd better not try messing with you, Lord Ned," Colonel Biffle said.

Ned of the Forest hadn't thought of that. His hands closed hard on the reins. "You're right, Biff. He'd better not try that. He'd be one of the sorriest men ever born if he did."

But he did his best to stay cheerful as he rode back toward the Army of Franklin's encampment outside Rising Rock. Maybe Thraxton was finally deciding to try to get between the southrons and their supply base over in Ramblerton. Maybe it wasn't too late for him to do that.

But if that was the reason he wanted the unicorn-riders back, why were all the high officers screaming at one another?

He brought his men into Thraxton's encampment a little before sunset. He'd hardly dismounted before excited footsoldiers started passing gossip to his riders, gossip that quickly reached him: Leonidas the Priest and Dan of Rabbit Hill sacked, James of Broadpath screaming to Nonesuch, and every sort of story under the sun about Count Thraxton. Even Ned, who was inclined to believe almost anything of his commander, found the rumors swirling through the encampment hard to swallow.

And then a runner came up to him and said, "Sir, you are requested and required to report to Count Thraxton's headquarters immediately upon your arrival."

"Oh, I am, am I?" Ned said. "Why didn't Thraxton order me to come in to him *before* I got back?" The runner just stared in confusion. Ned sighed. "Never mind, sonny boy. Lead me to him. I'll follow you."

He hadn't bothered finding out where Count Thraxton now made his headquarters. It wasn't anywhere he much wanted to go. Thraxton proved to be inhabiting a farmhouse near Proselytizers' Rise: a prosperous farmhouse, by its colonnaded front. *He doesn't do so bad for himself*, Ned thought, *no matter what he does to the poor army*.

Maybe it would just be business. *By the gods, I hope it'll just be business*. Ned made his face a gambler's blank as he strode into the parlor. He drew himself up straight and saluted Count Thraxton. "Reporting as ordered, sir."

Thraxton, as usual, looked as if his belly pained him. Perhaps he even looked as if it pained him more than usual. "Ah, Brigadier Ned. I am very pleased to see you." If he was pleased, he hadn't bothered telling his face about it.

"What can I do for you, sir?" Ned asked. The sooner he was gone, the happier he would be.

"I am not pleased that you led your men so far afield while chasing Whiskery Ambrose's unicorn-riders," Thraxton said, pacing back and forth through the parlor and looking at the wall rather than at Ned of the Forest.

"Would you have been more pleased if they'd come down on us and rampaged all around?" Ned demanded.

"I would have been more pleased had your men been closer to my hand and more ready to obey my orders," the Braggart answered. *What orders?* Ned thought scornfully. *If you'd had any halfway sensible orders to give, we'd be in Rising Rock by now*. Thraxton went on, "Accordingly, I am detaching three regiments from your command and transferring them to the control of Brigadier Spinner, the

cavalry commander for the division led—formerly led,
I should say—by Dan of Rabbit Hill."

Ned most cordially loathed Brigadier Spinner.
From everything he could tell, the feeling was mutual.
"You can't do that!" he blurted.

"You are mistaken." Thraxton's voice came cold as
a southron blizzard. "I can. I shall. I have." Relent-
ing ever so slightly, he added, "These regiments will
be returned to you after Spinner comes back from
his planned raid east of Rising Rock."

"If you want my men, why in the seven hells don't
you send me out?" Ned barked.

"Because if I send Spinner, I have some assurance
he will do as I command and return when I command," Count Thraxton replied, more coldly still.
"You have given me no reason for any such confidence. You may pick the regiments you wish to turn
over to him." Another tiny concession.

Too tiny—far too tiny. But the order was legal. Ned
knew that all too well. If he refused it, Thraxton would
sack him, too. Choking back his fury—he wouldn't give
the Braggart the satisfaction of showing it—he snarled,
"Yes, sir," saluted again, and stalked out.

Had Brigadier Spinner been standing outside the
farmhouse, Ned might have drawn sword on him. But
the other general of unicorn-riders was nowhere to
be seen. Still fuming, Ned of the Forest stomped
back to his own men. Soldiers who saw him had the
good sense to stay out of his way and not ask unfortunate questions.

He arrived among the unicorn-riders in the foulest
of foul tempers. Seeing his visage, Colonel Biffle
hurried over to him in some alarm, asking, "Is something wrong, sir?"

"Wrong? You just might say so, Biff. Yes, you just

might." The whole story poured out of Ned, a long howl of fury and frustration.

"He can't do that," Biffle blurted when Ned finally finished.

"I told him the same thing, but I was wrong, and so are you," Ned said. "If he wants to bad enough, he bloody well can. That's what being a general is all about." He said something else, too, something his beard and mustache fortunately muffled. After a moment spent recapturing his temper, he went on more audibly: "The one reason I'll sit still for it at all is that he did promise he'd give me my men back once Spinner was done with them. If it wasn't for that . . ." His left hand dropped to the hilt of his saber.

"Whose regiments will you . . . lend to Brigadier Spinner, sir?" Biffle paused in the middle there to make sure he found and used the right word, the word that would not ignite Ned further.

"I was thinking yours'd be the one I keep for my own self," Ned replied, and Colonel Biffle preened a little. Ned of the Forest slapped him on the back, hard enough to stagger him. "He's a pile of unicorn turds, Biff, but there's not a single stinking thing we can do about it." He yawned. "Only thing I want to do now is sleep. When I wake up, maybe I'll find out Thraxton the Braggart was nothing but a bad dream. Too much to hope for, I reckon." He went into his tent.

When he woke up the next morning, Count Thraxton and what he'd done remained all too vivid in his memory. But, as he'd told Biffle, he couldn't do anything about the Army of Franklin's sour commanding general. What he could do was get himself some breakfast; his belly was empty as, as . . .

*Empty as Thraxton's head*, he thought happily, and went out to get some food in better spirits.

He was sitting on the ground, eating fried pork and hard rolls and talking things over with Colonel Biffle, when a runner came up, saluted, and said, "Count Thraxton's compliments, sir, and he asked me to give you this." He handed Ned a rolled sheet of paper sealed with Thraxton's seal, saluted again, and hurried off.

"What's he want now?" Biffle asked.

"Don't know. Suppose I'd better find out." Ned broke the wax seal with a grimy thumbnail. He wasn't fluent with pen in hand, but he had no trouble reading. And Thraxton's hand, though spidery, was more legible than most. *Upon due consideration*, he wrote, *I have decided that, with a view to the best interests of the Army of Franklin as a whole, your cavalry regiments shall in fact be permanently transferred to the command of Brigadier Spinner. Trusting this meets with your approval, I remain*... He closed with the usual polite, lying phrases.

Ned of the Forest sprang to his feet, rage on his face. So did Colonel Biffle, alarm on his. "What's wrong, sir?" he asked, as he had so often lately.

"That lying son of a bitch!" Ned ground out. "I'm going to tell him where to go and how to get there, and I may just send him on the trip." He stormed off toward Thraxton's headquarters, Biffle in his wake.

An adjutant tried to turn him aside from Count Thraxton. He brushed past the man as if he didn't exist and roared into the parlor. Thraxton gave him an icy stare. "What is the meaning of this intrusion?" he demanded.

Ned of the Forest took a long, deep, angry breath. "I'll tell you what. You commenced your cowardly and contemptible persecution of me soon after the battle of Pottstown Pier, and you have kept it up ever since. You did it because I reported to Nonesuch facts, while you reported gods-damned lies. You have begun again your work of spite and persecution and kept it up. This is the second formation of unicorn-riders organized and equipped by me without thanks to you or King Geoffrey. These men have won a reputation second to none in the army, but, taking advantage of your position as the commanding general in order to humiliate me, you have taken these brave men from me."

He thrust his left index finger at Count Thraxton's face. Thraxton retreated into a corner and sank down onto a stool. Ned pressed after him. "I have stood your meanness as long as I intend to. You have played the part of a gods-damned scoundrel, and are a coward, and if you were any part of a man I would slap your jaws and force you to resent it. You have threatened to arrest me for not obeying your orders promptly. I dare you to do it, and I say to you that if you ever again try to interfere with me or cross my path it will be at the peril of your life."

Thraxton said never a word. He sat there, pale and shaking, while Ned kept prodding with that finger. At last, snarling in disgust, Ned turned on his heel and stormed out of the farmhouse. Colonel Biffle followed. Once Biffle was outside, Ned thunderously slammed the door.

As the headed back toward the unicorn-riders' camp, Biffle remarked, "Well, you are in for it now."

"You think so?" Ned shook his head to show he didn't. "He'll never say a word about it. He'll be the last man to mention it. Mark my word, he'll take no action in the matter. I will ask to be relieved and transferred to a different part of the fight, and he will not oppose it."

"I hope you're right, sir." The regimental commander didn't sound convinced.

"I reckon I am," Ned said. "And if I chance to be wrong, I'll kill the mangy son of a bitch and do King Geoffrey a favor."

"Geoffrey won't thank you for it," Colonel Biffle said.

"I know," Ned answered. "Nobody ever thanks the fellow who kills the polecat or drains the cesspool or does any of the other nasty, smelly jobs that need doing just the same. But I don't think it'll come to that." He sighed. "By the gods, though, Biff, I wish it would."

# VIII

Peering down into Rising Rock from the height of Sentry Peak, Earl James of Broadpath grunted in dissatisfaction. He turned to the officer commanding one of the regiments holding Sentry Peak for King Geoffrey. "Correct me if I'm wrong, Major . . . ?"

"Thersites, sir," the officer replied. He was an ugly customer, and would probably be dangerous in a fight.

"Major Thersites, yes." James nodded. "Correct me if I'm wrong, as I say, but doesn't it look to you as if the stinking southrons are bringing more and more men into Rising Rock?"

"It surely does, your Excellency," Thersites said. "I've been telling that to anybody who'd listen, but nobody cares to listen to the likes of me. If you don't have blue blood, if you're from Palmetto Province instead of Parthenia . . ."

James of Broadpath did have blue blood, but he was from Palmetto Province, too. Sure enough, the Parthenians looked down their noses at everybody else. He said, "Count Thraxton will hear about this. I'll make sure Thraxton hears about it." He liked saying *I told you so* as much as any other man.

"Is it true what they say about Thraxton and Ned?" Major Thersites asked.

"To the seven hells with me if I know," James answered. He told the truth: neither Ned of the Forest nor the commanding general of the Army of Franklin was saying much about whatever had passed between them. Rumor, though, rumor blew faster and stronger than the wind. But James was not about to gossip with a lowly major he barely knew.

Thersites said, "Anybody wants to know what I think, I wish Ned would've cut his liver out and fed it to the Lion God. Maybe then we'd get ourselves a general with some notion of what in the hells he was doing."

"Maybe," James said, and said no more. He'd learned his discipline in the stern school of Duke Edward of Arlington. No matter how much he agreed with this regimental commander, he wouldn't show it. In fact . . . "If you'll excuse me . . ." He bowed and started down the northern slope of Sentry Peak, the less steep slope that faced away from Rising Rock.

A puffing runner met him while he was still half-way up the mountain. "Your Excellency, you are ordered to Count Thraxton's headquarters over by Proselytizers' Rise as fast as you can get there."

"Oh, I am, am I?" Earl James wondered what sorts of plots and counterplots were sweeping through Thraxton's army now, and what the commanding general wanted him to do about them. Cautiously, he asked, "Why?"

"Because . . ." The messenger paused to draw in a deep, portentous breath. "Because King Geoffrey's there, your Excellency. He's come east from Nonesuch to find out what the hells is going on here."

"Has he?" James said. He'd been with the Army of Franklin for three weeks now, and he wondered about that himself. But regardless of what he wondered, only one answer was possible, and he gave it: "I'll come directly, of course."

He hurried down the mountain, so that he was bathed in sweat when he got to flatter ground. Heaving his bulk up onto the sturdy unicorn that bore him, he booted the beast into a gallop as he went off toward the southwest.

The unicorn was blowing hard when he reined in beside the farmhouse from which Thraxton led the army. He hadn't made the acquaintance of the sentry who took charge of the beast. After a moment, he realized why. *He's not one of Thraxton's men. He's one of the king's bodyguards.*

"Go on in, your Excellency," the sentry said. "You're expected." James nodded. What would have happened to him had he not been expected? Nothing good, most likely.

As he started for the farmhouse, Leonidas the Priest rode up, gaudy in his crimson ceremonial robes. Leonidas waved to him and called, "Now, if the Lion God so grant, we shall at last see justice done."

James of Broadpath cared less than he might have about justice. Victory mattered more to him. He just nodded to Leonidas the Priest and strode into the farmhouse. Baron Dan of Rabbit Hill waited there. So did Count Thraxton. And so, sure enough, did King Geoffrey. Careless of his pantaloons, James dropped to one knee and bowed his head. "Your Majesty," he murmured.

"Arise, your Excellency," Geoffrey said. His voice was light and true. Like his cousin and rival king, Avram, he was tall and thin as a whip. There the resemblance ended. Avram looked like a bumpkin, a commoner, a railsplitter. Geoffrey was every inch the aristocrat, with sculptured features, a firm gaze, and a neatly trimmed beard than ran under but not on his chin. As James got to his feet, Leonidas the Priest came in and bowed low to the king: he went to his knees only before his god. Geoffrey nodded to him, then spoke in tones of decision: "Now that we are met here, let us get to the bottom of this, and let us do it quickly."

Count Thraxton looked as if he'd just taken a big bite from bread spread with rancid butter. "Your Majesty, I still feel your visit here is altogether unnecessary. This army has done quite well as things stand."

"I know how you feel, your Grace," Geoffrey said. He was not normally a man to care much for the feelings of others, but Thraxton was a longtime friend of his. Nevertheless, having made up his mind, he went ahead; he was nothing if not stubborn. "I have had a number of complaints from these officers here" —he waved to James, Leonidas, and Dan— "and also from several brigadiers about the way the Army of Franklin has been led since the fight at the River of Death. As I told Earl James, for the sake of the kingdom I intend to get to the bottom of these complaints, and to set the army on a sound footing for defeating the southrons."

"Very well, your Majesty." Thraxton still looked revolted, but he couldn't tell King Geoffrey what to do and what not to do.

Geoffrey swung his gaze from the unhappy Thraxton to the Army of Franklin's subordinate—and insubordinate—generals, who were just as unhappy for different reasons. "Well, gentlemen?" the king asked. "What say you? Is Count Thraxton fit to remain in command of this host, or is he not?"

James of Broadpath blinked. He'd never expected King Geoffrey to be so blunt. Geoffrey was a good man, a clever man, a brave man, an admirable man . . . but not a warm man, not a man to make people love him. James could see why. Avram would have handled things more deftly—but Avram wanted to wreck the foundations upon which the northern provinces were built. And so James, like the rest of the north, had no choice but to follow Geoffrey.

And, like Leonidas the Priest and Dan of Rabbit Hill, he had no choice but to answer Geoffrey's question. Leonidas spoke first: "Your Majesty, in my view you must make a change. Count Thraxton has shown he has no respect for the gods, and so we cannot possibly expect the gods to show him any favor."

"I agree with the hierophant, though for different reasons," James of Broadpath said. *I must not hang back*, he thought. *As the king said, it's for the kingdom's sake.* "Once we beat the southrons, we should have made a proper pursuit. We should have flanked them out of Rising Rock instead of chasing them back into the town and letting them stand siege there—not that it's a proper siege, since we don't surround them and since they keep bringing in reinforcements."

"They have a demon of a time doing it," Thraxton broke in, "and they will have an even harder time keeping all those men fed."

"They never should have had the chance to get

them into Rising Rock in the first place," James returned, his temper kindling.

King Geoffrey held up a slim hand. "Enough of this bickering. Too much of this bickering, in fact. And I have not yet heard from Baron Dan. How say you, your Excellency?"

"Oh, I agree with Leonidas and James here," Dan of Rabbit Hill replied without hesitation. "An army is only as good as its head. With Thraxton in charge of the Army of Franklin, we might as well not have a head."

Thraxton glared. Dan glared back. James wondered whether, in all the history of the world, a commanding general had ever had to listen to his three chief lieutenants tell his sovereign that he wasn't fit to hold the post in which that sovereign had set him.

By King Geoffrey's expression, he hadn't expected those chief lieutenants to be quite so forthright, either. But he could only go forward now. "Very well, gentlemen," he said. "You tell me Count Thraxton does not suit you. To whom, then, should command of this army go?"

Again, Baron Dan didn't hesitate: "The best man this army could possibly have at its head is Duke Edward of Arlington."

*Well, that's true enough*, James thought. He'd asked James of Seddon Dun for Duke Edward himself. Edward was the best man any Detinan army, northern or southron, could possibly have at its head. King Avram had thought so, too. He'd offered the duke command of the southron armies as the war began. But Edward, like most northerners, had chosen Geoffrey as his sovereign, and had been making the southrons regret it ever since.

King Geoffrey knew exactly what he had in Duke

Edward. He didn't hesitate, either, but shook his head at once. "No," he said. "I rely on Edward to hold the southrons away from Nonesuch."

Dan of Rabbit Hill had to bow to that. But, as he bowed, he muttered under his breath, loud enough for James to hear: "If we hang on to Nonesuch and nothing else, we've still lost the stinking war."

The king, perhaps fortunately, didn't hear him. "Earl James," Geoffrey said, "perhaps you have another candidate in mind?"

"Perhaps I do, your Majesty," James of Broadpath said. "If you cannot spare Duke Edward from the west, Marquis Joseph the Gamecock might do very well here. The kingdom has not got all the service it might have from him since he was wounded last year and Duke Edward took charge of the Army of Southern Parthenia. He's a brave and skillful soldier, and I happen to know he is quite recovered from his wound."

King Geoffrey was not a warmhearted man—that had already occurred to James. But the icy stare the king gave him now put him in mind of a blizzard down by the Five Lakes country. As Geoffrey had once before, he said, "No," again, this time even more emphatically. "Whatever Marquis Joseph's soldierly qualities—and I do not choose to debate them with you—he does not hold my trust. He who names him again does so on pain of my displeasure."

Like Dan of Rabbit Hill, Earl James bowed his head. He knew too well why the king and Marquis Joseph didn't get along. Joseph had the habit of telling the truth as he saw it. Such men did not endear themselves to princes.

"Holy sir, have *you* a suggestion?" Geoffrey asked Leonidas the Priest.

"Either of the men my comrades named would improve this army," Leonidas replied, drawing another black look from Count Thraxton. Ignoring it, he went on, "If, however, they will not do, you could also do worse than Marquis Peegeetee of Goodlook."

But, once again, King Geoffrey shook his head. "All the objections pertaining to Marquis Joseph also pertain to him in equal force. And he is better at making plans than at carrying them to fruition."

That held some truth. Marquis Peegeetee had seized a fort in Karlsburg harbor, a blow that marked the formal break between King Geoffrey and King Avram. Between them, he and Marquis Joseph had won the first battle at Cow Jog, down in southern Parthenia. Since then, though, his luck had been less good. Even so, James would have preferred him to Count Thraxton. James, by then, would have preferred a unicorn in command to Thraxton.

King Geoffrey said, "General Pembert is a skilled soldier, and available for service here."

That produced as much horror in the generals as their suggestions had in the king. "He's not even a proper northern man!" Leonidas exclaimed, which was true—Pembert came from the south, but had married a Parthenian girl, and had chosen Geoffrey over Avram perhaps because of that.

"He surrendered the last fortress we held along the Great River, your Majesty," James added. "He hauled down the red dragon and gave the place to General Bart."

"He was forced to yield by long siege," the king said. "In his unhappy situation, who could have done better?"

"Your Majesty, I'm sorry, but you can't pretty it up like that," Baron Dan of Rabbit Hill said. "If you put General Pembert in charge of the Army of Franklin, my guess is that the soldiers will mutiny against him."

Geoffrey glared. No king ever cared to hear that he couldn't do what he wanted to do. His mouth a thin, hard line, Geoffrey said, "I cannot accept the men your officers proposed to head this army, and it seems the officer I named does not suit you. That being so, I find myself left with no choice but to sustain Count Thraxton here in command of this force."

Leonidas the Priest came out with something James of Broadpath had not expected to hear from a hierophant. "I thank you, your Majesty," Count Thraxton said quietly.

"You're welcome, my friend," King Geoffrey replied. *If Thraxton weren't his friend, he'd be heading into the retirement he deserves*, James thought. But the king hadn't finished: "Since you remain in command, I also confirm your dismissal of your wing commanders."

Leonidas said something even more pungent than he had before. Dan of Rabbit Hill threw his hands in the air in disgust. Geoffrey's decision there followed logically from the one that had just gone before. Even so, Earl James was moved to say, "Your Majesty, I hope you won't regret this."

Geoffrey stared at him out of eyes as opaque and unblinking as a dragon's. "I never regret anything," the king said.

Having had King Geoffrey sustain him, Count Thraxton should have felt relief and pride. Try as he would, though, he could muster up no more than a shadow of either emotion. What filled him most of all was overwhelming weariness. *I have fought so hard for this kingdom,* he thought dolefully, *fought so hard, and for what? Why, only to see the men I led to victory turn on me and stab me in the back.*

Even dismissing Leonidas and Dan brought scant satisfaction. As he strode through the front room of his farmhouse headquarters, candlelight made his shadow swoop and slink after him, as if it too were not to be trusted when his back was turned.

He sighed and scowled and sat down at the rickety table that did duty for a desk. His shadow also sat, and behaved itself. He found himself actually letting out a small sigh of relief at that. When his shadow didn't leap about the room like a wild thing, it reminded him ever so much less of Ned of the Forest.

He ground his teeth, loud enough to be plainly audible, hard enough to hurt. Why in the name of the gods hadn't he done more when that backwoods savage stormed in here, fire in his eye and murder in his heart? Thraxton was no coward; no man who'd ever seen him fight would claim he was. No, he was no coward, but there for a few dreadful minutes he'd been thoroughly cowed.

But he was still the commanding general, and thanks to King Geoffrey he would go on holding that post. And, if Ned had briefly cowed him, he didn't have to keep the man around to remind himself of his humiliation. He inked a pen and began to write.

*Headquarters, Army of Franklin, Proselytizers' Rise.* The familiar formula helped steady him, helped ease the perpetual griping pain in his belly. *Count Thraxton to King Geoffrey of Detina. Your Majesty: Some weeks since I forwarded an application from Ned of the forest for a transfer to the Great River for special service. At that time I withheld my approval, because I deemed*

*the services of that distinguished soldier necessary with
this army.*

After looking at what he'd written, he slowly shook
his head. *By the gods, what a liar I am!* went through
his mind. All he wanted was to get Ned of the Forest
as far away from him as he could, and to do it as
fast as he could. If that meant telling polite lies, tell
polite lies he would. He would do almost anything
never again to have to face the murder in Ned's eyes.

Pen scritching across paper, he resumed: *As that
request can now be granted without injury to the
public interests in this quarter, I respectfully ask that
the transfer be made at this time. I am, your Majesty, very respectfully, your obedient servant, Count
Thraxton, general commanding.*

There. It was done. He sprinkled fine sand over
the ink to dry it, then folded the letter and sealed
it with his signet ring. Once the wax was dry, he
called for a runner. Handing the young man the letter,
he said, "Take this to the king at once."

"Yes, sir," the runner said, and hurried away. He
asked no questions. That was as well, for Thraxton
knew he had few answers.

If he went over to the crest of Proselytizers'
Rise—not a long journey at all, less than a mile
from this farmhouse—he could look down into
Rising Rock and see the scores, the hundreds, of
fires of the southron soldiers encamped there. James
of Broadpath's words came back to haunt him. *You
wanted to chase Guildenstern out of Rising Rock,
and you ended up chasing him into it instead.*

Thraxton stepped outside and stared up at the
stars. A mosquito bit him on the neck. Absently,
hardly noticing what he was doing, he cursed the
buzzing pest. The curse he chose might have slain

an unwarded man. Used against a mosquito . . . The bug, which was flying off, burst into flame as if it were a firefly. But fireflies burned without consuming themselves. The mosquito's whole substance went into the fire, and it abruptly ceased to be.

*If only I could do to the southrons what I did to the mosquito.* But the men who followed King Avram *were* warded, worse luck. He'd managed to break through those wards and cast confusion into General Guildenstern's mind, but the effort had left him all but prostrated. And, because he did break through, the Army of Franklin had won the fight by the River of Death. But the effort winning took had left the army all but prostrated, too. Everyone who called for a hard, fierce pursuit of the southrons conveniently failed to notice that.

*You swore an oath you would take back Rising Rock. You swore an oath you would chase the southrons all the way out of the province of Franklin.* That didn't look like happening any time soon.

Now, in the recesses of his mind, the caverns where insults and reproaches lay unforgotten, Ned of the Forest fleered at him once more: not this latest outburst, but the one back in Rising Rock. Thraxton knew plenty of men called him the Braggart, but few had the nerve to do it to his face.

Thraxton looked up at the stars again. *I did everything I could*, he thought. He'd had one man in four killed or wounded in the latest battle; the River of Death had lived up to its name. How could he pursue after that?

"I couldn't," he muttered, drawing a curious look from a sentry. Fortunately, the man had the sense to ask no questions.

But Thraxton held his thoughts to himself. *They*

*want me to get east of the southrons, to slip between them and their supply base at Ramblerton. How can I do that when the army has no bridges to cross the Franklin River? If I send men across at the fords and the river rises—as it might, after any thunderstorm—they'll be cut off from any hope of aid. Can people see that? It doesn't seem so.*

He went back into the farmhouse, took off his boots, and lay down on the iron-framed cot that did duty for a bed: the softer one the farmer who'd abandoned the place left behind had proved full of vermin, and they, like the southrons, showed a higher degree of immunity to his spells than he would have liked.

Most of the bugs, unlike most of the southrons, were finally deceased. The ones that survived didn't bother Thraxton much. Even so, sleep was a long time coming. He knew as well as his fractious generals that he might have got more from the fight by the River of Death, and knowing that ate at him no less than it ate at them. They were full of bright ideas. He didn't think any of their bright ideas would work. Unfortunately, he'd come up with no bright ideas of his own. That left him . . . sleepless on a hard cot near Proselytizers' Rise, when he'd hoped to go back into Rising Rock in triumph.

When sleep did come, it did a better job of ambushing him than he'd done of catching the southrons unaware as they pushed into Peachtree Province. He woke with a feeling of deep surprise, almost of betrayal: what else might his body do to him while he wasn't looking?

He broke his fast with a couple of hard rolls and a cup of rather nasty tea. Southron galleys prowled outside the ports of the north, those that hadn't fallen to King Avram's men. Getting indigo out, getting proper tea in, grew harder month by month.

Count Thraxton had just finished his abstemious meal when a runner came in and said, "Your Grace, the king will see you now."

"Very good." Thraxton got to his feet. "I'll come." Only after he'd got moving did he reflect on the absurdity of that. If King Geoffrey wanted him to come, of course he would. He had no business speaking as if he were doing his sovereign a favor. He'd been commanding the Army of Franklin a long time; maybe he'd got used to the idea of having no one around of rank higher than his.

He ducked his way into the pavilion he'd had run up for the king. Dropping to one knee, he murmured, "Your Majesty."

"Arise, old friend," Geoffrey said. Thraxton straightened. The king seemed in a mood to put aside some of the formality of his office. He waved Thraxton to a stool and sat down on another one himself, though he sat very straight, as if his back pained him. "What can I do to help you win back Franklin?"

"Give my army another wing the size of James of Broadpath's," Thraxton replied without the least hesitation. "Give me the unicorn-riders and siege train and artisans that go with such a force. If I had them, I would sweep the southrons from this province as a cleaning wench sweeps dust from a parquet floor."

"If I had such men, I would give them with both hands," King Geoffrey replied. "I have them not, I fear. To give you Earl James and his followers, I had to rob Duke Edward in Parthenia and pray the southrons would stay quiet. We are . . . stretched very thin these days, you know."

"Yes." Thraxton's doleful nod matched his doleful countenance. "You do know, however, that the southrons have sent reinforcements into Rising Rock?"

"I know it," Geoffrey said. "The more men they have there, the faster they will starve. So I hope, at any rate."

"Indeed." Thraxton nodded again, this time in more willing agreement. "We have our hand on their windpipe to the east of here. I will do everything I can to squeeze it shut." *Maybe I'll parade through the streets of Rising Rock yet. Maybe.*

King Geoffrey nodded, too. "Good. May the gods favor our cause, then. Now . . . I shall transfer Ned of the Forest to the vicinity of the Great River, as you ask. I gather the two of you have known a certain amount of friction trying to work together."

"You might say so, yes." Thraxton remembered Ned's index finger stabbing at his face like the point of a sword.

"Very well. I was given to understand as much." Geoffrey paused, looking thoughtful. *He's going to tell me something I don't want to hear*, Thraxton thought; he needed no magecraft to realize as much. And, sure enough, the king went on, "In his own way, Ned is valuable to the kingdom. I understand why he needs to leave this army, but I would not have him leave while feeling ill-used. That being so, I intend to promote him from brigadier to lieutenant general before sending him east toward the Great River."

"You will of course do as you please in this regard," Thraxton said woodenly. "If it were up to me . . ." *If it were up to me, Ned of the Forest would face the worst of the seven hells before I finally let him die.*

But he couldn't very well tell that to King Geoffrey, not after what the king had just told him.

"Sometimes these things can't be helped," Geoffrey said. "Winning the war comes first. If we do not win the war, all our petty quarrels crash to the ground along with all our hopes. Do you want to live in a world where our serfs are made into our liege lords?"

"No, by the gods," Thraxton replied, as he had to. And he told the truth. But he didn't care to live in a world where Ned of the Forest was allowed to prosper, either.

"I'm glad that's settled, then," the king said. It wasn't settled—it was a long way from settled—as far as Count Thraxton was concerned. But, though Geoffrey was his friend, Geoffrey was also his sovereign. He couldn't say what lay in his heart. His stomach twinged painfully. Of itself, his left hand rubbed at his belly. So far as he could tell, that did no good at all, but sorcery and medicine had failed him, too. Geoffrey went on, "Having dismissed Dan of Rabbit Hill and Leonidas, with whom do you intend to replace them? You will need men you can trust."

"Indeed, your Majesty," Thraxton said, in lieu of laughing in King Geoffrey's face. Men he trusted were few and far between. When he thought about how many men put under his command had shamelessly betrayed him, he found it altogether unsurprising that that should be so.

"What do you say to Roast-Beef William, then?" Geoffrey asked.

Count Thraxton stroked his graying beard. The year before, he and Roast-Beef William had commanded armies moving more or less together down into Cloviston, toward the Highlow River. They'd had to come back to the north after accomplishing less than Thraxton would have liked, but he'd got on with the other general about as well as he got on with anyone: faint praise, perhaps, but better than no praise at all.

Geoffrey could have proposed many worse choices. If Thraxton hesitated much more, perhaps Geoffrey would propose somebody worse. And so he nodded. "Yes, your Majesty, I think he would suit me."

"Good," Geoffrey said. "I think his appetite for fighting matches his appetite for large slabs of red, dripping meat."

"Er—yes." Thraxton wondered if he'd made a mistake. He would, from time to time, have to eat with his wing commanders. His own appetite was abstemious. Having to watch Roast-Beef William demolish a significant fraction of a cow at suppertime would do nothing to improve it. *The sacrifices I make for the kingdom.*

"All right, then." The king seemed to tick off another item on his agenda. "You may choose your second wing commander in your own good time. Getting one man named, though, is important."

"As you say, your Majesty. Is there anything more?" As far as Thraxton was concerned, there'd been quite enough already.

But King Geoffrey nodded. "It is essential that you drive the southrons from as much of Franklin as you possibly can. Essential, I say. We should be hard pressed to make a kingdom without this province."

"I understand." Count Thraxton made himself nod. Making himself smile was beyond him. "I shall do everything as I can to carry out your wishes, your Majesty. Without more men, though . . ." The king glared at him so fiercely, he had to fall silent. But if the north could not get more men where they were needed most, how was it to make any sort of kingdom, with or without Franklin?

General Bart was not a happy man as the glideway brought him into Adlai, the town in southern Dothan Province closest to Rising Rock. He wasn't happy that King Avram had had to send him to Rising Rock to repair matters after General Guildenstern met disaster by the River of Death, and he was in physical pain. A few days before, up in the steaming subtropical heat of Old Capet, General Nat the Banker had lent him a particularly spirited unicorn, and he'd taken a bad fall. His whole right side was still a mass of bruises. He could ride again, but walking remained a torment.

His aide, a hatchet-faced young colonel named Horace, strode onto the glideway carpet and said, "Sir, we're in luck—General Guildenstern is here in Adlai, on his way south after King Avram recalled him."

"Is he, your Grace?" Bart said, and Colonel Horace nodded. Horace was a duke's son. That amused Bart, whose father had been a tanner. He knew he took perhaps more pride than he should at giving nobles orders; in the south, what a man could do counted for at least as much as who his father was. That was much less true in the north, where the nobles' broad estates gave them enormous power in the land.

"He would speak to you, sir, if you care to speak to him," Horace said.

"Of course I will," Bart answered. "I wish I hadn't had to make this trip, and I expect he wishes the same thing even more than I do. It's good of him to want to talk to me at all, and not to spit in my eye."

Colonel Horace contemplated that. "Sometimes, sir, I think you're a little too good at seeing the other fellow's point of view."

"Maybe, maybe not." Bart shrugged, which hurt. "Don't forget, Colonel, I went to the officers' collegium with these other fellows and served alongside 'em—our officers and the ones who chose Geoffrey. Knowing how the other fellow thinks is a big help in this business."

"If you say so, sir." To Colonel Horace, everything that had to do with fighting was simple. You found the enemy, and then you went out and hit him. As far as Bart was concerned, that made him an excellent subordinate and would have made him a very dangerous commander.

"I do say so," Bart replied. "Well, if Guildenstern wants to talk to me, I'm glad to talk to him, as I say. Bring him aboard."

"Yes, sir." His aide's salute was as precise as if it came straight from a manufactory. Colonel Horace stalked off the glideway carpet, returning a couple of minutes later with the general formerly in command at Rising Rock.

A cloud of brandy fumes preceded and accompanied Guildenstern. General Bart felt more than a little sympathy for his fellow southron officer. He was fond of spirits himself; there had been times in his life when he'd shown himself much too fond of spirits. He fought shy of them these days for just that reason.

General Guildenstern gave him a sloppy salute. "Here you are, sir. I hope you lick the gods-damned traitors right out of their boots."

"I hope I do, too," Bart said. "I wish I didn't have to try it in the wake of your defeat, General."

"So do I, gods damn it. So do I." Guildenstern wore a flask on his belt. He liberated it and took a long, healthy swig, then extended it to Bart. "Want a nip?"

Bart's face froze. He was not a big man, nor a particularly impressive one, save that, when he chose, he could make his eyes extraordinarily cold and bleak. A man seeing him when such a mood took him was well advised to give way, for Bart never would. He'd got more through dogged persistence than other, cleverer, generals had from military genius.

That cold, dark stare got through even to Guildenstern, already elevated from brandy though he was. Smiling a placating smile, he said, "Er, well, maybe not," and put the flask away in a hurry.

"Tell me of your dispositions," was all Bart said.

"My disposition? By the Thunderer's prick, it's not all it might be," Guildenstern said, and guffawed. Bart didn't, and that cold, intent look never left his face. General Guildenstern's chuckles died away to uneasy silence. At last, he asked, "Have you got a map of Rising Rock and the surrounding country, General?"

"I do." Bart pulled one from a red leather folder.

"All right, then." Brandy fumes or no, Guildenstern settled down to business and showed Bart where his men were posted and where Thraxton the Braggart's lines ran.

"Pity you let them take Sentry Peak," Bart said. "The top is a prime observation post, and engines on the forward slope can reach south across the Franklin River and just about into Rising Rock."

"I would be a liar if I said I was very happy about that myself, sir," Guildenstern replied. "Still and all, though, there are several things you might do, there and elsewhere, to shore up your lines."

Tracing ideas out with his finger, he showed Bart what he meant.

"Those are all good notions," Bart said when he was through. He meant it; he was not and never had been a man to whom hypocrisy came naturally. All the same, he fixed Guildenstern with that piercing glance once more. "Yes, they're excellent notions. Why didn't you use them yourself, instead of saving them up to give them to me?"

Guildenstern stared. He opened his mouth, but not a word emerged. Slowly and deliberately, without any fuss, General Bart put the map back in its folder. By the time he'd stowed the folder in amongst his baggage, Guildenstern found his power of speech once more: "What I did or didn't do doesn't matter, not any more. I'm off to the south, along with Thom and Alexander and Negley. Negley can go back to his flowers. The rest of us . . . If we're lucky, King Avram will send us out to the eastern steppe and let us chase louse-ridden blond nomads for the rest of the war. If we're lucky, I say."

The brandy he'd taken on no doubt helped fuel his self-pity. With a sigh, Bart said, "You could expect better, General, if the four of you hadn't left the field before the fight was over."

"We got swept away in the rout," Guildenstern said hotly. "The whole fornicating army got swept away in the rout. That's what makes a rout, the whole fornicating army getting swept away."

"Lieutenant General George didn't," Bart pointed out. "If he had, if the traitors had pushed him off Merkle's Hill, none of you would have come back safe to Rising Rock."

"To the seven hells with Doubting George!" Guildenstern cried, and stormed away.

General Bart started to go after him, then checked himself. He could understand why Guildenstern was angry and upset. Doubting George had had to fall back from the River of Death, but he'd done it with his chunk of the army in good order, and after fighting Thraxton's men to a standstill. Guildenstern and the other high-ranking officers had left too soon, and they would have to pay the price for the rest of their careers, if not for the rest of their lives.

When morning came, Bart set out for Rising Rock himself. He didn't go by glideway, not when the traitors could reach the line into town with their engines. He had to ride a unicorn for those last thirty miles or so. It was one of the less pleasant journeys of his life, since the bruises he'd taken in the fall up north were far from healed; his whole right side, from ankle to shoulder, was black and yellow and purple and, here and there, green.

Worse still, the road between Adlai and Rising Rock hardly deserved the name. It was rough and narrow, and flanked by broken-down wagons and the scrawny carcasses of asses and unicorns. Getting supplies into Rising Rock wasn't easy. Every so often, the officers with Bart had to dismount and lead their unicorns up and down gullies too steep for riding. When they did, they had to put Bart in a litter and carry him till the going got better. He could ride, though it hurt. He wasn't up to much in the way of walking, even with a stick in each hand.

To Colonel Horace, he said, "It's a good thing Thraxton hasn't got unicorn-riders out prowling in these parts. I can't run away, and I can't fight, either."

"Is it true that Ned of the Forest has gone off to fight somewhere else?" By Horace's tone, the aide expected the northern officer to come charging out of the trees if it weren't true.

"I believe it is," Bart answered from the embarrassing comfort of the litter. "I've seen the same reports you have, Colonel. Unless the northerners are bluffing us, he's gone. I hope he is. He caused me endless grief over by the Great River last winter, and I'd just as soon not have to cope with his marauders again."

He got into Rising Rock just after nightfall, and after surviving a challenge from nervous southron sentries. He was glad to get past the men from his own side. More than one general in this fight had already fallen victim to crossbow bolts from soldiers mistaking their own commanders for the foe.

Lieutenant General George greeted him in front of the hostel that had been General Guildenstern's headquarters, and before him Count Thraxton's. "Good to see you, sir," George said, saluting. "I know we're in good hands now."

"Thanks," Bart replied, slowly and painfully dismounting and then reaching for the sticks he'd tied behind the saddle. "It's mighty fine to see you here, George, speaking of good hands." He'd always had a high regard for the lieutenant general, higher than he'd felt for Guildenstern even before the battle by the River of Death.

"Come in, come in," Doubting George said now. "There's a capon waiting for you, and a nice, soft bed. I can see by the way you're standing that you could use one. How do you feel?"

"I've been better," Bart admitted. "But food and sleep and maybe a long, hot soak between one and the other would go a long way toward setting me right."

After supper, one of the blond maidservants at the

hostel offered to scrub his back in the tub and take care of anything else he had in mind. "General Guildenstern, he liked me fine," she boasted.

"I can see why," Bart answered; she was pretty and shapely. "But my lady down in the south wouldn't be happy if I spread it around, so I don't."

With a shrug, she answered, "That other fellow had a lady down south somewheres, too, but it didn't bother him none."

From everything Bart had heard about Guildenstern, that left him unsurprised. "Well, it bothers me," he said, and then, "I'm sure you won't have any trouble finding someone else who'd want to be friendly with you."

"Oh, so am I," she answered with a good-looking woman's certainty. "Still and all, though, I was on top before, and I was hoping to stay on top now that you're here." She shrugged again. "Well, if nobody's on top, I guess taking a step or two down won't be *so* bad." She strode out of the bathroom, waggling her hips a little to show him what he was missing. He laughed, although, being a polite man, he held off till she'd closed the door after her. Who would have thought serving girls ranked themselves by which generals they'd slept with?

Sleeping alone suited him just fine that evening. He felt much more nearly himself when he got up the next morning. After breakfast, Doubting George asked him, "Would you care to ride out and see some of the line we set up after we came back here to Rising Rock?"

"Can't think of a solitary thing I'd like better," Bart replied, even if he didn't look forward to the process of climbing up onto unicornback again. "If you don't get a good look at the ground with your own eyes, you'll never understand everything you might do."

"I couldn't have put it better myself," George said. They nodded to each other. Bart had always reckoned the lieutenant general a solid soldier. The more he spoke with him, the more he looked forward to working with him here.

Along with Colonel Horace, the two of them rode north and a little east toward Rising Rock Creek, which lay between the town of Rising Rock and Sentry Peak, and which marked the front between the army now Bart's and that of Count Thraxton. George said, "There's a sort of a truce here, so both sides can draw water from the creek without worrying about getting a crossbow quarrel in the brisket."

"Fair enough," Bart said. "Sentries could shoot at each other from now till the last war of the gods without changing how this fight comes out." He asked Doubting George, "Whose men are in the line here for the enemy?"

"James of Broadpath's, from out of the west," George answered. "Do you know him well?" Almost all the officers from Detina's old army knew each other to one degree or another.

"I should hope I do," Bart replied. "He was a groomsman at my wedding." He reined in and dismounted, continuing, "The rest of you kindly stay back here. I should like to go up to the creek alone, so as to get my observations without drawing the enemy's notice."

Like one of King Avram's common soldiers, he wore a plain gray tunic. But, as he made his slow, painful way forward with the aid of his sticks, a sentry in gray spotted his epaulets and called, "Turn out the guard—commanding general!" The other pickets in gray shouldered their crossbows and saluted.

And then, across the creek, one of King Geoffrey's blue-clad soldiers, a wag, heard the call and raised one of his own: "Turn out the guard—General Bart!" Grins on their faces, the traitors saluted him, too.

Bart acknowledged them by lifting his hat. "Dismissed!" he called to them, and limped back to his unicorn. As he remounted, he remarked, "I knew we were fighting a civil war, but that was more civility than I expected." He and George and Colonel Horace rode on down along the creek.

Doubting George studied the map with General Bart. "The road we have to the east is bad, but will serve us tolerably well as long as the weather stays dry," he said. "When the winter rains start, though, we'll starve if we have to depend on it. Rations are too low as things stand."

"Well, then, we've got to do something about it," Bart replied.

"What have you got in mind, sir?" Doubting George asked. He was particularly dubious here. General Guildenstern had been splendid at proposing this, that, or the other scheme to get Rising Rock out of its fix. He'd proposed all sorts of things, but done nothing. Bart had made a different sort of name for himself in the fighting farther east, but George wanted to see him in action before judging.

Bart's finger came down on the little hamlet of Bridgeton, about twenty-five miles east of Rising Rock. "If we can get a secure road from Bridgeton to here, we're safe as houses."

"Yes, sir," George agreed. "If we can do that, we're fine. Looks like a pretty good *if* to me."

"Shouldn't be," Bart said. "I've got a solid division under Fighting Joseph in Bridgeton right now; they were starting to come into Adlai, a little east of there, when I left Adlai for Rising Rock here. If they can move up to the Brownsville Ferry here" —he pointed again, this time only about eight miles east of town— "while we send men out that far, we'll hold either the river or a good road all the way from Bridgeton to here."

George studied the map. "That's not a bad notion," he said at last. "It might be worth trying." Fighting Joseph was a pretty good division commander, though he'd failed as head of an army in the west.

"Glad you agree," Bart said. "I've already given the orders. Joseph will move out today, and Brigadier Bill the Bald goes out of here tonight under cover of darkness with all the bridging equipment he needs to span the Franklin at Brownsville. He's a good officer and a pretty good soldier. He shouldn't have any trouble at all."

"You've . . . already given the orders?" George said.

"That's right." Bart nodded. "I don't see any point to wasting time. Do you?"

"When you put it that way, no sir," George answered in some bemusement. General Guildenstern would have spent endless hours bickering in councils of war, and would have ended up sitting on his haunches while Rising Rock starved. That was what Count Thraxton hoped would happen.

"All right, then," Bart said. "I already told you— if we're going to set about fixing things, we'd better fix them."

"True enough." Doubting George studied the new commanding general. "I don't think enough people know what to expect from you, sir."

"If they don't, they'll find out," Bart said. "If the traitors we're up against don't find out quite soon enough, that won't break my heart." He laughed briefly. "James of Broadpath's men are holding that stretch of line. Nothing like giving my old grooms-man a little surprise."

"You're looking *forward* to this!" George exclaimed.

"You bet I am," General Bart replied. "George, you know it as well as I do—the northerners have got no business tearing this kingdom apart. If you thought different, you'd be fighting for Geoffrey, not Avram."

"So I would—a lot of men from Parthenia are," George said. "Brave men, too, most of them."

"Brave men don't make a bad cause good by fight-ing for it, and they're fighting for a bad cause—a couple of bad causes, in fact," Bart said. "Making their living from the sweat of serfs is a nasty busi-ness, nothing else but." He paused. "I don't mean that personally, of course."

"Of course," Doubting George said dryly. "I have no serfs, not any more—Geoffrey confiscated my lands when I declared for Avram."

"Yes, I'd heard that." Bart did something George had rarely seen him do: he hesitated. At last, he asked, "Does it bother you?"

"Having my property confiscated? Of course it does," George answered. "I don't imagine Duke Edward is very pleased with King Avram for doing the same thing to him." He eyed his superior. "Or did you mean, does it bother me that I have no serfs any more?"

"The latter," Bart replied. "Forgive me if the ques-tion troubles you. But there are few men who were liege lords serving in King Avram's army, for in the south the serfs have been unbound from the land for a couple of generations. If my curiosity strikes you as impertinent, do not hesitate to say so."

"By no means, sir." George had had other southron officers ask him similar questions, though few with Bart's diffidence—and Bart, being his commander, had the least need for diffidence. George went on, "I would sooner this were only a fight to hold the kingdom together, that everything else could stay the same. But I see it is not so, and cannot be so, and that the nobles in the north are using their serfs in every way they can short of putting crossbows in their hands to further the war against our rightful king. That being so, I see we have to strike a blow not just against Geoffrey but also against the serfdom that upholds him. But the kingdom will not be the same afterwards."

He waited to see how General Bart would take that. The commanding general stroked his close-cropped beard. "I have judged from how you have conducted yourself in the fights you've led that you were a man of uncommon common sense, if you take my meaning. What you said just now has done nothing to change my opinion."

"Thank you very much, sir." Doubting George did not have his nickname for nothing; he'd been born with a cynical cast of mind. He was surprised at how much the commanding general's praise pleased him—a telling measure of how much Bart himself had impressed him. "Do you know, sir, there's a great deal more to you than meets the eye."

"Is there?" Bart said, and George nodded emphatically. The commanding general shrugged in a self-deprecating way. "There could hardly be less, you know."

Even in the north, he would never have been a

liege lord. Everything he was, he owed to Detina's army. Without his training at the officers' collegium, he might have ended up a tanner himself. When he'd left the army before King Avram's accession, he'd failed at everything he tried. People said he'd dived down the neck of a bottle. Maybe it was true; something in his eyes suggested to George that it was: a certain hardness, perhaps. But Guildenstern drank to excess in the middle of a battle, and George doubted General Bart would ever do such a thing. Bart had been through that fire, and come out the other side.

Now the commanding general shook his head slightly, as if to divert the conversation away from himself. "Once we have the road to Bridgeton secured," he said, "once we make certain we shall not be starved out of this place, and once all our reinforcements have arrived, I believe we can lick Count Thraxton clean out of his boots. Don't you agree?"

"Do you know, sir, I think I do." With General Guildenstern in command, George would have had his doubts. With General Bart . . . "I don't care how good a wizard Thraxton is. I don't think his spells would faze you a bit."

"Well, I hope not," Bart said. "In the long run, wizardry strikes me as being like most other things— it will even out."

"May the gods prove you right, sir," George said. That was in large measure his view of things, too, though a good many southron generals had a different opinion. As a general working rule, the mages who backed King Geoffrey were stronger than those who'd stayed loyal to King Avram. Thraxton the Braggart, for instance, had more power than any one southron mage George could think of.

But Bart said, "If wizards were so much of a much,

the traitors would be over the Highlow River in the east and pressing down toward New Eborac in the west. They may have fancier mages than we do, but we've got more of them, the same as we've got more soldiers and more manufactories. We can use that to our advantage. We *have* used that to our advantage—otherwise, we wouldn't be up here on the northern border of Franklin. We haven't done everything we might, but things aren't so very bad."

"If we'd done everything we might, we'd be marching up toward Marthasville today, not penned here in Rising Rock," George replied.

"That's true." Bart nodded. "But we can do more. We will do more. When Thraxton beat us there by the River of Death, he showed us we needed to do more. And we can—it's as plain as the nose on your face that we can. Thraxton won't get any more soldiers: where would they come from? But we've already reinforced this army, and we've got lots more men on the way. Once they're here, we'll take care of business the right and proper way."

George studied him. Bart didn't shout and bluster, as General Guildenstern had been so fond of doing. But the new commanding general's quiet confidence made him more believable, not less. When he said his army would be able to do something, he left little room for doubt in the mind of anyone who heard him. He might have been a builder talking about a house he intended to put up. How could you doubt a builder when he said the walls would stand so, the doors would be there and there, and the windows would have shutters in the latest style?

Thoughtfully, George said, "I do believe you're right."

"I hope so. I wouldn't be trying it if I didn't think

I was." Bart might have been saying, *Yes, this house will stand up to a storm.* He raised a forefinger. "Oh, I almost forgot. I've taken the liberty of attaching a couple of your regiments to the force Bill the Bald will lead. They were conveniently situated, and could join in his movements without drawing the northerners' notice."

"Whatever you think best, of course," Doubting George replied. Had Guildenstern done such a thing without telling him, it would have irked him. He found himself meaning what he'd said to General Bart.

"I'm glad it's all right with you." Bart sounded genuinely relieved. As if explaining why he'd used stone instead of brick, he went on, "When I strike a blow, I always try to strike the hardest one I can."

"Good!" George said. "That was what cost us so much not long ago. We were spread out over the whole landscape, and could hardly strike at all."

"I suspect that wasn't your idea." Before George could answer, Bart held up a hand. "Never mind, Lieutenant General; never mind. I don't need to know every gory incident, and General Guildenstern isn't around any more to give his side of things." His eyes twinkled, just for a moment. "Can't say I'm sorry about that. I expect I would have heard about it in *great* detail."

King Avram's army was full of backbiting. So was King Geoffrey's. So, no doubt, was every army back to the beginning of time, or perhaps before that—the gods were supposed to squabble among themselves, too. Rarely, though, had George heard such a good-natured snide remark.

Just for a moment, he even stopped doubting and said, "If we can keep on like this, sir, I think we'll do fine. One of the things we need to do is believe in ourselves, and you make us do that."

"I don't *make* us do a solitary thing except for what I order," Bart said.

Now George laughed. "Oh, I doubt that, sir."

But General Bart ignored the joke—which he'd hardly even heard before—and went on as if George hadn't spoken: "I do believe a united kingdom is stronger than a divided one can hope to be. That may give us an edge against the traitors. I hope it does. But what good is an edge unless you go out and take advantage of it? None, not that I can see."

That was nothing but good, hard common sense. Good, hard common sense had been in moderately short supply in this camp lately: one more thing about which even Doubting George entertained no doubts. He came to stiff attention and saluted. "With you in charge in these parts, I think we'll grab every edge we can find."

"No, no," Bart said mildly. "You don't grab the edge. You grab the hilt and give the enemy the edge." He chuckled.

So did George, rather dutifully. *He's fond of foolish jokes*, he thought, and then decided it didn't matter much. He'd known worse commanders with habits much more obnoxious than that.

Out in the street, a newly arrived regiment of Avram's soldiers tramped by, band blaring and thumping at their head. "More reinforcements," George said happily. "Even with the roads as bad as they are, even with the traitors where they are, we're bringing in what we need."

"So we are," Bart agreed. After some hesitation, he inquired, "Ah . . . what tune are they playing there?"

Now Doubting George doubted he'd heard

correctly. "Why, the Battle Psalm of the Kingdom, of course," he replied.

"Oh." General Bart let out another chuckle, this one aimed at himself. "I only know two tunes, you see. One's the Royal Hymn, and the other one—the other one isn't."

Another foolish joke. George laughed again, too. Then, seeing the wistful look on the commanding general's face, he wondered if Bart had been joking.

Rollant yawned enormously. He'd been doing that ever since Sergeant Joram gave him a boot in the backside and got him out of his bedroll. Beside him, Smitty was yawning, too. They weren't the only ones unhappy at having to make a night march. Everyone in the whole regiment seemed no better than half awake.

"This had better work," Smitty grumbled. "If they made me lose sleep on account of some gods-damned brainless noble's brainstorm, I'm really going to be hot."

Such talk still faintly scandalized Rollant, even though the former serf had been living in the free and easygoing south for some years. Back in Palmetto Province, no one—and especially no blond—would have mocked the nobility so. He tried to hide his feelings with raillery of his own: "I'm sure all the dukes and counts and barons are trembling in their boots, Smitty."

"They'd better be." Smitty sounded as if he meant it. "It's us commoners who do most of the work and make most of the money, and the bluebloods don't remember it nearly often enough."

That scandalized Rollant, too, and more than a little. He took the nobles and their privileges for granted; he was just glad to be out from under Baron Ormerod. "How would we run things if there weren't any nobles?" he asked.

"I don't know, but I expect we'd manage," Smitty said. "Free Detinans can do whatever we set our minds to do."

He did mean it. Rollant didn't know whether he was right or wrong, but he did mean it. Most Detinans thought that way. They were convinced they were going somewhere important, and they all seemed eager for the journey. Rollant, now, Rollant had his doubts. But he'd grown up on an estate where the only place he could go was where Baron Ormerod told him to. That made a big difference. Nobody had an easy time telling free Detinans what to do. Even here in the army, they talked back to their sergeants and officers, and tried to come up with better ideas than the ones the generals had.

"Let's go!" Sergeant Joram bellowed. "Come on! We can do it! We're gods-damned well going to do it."

No one talked back to him then. Rollant felt like it. Marching through the middle of the night wasn't his idea of fun. But nobody asked what his idea of fun was. People just told him to do things and expected him to do them. He didn't usually have too hard a time with that; he'd had practice obeying on Ormerod's estate. Tonight, though, he was very tired.

Tired or not, he marched. So did everybody else— the army treated flat-out disobedience from soldiers even more ruthlessly than northern liege lords rooted it out among their serfs. "Watch where you're putting your feet," somebody not far from Rollant grumbled—in the darkness, he couldn't see who.

"How can I watch?" somebody else said—maybe

the offender, maybe not. "I can't see the nose in front of my face."

"It ain't *that* dark, Lionel," yet another soldier said, "and you've got yourself a cursed big nose." Lionel expressed loud resentment of this opinion. Several other people spoke in support of it.

Rollant thought Lionel had a big nose, too. He thought most Detinans had pretty good-sized beaks. He didn't join the debate, though. The Detinans were willing to let blonds fight for them. They were much less willing to hear what blonds had to say. That didn't strike him as fair, but a lot of things didn't strike him as fair.

Then somebody stepped on his heel, almost stripping the boot from his foot. "Careful, there," he said.

"Sorry." Whoever was marching along behind him didn't sound very sorry, but he didn't step on Rollant any more, either.

They tramped east. It was, Rollant realized little by little, a large column. Whatever he was part of—nobody'd bothered explaining it to him—looked to be something important. He didn't suppose they would have sent out the column on a night march if it weren't important. He hoped they wouldn't, anyhow.

Somebody rode by on a unicorn. "Keep going, men," he called. "When we get to the river, we'll give the traitors a surprise." He raised his hat. Starlight gleamed from his shiny crown.

"That's Bill the Bald!" Smitty exclaimed. "He must be in charge of this whole move."

"I'd like it better if we had Doubting George in charge of us," Rollant said. "If he kept us from getting licked by the River of Death, I expect he can do just about anything." Smitty didn't argue with him.

Dawn began turning the eastern sky gray and then pink. Rollant started to be able to see where he was putting his feet. He tried to see more than that, to see where the enemy was. He couldn't, not yet.

Smitty said, "Next thing we've got to find out is if the pontoons make it to where they're supposed to be when we make it to where we're supposed to be. If we can't cross the river, we sure as hells can't do the fighting we're supposed to do."

"Cross the river?" Rollant said. "Nobody ever tells me anything."

"I'm telling you now, aren't I?" Smitty said. Rollant nodded, but he still meant what he'd said. He always got rumors more slowly than most of the others in the company. He knew why, too: he was a blond. He'd mostly given up complaining about it. Complaining didn't make people talk to him any more, and it did make them think he was a whiner. He didn't think so, but one of the lessons of serfdom and the army alike was that hardly anybody cared what he thought.

Lieutenant Griff still led the regiment; Captain Cephas wasn't fit to march or fight. Griff pointed ahead, toward the Franklin River. "That's Brownsville Ferry, where we're going," he called to the company. He actually sounded as if he knew what he was talking about. "We've got more men coming, I hear. Between them and us, we'll drive the traitors back and open up a proper supply route."

"Why didn't he tell us all that before we started marching?" Rollant asked.

"He probably didn't know himself," Smitty answered. "How much you want to bet somebody briefed him while we were on the road here?"

Rollant thought about it. It didn't take much

thought. He nodded. "That sounds right." As the company commander had, he pointed. "Look at those big wooden boxy things floating in the river."

"Those are the pontoons." Smitty's voice cracked with excitement. "And see? We've got the wizards in place to do what needs doing with 'em. By the gods, that didn't always happen when General Guildenstern was in charge of things."

Sure enough, the mages on this bank of the Franklin were busy incanting—and the northerners on the far bank of the river didn't seem to have any sorcerers in place to challenge their spells. Under their wizardry, the pontoons formed a line straight across the Franklin River. More mages—and some down-to-earth, unmagical artificers, too—spiked planks on the pontoons to form a makeshift bridge. The blue-clad traitors did have a few soldiers in place on the far side of the river. They started shooting at the artificers as soon as they got within range. They hit some of them, too, but not enough to keep the bridge from getting finished. Rollant whooped, even though that completed bridge meant he was going into danger. He wasn't the only one cheering, either—far from it.

Trumpets blared. Gray-clad soldiers swarmed onto the bridge and charged toward the enemy: unicorn-riders first, then pikemen, then crossbowmen like Rollant and his comrades. "We are to drive back the enemy wherever we find him," Lieutenant Griff said grandly.

Rollant set a quarrel in the groove of his crossbow and cocked the weapon. The rest of the soldiers in his company did the same. They couldn't do much in the way of driving unless they could shoot. More and more of King Avram's men flooded over the bridge. By now, the sun had risen. Rollant saw the men who followed King Geoffrey running away, some of them pausing every now and then to shoot at his comrades and him. It wasn't that they weren't brave; he knew too well that they were. But General Bart's sudden, strong move to seize this river crossing had caught them by surprise, and they didn't have enough troopers close by to stop it.

Then his own feet were thudding on the timbers of the pontoon bridge. "King Avram!" he shouted at the top of his lungs. "King Avram and freedom!"

He didn't hear anyone yelling for King Geoffrey and provincial prerogative. His boots squelched in the mud on the far riverbank. He looked around wildly for somebody to kill.

But there weren't that many northerners around. The men who'd gone over the pontoon bridge ahead of Rollant had killed some of them, while others had run away, seeing themselves so outnumbered. Rollant shot at one traitor who'd decided to run a little later than his comrades. His bolt caught the enemy soldier right in the seat of the pantaloons. The fellow let out a howl Rollant could clearly hear and ran faster than ever, one hand clapped to the wound.

"Nice shot!" Smitty said, laughing. "He'll remember you every time he sits down for the next year." He waved to Sergeant Joram. "Put it in the report, Sergeant—Trooper Rollant has made himself a pain in the arse to the enemy."

"What are you talking about?" Joram demanded—he hadn't seen the shot. Smitty explained. The sergeant condescended to chuckle. "All right, that's not bad. But our job is to kill the whoresons, not just stick pins in their backsides."

All Rollant said was, "Yes, Sergeant." He wanted

to kill the traitors, too. He didn't want to kill them because they were traitors, or because they were trying to tear the kingdom to pieces. All that was for ordinary Detinans. He wanted to kill them because one of their number had used him like a beast of burden till he was a grown man and able to run away, because uncounted thousands of them used other blonds the same way (and used their women worse), because almost every Detinan in the north wished he were a liege lord and able to use blonds so. If that wasn't reason enough to want the traitors dead, Rollant was cursed if he knew what would be.

"Soldiers coming!" somebody called. "Coming out of the east!"

Rollant wasted no more time worrying about reasons to want to kill the enemy. The most basic reason was simplicity itself: if he didn't kill northerners, one of them would be delighted to kill him. He put a new quarrel in his crossbow with frantic haste, then yanked back the string to cock the weapon.

Smitty had sensibly found shelter behind a low stone fence. Rollant got down behind the fence with him. Crouching on one knee, he peered over the fence in the direction of the rising sun. Sure enough, there came the cloud of dust that bespoke marching men.

It was a large cloud. "A lot of those bastards heading this way," Smitty said.

"I know," Rollant answered. "Well, we wondered where they were. Now we know. They want us, they'll have to pay for us."

"That's right," Smitty said. "They made us charge fences, back there in front of Rising Rock. Now we'll see how well they like it, gods damn them."

Rollant nodded. One of the things soldiers in this

war quickly learned was how much protection mattered. A man behind a solid stone wall could stand off several out in the open—provided an engine or a wizard didn't knock down the wall. That, unfortunately, happened, too.

And then, to his surprise, Rollant heard cheers from King Avram's soldiers farther east. Some of the cheers had words attached to them. And those words were among the most welcome he'd ever heard: "They're ours!"

When he heard those words, he cheered, too. He cheered, yes, but he didn't show himself, not yet. When Detinans fought Detinans, one army looked all too much like another. Men had killed their own generals before, and you were just as dead with a friend's bolt through you as with a foe's.

But then somebody yelled, "Those are Fighting Joseph's men, come to help us hold the supply line against Geoffrey's traitors."

At that, Rollant did get to his feet. If people could see who led the newcomers, he was willing to believe they followed King Avram. Then he saw the general himself, and did some yelling of his own: "There's Fighting Joseph!"

A lot of men were yelling Fighting Joseph's name, and he waved to the ordinary soldiers. He was an extraordinarily handsome man, with ruddy features and a piercing glance. Back in the west, he'd promised to lead his army straight to Nonesuch. If he had, people wondered if his next move would have been to overthrow King Avram and seize the throne for himself. They'd stopped wondering in a hurry, when Duke Edward of Arlington used half as many men as Fighting Joseph led to whip him soundly at Viziersville. He still made a good division commander, though.

"Hello, boys!" he called now from the back of the fine unicorn he rode. "We're here, and there's plenty more coming along after us. Your days on short commons are done, and once you've filled your bellies, we'll throw the traitors out of here and boot them back to Peachtree Province once and for all."

Everybody cheered. Rollant shouted himself hoarse. Smitty threw his hat in the air—and then recovered it in a hurry, before Sergeant Joram could growl at him for going without it. As he put it back on his head, he said, "It may not be so easy. Geoffrey's men'll try and knock us out of here, you wait and see if they don't."

# IX

"Those sons of bitches!" Major Thersites shouted in a perfect transport of rage. "Those idiotic, gods-damned sons of bitches! What in the hells have we got generals for in the first place, if they can't keep things like that from happening?"

Captain Ormerod had never seen him so furious. He wished Colonel Florizel were still commanding the regiment; Florizel was gentleman enough to keep his annoyance under control. He was also gentleman enough to tell the officers under him why he was annoyed. Cautiously, Ormerod asked, "What's gone wrong now, sir?"

"I'll tell you what's gone wrong," Thersites snapped. "The great mages and mighty scholars who command us have let the stinking southrons put a decent supply line back together, that's what. How are we supposed to starve those buggers out of Rising Rock if they can bring in as many victuals as we can?"

"Oh, dear," Ormerod said, in lieu of something a good deal stronger. "How did that happen?"

"How? I'll tell you how," Thersites growled. "All our bright boys were sound asleep, that's how. They hit Brownsville Ferry from east and west at the same time, and ran our soldiers right out of there. Of course we never expected it. Why would the southrons want to keep themselves fed?"

Maybe he was right about how the unfortunate event had happened, maybe he was wrong. He was, as always, so full of bile against those set above him that Ormerod had trouble trusting his own judgment there. But Thersites was surely right about what the southrons' advance meant. "We have to push them back," Ormerod said.

"*You* can see that." Thersites didn't have any trouble with Ormerod—he outranked him. "*I* can see that. But can the great philosophers over on Proselytizers' Rise see that? Not bloody likely!" He spat in fine contempt.

A couple of hours later, though, Earl James of Broadpath came riding up to the base of Sentry Peak on a unicorn that would have done better hauling a winery wagon. "Come on, you lazy good-for-nothings," he called. "We've got some southrons to clear out east of here."

"How did they get there in the first place?" Thersites asked him.

"Pulled a march on us, caught us by surprise," James of Broadpath answered. "It's war. These things happen. What matters is whether you fix them or not. Get your men ready to fight, Major."

"Yes, sir," Thersites said. James nodded and rode

on. Thersites turned to Ormerod. "You heard the man. Let's get ready to move."

"Yes, sir," Ormerod said, as Thersites had before. "Who will take our place here?"

"I have no idea, Captain," the regimental commander answered. "But I'm not going to worry about it, either. I hope the big brains will see they need to move somebody else in if they move us out. I hope so, but you never can tell."

With that something less than ringing reassurance, Ormerod had to be content. He hurried back to his own company, shouting for the men to line up ready to march. "What now?" Lieutenant Gremio asked in some exasperation. "Are they going to throw us at Rising Rock? They're asking for us to get slaughtered if they do."

"No, it isn't that," Ormerod said, and explained what it was. He added, "Remember what happened to Dan of Rabbit Hill and Leonidas the Priest. Criticizing the commanding general isn't smart."

"Getting ourselves in this mess isn't smart, either," Gremio retorted. "If I see that someone is an imbecile, should I keep quiet about it?"

"I don't know. Should you?" Ormerod said. "Thersites certainly hasn't. Do you want to be just like him?"

As he'd thought it would, that gave Gremio pause. The barrister from Karlsburg grimaced and said, "All right, Captain, you've made your point. And this is something that needs doing, no doubt about that. Will anyone replace us here?"

"I don't know," Ormerod said. "Nobody bothered to tell me." Gremio grunted and rolled his eyes.

Ormerod's company was the second one ready to march. That spared him and his men the rough side of Major Thersites' tongue. "This isn't a ladies' social,

Captain," Thersites snarled at the commander of the last company to assemble. "If you don't care to run the risk of getting shot, you shouldn't have come along in the first place. You could be back in Palmetto Province happy and safe, you know."

"Yes, sir. I'm sorry, sir," the luckless company commander said through clenched teeth. Colonel Florizel would never have used him so; Colonel Florizel was a true northern gentleman. Major Thersites, as far as Ormerod could see, was a first-class son of a bitch. But, with Florizel wounded, he was also the regimental commander, and the company commanders had to put up with him.

"Let's go," Thersites said. Off went the regiment, along with several others from the slopes of Sentry Peak. Ormerod wondered if they would have enough men to shift the southrons. He couldn't do anything about that except wonder. When he wondered out loud, Gremio said, "They've been getting plenty of reinforcements. Where are *our* fresh troops coming out of the east? Or anywhere else, for that matter?"

"Haven't seen 'em," Ormerod answered, just as the regiment began to move. He raised his voice: "Come on, men! We can do it! Forward—march!" *What a liar I'm turning into*, he thought, not having the faintest idea whether they could do it or not.

"We should have come this way weeks ago," Gremio said. "If we had, we really could have starved the southrons out."

"What did I tell you before?" Ormerod asked.

"If you want to report me to Thraxton the Braggart, go right ahead," Gremio said. "He's sent away better officers than the ones he's kept, with the possible exception of Leonidas the Priest."

Ormerod didn't want to report him to Count

Thraxton. For one thing, he'd have to report him through Major Thersites, and Thersites said worse things about Thraxton than Gremio ever had. For another, Ormerod wanted nothing more than to close with the southrons and to drive them out of the north. Here he was, finally getting his chance. He just shook his head and kept marching.

It wasn't going to be easy. The closer he got to the southrons' positions, the more obvious that became. Avram's men were taking advantage of every fence and clump of trees and tiny hillock they could. Whoever was in charge of them plainly knew his business.

And they had unicorn-riders, too, men who galloped out, shot their crossbows at the advancing northerners, and then hurried away before anything very much could happen to them. It was like getting stung by gnats, except that some of the stings from these gnats killed.

"Where's Ned of the Forest when we really need him?" Lieutenant Gremio said.

"Off to the Great River," Ormerod answered. Gremio's expression was eloquent.

As the northern force approached the enemy line, engines opened up on them. The engines opened up a little too soon, as a matter of fact, almost all the stones and bursting firepots falling short. Ormerod felt better to see that: it was nice to know the southrons could make mistakes, too.

In a great voice, Major Thersites shouted, "Form line of battle!"

"Form line of battle!" Ormerod echoed to his men. Veterans, they knew how to go quickly from column into line, where raw troops would have been all too likely to make a hash of the job. And, he saw, they would have a good, solid screen of pikemen in front of them. That would help. If anything helped, that would help.

Someone off to one side winded a horn. Ormerod knew the horn calls, too. "Forward!" he shouted, along with the other officers in the force James of Broadpath had collected. Forward the men went, roaring like lions with the northern battle cry that often seemed worth a couple of regiments all by itself.

But the southrons were not inclined to give up without a fight the positions they'd taken. Some of their engines had started shooting a little too soon. That had let Geoffrey's men form their battle line without harassment. But as that battle line rolled toward the enemy, more stones and bursting firepots took their toll. A couple of repeating crossbows began scything down soldiers in blue.

*When they got here, they brought everything they needed to stay*, Ormerod thought. *I wish we were able to do that more often.*

Wishing, as usual, did him very little good. All he could do was trot forward, roaring at the top of his lungs and urging his men on. The sooner they closed with the southrons, the sooner the engines wouldn't matter any more. And the enemy didn't have enough engines to stop the charge cold—he gauged such things with the practiced eye of a man who'd gone toward a good many strongly held positions.

Now he was close enough to see individual southron soldiers—and they were close enough to start shooting at his comrades and him. A few of them had yellow hair under their gray caps. Was one of them Rollant, his runaway serf? *I should have killed him, back there near the River of Death.*

A few field engines had come along with the

northerners' hastily mustered force. A stone landed among the southrons, and suddenly there was a gap, three men wide, in their line. More soldiers in baggy gray pantaloons strode forward to fill it.

With a buzz like that from the wings of an angry hummingbird, a crossbow quarrel zipped past his head. They started shooting, too, shooting as they advanced. The waiting southrons were bound to be more accurate, but some of the bolts from the advancing northerners struck home, too. A gray-clad soldier threw up his hands and pitched over backwards.

Ormerod yanked his sword from its scabbard. Before long, this work would be hand to hand. "King Geoffrey!" he yelled, and let out another roar.

"King Avram!" the southrons shouted. That only made Ormerod more furious. That they should want to be ruled by someone who would twist the ancient laws and customs of Detina all out of shape was bad enough in and of itself. That they should want to force Avram's rule on the part of Detina which wanted nothing to do with him was much, much worse, at least to Ormerod's eyes.

"Provincial prerogative!" he cried.

"Freedom!" the southrons yelled back.

"How is it freedom when you want to take my gods-damned serfs off my gods-damned land?" Ormerod demanded. He didn't get an answer to that, or at least not a carefully reasoned one. His regiment and the southrons collided, and the argument between them went on at a level much more basic than words.

He stabbed a southron in the shoulder. The fellow howled like a wolf and twisted away, blood darkening his tunic. The men of Ormerod's regiment and the southrons pounded away at one another with shortswords and with crossbows swung club-fashion.

They kicked and bit and punched and wrestled and cursed one another as they grappled.

"Come on, boys!" Ormerod yelled. "We can do it!"

But more southrons, some armed with crossbows, others with pikes, came up to help hold back King Geoffrey's men. More northerners came forward, too, but not so many: for one thing, the southrons seemed to have more men on the spot, and, for another, their engines did a better job of hindering the advance of the northern reinforcements.

Back and forth the fight swayed. If the northerners could drive their foes back to and over the pontoon bridge, the southrons' supply route to the east would break once more. If not . . . Ormerod preferred not to think about *if not*. All he thought of was the man just ahead of him and, after that son of a bitch fell to his sword, the next closest southron. He stormed past the body of the soldier he'd just slain, shouting, "King Geoffrey! Provincial prerogative forever!"

Then, to his horrified dismay, a new shout rose off to the flank: "Unicorn-riders! Southron unicorn-riders!"

His men and the men close by all howled in alarm. A compact group of soldiers had little trouble holding unicorns at bay, but the beasts and the warriors aboard them could be dangerous to men in loose order, especially when those men were already fighting for their lives. He saw a couple of men in Geoffrey's blue break off their struggle with the southrons and speed toward the rear.

"No!" he cried. "Stand your ground! It's your best chance!"

But they would not listen to him. And they were the first of many. Before long, it wasn't a matter of driving the southrons back over their pontoon bridge.

Rather, the struggle was to keep the enemy from turning victory into rout.

Cursing, Ormerod had to fall back or risk getting cut off from his comrades and captured or killed. He shook his fist toward the east, toward the unicorn-riders who'd ruined his side's chance for a win. A moment later, he was cursing even louder and more sulfurously.

"Stand!" he shouted. "Stand, gods damn you! Those aren't unicorns! Those are a bunch of wagon-hauling asses, and you're a bunch of stupid asses for letting them panic you like this! Stand!"

His men, King Geoffrey's men, would no more stand their ground than they'd listen to him. They thought they knew what had happened, and they weren't about to let facts bother them when their minds were made up. They streamed back toward Sentry Peak.

Ormerod kept on cursing, which did him no good whatever. And then, hating himself, hating his men, and hating the asses most of all, he joined the retreat. "We've got trouble here," he growled to Lieutenant Gremio. He wished Gremio would have argued, but the other officer only nodded.

There were times when Lieutenant General Hesmucet wondered why his parents had named him after the blond chieftain who'd fought the Detinans so ferociously during the War of 1218. When he was a boy, he'd had endless fights because of his name. Now that he was grown to be a man, he found it more useful than otherwise: people remembered him on account of it.

And he aimed to be remembered. He looked back at the long column of men in King Avram's gray he led. They'd started out from their base by the Great River when news of the disaster north of Rising Rock reached them. Now, at last, after much travel by glideway and a good deal of marching, they'd come east to Rising Rock to help General Bart defend the place against the traitors and drive them out of Franklin and back into Peachtree Province.

Hesmucet took one hand off the reins of his unicorn and scratched his close-cropped dark beard. Even after two and a half years of war, he found the idea that the northerners were traitors to the Kingdom of Detina strange. When Geoffrey declared himself king in Avram's despite, Hesmucet had been provost at a military collegium up in the north. His friends there had tried to persuade him to fight for Geoffrey, but he hadn't been able to bear the thought of tearing the kingdom apart like a chicken wing. He'd gone south once more to take service with Avram, and none of the northerners had tried to stand in his way.

His aide-de-camp rode up to him and said, "Sir, we're coming up to the battlefield by Brownsville Ferry."

"Yes, I can see that for myself, Major Milo; thank you," Hesmucet said. "I didn't think those bodies scattered over the ground had got there by themselves."

Major Milo flinched a little. Anyone who dealt with Hesmucet had to deal with his sharp tongue. "It was a noble victory," the aide-de-camp said. "Two noble victories, in fact."

Hesmucet shrugged. "It was a battle. Battles are hells on earth, nothing else but. We may need to fight them, but we don't need to love them."

Milo said, "If you don't mind my saying so, sir, that strikes me as an . . . unusual attitude for a soldier."

"I don't mind your saying so—why should I?" Hesmucet replied with another shrug. "But I know the kind of business I'm in. Do you think a garbage hauler expects to stay clean as he goes about his job?"

Milo must have thought he'd gone too far. His voice was stiff as he said, "We don't haul garbage, sir."

"No, indeed." Lieutenant General Hesmucet waved at the field, and at the twisted, bloated, stinking corpses lying on it. The motion disturbed a few ravens close by. They flew up into the air with indignant croaking squawks. "We don't haul garbage, Major. We make it."

His aide-de-camp pondered that, then shook his head, rejecting the idea. Hesmucet laughed quietly to himself. Major Milo came from a family with noble blood, and naturally looked on war as a noble pursuit. Hesmucet had a different view: to him, war was what you needed to do when the fellow with whom you were arguing wouldn't listen to reason. You hit him, and you kept on hitting him till, sooner or later, he fell over. Once he went down, he wouldn't argue any more.

Several asses had been put out to graze among the unicorns. Hesmucet pointed their way. "What's that in aid of?" he wondered aloud. "They're supposed to be kept off by themselves."

"Shall I find out, sir? I see some of our men nearby there," Major Milo said. He might be prissy, but he was conscientious.

And Hesmucet had had his bump of curiosity tickled. "Yes, why don't you?" he said, and rode off to one side of the track so his men could keep moving while he waited. Milo trotted his unicorn over to the soldiers watching the foraging beasts, spoke briefly with them, and then came back toward Hesmucet. To the general's surprise, his aide-de-camp wore a grin. "What's so funny?" Hesmucet called.

"Well, sir, it seems those asses *are* unicorns, in a manner of speaking." Sure as hells, Major Milo was grinning.

"They sure look like asses to me." Hesmucet was a man for whom what he saw, and only what he saw, was real.

But now Milo laughed out loud. "Oh, but sir, those asses are *brevet* unicorns. They broke loose from their wagons during the last fight, and they helped panic Geoffrey's men, so they've been promoted for the duration."

"I see." Hesmucet laughed, too. "I quite like that, Major. Already more brevets in this war than you can shake a gods-damned stick at."

Detina's regular army, its professional army, was tiny. Through most of the kingdom's history, its main role had been to subdue the wild blond tribes in the far east. But now both King Avram and Grand Duke Geoffrey had recruited vast hosts to enforce their vision of what Detina ought to be. A man who'd been a captain in the regular army might command a division these days. He'd be breveted a brigadier or even a lieutenant general.

But, unless his sovereign chose to confirm that rank among the regulars, he'd go back to being a captain when the war finally ended, if it ever did, with only a captain's pay and only a captain's prospects, and very likely with all his chances for glory behind him forever. Hesmucet knew a good many human asses breveted up beyond their proper rank, so why not the kind that went on four legs as well? Who could guess what sort of unicorns they'd make?

"Well, I hope they enjoy their privileges," he said, and used the reins and the pressure of his knees to urge his own veritable unicorn forward to the head of his army. Major Milo stuck close by his side. There ahead lay the pontoon bridge Bill the Bald had stretched across the river. The unicorns' hooves thudded on it. Shading his eyes with his hand, Hesmucet could see Rising Rock ahead.

"There'll be a great wailing and gnashing of teeth among the traitors when they find out we're here," he said.

His aide-de-camp nodded. "They haven't been able to keep reinforcements out, and they haven't been able to keep supplies out, either. I think they're going to be sorry before very long."

"So do I," Hesmucet agreed. But then he checked himself. "Of course, General Guildenstern no doubt thought the same cursed thing. Still, General Bart will have a lot more to throw at the northerners than Guildenstern did—and he'll do a better job with what he's got, too, unless I miss my guess."

As if to underscore his words, the troopers he led began marching over the bridge that led toward Rising Rock. Their footfalls were a dull thunder—Hesmucet glanced up to the sky, thinking of the might of the Thunderer—that went on and on and on. No traitors were about to hear that sound, but it would have brought only dismay to them if they had.

General Bart met Hesmucet at the eastern outskirts of Rising Rock. "Good to see you," Bart said, a broad smile on his face. "Now we have the old team back again."

Hesmucet clasped his superior's hand. "Good to be here, sir. We've always whipped the traitors when we fought them together. I don't see any reason why we shouldn't do it again."

"I hope you're right." Bart eyed the long columns of men in gray tunics and pantaloons tramping into Rising Rock. "Now that you're here, now that Thraxton can't starve us out of this place any more, we're going to give it a try, anyhow."

"We've beaten Thraxton before. We can beat the son of a bitch again," Hesmucet said. Bart frowned slightly: not so much a turning down of the mouth as a vertical line between his eyebrows. He was as hard-driving a general as any, but he had little taste for harsh language.

But he was also willing to make allowances for Hesmucet he wouldn't have for most officers. "I think our chances are good," he said. "Doubting George could have held Rising Rock against Thraxton the Braggart by himself, provided only that Thraxton didn't cut off his victuals altogether. We've got his army—he has command over what was Guildenstern's whole force—and the divisions Fighting Joseph brought from the west (if Duke Edward sent James of Broadpath here, we could afford to bring men east, too), and now you're here as well. When we hit, we'll hit hard."

"That's what the whole business of war is all about, sir," Hesmucet said.

"I *am* glad you're here, by the gods," Bart said. "When it comes to matters of fighting, we think alike, you and I. There's no one better than Lieutenant General George for receiving a blow from the enemy, but he's slower than I wish he were when it comes to striking. And as for Fighting Joseph . . ."

Voice dry, Hesmucet said, "I don't expect King Avram is brokenhearted at having an excuse to send

Fighting Joseph out here to the east, a long way away from Georgetown and the Black Palace."

"I don't expect you're wrong." Bart's voice was dry, too. "I don't suppose he could have tried a usurpation after losing at Viziersville this past spring, but I don't suppose he was very comfortable to have around just the same."

"No doubt that's so, sir." Hesmucet leaned forward in the saddle. "Will he give *you* trouble?"

"He may," Bart answered. "He thinks of glory for himself first and everything else afterwards. He always has; it's the way the gods made him. He will try to seize as much independent command as he possibly can—that's the way the gods made him, too. But he will also fight hard. I know that. He didn't get his nickname for nothing. I don't mind him getting some of what he wants, so long as he gives me what I want."

Hesmucet chuckled. "Well, sir, if any man can keep asses and unicorns in harness together, you're the one." He snapped his fingers. "And speaking of which, did you hear about the asses breveted as unicorns?"

"I did indeed," Bart said. "By all accounts, they deserve their brevets a good deal more than some two-legged officers who've got them."

"I thought the very same thing," Hesmucet said. "I wouldn't be surprised."

"Come into the city now," Bart urged. "I'll show you the enemy's dispositions north and west of here, and we can start planning how best to strike them."

"Nothing I'd like better, sir," Hesmucet said. "Is it true that Ned of the Forest isn't leading the traitors' unicorn-riders any more? I heard that, and I believed it because I wanted it so much, but is it so?"

Bart nodded. "It is. Thraxton, you know, will quarrel with anyone."

"That he will," Hesmucet said. "I'm not sorry he quarreled with Ned. I don't know where Ned's gone—"

"Off toward the Great River, I hear, while you were coming this way," Bart told him.

"Is that a fact?" Hesmucet said. "Well, our unicornriders over there can try to get rid of him. I don't think we'll ever have peace in Franklin or Cloviston till Ned of the Forest is dead. But to the hells with me if I'm sorry we won't be facing him here. He'd make bringing supplies into Rising Rock a much tougher job than it is now, and you can't tell me any different."

"Nobody ever could tell you any different about anything," Bart said. "That's one of the things that makes you a good soldier."

"I don't know about that, sir." Hesmucet plucked at his beard as he pondered. "I have my doubts, in fact. You have to keep your eye on the enemy every minute, or else he'll make you sorry."

"That's not what I meant," Bart said. "Of course you keep your eye on the enemy. But you do what *you* want to do; you don't do what he wants you to do. You always try to make him dance to your tune." He laughed. "I try to do the same, the only difference being that I can't recognize my tune even if a band starts playing it right in front of my face."

"Ah." Hesmucet ignored the feeble joke, whose like he'd heard before, to bring his wit to bear on the essence of what Bart said. "I think you're right. That's the way you've run your campaigns—I know that for a fact."

"All but once, when Ned got into my rear as I was

coming north along the Great River," Bart said. "Ned fights the same way, and when he hits a supply line, it *stays* hit, by the gods. I had to pull back. It was that or starve."

"But you went north again later, after Ned rode off somewhere else," Hesmucet said. "Ned left. You stayed. And you won: King Avram holds every inch of the Great River these days, and what Geoffrey wanted to be his realm is torn in half."

"If you keep moving forward, if you make the foe respond to you, good things are pretty likely to happen," Bart said. "And if you keep your army together. General Guildenstern is a brave officer—no one ever said differently—but he split his in three pieces, and he's lucky worse didn't happen to it. I make plenty of mistakes, but I won't make that one."

"No, I don't suppose you would, sir," Hesmucet said. "You haven't made many mistakes, not that I've seen." From many men, that would have been flattery. He made it a simple statement of fact, and wouldn't have said it if he hadn't believed it.

"Thank you kindly," Bart told him. "Now would you care to ride into Rising Rock with me?"

"I would indeed," Hesmucet said, and into the town they rode without the least concern for whose rank was higher than whose.

Count Thraxton was not a happy man. Count Thraxton rarely was a happy man, but he found even more reasons for gloom than usual when he peered east from Proselytizers' Rise toward Rising Rock. Oh, on the surface things looked good enough. King Geoffrey had sustained him in his command. He'd got rid of the officers who'd libeled him to the king. Everyone who led men under him was either loyal to him or knew how to keep his mouth shut in public.

And yet . . . He knew the grumbling went on. He didn't need any great skill in magecraft to understand that. His officer corps might be cowed, but it was not satisfied. The only thing that would satisfy his officers was marching into Rising Rock. And how was he supposed to manage that?

*You should have done it after we beat the southrons by the River of Death.* He could still hear his officers bleating like so many sheep. He looked up into the heavens, toward the mystical mountain beyond the sky where the gods lived. "You tell me, Thunderer; you tell me, Lion God: how was I supposed to make my army move fast when the enemy had just shot one man in four?" he said. A sentry gave him a curious look. His glare sent the man back to dutiful impassivity in a hurry. If it hadn't, Thraxton would have done a great deal more than just glare.

The gods didn't answer him. They never did. That might have been one of the reasons he was always so melancholy, so bad-tempered. *The gods speak to an idiot like Leonidas the Priest. He says so, and I believe him. But they will not speak to me, not face to face. What does that say about Leonidas? What does it say about me? Even more to the point, what does it say about the gods?*

A messenger came up to Thraxton. "Excuse me, your Grace," the fellow said. "I have here Earl James of Broadpath's report on the failed attack against the southrons by the Brownsville Ferry a few days past." He held out a couple of sheets of closely written paper.

"Thank you so much," Thraxton said, accepting the papers with a sour sneer. "I shall be fascinated to learn how the brilliant Earl James, schooled under the even more brilliant Duke Edward, explains away the ineptitude that kept him from success."

"Er—yes, sir," the messenger said, and left in a hurry.

Thraxton needed hardly more than a glance at the report to see how James exculpated himself: partly by blaming Leonidas the Priest, and partly by complaining he hadn't had enough men to do the job Thraxton had set him. Thraxton's sneer grew wider. *You don't think it's so easy when you're in command, do you? But you expected the sun and moon from me.*

All at once, his revulsion against James swelled to the point where it was more than he could stand. He shouted for a messenger. The one who came running looked suitably apprehensive. "Let the illustrious James of Broadpath know I require his presence at his earliest convenience," Thraxton said.

"Yes, sir." The runner trotted off to do Thraxton's bidding, obeying without fuss or back talk. *If only the rest of the Army of Franklin would do the same.*

James of Broadpath came, but in his own sweet time. It was a couple of hours before he guided his big, ungainly unicorn up to Count Thraxton's headquarters. When he slid down—to the poor beast's obvious relief—he saluted and said, "Reporting as ordered, sir."

"So you are," Thraxton said. "Good of you to do so—at last." James glowered, but could only glower. Thraxton went on, "I have a new task in mind for your wing, your Excellency." *One that will get you out of my hair for some time to come.*

"Sir?" James of Broadpath said.

He was giving Count Thraxton as little as he could;

Thraxton saw that at once. *Go ahead, James, wriggle on the hook as much as you care to. It will do you no good.* "As I said, I have something special for you, your Excellency, and for the soldiers you brought here from the magnificent Army of Southern Parthenia."

By the way he said it, he reckoned that army something less than magnificent. James heard that, but could only frown as he replied, "I shall endeavor to do anything you may require of me, your Grace."

"So you showed by the Brownsville Ferry," Thraxton said, for the pleasure of watching James scowl and fume. "What I have in mind this time, however, is a more nearly independent command for you."

"Ah?" James of Broadpath said. Thraxton didn't smile, though another man might have. The fish was nibbling at the hook. After plucking his bushy beard, James went on, "Tell me more."

*Hooked, sure enough,* Thraxton thought. Aloud, he said, "Whiskery Ambrose has been making a nuisance of himself for some time now, southwest of us in Wesleyton. I purpose detaching your force from the Army of Franklin and sending you forth to lay siege to him there or to drive him from our land altogether."

Earl James frowned. "I see the need for doing it," he said at last, "but I have to say, your Grace, that I question the timing."

"How do you mean?" Thraxton always bristled when anyone questioned him.

"Do you really want to detach a large part of your force when the southrons are bringing fresh soldiers into Rising Rock?" James asked. "If you were going to send me against Wesleyton, you might have done better to try it just after we won at the River of Death."

"Back then, you were all for my moving men east of Rising Rock, not to the southwest," Thraxton reminded him in tart tones.

"I was all for your doing *something*, your Grace," Earl James said. "I was all for your doing *anything*, as a matter of fact. Sitting in front of Rising Rock frittering away the time does King Geoffrey's cause no good."

Count Thraxton glared at him. Sacking James of Broadpath wouldn't be easy. Thraxton didn't care to squabble with Duke Edward of Arlington, who was even more likely than he to have the king's ear. But he could send James away. He could—and he would. "I judge a move against Wesleyton to be in our best interest at this time. Too many would-be betrayers in western Franklin take aid and comfort from having Whiskery Ambrose and his army close by."

"That's so," James said. Had he denied it, Thraxton would have called him a liar on the spot. Most of Franklin was and had been strongly for Geoffrey, but the mountainous west, where there were few estates of any size and only a handful of serfs, remained a hotbed of Avramist sentiment.

"Well, then," Thraxton said, as if it were all settled.

But James of Broadpath persisted, "They can't hurt us here. A screen of unicorn-riders could keep Whiskery Ambrose away if he got a rush of brains to the head and tried to move on Rising Rock. Ned of the Forest was doing fine there. Shouldn't we settle more important business in these parts before we go on to the less?"

"I want Wesleyton taken," Thraxton said. "I want Whiskery Ambrose killed or chased away. And, your Excellency, it is my express command that you undertake this campaign against him." *Because, your Excellency, I want you and your carping criticism as far away from me as possible.*

James of Broadpath gave him a precisely machined salute. "Yes, sir," he said, no expression whatever in his voice. "When is it your express command that my force and I should leave for Wesleyton?"

"Day after tomorrow," Thraxton answered. "Go down there, settle with Whiskery Ambrose, and return once he is beaten—but not until then. Do you understand me?"

"Yes, sir," James said, as tonelessly as before. "And if you are attacked while I'm operating against Wesleyton?"

"I assure you, your Excellency, this army is capable of defending itself," Thraxton said. "Our positions are as strong as the craft of field fortification allows them to be. Do you deny that? How could an enemy possibly hope to sweep up the slopes of Proselytizers' Rise with fierce, alert soldiers shooting at him from the top?"

"I don't know, your Grace, and the gods grant that we need never find out," James replied. He saluted Count Thraxton. "If you would have me go, sir, I shall, and do what I can for the kingdom."

"Good," Thraxton said, which earned him another sour look from the officer from the Army of Southern Parthenia. Muttering something his bushy beard muffled, James of Broadpath mounted his burly unicorn and rode away.

Once he was gone, Thraxton called for two more runners. To one, he said, "Tell Roast-Beef William I would see him at once." He told the other, "Order Duke Cabell of Broken Ridge here immediately." Both messengers saluted and went to do his bidding.

Thraxton enjoyed nothing more than sending men to do his bidding.

Roast-Beef William, who'd taken over for Leonidas the Priest, reported to Thraxton fast enough to keep even that sour-tempered soldier reasonably sweet. His other nickname was Old Reliable; he'd written the tactical manual on which both Geoffrey's army and Avram's based their evolutions.

"What can I do for you, sir?" he asked now. His fondness for big chunks of meat had given him his more common sobriquet, but he also had a red, red face.

"I would sooner wait for the duke," Thraxton replied. "Then I need say this only once." Roast-Beef William just shrugged and nodded. He got on well with almost everyone. He got on well enough with Thraxton, which proved the point if it wanted proving.

Cabell of Broken Ridge strode up to Thraxton's headquarters only a couple of minutes later. He now commanded the wing Dan of Rabbit Hill had led before. Count Thraxton had hesitated more than a little before naming him to the post, not least because his blood was higher than Thraxton's. When old King Buchan died, there'd been some talk in the north of raising Cabell to the throne, though Geoffrey soon solidified his claim to rival Avram. Cabell seemed content as one of Geoffrey's officers. Thraxton, who was never content himself, mistrusted that, but found no better choice despite his misgivings.

"At your service, your Grace," Cabell said now, bowing courteously. He was a darkly handsome man with a round face and long, dark mustachios that swept out like the horns of a buffalo.

"Good," Thraxton said. Cabell hadn't got there fast enough to suit him, but hadn't been so slow as to disgrace himself, either. And Thraxton was much more cautious about offending a duke than he would have been with an earl or a baron or a man of no particular breeding like Roast-Beef William.

"What's in your mind, sir?" Old Reliable asked now.

"I have ordered James of Broadpath south and west to strike against Whiskery Ambrose at Wesleyton," Thraxton answered. "After he has beaten Ambrose, he will return here or strike farther south, as opportunity presents itself."

"That's a bold strategy, sir," Cabell of Broken Ridge said.

"Bold, yes. Bold but risky." Roast-Beef William plucked at his graying beard. "We could find ourselves in trouble if the southrons strike while James is away. Dividing your force in the face of the enemy . . . It's how Guildenstern came to grief, you know."

"But Guildenstern did not know where we were." Thraxton pointed down toward Rising Rock. "We see everything the southrons do at the moment they do it. They cannot possibly surprise us."

"With our position, we can hold them anyhow," Cabell said.

"I hope you're right, your Grace," Roast-Beef William said.

"Of course I am." Cabell of Broken Ridge had no doubts whatever.

Thraxton always had doubts. More often than not, he had doubts about the men who served under him. He said, "We can hold, and we shall hold, provided that my wing commanders stay alert to any movement the southrons might seek to prepare." He spoke as if expecting to discover Cabell and Roast-Beef William snoring in their tents: if he couldn't find a quarrel any other way, he would make one.

Roast-Beef William only shrugged; he never had been a quarrelsome sort. But Duke Cabell, predictably, bristled. "Why did you pick us to command the wings, if you didn't think we could do what you wanted?" he demanded.

Hearing the question made Thraxton regret his choice. He snapped, "That's my concern, not yours."

"Gentlemen! Gentlemen!" Roast-Beef William said in some alarm as Thraxton and Cabell glared at each other. "Remember, gentlemen, the more we fight among ourselves, the happier General Bart will be down there in Rising Rock."

Duke Cabell of Broken Ridge nodded and half bowed. "That is well said, sir, and I shall try to take it to heart."

"If my subordinates were more subordinate and less insubordinate, we should not have these problems," Thraxton said. Roast-Beef William coughed gently, from him as strong as a string of oaths from another man. Thraxton turned his scowl on the other officer, but the man called Old Reliable looked back out of steady and innocent eyes, and Thraxton was the first to look away. He gave a slow, reluctant nod. "As you say, William. The point *is* well taken."

"Thank you, sir," Roast-Beef William said. "And I know one other thing we should do."

"And that is?" Thraxton's voice got some of its usual rasp back. If Roast-Beef William presumed to try to give him orders . . .

But the wing commander said, "Sir, we should pray to the Thunderer to keep the weather good, so we can go on watching Rising Rock," and Count Thraxton found he had to nod.

❖　　　❖　　　❖

Earl James of Broadpath and his men marched south and west out of Rising Rock in the midst of a driving rain. The autumn had been mild up till then. "Just my luck," he muttered under his breath, as rain beat down on his broad-brimmed traveler's hat. "Just my fornicating luck."

"Sir?" said an aide riding nearby.

"Never mind," James replied. "Just talking to myself. In the temper I'm in, I'm the only one I'm fit to talk to."

His heavy-boned unicorn squelched along. When the rain first started falling, he hadn't been sorry; it would lay the dust on the road. But, of course, more than a little rain was worse than none at all when it came to movement, for it quickly turned roads to bogs. This one was well on the way. And James of Broadpath rode at the head of the army. Once some thousands of footsoldiers had churned up the mud, how would the asses and unicorns hauling supplies and siege engines fare? None too well, and James knew it.

"Glideway," he said, again more to himself than to anyone else. "We have to get to the glideway port at Grover. Once we do, we'll be all right." Grover was thirty miles away: less than two days' march in good weather, considerably more than two days' march through muck.

How much more, James soon discovered. His weary, filthy men got into the little town in north-western Franklin on the fourth day out from Pros-elytizers' Rise. He rode to the glideway port there. At the port, he discovered that none of the glideway carpets he'd been promised were anywhere about.

At that point, he lost his temper and began bellowing like a bull just before a sacrifice. His roars routed out a buck-toothed clerk who looked like nothing so much as a skinny, frightened rabbit. The poor clerk's terror meant nothing to James. "Where in the seven hells are my carpets, you son of a bitch?" he roared.

"Sir, I don't know anything about them," the clerk quavered.

"Well, the Lion God rip your throat out, why don't you?" James said. "If the fornicating glideway clerk doesn't know where the devils my stinking carpets are, who the devils does?"

"All glideway carpets in the military district of the Army of Franklin are under the personal control of Count Thraxton, sir," the clerk said.

James of Broadpath clapped a hand to his forehead. "He was supposed to send them here, or enough to let my ragtag and bobtail deliver some sort of attack on Whiskery Ambrose up in Wesleyton. How in the hells am I suppose to deliver any sort of attack on him if half my men drown in the mud before we get to Wesleyton?"

"I wouldn't know about that, sir," the glideway clerk said primly. "No, sir, I wouldn't know about that at all. If you want to find out about that, sir, you'd have to take it up with Count Thraxton his own self."

"I thought I bloody well had, before I started for this miserable, stinking hole in the ground of a village," James snarled. The clerk looked furious—in a rabbity sort of way—but James was too irate himself to care a copper for his feelings.

At that moment, a scryer came up to James and said, "Excuse me, your Excellency, but I've just received a message from Count Thraxton's scryers, inquiring as to where we are and asking why we haven't made better progress toward Wesleyton."

James of Broadpath stared at the sorcerer. His expression must have been something to behold, for the fellow drew back in alarm. "He complains that we haven't got closer to fornicating Wesleyton?" he whispered.

"Yes, sir," the scryer answered.

"Oh, he does, does he?" From a whisper, Earl James' voice rose to a deep-throated rumbling roar, rather like the precursor to an earthquake, that sent both the scryer and the glideway clerk backing away from him in alarm not far from terror. "He does, does he? Why, that . . ." James proceeded to express his detailed opinion of Thraxton's ancestry, likely destination, and intimate personal habits—matters on which he had nothing save opinions, but those strongly held ones.

"Shall I . . . respond that we're doing the best we can, sir?" the scryer asked when his fulminations finally faded.

"No, by the gods," James said, his outrage kindling anew. "Get your fornicating crystal ball. I'll tell Thraxton what I think of him and his nagging myself, to the hells with me if I don't."

"Sir—"

"Get it!" James shouted, and the scryer fled. When he returned, he had the crystal ball with him. "Good," James said grimly. "Now get me that two-faced son of a bitch, so I can talk with him face to face to face." He laughed at his own wit.

Looking distinctly green, the scryer murmured the spells he needed to activate his crystal ball. An image appeared in it. It wasn't Thraxton's, but that of his chief scryer. James' scryer spoke briefly to him, then said, "Count Thraxton is not available, your Excellency. He's plotting strategy with

Roast-Beef William and with Duke Cabell. The scryer says it's urgent."

Elbowing aside his own scryer, James stared at the fellow who served Count Thraxton. "Plotting, indeed," he ground out. "He is plotting against *me*, and you're welcome to tell him I said so."

"Your Excellency, I am certain you are mistaken," the scryer back by Proselytizers' Rise said smoothly. "Count Thraxton wishes you every success."

"Count Thraxton wishes I would jump off a cliff," James of Broadpath retorted. "Why did he send me out without any proper help on the glideways here?"

"I'm sure that's an oversight on the part of someone else," Thraxton's scryer said.

"Are you? I'm not," James answered. "Who controls routing for the glideways in this part of the kingdom? His Grace does, his Grace and no one else."

"Why would he want you to fail, your Excellency?" the scryer asked. "There's no sense to it, as you'll see if you think about things for just a moment."

"No, eh?" James sounded thoroughly grim. "Why would he send me forth without arranging the glideways unless he wanted me to fail? He has to know I need them; whatever else he is, he's no fool. And why would he order me to hurry without giving me any possible chance to do so? To put himself on the record as hustling me along, that's why. Of course, nothing about the glideways is on the record, is it?"

"I'm sure I wouldn't know, sir," the scryer answered. "I am not privy to Count Thraxton's thoughts."

A lot of those thoughts surely went through him to the officers Thraxton commanded. Even so, James had trouble getting angry at the fellow. He would not have wanted a scryer who blabbed his ideas to the world at large. Still . . . He took a long, deep, angry breath. "You tell Count Thraxton for me that I want to see enough glideway carpets to move my army get here to Grover pretty gods-damned quick. And you tell him that, without those carpets, I can't move against Whiskery Ambrose in Wesleyton. I can't, and I won't. Have you got that?"

"I certainly do, your Excellency," Thraxton's scryer said. "The count will hear of this."

"He'd bloody well better," James rumbled. He made a sharp chopping gesture to his own scryer, who broke the mystical link between the two crystal balls.

Eyes wide, his scryer asked, "Would you really stop the advance on Wesleyton, sir?"

"Of course I would," James growled. "How in the hells can I go on with it unless I've got glideway carpets? If these rains keep up, we'd be a fornicating month getting there by road, and we'll all starve by the time we did." He knew he was exaggerating. He also knew he wasn't exaggerating a great deal.

He got his glideway carpets. They started coming in the next day. That surprised him. He hadn't expected them in the least. Maybe Count Thraxton had some vestigial sense of shame after all. No sooner had that thought crossed James' mind than he shook his head. He wouldn't have bet anything on it that he couldn't afford to lose.

Loading men and unicorns and wagons and engines onto the carpets was another adventure, especially since the rain kept falling—and especially since Thraxton the Braggart kept haranguing James for more speed. James made a point of having his scryer tell Thraxton he was busy whenever the general commanding the Army of Franklin asked for him.

Had he spoken with Thraxton, he knew what he would have said—and he knew the other man would not have cared to hear it.

At last, several days after it should have, James' force started southwest down the glideway. Even that went more slowly than it should have. James didn't know why. The mages claimed the wretched weather had nothing to do with it. But when James bellowed, "What in the seven hells does, then?" they only shrugged and shook their heads.

And, of course, they couldn't simply take the glideway straight to Wesleyton, climb off the carpets, and come out fighting Whiskery Ambrose's men. The southrons were in possession of the glideway for about the last third of the distance to Wesleyton. As soon as James' men got down to the Little Franklin River, the glideway journey was over. They had to go back to being soldiers again.

James of Broadpath hoped Whiskery Ambrose would come out and fight him with his whole army. He'd fought Ambrose when the southrons attacked the Army of Southern Parthenia, and Duke Edward had crushed him without any great effort. Ambrose was unquestionably brave. Having said that, one said everything there was to say about his military virtues. If he'd attacked the position Duke Edward had taken for the next hundred years, all he would have done was kill every southron man born of the next several generations. In the field, in a standup fight, James was sure he could beat him.

But Whiskery Ambrose refused to give James a standup fight. His unicorn-riders and a few foot-soldiers skirmished with James' men, delaying them, falling back, skirmishing again, and again retreating toward Wesleyton. James, who had been frustrated from the very beginning of this misbegotten campaign, soon felt ready to bite nails in two.

Lacking nails, he also felt ready to bite in two the captured southron captain who was brought before him. "Gods damn you, why don't you sons of bitches fight?" he shouted into the man's startled face.

"Sir, you'd have to ask General Ambrose about that," the captain said.

"To the hells with General Ambrose," James said. "If he *is* a general, why doesn't he come out and give battle?"

The captain raised an eyebrow. "If *you're* such a fine general, why don't you make him?" James glared at him. The southron looked back steadily enough. He went on, "General Ambrose has orders to hold Wesleyton, and that is what he intends to do."

Cursing under his breath, James sent the prisoner away. Whiskery Ambrose always followed orders to the limit, presumably because he couldn't come up with any better ideas on his own. Had he been ordered to drive James away, he would have bravely done his best—and played straight into James' hands.

As things were, James had no choice but to press on despite wretched roads and worse weather. He had his orders, too, and he had Count Thraxton back outside Rising Rock nagging him ahead through the scryers. They faithfully delivered all of Thraxton's messages. James ignored some and answered those he couldn't ignore. He didn't want Thraxton to be able to make a case that he'd been derelict.

"I know where the dereliction lies," he told Thraxton's chief scryer. "King Geoffrey will know it, too—you mark my words."

"King Geoffrey and the count are intimate friends," the scryer answered. "You slander Count Thraxton at your peril."

"I fail to tell the truth about him at the kingdom's peril," James retorted. "And his Grace is the greatest slanderer left at large."

"Shall I convey that opinion to him?" the scryer asked acidly.

"Why not?" James said. "He already knows my view of him, and his of me is unlikely to go lower."

"Very well." The scryer did his best to sound ominous. James of Broadpath laughed in his face. The scryer mouthed something that was surely not a compliment. A moment later, the crystal ball in front of James went dark.

He laughed again. He'd had the last word, and he hadn't even said anything.

In spite of everything, he got his army moving again the next morning. The men went forward with a will. They thought they could take Wesleyton. They thought they could do anything. Under Duke Edward, they'd proved they could time and again.

*Can they do it without Duke Edward?* James wondered, and then, even more to the point, *Can they do it under me?* He was going to find out. He'd always longed for independent command. Now he had it, even if not quite under the circumstances in which he'd wanted it.

That afternoon, his little army came up against the outworks around Wesleyton. He looked from them to the keep at the heart of the town, then let out a long, sad sigh. One glance was plenty to tell him Whiskery Ambrose had orders much easier to obey than his own.

❖    ❖    ❖

After Rollant's regiment helped drive the traitors back from the Franklin River and helped open the way for supplies and for the forces led by Fighting Joseph and by Lieutenant General Hesmucet, it had little fighting to do for a while. That suited him fine. He and Smitty made their tent as comfortable as they could, adding scrounged extra cloth to make it more wind- and waterproof and piling up springy, fragrant pine boughs on which they could lie snug and warm in their blankets.

Rollant was sitting in front of the tent spooning up mush mixed with salt pork from his mess tin when somebody not far away let out a cheer. His head whipped around. Several more people started to whoop and holler. A moment later, Rollant did, too.

Smitty stuck his head out of the tent. "What in the hells?" he said. "How am I supposed to write a letter to my folks if you're yelling your fool head off?"

"Captain Cephas is back—for good, this time, looks like," Rollant exclaimed. "See? There he is."

"What?" Smitty said, this time in an altogether different tone of voice. Then he started cheering, too.

The wounded officer made his way through the company, shaking hands with all his men. He remained thinner and paler than Rollant remembered, but he was back, and that was all that mattered. "Good to see you, sir!" Rollant said.

"Good to be seen, believe me." Cephas' hand went to the right side of his ribcage. "For a while there, I didn't think anyone would see me again." He clasped Smitty's hand after Rollant's, and asked him, "Are you still raising trouble?"

"Every chance I get, sir," Smitty said proudly.

"Good. Keep it up," Cephas said with a grin, and went on to the next tent.

Smitty looked about ready to burst with pride. Rollant said, "Remember, now, he won't tell you that when Sergeant Joram brings you up before him."

"Spoilsport," Smitty said. After a moment, he added, "I can think of one man in the company who isn't happy to see the captain again."

"Who, Lieutenant Griff?" Rollant shook his head. "You're wrong, Smitty. I saw him—he was grinning fit to burst."

"So he was," Smitty agreed. "But he's not the fellow I meant. It's Hagen who isn't happy to see Captain Cephas back, and that's because Corliss *is*."

"Oh." Rollant glanced toward the serfs he'd brought in from just outside of Rising Rock. Sure enough, smiles wreathed Corliss' pretty face. And, sure enough, her man scowled at Cephas' back. "I don't like that," Rollant said. "I don't like that one bit, as a matter of fact. That could be trouble. It could be a lot of trouble."

"You're repeating yourself," Smitty remarked. "Not only that, you're saying the same thing over and over."

"Well, what if I am?" Rollant said. "I'll tell you something else—once. I wouldn't want to be Captain Cephas if he docs start messing around with Corliss, or even if Hagen just thinks he is."

"You're worrying too much," Smitty said with a dismissive wave. "Gods above, Rollant, Hagen is only a—" Several words too late, he broke off. Even with his swarthy skin, his flush was plain to see.

Rollant took off his cap and displayed his own head of blond hair. "Just in case you'd forgotten, I'm only a serf, too. Only a runaway serf, come to that. If you want to take me across the lines to my old liege lord, you'd put some gold in the pockets of your pantaloons."

"Oh, shut up," Smitty said. "I didn't mean it like that. You've proved *you're* a man, by the gods."

"And Hagen hasn't?" Rollant was unwilling to let it go. "Is that on account of the color of his hair?"

"Gods dammit, it's on account of he's not a soldier." Now Smitty was starting to sound angry, too. "Anybody who's no soldier and tries to take on one of us'll be sorry he was ever born—but not for very long, because it's the last thing he'll ever do."

That held some truth—enough to melt some of Rollant's anger. Not all of it, though. "How long are blonds going to have to keep on proving themselves in Detina?" he asked bitterly. "We didn't invite you black-bearded bastards to sail over here. How long are we going to stay strangers in our own land?"

With anyone but Smitty, that would have put him in trouble. It was one step over the line, or more likely two. Before King Avram succeeded, Rollant never would have dared say such a thing to an ordinary Detinan: he would have been too likely to end up in gaol as an insurrectionary. But Avram had taken over the Black Palace promising to free the northern serfs from their bondage to the land and, by implication, to turn them into something like ordinary Detinans themselves. If that didn't let Rollant speak his mind every now and again, what ever would?

Slowly, Smitty said, "The more you look at things, the more complicated they get, don't they?"

It wasn't an apology, but it felt like a step toward one. Rollant said, "That's what this war is all about— to make sure Detina doesn't stay the way it used to be."

"All I joined up for was to make sure Grand Duke Geoffrey didn't change Detina into two different kingdoms," Smitty said. "That's all most of us joined up for. This other business, it . . . just happened."

Rollant should have got used to being an afterthought in Detinan affairs. He should have, but somehow he hadn't. And, if blonds were an afterthought, why had the north tried to set up its own kingdom to keep them tied to the land?

He almost threw that in Smitty's face, too. Almost, but not quite. A blond who pushed too hard only ended up pounding his head against a wall. And most of Smitty's heart was in the right place. If not quite all of it was, when had the world ever been perfect?

Sergeant Joram strode by. He nodded to Rollant. "Nice day, isn't it?" he remarked.

Incautiously, Rollant answered, "If you ask me, it's chilly."

Sergeant Joram beamed. "Then you need some work to warm you up, don't you? Draw yourself an axe and chop firewood."

"Sergeant!" Rollant said, cursing having grown up in the milder autumns that prevailed down in Palmetto Province. He didn't think Joram was picking on him because he was a blond. Joram picked on people because he was a sergeant, and that was all sergeants were good for—or so things seemed to common soldiers, at any rate.

Incautiously, Smitty laughed at Rollant's fate. Joram beamed at him, too. "Misery loves company," the sergeant observed. "You can chop wood, too."

"Have a heart, Sergeant!" Smitty howled. Joram went on his merry way. For a heartless man, he walked very well. Even the blond warriors who'd fought against Smitty's ancestors had surely known hearts were in short supply among underofficers.

"Misery loves company," Rollant repeated spitefully.

What Smitty said to him was a good deal more pungent than *have a heart*. Smitty didn't have to waste politeness on a common soldier who was a blond to boot.

Mist shrouded the top of Sentry Peak and turned Proselytizers' Rise, off to the west, into a vague dark gray shape hardly visible against the lighter gray of the sky. Smitty, still grumbling at everything, said, "This stinking fog means we can't see what Thraxton the Braggart's up to."

"He can't see what we're up to, either," Rollant pointed out as his axe thudded into a log. "Which counts for more?"

"I don't know," Smitty answered. "But after what that old he-witch did to us there by the River of Death, I want to keep an eye on him every godsdamned minute of the day and night." He attacked the log in front of him as if it were Count Thraxton.

Rollant grunted with effort as he swung his own long-handled axe. Smitty had a point, perhaps a better one than he realized. To Detinans, magic was just another craft, just another skill. A man could be a fine mage in the same way as he could be a good cook. Rollant lived in that world, but wasn't altogether of it. Among his people, magic was more personal, more dangerous. He dreaded a man like Count Thraxton in a way Smitty didn't.

*But when our magecraft met theirs, they smashed ours again and again*, he thought. *That must mean they're right, or closer to right than we were, mustn't it?* However little he liked the idea, he supposed it had to be true.

He'd been sure Joram would come by to see how they were doing. The sergeant smiled sweetly. "Feeling warmer now?" he inquired.

"Just fine," Smitty said. Rollant didn't say anything. Joram might have turned whatever passed his lips into an excuse to pile more work onto his shoulders. Of course, if Joram was looking for an excuse to pile more work onto his shoulders, he could always just invent one.

But he said, "All right, boys, that will do for now. Get Hagen to haul it off to the cooks." He raised his voice to a shout: "Hey, Hagen! Got a job for you."

"What do you need, Sergeant, sir?" The serf treated Joram as if the underofficer were his liege lord. "You tell me what to do, I do it." He grinned. "Not only that, you even pay me to do it." He liked money. And Sergeant Joram had never bothered his wife—if Corliss was bothered.

"Take this firewood to the cooks," Joram said.

"Yes, sir, Sergeant, sir," Hagen said. Joram grinned, enjoying every word of that. Rollant did his best not to grin, too. His amusement sprang from rather different sources. He'd laid flattery on with a trowel a few times himself, or perhaps rather more than a few. He remembered getting out of trouble with Baron Ormerod more than once by pretending Ormerod was just this side of a god. The Detinan noble had eaten it up. What man wouldn't?

As the blond whom Rollant had brought in to the company picked up a big armload of wood, Rollant and Smitty quietly got out of Joram's sight, lest the sergeant find them something else to do. They were gone before Joram bothered to look for them. He could have yelled and called them back, but he didn't bother. He could pick on any common soldier in the company; he didn't need to concentrate on the two of them.

"He's not a bad sergeant," Rollant said.

"There are worse," Smitty allowed. "But there are better ones, too. Some of those bastards only want to sit around and get fat, and they don't make their men work any harder than they do themselves."

"I think you're dreaming," Rollant told him. "Serfs still tell the story of a kingdom out in the east someplace, where the blonds rule everything and they make the Detinans grow things and make things for them. It isn't real. I think most of the blonds who tell the story know it isn't real. But they tell it anyway, because it makes them feel good."

"Turning the tables, eh?" Smitty said, and Rollant nodded. Smitty pointed. "Who's the fancy new tent for? That wasn't here last night."

"Captain Cephas wasn't here last night, either— he was back in Rising Rock," Rollant pointed out, adding, "And you people say blonds are dumb."

Smitty thumped his forehead with the heel of his hand, as if to proclaim himself an idiot to the world at large. "Got to keep the captain feeling good," he said.

Someone came out of the fancy tent: Corliss, Hagen's wife. She looked as if someone—presumably Captain Cephas—had just made her feel good; Rollant had seen that slightly slack smile on his own wife's face too many times after they made love to mistake it on another woman's.

Corliss hurried away, back toward her own, smaller, tent. Smitty pursed his lips to whistle, but no sound came out. That might have been just as well. He turned toward Rollant. "She's not trying to hide it, is she?"

"No." Rollant felt . . . He didn't know what he felt. How many blond women had had to lie down with Detinans since the invaders came over the Western Ocean? How many half-breed serfs remained tied to their noble fathers' lands? More than any man, blond or dark, could easily reckon.

He didn't think Cephas had forced himself on Corliss. He had no reason to think that. By all the signs, she'd been as eager as the officer. That should have made a difference. It did—and yet, it didn't. What Rollant knew to be true had very little to do with what he felt.

As he had before, he said, "There's going to be trouble."

This time, Smitty picked his words with a little more care: "You worry too much, I think."

"Well, let's hope you're right," Rollant answered, which didn't mean he agreed with the other soldier. He wished he knew what to do. He wished he thought anyone could do anything.

"Are we ready?" Lieutenant General Hesmucet demanded.

General Bart shook his head. "Not quite yet," he answered.

"What in the hells are we waiting for, then?" Hesmucet asked. "I'm here. Fighting Joseph is here. We've got unicorn-riders here all the way from Georgetown. What more do we need, sir? A fancy invitation from Thraxton the Braggart?" He was a hot-tempered man, and wanted nothing more than the chance to close with the traitors and beat them.

But Bart shook his head. "We're still light on rations. Harvest is done, and there's no foraging to speak of. I don't want to move without being sure we won't bog down because we're too hungry to go forward."

"Oh, very well," Hesmucet said testily. "How long

do you think we'll need to build up the stores you want?"

"A couple of weeks more, unless Thraxton the Braggart pulls a sorcerous rabbit out of his hat," Bart replied. "And I want to keep an eye on what's happening off to the southwest. I may have to send out a detachment to help Whiskery Ambrose against Earl James. I hope I don't, but you never can tell." He sighed.

"Something wrong, sir?" Hesmucet asked. A sigh from General Bart often had more weight than a tantrum from a man with a spikier disposition.

"Only that I'd really rather not be fighting James," the commanding general answered. "Back in the old army, back in the days when there was just one army, we were the best of friends."

"That sort of thing *will* happen in a civil war, sir," Hesmucet said. "I have plenty of friends among the traitors, too. But that doesn't mean I don't want to lick them."

"It doesn't mean I don't want to lick them, either, as you ought to know by now," Bart said—a sharper comeback than he usually made. "It only means I wish I didn't have to fight James. That's all I said, and that's all I meant."

"Yes, sir," Hesmucet replied, accepting the rebuke.

Bart chuckled. "I know you're not a reporter or anyone else who claims he can read minds."

"Ha!" Hesmucet's answered smile was savage. "That would be funny, if only you were joking. You read what people have to say in the papers, they know what you'll be up to six months from now."

"Oh, I read them all the time," Bart said. "I read them—I just make sure I don't believe them."

Hesmucet laughed out loud. Bart had a deadpan

way of being funny he'd never met in another man.
Here, though, the commanding general gave him a
quizzical stare. He might have been funny, but he
didn't seem to have intended to. Hesmucet said,
"When we do move, we'll whip 'em."

"That's the idea," Bart agreed. "Not much point
to moving unless you move intending to whip the
other fellow and then keep after him. I don't know
why so many generals have trouble with that notion,
but they seem to."

He made it sound so simple. When he fought, he
made it look simple, too. Maybe it was, to him.
Hesmucet felt the same way, and also tried to fight
the same way. Bart was right: a lot of officers on both
sides either wouldn't move at all or moved for the
sake of moving. And when they fought . . .

"If Thraxton had known what to do next after he
beat Guildenstern by the River of Death, this army
would have been in a lot more trouble than it was,"
Hesmucet said.

"Well, I can't tell you you're wrong, because I think
you're right," General Bart said. "When you've got
somebody in trouble, you'd better go after him immediately." He pronounced the word *immejetly*; aside
from an eastern twang, it was one of the very few
quirks his speech had. He nodded, as if to emphasize
the point to Hesmucet. "If you don't go after him, he'll
come after you sooner than you'd like."

"That's the truth," Hesmucet said. "That's the gods'
truth, and we're going to prove it to the Braggart.
And now, if you excuse me, I aim to make sure we're
good and ready to do just that."

"Good." Bart waved a hand in genial dismissal.

For the rest of the day, Hesmucet prowled through
the force he'd brought west from along the Great

River. He made sure the men had plenty of food and the unicorns and asses plenty of fodder. Considering the state Rising Rock had been in before the supply line back to Ramblerton opened up, victuals were his most urgent concern. As he'd expected and hoped, everything there was as it should have been.

But he didn't stop with smoked meat and hard biscuits and hay. He spent a lot of time with the armorers, checking to be certain his men had enough crossbow bolts to fight a battle, and that the siege engines had more than enough darts and firepots.

"We'll be fine, sir," an armorer assured him. "Don't you worry about a thing—we'll be just fine."

"If I didn't worry, we might not be fine," Hesmucet answered, which left the armorer scratching his head in bemusement.

And Hesmucet conferred with his mages. He knew from experience that magecraft got short shrift in most southron armies, sometimes including his own. The south was a land where artificers earned more respect than wizards, and a good many southron generals reckoned that having enough munitions would get them through almost any fight. Sometimes they were right. But sometimes they were wrong— and when they were wrong, they were disastrously wrong.

Hesmucet was not that sort of southron general. Maybe that was because he'd spent some time teaching at a northern military collegium, and seen how important sorcery was to the serf-keeping nobility of the north. If the traitors used it as an effective weapon of war—and they did, over and over again— he was cursed if he wouldn't do the same.

One of his mages said, "You do realize, sir, that we are not fully a match for our northern counterparts.

I am embarrassed to admit that, but I would be lying were I to deny it."

A good many southron generals would have thrown their hands in the air at hearing such a thing. Again, Hesmucet was not that sort of southron general. He said, "Don't worry about it."

"Sir?" the mage said. His colleagues, especially those newly attached to Hesmucet's command, looked startled, too.

"Don't worry about it," Hesmucet repeated. "I don't ask you to beat Thraxton the Braggart all by yourselves with your magecraft. I ask you to make the son of a bitch work hard to get anything past *you*. If we can hold the traitors anywhere close to even when it comes to magic, we ought to whip them, because we're stronger than they are every other way."

Again, the mages—especially the new ones—gaped. "What a refreshing attitude," said the one who'd spoken before.

"I wish more officers had it," another added wistfully.

"Don't fall down on the job, now," Hesmucet warned. "We can't afford to let the traitors ride roughshod over us."

"Of course not, sir," a mage said, as if northern wizards hadn't ridden roughshod over their southron counterparts too many times.

But Hesmucet couldn't rub the sorcerers' noses in that. He was trying to build them up, not to tear them down. He said, "I'm sure you'll all give your best for the king and for Detina."

One of the mages, a youngish fellow with an eager gleam in his eye, stuck up a hand as Hesmucet was about to leave. When Hesmucet nodded to him, he said, "Sir, would it be useful to keep these clouds and this mist around for a while longer?"

"Useful? I should say so," Hesmucet answered. "With the traitors peering down on us from Sentry Peak and Proselytizers' Rise, the more bad weather, the better. But can you do anything about that? By what I've heard, weather magic is a nasty business."

"It is, sir, if you try to make it sunny in the middle of a rainstorm or to bring snow in the summertime," the sorcerer said. "But it's a lot easier to ride the unicorn in the direction he's already going—that's what the proverb says, anyhow, and I think it's true. This time of year, low-hanging clouds and fogs and mist happen all the time around Rising Rock."

"So you can keep them happening?" Hesmucet said, and the mage nodded. Hesmucet stabbed out a finger at him. "But can you keep them happening *and* keep Thraxton the Braggart from noticing you're doing it?"

"I think so, sir," the wizard replied. "He might notice, he or his mages, if they really set their minds to investigating—but why would they? They know the weather around Rising Rock as well as we do—better than we do, in fact. Chances are, they'd just grumble and go on about their business."

"I like the way you think," Hesmucet said. "What's your name?"

"I'm Alva, sir."

"Well, Alva, you just talked yourself into a good deal of work, I'd say," Hesmucet told him. "What happens if Thraxton decides to try a spell to lighten things up around these parts?"

"For one thing, sir, he's working against the way the unicorn's going," Alva answered. "He's a mighty mage, but he could try a spell like that and have it rain for a week afterwards—and he knows it, too. For another, even if he did try his spell and had it work, he probably wouldn't notice mine. And even if he did notice mine, how are we worse off for trying?"

There was a question to warm Hesmucet's heart. "We aren't, by the gods," he said. "Go ahead and take a shot at it, Alva. And you're right—Thraxton's spells have a way of going wrong just when he needs them most."

Some of the other sorcerers congratulated Alva. Rather more of them looked jealous. That surprised Hesmucet not at all. People who wanted to get out there and do things, from all he'd seen, were more likely to draw people trying to hold them back than people trying to push them ahead.

He thought about warning the wizards. In the end, he held his tongue. Again, he was trying not to put pressure on them. *I wouldn't treat my brigadiers so tenderly*, he thought. But mages weren't brigadiers. If you tried to treat a tiger like a unicorn, you'd be sorry.

*And if you treat southrons like men of no account and don't believe they'll do as they said and fight to keep the kingdom one, you'll be sorry.* Hesmucet looked toward Thraxton's headquarters on Proselytizers' Rise and nodded. Thraxton couldn't see or hear him, of course, but he didn't care.

Full of restless energy, Hesmucet hurried back to General Bart and told him what Alva had in mind. Bart nodded. "That's worth a try," he said. "It'll be good, if he can bring it off."

"Just what I thought, sir," Hesmucet said.

Bart nodded again. "And even if it doesn't work, it'll give Thraxton and the other northerners something new to flabble about. Having 'em run every which way after something we're trying is a lot better than letting 'em plan their own mischief and making us pitch a fit."

"That's . . . true." Hesmucet gave the commanding general a thoughtful look. "That's very true, as a matter of fact, and I hadn't thought of it."

"You don't want to make things too complicated," Bart said. "If you push first, the other fellow has a harder time pushing back. And if you've known the other fellow for years, you've already got a pretty good notion of what he'll do and what he won't do. We went to the same military collegium as the traitors' generals. We fought alongside 'em before they tried to pull out of Detina. We know who's smart and who's a fool. We know who's brave and who isn't, and who gets drunk when he shouldn't."

Was he talking about himself? Even more than General Guildenstern, before the war he'd had a reputation as a hard-drinking man. But Guildenstern had kept right on tippling, while Hesmucet couldn't recall seeing General Bart with a glass of brandy or even wine in his hand since the fight against Grand Duke Geoffrey started.

Bart went on, "And, by the gods, we know who can get along with people and get the most of out of them and who can't, don't we?"

At that, Hesmucet threw back his head and laughed out loud. "Now who could you be talking about, sir? The chap who changes his wing commanders the way a dandy changes his pantaloons?"

"Count Thraxton is a fellow with a little bit of a temper on him," Bart said, "and since we know that, we ought to take advantage of it, don't you think?"

He did make things sound simple, simpler than they'd seemed to Hesmucet. He made good sense, too. Hesmucet could see that. He ran a hand along his closely trimmed beard. Maybe, as Bart said, the simple ability to see and to do all the obvious and important things—and to realize they *were* obvious and important—was what set fine generals apart from their less successful counterparts.

*In that case*, Hesmucet thought, *we're in pretty good shape here in Rising Rock.*

"No, no, no," Doubting George said, not for the first time. "I don't mind in the least. This is one of the things that happen in a war."

Absalom the Bear shook his big, shaggy head back and forth, as if he were indeed the great beast that gave him his ekename. "It's not fair, sir," the burly brigadier said. "It's not right. This ought to be your army now. You're the one who made sure it'd still *be* an army."

"It wasn't my army when I did that—not that I did so much," Lieutenant General George replied. "It was General Guildenstern's."

"So it was." Absalom snorted. "And a whole great whacking lot of good *he* did with it, too."

"What should I do—raise a rebellion?" George asked. "If I do, how am I different from Geoffrey?"

After that, Absalom looked like a flustered bear. "I certainly didn't mean you should do anything of the sort, sir."

"I doubted that you did," George said dryly. "If you don't want me leading my soldiers against General Bart and Lieutenant General Hesmucet, what *do* you want?"

"I want you to get the credit you deserve for saving this army," Absalom said stubbornly. "You did that, and everybody knows it. You ought to be commanding here—you and nobody else."

"No, no, no," Doubting George said yet again. He was more flattered than angry, but he knew he had to look more angry than flattered, and he did.

"But why not?" Absalom the Bear demanded. "You saved the army, and—"

"Enough," George broke in. Now he really was starting to get angry. "For one thing, I'm a long way from the only one who's done something like that, you know. Bart saved King Avram's army at Pottstown Pier, sure as sure he did, and that was an even bigger fight than the one by the River of Death."

Absalom tried again: "But—"

"No, no, no." George cut him off again. "I named one thing, but it's the small one. Here's the big one coming up. The big thing, the important thing, the thing that really matters, is that we lick Grand Duke Geoffrey and the traitors. How that happens doesn't matter a copper's worth. *That* it happens is the biggest thing in the world. Have you got that, Brigadier?"

Absalom the Bear was eight years younger than Doubting George, and close to a head taller. Had he so desired, he could have flattened George without breaking a sweat. George knew that. If he knew it, Absalom had to know it, too. But the big, muscular brigadier quailed before him like a young lieutenant taking a dressing-down from the king. "Yes, sir," Absalom said earnestly. "I'm sorry, sir. I didn't mean any harm, sir."

"No one will use me to play the game of factions in King Avram's army. No one," George said. "Have you got *that*?"

"Yes, sir," Absalom repeated. "I . . . I hadn't seen it like that. Now that you point things out to me, I know you're looking at them from higher ground than I was."

"All right, then. I'll say no more about it." But Doubting George held up a forefinger. "No, I will say one thing more after all. If by any chance you have friends who think the same way you did, make it very plain to them that I will not be a party to any of this. I ask no names. I don't want to know. But if there has been some stupid conspiracy, I expect it to dissolve."

"Yes, sir. It will, sir." Absalom the Bear fled as precipitately as most of General Guildenstern's army had when James of Broadpath threw his soldiers into the gap in the southrons' line. But he hadn't fled quite fast enough. He'd told George what George hadn't wanted to hear.

Now alone on the streets of Rising Rock, George sighed. His breath smoked in front of his face. The day, like a lot of days lately, was cool and damp and misty. Maybe that mage Hesmucet had found was doing his job. Maybe the weather would have been like this anyway. How could anyone not a mage tell?

At the thought of Hesmucet, Doubting George sighed again. He did want a larger command, and recognized that the other lieutenant general was more likely to get it. But that mattered only so much. He'd meant every word he said to Absalom the Bear. As a Parthenian, he, like Duke Edward of Arlington, had had to choose between ties to Detina and ties to his province. Unlike Edward, he'd chosen the large kingdom. He knew the choice he'd made, and didn't regret it.

*Smashing the traitors is the most important thing.* Doubting George had to make himself believe that beyond the shadow of a doubt. He'd given up too much not to believe it. He would get his confiscated estate in Parthenia back if Avram beat Geoffrey, but how much would it be worth with the serfs freed, with no hope of bringing in the crops that supplemented his meager army pay?

"I don't care," he said, as if someone had asked him the question aloud. "By all the gods, I don't." If that weren't true, he would have been wearing blue pantaloons and calling Geoffrey his sovereign. And, as if that weren't bad enough, he might have been serving under Thraxton the Braggart. Next to that dreadful prospect, the thought that Hesmucet might gain some extra preferment didn't look so bad.

George looked toward Proselytizers' Rise and then toward Sentry Peak. He couldn't see them, which meant the northerners there couldn't see him, either. He wondered what Count Thraxton was planning. He couldn't have much of an attack in mind hereabouts, not if he'd sent James of Broadpath off towards Wesleyton.

*I wouldn't have done that.* Doubting George shook his head. *No, I wouldn't have done that at all.* He was a defensive fighter, first, last, and always. *You have to be daft to send a big part of your army away when the other fellow is building up his forces. Well, maybe you don't* have *to be daft, but it certainly helps.*

Did Thraxton really think his magecraft could make up for his lack of men? Maybe he did. It hadn't at several other fights, but maybe he did. That, in George's opinion, was another bit of daftness. Well, Thraxton's troubles weren't his, for which fact he heartily praised the gods.

He began walking toward the north end of town, toward the trenches and barricades he'd ordered built after General Guildenstern's army had had to fall back to Rising Rock from the River of Death. Magecraft or no magecraft, anyone who tried to take those fieldworks would have his work cut out for him. The works were stronger now than they had been when first made right after the grinding retreat from Peachtree Province, and better manned, too, but the traitors wouldn't have enjoyed trying to take them even then. No one enjoyed trying to take a position Doubting George chose to defend.

"Here's the general!" someone called from the trenches. Southron soldiers whooped and cheered. A couple of them scaled their hats through the air.

"Careful, boys," George said. "You'll make old Thraxton and his pet he-witches try and curl my beard for me if they find out I'm around."

"And do you think they can do it?" a soldier asked, as if delivering a cue in a play.

"Oh, I have my doubts," George answered. The soldiers cheered louder than ever. They played up the nickname he'd got back at the military collegium, and enjoyed it when he did the same.

"Shut up, you gods-damned noisy fools!" a northern sentry yelled from his post not far beyond the line.

"To the hells with you!" the southrons yelled back, and much else besides. They finally made the enemy soldier so angry, he shot his crossbow at them. The bolt harmlessly buried itself in the ground. A southron added, "And you can't shoot worth a gods-damn, either!"

"Why don't you southron bastards go back to your own kingdom and leave us alone?" the sentry called.

"This *is* our kingdom!" George yelled before any of his men could answer. "Detina is one kingdom. It always has been. It always will be."

"Liar!" the northerner shouted back. "If you think we're going to let that son of a bitch of an Avram turn all our blonds into nobles, you can gods-damned well think again."

"He's never said he wanted to do anything of the kind." George rolled his eyes in exasperation. "All he wants to do is turn them into Detinans."

"That's bad enough!" the sentry said, and shot another crossbow quarrel in the direction of the southrons.

"Don't worry about him, sir," said one of the soldiers in gray tunic and pantaloons. "He shoots at us all the time, but he hasn't hit anybody yet."

"You ought to send out a couple of fellows with knives and get rid of him once for all," George said.

Eyes wide, the soldier shook his head. "By the Lion God, no! If we sneak over and cut that bastard's throat, the stinking traitors are liable to put somebody there who really knows how to handle a crossbow."

"All right." Doubting George yielded the point. He had to fight hard not to yield to laughter, too. "Leave him there, then, if it makes you happy. In that case, though, you have to go on listening to him."

"He's a fool," the soldier said dismissively. But the question he asked next showed he wasn't quite so sure: "Sir, do you think a blond could ever become a Detinan nobleman? Do you think that could ever happen?"

George had his doubts but, for once, didn't voice them. He didn't much care for the idea, but he also didn't tell the soldier that. What he did say was, "I don't know and I don't care and I'm not going to worry about it. Don't you worry about it, either. Like I said, the only thing that matters is holding the kingdom together. If we can do that, the gods will take care of us, right?"

"Yes, sir," the fellow said. "That's a good way to look at things, sir."

"I hope it is," Doubting George said. He hadn't thought about the question the trooper had put to him. He wondered whether King Avram had thought it all the way through. If blonds were to become the same as real Detinans in law, what was to keep them from becoming part of the nobility? What was to keep them, even, from marrying into the royal family? Nothing he could see.

He shrugged. It wasn't his worry, for no blonds would marry into *his* family any time soon. He was perfectly happy with his wife, who was now living in a rented house in Georgetown. He hadn't even tomcatted around his Parthenian estate when he was there, as so many nobles did. Unlike a lot of his neighbors, he wasn't liege lord to young serfs who looked like him.

*How will the blonds make their way in the world if they aren't serfs any more?* he wondered. He shrugged again. He didn't see any of them in this regiment, but he'd had a fair number under his command, and they'd fought as well on Merkle's Hill and other places as anybody else. That had surprised him at first, but one thing he didn't doubt was what he saw with his own eyes.

Having looked over the fieldworks with his own eyes, he went back into Rising Rock. When he got to the hostel where General Bart made his headquarters, Colonel Andy said, "Oh, there you are, sir."

George looked around behind himself, as if he might have been somewhere else. "Well, yes, I think so. What of it?"

"Only that the commanding general's been looking for you, sir," his adjutant replied.

"Ah." That was business. Doubting George nodded.

"Well, he'll probably find me pretty soon. Will he find me in his rooms, do you suppose?"

"Er, yes, sir, I believe he will." Andy suffered George's occasional fits of whimsy in much the same way as he might have suffered a bout of yellow fever.

"Good," George said. "I'll wander upstairs, then, and see if he does find me there." He headed for the fancy spiral staircase, leaving his adjutant scratching his head behind him.

When he knocked on the commanding general's door, Bart opened it himself. General Guildenstern would have, too, but Guildenstern likely would have had to shoo a scantily clad blond wench out of the chamber first. Not being a noble had never stopped him from tomcatting. "Good day, George," Bart said. "Good to see you."

"Good to be seen, sir," George said, deadpan as usual.

Bart scratched his head. His quizzical expression looked very much like Andy's. He rallied faster than George's aide-de-camp had, though, saying, "How would you like to look over the latest plan for attacking Count Thraxton's army?"

"I think I'd like that pretty well, sir," George answered.

"Do you, eh?" Bart said. "I was wondering if you'd tell me you didn't care."

Innocent as a sneakthief who'd seen a judge more times than he could count, George said, "I can't imagine why, sir."

"No, eh?" General Bart's eyes glinted—or maybe it was just a trick of the light. "I doubt that."

"I can't imagine why, sir," George repeated, and stepped into the commanding general's chamber.

✦      ✦      ✦

Rain drummed down out of a chilly, leaden sky. Captain Ormerod's boots squelched in mud when he stepped out of his tent. Peering south from the forward slopes of Sentry Peak toward Rising Rock, he saw rain and mist and not much else. He cursed. Even his curses sounded dull and commonplace and gray.

Then he said, "If this is what licking the southrons up by the River of Death got us, gods damn me to the hells if I don't think we'd've been better off getting whipped."

Lieutenant Gremio was looking south, too, with rain dripping from the brim of his hat and from a threadbare cape some southron didn't need any more. He shook his head. "Losing is always worse," he said, ready as ever for an argument. Sure enough, he was a barrister to the very core of his being.

But Ormerod said, "No. Look at the southrons."

"I can't, not with all this rain and fog." Gremio was also relentlessly precise.

Precision notwithstanding, Ormerod ignored him. "Look at the southrons," he repeated. "They lost by the River of Death. They had to run back here and hole up in Rising Rock. And they went and did things. They brought in more men. They made sure they kept their supply lines open. What can we do to them now?"

"Beat them again," Gremio answered.

"Fine," Ormerod said. "Let's beat them. How do you propose to do it?"

"I'm not a general," Gremio said. "Even you have a higher rank than I do, sir." He let reproach creep into his voice—probably reproach for Ormerod's having that higher rank. "But I am sure those in command must have some notion of how to go about it." Maybe that was where the reproach came from. Maybe. Ormerod didn't believe it.

He said, "If they do, they've done a hells of a good job of keeping it secret from everybody else."

Gremio grunted. He couldn't very well deny that, not when it was staring not only him but the whole Army of Franklin square in the face. At last, sounding a good deal less than happy, he said, "We can only hope that all the changes the army has seen will lead to a happy result."

"Not fornicating likely." That wasn't Ormerod; he and Gremio both jerked in surprise. When Ormerod whirled, he found Major Thersites standing behind them. Thersites could move quiet as a cat when he chose. He stood bareheaded in the chilly rain, letting it drip down his face. "Not fornicating likely," he said again, relishing the phrase. "We had our chance, had it and didn't take it. Now we're just waiting for the other boot to drop—on us."

Ormerod wished Colonel Florizel still commanded the regiment. Florizel was a good, solid fellow; even when he worried, he never showed it. Thersites, on the other hand, spoke his mind in a thoroughly ungentlemanly way—and would gleefully gut anyone who accused him of being ungentlemanly. Picking his words warily, Ormerod said, "It is true that we might have done better after the fight by the River of Death." Finding himself agreeing with Thersites made Ormerod wonder about his own assumptions.

"Better?" Thersites snorted now. "We couldn't have done worse if we'd tried for a year. I've seen plenty of mugs of beer with better heads on 'em than Thraxton the Braggart's got." That jerked a laugh out of Ormerod. Thersites went on, "Not chasing Guildenstern hard—that was plenty smart, wasn't it? And sending James of Broadpath off to the hells and gone when the southrons are getting ready to up and kick us in the ballocks—why, gods damn me to the hells if that wasn't even smarter."

It was true. Every word of it was true. Ormerod knew as much in his belly. He still wished Thersites hadn't come right out and said so. The man had a gift for pointing out things that would have been better left unnoticed.

Gremio spoke with as much care as he would have used before a hostile panel of judges: "I think Count Thraxton ordered Earl James away because the two men had a certain amount of difficulty working together." As a barrister, he saw the world in very personal terms.

Thersites saw it that way, too. He also saw it in very earthy terms. "James is no fool. He knows Thraxton is a dried-up old unicorn turd, same as everybody else with an ounce of common sense does. No wonder Thraxton sent him off to Wesleyton. He knows what a proper general's supposed to be like, James does. Thraxton ran Ned of the Forest out of this army, too, and don't think we won't regret *that*."

He'd complained about Ned's departure before. *Ned*, Ormerod thought, *is what he wishes he were*. Gremio said, "We can't do anything about it now."

"Of course we can, by the Thunderer's hammer," Thersites said. "We can pay for it—and we will." He squelched away.

"What a disagreeable man," Gremio said. But he said it in a low voice. He was right, too, no doubt of that. But being right about a disagreeable man's disagreeability (Ormerod wondered if that was a word, and rather hoped it wasn't) could have disagreeable consequences.

"He says what he thinks," Ormerod observed.

"If that doesn't prove my point, curse me if I know what would," Gremio answered.

Ormerod went back to what they'd been talking about before Thersites made his appearance: "What *are* we going to do here? What *can* we do here, except wait for the southrons to hit us and hope we can beat them?"

"I don't know," Gremio said—not the most common admission for a barrister to make. "As I told you before, I hope our generals do."

"Well, I hope so, too," Ormerod said. "I hope for all kinds of things. But hoping for 'em doesn't mean I'm going to get them. If Count Thraxton doesn't know what in the hells he's doing, he could have fooled me."

Lieutenant Gremio raised an eyebrow. But he was too smooth to contradict his superior too openly. Instead, he changed the subject: "If you had everything you hope for, what would it be?"

"Why, for us to have our own kingdom," Ormerod answered at once. "For us to whip the southrons out of our land. That's what we're fighting for, isn't it?"

"And after we've won the war?" Gremio asked.

"All I want to do is go back to my estate and go on like nothing ever happened," Ormerod said. "That's what we're fighting for, too."

"Well, so it is." But Gremio had an ironic glint in his eye that Ormerod neither liked nor trusted. The barrister from Karlsburg asked an innocent enough question: "How likely do you think that is?"

Ormerod didn't like to reflect any more than he had to. "If we can lick the southrons, why shouldn't things go back to the way they ought to be?"

"They might," Gremio allowed. "They might, but

I wouldn't count on it. And if they don't, it's Avram's fault, the gods chase him through the seven hells with whips forever."

Even Ormerod figured out what he was talking about. "You mean the serfs, don't you? With King Geoffrey running things, they'll fall back into line soon enough, you wait and see."

"I hope you're right," Gremio said. "As I say, though, I wouldn't count on it. Avram's told the blonds they can be free, and they aren't going to forget. Ideas are corrosive things."

"Chasing the serfs through the fields with whips will bring them back into line," Ormerod said. "They've risen up before. We've whipped them every fornicating time they tried it. If we have to, we can bloody well do it again."

"We've done such a good job of sitting on them— the past hundred years especially—that most of them forgot things could be any other way," Gremio said. "It won't be like that any more."

"We can do it," Ormerod repeated, but he didn't sound quite so sure of himself any more. "Or we could do it, anyway, if the southrons didn't keep stirring up trouble in our land. That's another reason to have our own kingdom: to keep them from bothering the blonds, I mean."

"Yes, but can we?" Gremio asked. "If they don't respect provincial borders, why should they care about the bounds between kingdoms?"

With a grunt, Ormerod studied a new idea. The more he studied it, the less he liked it. As Gremio said, ideas were corrosive things. They kept a man from resting easy with the way the world had always worked. "We'd have to conquer the southrons, beat 'em altogether, to keep 'em from meddling. That's what you're saying." He sounded accusing. He felt that way, too.

"We can't conquer the southrons, not in a thousand years," Gremio said. "The south is bigger than we are."

He was right. Ormerod knew it. Keeping Avram's men from conquering the north was hard enough—more than hard enough. "You're saying we'll never have peace!" Ormerod cried in dismay.

Gremio shrugged a barrister's shrug. "I didn't say that. You did."

For a moment, Ormerod accepted the remark. Then he wagged a finger at the lieutenant. Voice sly, he said, "I know what you barristers do. You trick a man into saying what you wanted him to, and then you act like it wasn't your fault at all."

"I haven't the faintest idea what you're talking about." Gremio did his best to sound innocent. His best wasn't quite good enough, for he also ended up sounding amused.

"A likely story," Ormerod told him. "If you don't think we'll ever have peace even if we do lick the southrons, why'd you join the army in the first place?"

"On the off chance I might be wrong," Gremio replied—and to that, Ormerod had no answer whatever.

When he walked off shaking his head, he heard Gremio quietly chuckle behind him. The lieutenant had won this round in their ongoing skirmish, and they both knew it. Ormerod stared south toward Rising Rock. He would have relished a fight with the southrons just then. When he was fighting, he didn't have to think. Encamped—becalmed—here on the lower slope of Sentry Peak, he couldn't do much else. And, little by little, the Army of Franklin had stopped being the force besieging the town. These days, it felt more as if they were the besieged.

He wondered if Rollant was down there somewhere, or if the runaway serf had perished during the fighting by the River of Death. Rollant had been fighting under Doubting George, who'd made the stand on Merkle's Hill. He'd had plenty of chances to come to grief. Ormerod hoped he had. No serf-catcher would bring the blond back to Palmetto Province, not from out of the south. Even before the war, the southrons had laughed at the runaway-serf laws intended to bind blonds to the land. They surely wouldn't pay those laws any attention these days.

"Bastards," Ormerod muttered under his breath. There weren't so many blonds in the south and the southeast; the real Detinans there could afford to pretend blonds were as good, or almost as good, as anybody else. Up in the north, that would never do. Ormerod was as sure of it as he was of the power of the gods. But King Avram, that gods-damned fool, couldn't see it, and so . . .

*And so my crops have gone to the hells these past three seasons*, Ormerod thought resentfully. *And so I'm here in the middle of nowhere, instead of taking care of my estate the way I ought to.* He shook his fist in the direction of the southrons down in Rising Rock. *Why don't you go away and leave us alone?*

But they wouldn't, and so they had to be driven away. Ormerod shook his fist at mist-shrouded Rising Rock again. Then he turned and shook his fist at Proselytizers' Rise, too, and at Count Thraxton's headquarters there. If Thraxton had pursued, maybe . . .

Ormerod heard a thud behind him. He whirled, hand flashing toward his swordhilt. Shaking your fist at a mage wasn't always a good idea, even when the mage couldn't—or wasn't supposed to be able to—see you. And Thraxton the Braggart had always been a bad-tempered son of a bitch. If he somehow knew, if he'd somehow shaped a sending . . .

"Sorry, sir," the blue-clad soldier in back of Ormerod said sheepishly. "Kicked that gods-damned rock hard enough to hurt. I expect I'd trip over my own two feet if there was nothing else handy."

"Heh," Ormerod said, still jumpy. The soldier sketched a salute and ambled away. He didn't know what he'd done to his company commander's peace of mind. Ormerod hoped he never found out, either.

One of the sergeants was doing a good, thorough, systematic job of chewing out a man who'd forgotten something the underofficer thought he should have remembered. The soldier was giving about as good as he got, denying everything and loudly proclaiming that the sergeant hadn't told him about whatever it was and had no business bothering about him anyway, as it shouldn't have been his job in the first place.

Instead of spraying flames all over the place like a firepot, the sergeant said, "Ahh, to the hells with it. What we both want to do is rip another chunk off the gods-damned southrons. Till then, we're just chewing on each other on account of we can't get at them."

"Gods-damned right," the common soldier said. "We'll tear 'em a new one when we do, though." The sergeant grunted agreement. Neither had the slightest doubt in his mind.

And their certainty made a small, tender, flickering hope live in Captain Ormerod.

❖　　　❖　　　❖

General Bart eyed his wing commanders and brigadiers. "Gentlemen, we are just about ready to attack,"
he said. Some of them really *were* gentlemen—
Doubting George, for instance. Bart was a tanner's
son. But he had the rank. That was all that mattered.
If he did the job right, he would keep the rank and
keep on giving orders to his social betters. If he
didn't, he would deserve whatever happened to him.
That was how things worked. It struck him as fair.
But things would have worked the same way even
if it hadn't.

Fighting Joseph said, "Turn me loose, General. Just
turn me loose, and I'll show you what I can do."

"You'll be in the fight, never fear," Bart said.
Joseph's handsome, ruddy face showed nothing but
confidence. Earlier in the year, he'd commanded the
whole western army after Whiskery Ambrose failed
so spectacularly with it. And Joseph had failed, too,
letting Duke Edward of Arlington trounce him at
Viziersville with about half as many men as he commanded. Joseph would never have charge of a whole
army again.

He had to know that. He wasn't a fool—no, he
wasn't that particular kind of fool. But he remained
an ambitious man. He would try to stretch what command he had here in the east as far as Bart would
let him, and then a little further. Bart didn't intend
to let him get away with much of that.

But what he intended and what would actually
happen were two different beasts. Fighting Joseph
had a will of his own, and Thraxton the Braggart had
a will of his own, too—*quite a will of his own*, Bart
thought with wry amusement. Nothing would go
exactly as planned. *No, not exactly. Still and all, I
aim to have* my *will be the one that prevails.*

"Will you be ready to move on Sentry Peak when the day and the hour come?" he asked Fighting Joseph.

"Of course, sir." Joseph sounded affronted. "I am always ready to move."

There Bart believed him. Joseph might prove too aggressive, but he was unlikely not to be aggressive enough. Bart turned to Doubting George. "What about you, Lieutenant General?"

"Give the order, sir, and my men and I will obey it," George replied. "You have only to command."

Bart hoped he meant that. George was no glory hound, as Fighting Joseph was. He made an indomitable defender; they were calling him the Rock in the River of Death these days. But he wasn't so good at going forward as he was at not going back. "I shall rely on you," Bart said, and Doubting George nodded.

"Tell me where to go," George said. "Tell me what to do. By the gods, I'll do it. If you think you have another man who can do it better, give it to him. The kingdom comes before any one soldier."

"Well said," Bart replied. "An example for us all, as a matter of fact." He looked at Fighting Joseph. Joseph stared blandly back, as if he didn't have the slightest notion of what Bart had in mind. Maybe he didn't. Maybe he truly was blind to what other people thought of him. Maybe. Bart wouldn't have bet anything on it he couldn't afford to lose.

Bart wouldn't have bet anything on it anyway. Spirits had been his vice, not rolling dice or a spinning wheel of chance. Fighting Joseph had been rich and then poor several times in quick succession in silver-rich Baha out in the far east. He would gamble on anything, including his superiors' patience.

With some relief, Bart turned away from him and

toward Lieutenant General Hesmucet. "Are you ready to fight?" he asked, already confident of the answer.

Sure enough, Hesmucet nodded. "I've been ready for days, sir. So have my men. We're just waiting for you to turn us loose."

"Don't worry. I intend to," Bart replied. Hesmucet didn't puff himself up the way Fighting Joseph did. He didn't prefer the defensive, as Doubting George did. He wanted to go forward and grapple with the enemy. In that, he was very much like Bart himself. If a strong man and a weak man grappled and kept on grappling, sooner or later the strong man would wear down the weak one.

"When we start fighting the northerners, we have to hit them with everything we've got and go right on hitting them till they fall over," Bart said. "That's what will win the fight for us."

"We shall win glory for King Avram," Fighting Joseph declared.

"As long as we win the fight," Doubting George put in. Bart decided George really didn't care about glory, and that he'd meant what he said when he urged his own replacement if Bart thought that would help defeat Thraxton's men. It wasn't that he had no pride; Bart knew better. But he really did put the kingdom ahead of everything else. Bart had to admire that.

He said, "All right. I think we know what we're supposed to do. That was the point of calling you together, so we're through here. Lieutenant General Hesmucet, stay a bit, if you'd be so kind. I want to talk with you about weather magic when we do attack the traitors."

"Yes, sir," Hesmucet said as the other officers rose from their seats and headed back to their own commands. "At your service, sir."

"At King Avram's service," Bart said, and Hesmucet nodded. Bart resumed: "He made us, and he can break us. That's what being a king is all about."

"Yes, sir," Hesmucet repeated. "But we can make him or break him, too. That's what fighting a civil war is all about."

Had Fighting Joseph said that, he would have meant trying to break the king and seize the throne himself. Hesmucet's mind didn't work that way. Neither did Bart's. He said, "Can we do this the way we've planned it?"

"I think so," Hesmucet answered. "We've got more men. We've got more engines. We've got more of everything, except . . ." His voice faded.

"Except fancy magecraft," Bart finished for him. Hesmucet nodded. Bart shrugged. "Most of the time, it doesn't work the way it's supposed to. If it did, the northerners would have licked us by now."

"I know that," Hesmucet said calmly. "But Thraxton's sure to throw everything he's got at us. He doesn't want to have to fall back into Peachtree Province again."

"We just have to stop him," Bart said.

"Guildenstern couldn't," Hesmucet said. "His mages couldn't, either. If the traitors are playing with loaded dice, we have trouble. You know that's so."

"Yes, I know that's so—if they are," Bart agreed. "But I also know I'm not going to lose much sleep over it. I'll tell Phineas and the others to do their best. That's all they can do. If they do their best, and if our soldiers do *their* best, I think we're going to win."

"Yes, sir." Hesmucet didn't sound as if he believed it himself, not at first. But then he paused, stroking that short beard, hardly more than stubble, he wore. His smile, Bart thought, was quizzical. "Do you know, sir," he said, "there are a lot of generals who, if they said something like that, you'd right away start figuring out what would go wrong and how you'd keep from getting the blame for it. But do you know what? When I listen to you, I think you're going to do exactly what you say you'll do. And if that's not pretty peculiar, to the seven hells with me if I know what is."

"Thraxton the Braggart's just a mage. He's not a god," Bart said. "He makes mistakes, the same as anybody else does. He did it down at Pottstown Pier, and he did it again at Reillyburgh. If we jog his elbow right when he's trying to do three or four things all at the same time, he'll likely do it once more. And if he does, we'll lick him."

"But if he doesn't . . ." Hesmucet still had doubts.

Bart sighed. "Look at it this way, Lieutenant General: the traitors have to do everything perfectly to have a chance of beating us. We can make some mistakes and still beat them. General Guildenstern made every mistake in the book, but they couldn't run him out of Rising Rock even so. Don't you think the Braggart knows that as well as we do?"

"He has to," Hesmucet said. "He's not stupid."

"No, that's never been his trouble," Bart agreed. Both men chuckled. Bart continued, "But it has to weigh on his mind, wouldn't you think? Knowing he's got to be perfect, I mean, knowing he's got no margin for error. It's easy to walk along a board lying in the middle of the road. But take that board to New Eborac and stretch it out between the top floors of a couple of blocks of flats, where you'll kill yourself if you fall off. How easy is it then? The more a mistake will cost, the more you worry about it . . ."

He waited. Either he'd convinced Hesmucet or he hadn't. Slowly, the other officer nodded. "That sounds good to me, sir. Now—did you still need to talk about Alva the weatherworker?"

"No, I don't think so," Bart answered. They both chuckled again. Hesmucet gave a salute so sloppy, some sergeant at the Annasville military collegium would have had an apoplexy seeing it. Bart returned an even sloppier one. When anybody could see them, they stayed formal. By themselves, they were more nearly a couple of friends than two of Avram's leading officers.

After Hesmucet left, Bart sent a runner to summon Colonel Phineas. The army's chief mage arrived looking apprehensive. "You wanted me, sir?"

"I certainly did," Bart said. "I want you and your wizards to start doing everything you can to annoy the Army of Franklin. I want you to make the traitors stretch their own sorcerers as thin as they'll go, and then a little bit thinner than that. Can you do it?"

"Of course we can, sir," Phineas said. "But I don't see how doing it will change things one way or the other."

"Oh, it probably won't," Bart said placidly. "Do it anyhow."

"Yes, sir," Colonel Phineas said. After a moment, he nerved himself to add, "I don't understand, sir."

*Shall I explain?* Bart wondered. *If he's too stupid to see for himself, isn't he too stupid to do us any good?* But, in the end, he relented: "If the traitors are busy putting out lots of little fires all along their line, it'll make them have a harder time noticing we're setting a big fire right under their noses."

"Ah. Deception." Phineas beamed. He could see

something if you held it under his nose and shone a lamp on it. "Very commendable. Who would have thought deception could play a true part in matters military?"

"Anyone who went to the military collegium, for starters," Bart said.

But the army's chief wizard shook his head. "Not from the evidence I've seen thus far, sir. By all the signs, the only thing most officers are good for is bashing the foes in front of them over the head with a rock. . . . No offense, sir."

"None taken," Bart said, more or less truthfully. "We do try to surprise the chaps on the other side of the line every now and again. They try to surprise us every now and again, too, but we try not to let that work."

"Yes, sir." But Colonel Phineas sounded even less convinced than Lieutenant General Hesmucet had. Then the plump, balding Phineas brightened. "Well, we will do what we can, I promise you. Deception? What a conceit!" Off he went, though Bart hadn't given him any sort of formal dismissal.

Colonel Horace came in a couple of minutes later. "What was the old he-witch muttering to himself about?" General Bart's aide inquired. "He sounded happy as a pig rooting for turnips."

"He's amazed that I have some notion of fooling the enemy instead of just pounding him to death," Bart replied. "We do try to play these little games with the least loss we can."

"Of course we do, sir." Horace bristled at the idea that anyone could think otherwise.

"And we'll have the chance to show the northerners just how we play them," Bart said. "Meanwhile, though, the less they see, the better."

"Absolutely, sir." Colonel Horace was fiercely loyal. That made him a splendid aide. "High time they get the punishment they deserve."

"I wish this weren't necessary," Bart said. "I wish we weren't fighting." *Even if that meant you were still a drunken failure? Yes, by the gods, even then.* "But since we *are* fighting, we'd better win. Having two kingdoms where there should just be Detina is unbearable."

"It won't happen." Horace was also an all but indomitable optimist. "When we hit Thraxton, we'll break him."

"May it be so," Bart said. "Our job is to make it so, and we're going to do our job. Wouldn't you agree, Colonel?"

Horace's expression declared that Bart hadn't needed to ask the question. "Thraxton will never know what hit him."

"That's the idea," General Bart said. "I don't want him knowing what's going to hit him, not till it does— and not then, not altogether."


"How are things back by Rising Rock?" James of Broadpath asked Count Thraxton's scryer after that scryer finished relaying Thraxton's latest demand that he take Wesleyton on the instant, if not sooner.

With a shrug, the fellow answered, "The southrons keep throwing little pissant magics at us every which way, so much so that nobody quite seems to know what's going on here right now, sir."

"Oh, really? Why does that not surprise me?" Earl James rumbled. A moment later, he realized the remark was odds-on to get back to Count Thraxton. A moment later still, he decided he cared not a fig. Thraxton the Braggart already knew what he thought of him. Thraxton, James thought, had many flaws, but stupidity was not among them.

"Along with everything else, sir, the weather around here's been so nasty and misty, there could be a southron—or a regiment of southrons—right outside the tent and I wouldn't know about it till the bolts started flying," the scryer said. "That's got something to do with it, too."

"The fog of war," James said vaguely. He forced his mind back to things he could hope to learn: "How is Brigadier Bell doing?"

"Damn me to the hells if he isn't healing up, your Excellency," the scryer answered.

James of Broadpath's eyebrows leaped. "Oh, really?" he said again, this time in honest amazement. Any man who could survive two wounds such as Bell had taken with so little time between them was made of stern stuff. "The gods must love him."

"I don't know about that, sir. He's still in pain, lots of it," the scryer said. "He pours down enough laudanum to knock a tiger on its tail, and it doesn't seem to help much. But he is talking about wanting to command again."

"That sounds like him," Earl James agreed. "He won't be leading from the front any more, though."

"No, sir," the scryer said. "Farewell, sir." The crystal ball went back to being no more than a sphere of glass.

James sighed. *Leading from the front is why Bell will be a cripple to the end of his days*, he thought, and shivered a little. It could happen to any commander who wanted to mix it up with the foe and to see at first hand how his men were fighting. At Viziersville, between Nonesuch and Georgetown, King Geoffrey's soldiers had shot Thomas the Brick Wall, Duke Edward's great lieutenant, off his unicorn and killed him. James shivered again, a bit harder this time. *A goose just walked over my grave*. His hand twisted in the sign the Detinans had borrowed from their blond serfs to turn aside omens.

He strode out of the scryers' tent and peered west toward Wesleyton. No fogs, no mists here: only the sun shining bright but cold out of a sky the blue of a swordblade. This time, James' shiver had to do with nothing but the weather, which came as rather a relief.

Looking toward Wesleyton, however, brought him no relief at all. Whiskery Ambrose had more men than he did and plainly intended doing nothing with them but trying to hold on to the town he'd taken. Given that defenders, shooting from entrenchments and from behind ramparts, were likely to take fewer losses than attackers, who had to show themselves to come forward, he didn't like his chances of breaking into the place.

When he sighed, his breath smoked, another sign that autumn was marching toward winter. Quick-marching, too—every day, the sun sped faster across the sky and spent less time above the horizon. The sun god always went north for the winter.

"I have to try to take Wesleyton," he muttered, and his breath smoked when he did that, too.

He looked around the camp. His men seemed more worried about staying warm than about attacking. He had trouble blaming them. He did wish Whiskery Ambrose wanted to come out and fight. That would have made his own life much easier. Unfortunately . . .

When he gathered together his wing commanders and leading mages, they seemed no more enthusiastic about attacking than he was. "Sir, the odds against our seizing the town strike me as long," said Colonel Simon, his chief mage.

Those odds struck James as long, too. Nonetheless, he said, "We have to make the effort. If the southrons stay here in western Franklin, they can stir up endless trouble for King Geoffrey." All the assembled officers grimaced. They knew only too well that he was right. Serfs were few on the ground in this mountain country, and a great many of the yeoman farmers hereabouts preferred Avram to Geoffrey. A southron army aiding and abetting them was the last thing the already beleaguered north needed. "We have to try," James repeated.

"Do you really think we can do it?" asked Brigadier Falayette, one of his wing commanders. "Should we risk breaking up this army with an attack unlikely to reach its goal?"

"As I said, taking Wesleyton back is important," James of Broadpath replied. "Count Thraxton is right about that." *No matter how little else he's right about.* James wished Brigadier Bell were well enough to have come with the army. He never counted the cost before an attack. Sometimes that was unfortunate. It had been unfortunate for him personally— the gods knew that was true. But sometimes an officer like that could lead men to victory where they would never find it otherwise.

"Not wrecking ourselves is important, too," Brigadier Falayette insisted. "If we need to come to Thraxton's aid against the southrons, or to return to the Army of Southern Parthenia in a hurry . . ."

"Suppose we think about how we're going to beat the southrons," James said, glowering from under bushy eyebrows at Falayette. "Let's let them worry about how to lick us."

"Yes, sir," the brigadier said. Any other choice of words would have brought more wrath down upon him.

James unfolded a map of Wesleyton and its environs. His plump, stubby forefinger stabbed down at one of the forts warding the eastern side of the town. "Here," he said. "If we can break in at Fort WiLi, we can roll up the southrons. Brigadier Alexander!"

"Sir?" said the officer in charge of James' engines.

"Concentrate your engines in front of that fort. Nothing like a good rain of firepots to make the enemy lose his spirit."

"Yes, sir." Brigadier Alexander was young and eager. Unlike Brigadier Falayette, he didn't worry about whether something could be done. He went out and did his best to do it.

But, given the dispositions of James' men . . . "Brigadier Falayette!" James waited for the wing commander to nod, then went on, "As your men stand before Fort WiLi, you shall make the assault upon it. As soon as you have gained control, rapidly send soldiers north and south so as to secure as much of the enemy's line as you can, easing the way for our other forces."

"Yes, sir," Falayette said.

James did his ponderous best to hide a sigh. He heard no eagerness there. "Colonel Simon!" he said.

"Sir?" Simon the mage replied.

"As with Brigadier Alexander's specialty, the attack on the fort will require all that your mages can give," James said.

"I understand, sir," Simon said. "You'll have it."

"Good." James wondered how good it was. Brigadier Falayette had a point. Wouldn't it be better to hang on to what they had now than to throw it away on an attack that held little hope of success? Earl James sighed again, openly this time. Count Thraxton had given the orders, and he had to obey. And retaking Wesleyton would be important—if they could do it.

He gave the order for the attack with more than the usual worries. Brigadier Alexander's engines pummeled the earthen walls of Fort WiLi. Stones battered them. Firepots sent flame dripping down them and over the battlements to burn the men inside. James of Broadpath wouldn't have cared to find himself on the receiving end of that bombardment.

And Simon the mage and his wizardly colleagues did all they could to punish the fort and the southrons inside it. Lightning struck from a clear sky. The ground trembled beneath James' feet, and presumably did more than tremble inside Fort WiLi. Batwinged demons shrieked like damned souls as they swooped down on the defenders.

Against the blonds in the old days, the days of conquest, the sorcerous assault would have been plenty to win the fight by itself. But the southrons knew all the tricks their northern cousins did, even if they weren't always quite so handy with them. Their lightnings smote James' men, too. The tremors died away as the southron mages mastered them. And as for the demons, as soon as they manifested themselves in the real world, they were as vulnerable to weaponry as any other real-world creatures. Once the stream of darts from a repeating crossbow knocked three of them from the sky in quick succession, the rest grew much more cautious.

And the southrons had many more engines to turn on James' men than Brigadier Alexander had to turn on them. One after another of the catapults brought with such labor from Rising Rock went out of action. Alexander's artificers shrieked as fire engulfed them.

James beckoned for a runner. "Tell Brigadier Falayette to start his footsoldiers moving right this minute. We're getting hammered harder than we're hammering."

"Yes, sir." The runner dashed off.

Despite the order, the pikemen and the crossbowmen who would follow them did not go forward. Fuming, James of Broadpath dispatched another runner to his reluctant brigadier, this one with more peremptory orders. After a little while, the second runner came back, saying, "Brigadier Falayette's compliments, sir, but he believes the enemy has strung wires in front of his position. Have we tinsnips or axes to cut them?"

"Tinsnips?" James clapped a hand to his forehead. "*Tin*snips?" The word might have come from one of the more obscure tongues the blond tribes used. "You tell Brigadier Falayette that if he doesn't get his men moving this instant—this *instant*, do you hear me?— we'll find out if we've got a pair of tinsnips big enough to fit on his gods-damned neck."

With a gulp, the runner fled.

And the pikemen and crossbowmen did go forward—straight into everything the southrons' still undefeated engines could throw at them, straight into the massed shooting of every crossbowman Whiskery Ambrose could put on the walls of Fort WiLi. They went forward roaring, plainly intending to sweep everything before them.

But, as Brigadier Falayette had said, the southrons did have thin wires strung in front of Fort WiLi. They slowed the attackers so that Whiskery Ambrose's men and engines could pound them without mercy, and the northerners were able to do little to reply.

"Where's Simon the mage?" James shouted in fury. When the wizard came before him, he growled, "Why didn't you clever sons of bitches notice those wires ahead of time?"

"I'm very sorry, sir, but we can't possibly notice everything," Simon said.

"Sometimes it seems as if you can't notice *anything*," James said. The colonel gave him an aggrieved look, which he resolutely ignored. "Is there anything you can do to get rid of the gods-damned wires? Conjure up some demons with sharp teeth and a taste for iron, maybe?"

Simon the mage shook his head. "We would need some considerable, time-consuming research, and we have no time to consume, I fear."

He was all too obviously right about that. Instead of going forward with roars, James' men were streaming away from the fort outside Wesleyton. They'd made their attack and seen it fail. They were veterans. They knew what that meant: no point in staying close to the enemy and getting hurt to no purpose.

After a while, Whiskery Ambrose sent out a young captain with a white flag. Northern soldiers led him to James of Broadpath. "The general's compliments, sir," the youngster said, "and he would be pleased to grant you two hours' truce to recover your wounded."

James bowed. "That is very courteous and gentlemanly of General Ambrose, and I accept with many thanks." They exchanged a few more compliments before the southron captain went back to Fort WiLi.

*Now I'll have to explain to Captain Thraxton how and why I didn't break into Wesleyton*, James thought gloomily. *That will be every bit as delightful as going to the dentist.*

A scryer came up to him, as if the thought of having to talk to Thraxton were enough to bring the fellow into being. "What now?" James asked.

The scryer looked worried. James felt his own temper, stretched thin by the repulse, fray even further. Had the illustrious Thraxton decided to sack him even in advance of knowing what had happened here? James didn't intend to disappear peacefully. But then the scryer said, "Sir, the fighting's started up by Rising Rock."

# XI

Another gray, foggy, misty day. Captain Ormerod was sick of them. "Is this what fall is like in these parts?" he asked, leaning closer to the campfire. "If it is, why in the hells does anyone live here?"

"It really isn't, sir," Lieutenant Gremio answered. "I've spoken with some men who come from this part of Franklin, and—"

"Looking for evidence, eh?" Ormerod broke in.

"Well, yes, as a matter of fact," Gremio said. "They tell me they can't recall seeing such a wretched run of weather. It's almost as if some mage were holding a blanket of clouds and mist over Rising Rock."

Ormerod raised an eyebrow. "Do you suppose some mage is? Some southron mage, I mean?"

"I wouldn't think so, sir," Gremio said. "Surely Count Thraxton would notice if that were so."

"Oh, surely." Ormerod put as much sarcastic venom in that as he could. "Thraxton is just like a god—he notices everything that goes on around him. Haven't you seen that for yourself?"

"It's foggy. I can't see anything much," Gremio said.

But then Ormerod said, "It is starting to clear out a bit, I suppose." The more he looked, the more and the farther he could see. If it had been a spell—and he didn't know about that one way or the other— the wizard who'd been casting it seemed to need it no longer. When he looked up to the top of Sentry Peak, he spied King Geoffrey's flag, red dragon on gold, floating where his regiment (though Major Thersites would have had something memorable to say had he put it that way in earshot of him) had placed it.

And when he looked east . . . When he looked east, his jaw dropped and his tongue clove to the roof of his mouth. Lieutenant Gremio was already looking east. Being a barrister, he'd likely had a tongue hinged at both ends since birth. "By the Lion God's mane," he said hoarsely, "if that isn't every stinking southron in the world out there, it might as well be."

"Oh, gods be praised," Ormerod said. "I was afraid I was imagining them."

"And they're all heading this way," Gremio added.

"I know," Ormerod said. That also made him afraid, but in a way different from, and more concrete than, he'd felt before.

Major Thersites saw the advancing enemy, too. "Stand by to repel boarders!" he called, as if the southrons were so many pirates about to swarm onto a fat, rich merchantman. But General Bart's men advanced with far better discipline than pirates were in the habit of showing.

"Can we hold them back, sir?" Lieutenant Gremio asked, in the voice of a small child looking for reassurance.

But Ormerod had no reassurance even for himself, let alone to give to anyone else. "To the hells with me if I know," he answered, while *Not a chance on earth or under it* ran through his mind.

Thersites was right, though: they had to try. Ormerod shouted orders to his men, who found the best cover they could and got ready to fight back. The Franklin River anchored the southern end of their line, the steep slopes of Sentry Peak the northern. Thersites said, "Gods damn it, where's that louse-ridden Thraxton the Braggart when you really need the son of a bitch? He ought to have a spell ready that'd sweep away these bastards like a blond wench sweeping out your bedroom."

The more the mist lifted, the more Ormerod saw. The more Ormerod saw, the more he wished he didn't. "I think Thraxton is liable to be busy somewhere else," he said unhappily.

From Sentry Peak here in the north to Funnel Hill, the extension of Proselytizers' Rise in the far southwest, southron troops advanced against the line the Army of Franklin had set up to hold them inside Rising Rock. How many soldiers had General Bart brought into the town? Ormerod didn't know, not in numbers, but the southrons were sending forth far more men than he'd thought they had.

He couldn't pay so much attention to the distant vistas of the battlefield as he would have liked. The southrons moving on his part of the line from the east drew closer by the minute. He cursed as he recognized the banners their regimental standard-bearers waved.

"Those are Fighting Joseph's troopers!" His voice rose to a furious shout. "Those are the sons of bitches we fought when we went west toward Brownsville Ferry. Some of you boys ran away from jackasses on account of you thought they were unicorn-riders. You're not going to let these bastards shift you now, are you?"

"No!" his men yelled, and he hoped they meant it.

"We haven't got enough of anything," Gremio said worriedly. "We haven't got enough men, we haven't got enough engines, we haven't got enough mages. How are we supposed to stop—that?" He pointed toward the gray flood rolling down on them.

"We've got to try," Ormerod said, echoing Thersites. "If you like, Lieutenant, I'll write you a pass so you can go to the rear." Gremio bit his lip but shook his head. Ormerod slapped him on the back. "Stout fellow."

"No, just a fool, ashamed of looking like a coward before my comrades," Gremio said. "I'd be smarter if I took you up on that, and we both know it."

"They haven't killed me yet," Ormerod told him. "Futter me if I think they can do it this time."

"I admire your spirit," Gremio said. "I would admire it even more if I thought Count Thraxton could send us reinforcements from elsewhere on the field."

"We'll manage," Ormerod said; he didn't think Thraxton the Braggart could send them reinforcements, either. "We have to manage."

King Geoffrey's soldiers were doing everything they could. Artificers turned engines away from Rising Rock and toward the east so they would bear on the advancing foe. Stones and firepots began to fly. So did streams of darts from the big repeating crossbows. Southrons in gray started falling.

But the southrons, along with everything else, were bringing their own wheeled engines forward. They started shooting first at the catapults and repeating crossbows that were tormenting them. That spared Ormerod and his fellow footsoldiers for a while, but only for a while. Gremio was right: the southrons had more engines here than did this part of Count Thraxton's army. Little by little, they battered Thraxton's engines down to something close to silence, and then turned their attention to his pikemen and crossbowmen.

By that time, Ormerod's soldiers were shooting at the oncoming enemy footsoldiers. "Avram!" the southrons yelled. "Avram and freedom! One Detina, now and forever!"

Some of the northerners gave their lion-roar of defiance. Others shouted Geoffrey's name or cried, "Provincial prerogative in perpetuity!" And still others yelled things like, "We don't want to stay in the same kingdom with you sons of bitches!"

Despite the crossbow quarrels hissing around the battlefield, Ormerod stood tall as he drew his sword. He flourished the blade, screaming, "You'll never take my blonds away!"

A ditch and an abatis of sharpened tree trunks held the southrons at bay. Ormerod's men shot a good many of them as they struggled through the obstacles. But the rest of the pikemen, still shouting their hateful battle cry, swarmed forward. One of them came straight at Ormerod, the point of the pike held low so it could tear out his guts.

He hated pikemen. He always had, ever since he first had to face one. Their weapons gave them more reach than his sword gave him. That anyone might kill him without his having so much of a chance to kill the other fellow instead struck him as most unfair.

He slashed at the pikestaff, just below the head. He'd hoped to cut off the head, but an iron strip armored the staff, too—a nasty, low, devious trick the southrons were using more and more these days. Still and all, he did manage to beat the point aside, which meant the fellow in gray tunic and pantaloons didn't spit him for roasting, as he'd no doubt had in mind.

"King Geoffrey!" Ormerod yelled, and stepped in close for some cut-and-thrust work of his own.

That was what he'd intended, anyhow, but things didn't work out the way he planned, any more than things for the Army of Franklin looked to be working out as Thraxton the Braggart had planned. Instead of either letting himself get run through or fleeing in terror, the enemy pikeman smartly reversed his weapon and slammed the pikeshaft into Ormerod's ribs.

"King Geoffr—*oof!*" Ormerod's battle cry was abruptly transformed into a grunt of pain. He sucked in a breath, wondering if he'd feel the knives that meant something in there had broken. He didn't, but he had to lurch away from the southron to keep from getting punctured—the fellow was altogether too good with a pike. *Why aren't you somewhere far away, training other southrons to be nuisances?* Ormerod thought resentfully.

Then a crossbow quarrel caught the pikeman in the face. He screamed and dropped his spear and rolled on the ground and writhed with his hands over the wound, just as Ormerod would have done had he been so unlucky. Another southron pikeman stepped on him so as to be able to get at Ormerod.

Once he got at him, he was quickly sorry. He

wasn't so good with his pike as the unlucky southron had been, and soon lurched away with a wounded shoulder.

"That's the way to do it!" Major Thersites shouted. Thersites himself was doing his best to imitate a whirlwind full of flail blades: any southron who got near him had cause to regret it, and that in short order. "Drive those sons of bitches back where they came from!"

But the southrons kept pressing forward, no matter how many of them fell to blades and crossbow bolts. Ormerod's comrades were falling, too, and reserves were thin on the ground in this part of the field. Here and there, men from his company began slipping off toward the west, toward Proselytizers' Rise.

"Hold your ground!" Lieutenant Gremio shouted.

"Hold, by the gods!" Ormerod echoed. "Don't let them through. This is for the kingdom's sake. And besides," he added pragmatically, "you're easier to kill if they get you while you're running."

That made the men from his company hang on a little longer. Major Thersites' profane urgings made the whole regiment hang on a little longer. But then a firepot burst at Thersites' feet. He became a torch, burning, burning, burning. He screamed, but, mercifully, not for long. That left the seniormost captain in the regiment, an earl named Throckmorton, in command.

"Hold fast!" Captain Throckmorton cried. But he sounded as if he were pleading, not as if he would murder the next man who dared take a backward step. And pleading was not enough to hold the soldiers in their places, not in the face of the oncoming southron storm. More and more of them headed for the rear.

"What can we do?" Gremio asked, watching them go.

"Not a gods-damned thing, doesn't look like," Ormerod answered grimly. "We aren't the only ones getting away from the enemy—not even close. That's the one thing that makes me feel halfway decent. Look at some of those bastards run! You could race 'em against unicorns and clean up." He spat in disgust.

"If we stay here—if you and I stay here, I mean— much longer, the southrons will kill us," Lieutenant Gremio said.

He was right, too; Ormerod could see as much. For a moment, rage so choked him that he hardly cared. But, at last, he said, "Well, we'd better ske-daddle, too, then. I haven't killed as many southrons as I want to, not yet, and I won't get the chance by staying here."

"I feel the same way, Captain," Gremio said. Ormerod wondered whether that was true, or whether the barrister simply sought an acceptable excuse to flee. He shrugged. It didn't really matter. They could fall back, or they could die. Those were the only choices left. They could not hold.

Dying here wouldn't accomplish anything, not that Ormerod could see. Along with other stubborn northerners, some from their regiment, others men he'd never seen before, they fought a rear-guard action that kept the southrons from overwhelming this wing of Count Thraxton's army. The soldiers fell back toward the protection of the lines on the height of Proselytizers' Rise.

"I wonder if those bastards will have cut and run, too," Ormerod grumbled.

"Doesn't look like it, sir," Gremio said, and he was

right. He added, "If you ask me, we can hold the crest of the rise forever."

"Here's hoping you're right, because we'd better," Ormerod answered. Some of his men went into line with the troopers already in place on Proselytizers' Rise. Others, exhausted by a long day's fighting and by the retreat they hadn't wanted to make, sprawled wherever they could.

Ormerod stayed in line till darkness ended the fighting. He was up before sunrise the next day, too, up and cursing. "What's the matter now?" Lieutenant Gremio asked sleepily.

"That's what, by the gods." Ormerod pointed back toward Sentry Peak. Above a thick layer of cloud, King Avram's gold dragon banner on red—an enormous flag, to be seen at this distance—had replaced Geoffrey's red dragon on gold. Ormerod knew he shouldn't have been surprised, but he misliked the omen.

At the same time as Fighting Joseph attacked the forward slopes of Sentry Peak, the northern end of Count Thraxton's line, Lieutenant General Hesmucet's soldiers went into action against Funnel Hill, the southwestern part of the unicornshoe Thraxton had thrown partway around Rising Rock. Runners reported that Fighting Joseph was driving the traitors before him. Hesmucet wished he didn't have to listen to any of those reports. Things were not going nearly so well for him as he would have hoped.

For one thing, Funnel Hill, like the nearby Proselytizers' Rise, had a steep forward face and a devils of a lot of northerners at the top. For another, Hesmucet rapidly discovered that the maps they were using had led him and General Bart astray. By what the maps said, Funnel Hill wasn't just near Proselytizers' Rise, but was the Rise's southernmost extension. The ground told a different story. Even if his men got to the top, they would have to fight their way down into a deep, unmarked valley and then up another slope to get where they really needed to go.

But, even though they had no hope of doing what he and Bart had thought they might, they had to keep fighting. If they didn't, the northerners on Funnel Hill would go somewhere else and cause trouble for General Bart's soldiers there.

A runner came up to Hesmucet and said, "Sir, they've got our right pinned down pretty badly."

Hesmucet managed a smile of sorts. "Well, it was our left a little while ago. If that's not progress, I don't know what is." He knew perfectly well it wasn't progress, or anything like progress. But if he didn't admit that to anyone else, he didn't have to admit it to himself, either.

Lightning bolts smashed down out of the clear sky. They didn't strike the men in gray struggling to advance, but they came too close to make Hesmucet happy. The runner said, "Where the hells are *our* wizards—uh, sir?"

"That's a good question." Hesmucet raised his voice to a shout: "Alva! Where have you gone and got to, Alva?"

"Here, sir!" The young mage came running up. "What do you require, sir?"

"Are you good for anything besides fogs and mists?" Hesmucet asked. "These northern whoresons are giving our boys a hard time. I want you to do something about that, gods damn it. Show me what you can manage."

"I'll do my best," Alva said. "I wish I could have

had a little more notice so I could have prepared more effects, but—"

"But nothing," Hesmucet said. "You're a mage who knew he was going to be in the middle of a battle. How much fornicating preparation do you need?"

"I don't need any fornicating preparation, sir," Alva answered with a grin. "All I need there is a friendly girl."

That stopped Hesmucet in his tracks, as surely as Doubting George's men had stopped the traitors on Merkle's Hill. Before Hesmucet could start up again, Alva began to incant. Hesmucet stared as the Lion God appeared in the sky over the battlefield. The god roared anger down at the northerners. Then, walking on air, his great tail lashing across a quarter of the sky, he stalked toward the place where the northern mages on Funnel Hill were likeliest to be standing.

"You don't do things by halves, do you?" Hesmucet knew he sounded shaken, but couldn't help it.

"I try not to, sir," Alva answered calmly. "Anything worth doing is worth overdoing, or that's what people say."

"Is it? Do they?" Hesmucet rallied. "Leonidas the Priest would not approve of you at all, young fellow." Alva laughed the clear, boyish laugh of someone feeling his full power for the first time. It occurred to Hesmucet to wonder just *how* great that power was. "Ah . . . Alva . . . That isn't *really* the Lion God up there, is it?"

"Just a simulacrum," the young mage said. "Nothing to worry about—and the real Lion God probably won't even notice. From everything I've been able to find out, the gods pay a lot less attention to what goes on down here on earth than most people think.

You almost wonder if it's worth your while believing in them."

"No, I don't," Hesmucet said. "What I wonder is what the younger generation is coming to. If we don't believe in the gods, our magic will fail, and then where would we be?"

"We'd manage." Alva sounded perfectly confident. "I think we could get along just fine with nothing but mechanical devices."

"Not bloody likely!" Hesmucet exclaimed. "How would you replace a firepot or a glideway, for instance?"

"I don't know, not off the top of my head," Alva admitted, "but I'd bet we could do it if we set our minds to trying."

"Easy enough for you to say when you haven't got anything riding on it," Hesmucet told him. "Next thing you know, you'll say you could make light without fire or magic, or else that you could capture sounds out of the air without a crystal ball."

"It might be interesting to try," Alva said in thoughtful tones.

Hesmucet cursed under his breath. He'd succeeded in distracting the mage, which was the last thing he needed. The image of the Lion God above the enemy was fading, fraying. "You might want to fix that up," he suggested.

"No, no point to it," Alva said. "They've figured out it's not real. I'll let their mages tear at it for a while. As long as they're doing that, they won't make any mischief of their own. I'll come up with something else in the meantime."

*Make them respond—don't respond to what they're up to*, Hesmucet thought. General Bart had said the same thing.

"You might make a general one day," Hesmucet told Alva.

"Not likely." The young mage didn't try to hide his annoyance. "The north treats its wizards much better than we do."

"You were the one who pointed out there are reasons for that," Hesmucet said. "Maybe you would have done better to stay with the mechanic arts."

"Maybe I would have," Alva said. "But it's rather too late to worry about that now, wouldn't you say? I've got work to do, even if it's work that won't ever get me fancy epaulets."

What sort of work he had in mind became evident in short order, for lightning bolts crashed down onto King Geoffrey's men on Funnel Hill from out of the clear sky. Unlike the manifestation of the Lion God that had appeared a few minutes before, the lightnings were unquestionably real.

When Hesmucet remarked on that, Alva nodded and smiled as if he were a clever child. "That's the idea, sir. You mix the real and the illusions together till nobody on the other side is sure which is which. Then the enemy has to test everything, and you can give him some nasty surprises."

"You're a menace, do you know that?" Hesmucet said. "All I can tell you is, I'm gods-damned glad you're on our side. You'd be worth as much to the traitors as Count Thraxton, I think."

He meant it as a compliment. Alva took it as an insult. "That old foof? He's not so much of a much."

"He's very strong," Hesmucet said. "If you don't believe me, go ask General Guildenstern. But you'll have to go a long way to ask him, because he'll be sent off to fight the wild blonds out on the steppes if he's lucky enough to stay in the army. Thraxton wrecked his career, and the bastard came within an eyelash of wrecking his whole army. If Doubting George hadn't held on, there at Merkle's Hill . . ."

When Alva answered, Hesmucet doubted his words had anything to do with anything: "Sir, have you ever seen a rhinoceros?"

"Yes, a time or two, in zoological parks," Hesmucet said, too surprised not to give back the truth. "So what?"

"A rhinoceros is a great big strong beast with a pointed horn, right?" Alva said, and Hesmucet had to nod. The young mage went on, "And most of the time, it isn't dangerous at all, because it can't see past its own ears. No matter how strong it is, it hasn't got any brains to speak of, either. Most of the time, it'll charge in the wrong direction. Every once in a while, it'll squash something flat, but not very often. That's Thraxton, sir. That isn't me."

"No, I can see that," Hesmucet said, doing his best not to laugh out loud. "You're practicing to be a viper."

"That I like," Alva said. "That suits me fine. I'll stay by the edge of the trail and bite from ambush—and what I bite will die."

"Splendid." Hesmucet pointed toward the top of Funnel Hill. "What do you say to biting some more of those traitors? We may take the hill yet." By now, though, the sun was sinking toward the western horizon. Even if his men did take Funnel Hill—which struck him as unlikely, despite his bold words—they wouldn't be able to turn and move on Proselytizers' Rise from the flank, which had been the point of the attack in the first place.

Maybe Alva saw the same thing. Maybe not—he wasn't a general, only a kid with more brains than he knew what to do with. He said, "I'll try my best, sir."

His best proved hair-raisingly good, even for Lieutenant General Hesmucet, who was, as he'd said, on the same side. Flames suddenly sprang into being all along the northerners' lines, as if one of the hotter hells had decided to take up residence on earth for a while. *They can't be real . . . can they?* Hesmucet thought.

He had to nerve himself before asking Alva. Partly, that was not wanting to distract the sorcerer. Partly, it was . . . Hesmucet would have hesitated to call it fear, but he would have hesitated to call it anything else, either.

When at last he did put the question to the mage, Alva smiled an unpleasant smile. "If you have trouble telling, sir, think how much more trouble the traitors must have. Often enough, an illusion you can't tell from the real thing is as good as the real thing."

Hesmucet nodded. He'd heard the like from other sorcerers, too. But he said, "I want a straight answer, if you don't mind."

"And if I do?" But Alva seemed to think twice about the wisdom of twitting a fierce-faced lieutenant general. "Well, sir, to tell you the truth, most of it's illusion. Most, but not quite all. Some of the traitors up there on the hillside are really roasting, and that makes them all thoughtful."

"I can see how it would," Hesmucet said. "It'd make *me* thoughtful, that's for gods-damned sure. Now—what can they do about it?"

"Cook," Alva said happily. Hesmucet laughed.

But Thraxton the Braggart wasn't the only mage the northerners had. Before long, the flames faded. Hesmucet wondered how many men they'd seared. Not enough for his purposes: he saw that quite soon. Shouting King Avram's name, his own men charged the enemy's trenches on Funnel Hill. They charged—and, not for the first time that day, they were driven off with heavy loss.

Now Alva sounded indignant: "Why can't the traitors just panic and flee?"

"Because they're Detinans, same as we are," Hesmucet answered, "and because they're a pack of stubborn bastards, too, maybe even more than we are. Would *you* like to try to stand up to the might of most of the kingdom when all you had to help you was the north?"

"I never thought about it like that, sir," Alva said. "As far as I'm concerned, they're traitors, and that's all there is to it."

"Oh, they're traitors, all right," Hesmucet said. "But that doesn't mean they're not brave men. I don't think I've ever seen braver."

"Or fighting for a worse cause," Alva remarked.

"Splitting the kingdom, you mean? Of course," Hesmucet said. Alva stirred beside him. Before the mage could speak, Hesmucet went on, "If you aim to talk about the blonds, I'm going to tell you something first. What I'm going to tell you is, I don't much care about them one way or the other. If you want to think they'll make good Detinans, go ahead. I have my doubts. But I obey my king, and my king is King Avram. I haven't got any doubts at all about that."

Alva eyed him as if he'd never seen him before. "You are a very . . . peculiar man, aren't you, sir?"

"Thank you," Hesmucet said, which only seemed to confuse the mage further. He added, "What I am right now, thank you very much, is an *angry* man. We aren't going to take that stinking hill. You've done everything you could—you've been splendid, Alva, and that'll go into my report—but we aren't. And we needed to. This whole army will have to work harder because we didn't."

"Don't you worry about it, sir," Alva said. "We'll lick them."

"How can you be so sure?" Hesmucet asked. "You're the one who said the gods don't worry about us so much as we think."

"Even so," Alva said.

"Well, then?" Hesmucet growled. He knew he sounded impatient. As far as he could see, he could hardly sound any other way. The fight on Funnel Hill wasn't going the way he wished it were.

"There's more of us, and we've got more engines," Alva said. "If we lose in spite of that, we should be ashamed of ourselves."

"General Bart says the same thing," Hesmucet replied. "He's right about the war. I'm pretty sure about that. But I don't know whether he's right about this fight here—and right this minute, this fight here is all that counts."

Lieutenant General George was not happy with the role General Bart had assigned to his army. The soldiers General Guildenstern had formerly commanded were making what amounted to a noisy demonstration against Proselytizers' Rise. Even if Bart hadn't spelled it out in so many words, their assignment was to keep Thraxton the Braggart's men busy in the center while Fighting Joseph and Hesmucet won glory on the wings.

Bart's orders did read, *If possible, your force shall scale the heights of Proselytizers' Rise and expel the enemy therefrom.* "I like that," George said to Colonel Andy. "I truly like that. If the gods themselves attacked Proselytizers' Rise from below, could they carry that position?"

"Sir, I . . ." His aide-de-camp spoke with all due deliberation, and with malice aforethought: "Sir, I doubt it."

"So do I," Doubting George said morosely. "By the Thunderer, so do I."

"General Bart doesn't think this part of the army can really fight," Andy said. "He doesn't think we're worth anything."

"I'm very much afraid you're right," George said. "And, as long as he gives us impossible positions to try to take, all he has to do is see that we haven't taken them to get all his assumptions proved for him."

"It isn't fair," Andy said. "It isn't even close to fair."

"Well, there I would have to agree with you." George raised a forefinger. "Now don't get me wrong. I want this whole great force to whip Count Thraxton. That comes first, and I've said so many times. But I don't want my men, so many of whom fought like heroes by the River of Death even though we lost, I don't want them slighted."

"I should say not, sir," Andy replied. "It's a reflection on them, and it's also a reflection on you."

Privately, Doubting George agreed with that. Publicly . . . He said what he'd been saying: "No one man's part is all that important. But I think we could serve the kingdom better with different orders."

"Do you want to complain to Bart?" Andy asked. "It might do some good."

"Unfortunately, I doubt that," George said. "It wouldn't make the commanding general change his mind, and it would get me a reputation as a whiner, which is not the reputation I want to have."

Pulling the brim of his hat down lower over his

eyes, he watched his men doing their best to go forward in the face of formidable odds. The eastern slope of Proselytizers' Rise was very high and very steep. No one could reasonably be expected to get close to it, let alone scale it with an enemy waiting at the top.

But, as long as George's men kept trying, Thraxton couldn't move any of his own soldiers away from Proselytizers' Rise to Sentry Peak or Funnel Hill. *We'd be a proper fighting army if Bart would let us*, George thought. Then, reluctantly, he checked himself. *As long as the battle is won, how doesn't much matter. And there will be credit to go around.*

*And if the battle isn't won, where will the blame land?* He imagined coming before the panel of Avram's ministers empowered to review the conduct of the war. He imagined some crusty, white-haired pen-pusher rasping, "You were requested and required to drive the traitors from this place called Proselytizers' Rise. Would you care to explain to us how you failed to carry out your duty?"

He wouldn't be able to. He knew he wouldn't be able to. If the king's ministers saw the ground, they might possibly begin to understand. Without seeing the ground? *Not a chance*, he thought. *Not a single, solitary chance, not in any one of the hells*. All they would see was that he'd got an order and failed to carry it out. And that panel was full of vindictive souls. They would remember he was a Parthenian. They would forget he was called the Rock in the River of Death. And they would, without the tiniest fragment of doubt, kill his soldierly career.

*By all the gods, we'd better win.*

Seeing where he was, seeing what lay ahead of him, seeing what his orders were, he had to rely on

Fighting Joseph to his right and Lieutenant General Hesmucet to his left. He wasn't going to win the battle by himself. He hated that. Relying on others came no easier to him than it did to most Detinans. If he had to do something, he wanted to be in charge of it. But this battle was too big to make that possible. *Come on, Fighting Joseph. Make them run.*

Colonel Andy pointed. "Look, sir! We've got a lodgement there, right at the base of the Rise."

"So we do," Doubting George said. "Next question is, can we keep it?"

They couldn't. George hadn't really expected that they would, not with the advantage in numbers the northerners held. The traitors rolled boulders down onto his men, sweeping them away as a blond scullery maid might sweep crawling ants off a wall. They rained firepots on the southrons, too, and plied them with crossbow quarrels. A few men in gray clung to the ground they'd gained, but more—even those who weren't hurt—fell back. George had a hard time blaming them.

"I thought we had something going there," Andy said dejectedly.

"I hoped we had something going there," George replied, which wasn't the same thing at all.

"The traitors will know they've been in a battle, by the Lion God's fangs." Colonel Andy looked and sounded as belligerent as a man could when he wasn't doing any actual fighting himself.

"I want them to know they've lost a battle," George said. "Right now, Colonel, I have to confess, I don't know how to make that happen, not on this part of the field."

"I wish I did, sir," his aide-de-camp said.

"I wish you did, too. I wish anybody did. I hope

we're doing well on the ends of the line, because we're in a devils of a fix here in the middle." Doubting George sighed. "We're all doing the best we can. I have to remember that."

"General Guildenstern was doing the best he could, too," Andy said acidly.

"Why, so he was," George said. "Guildenstern is a brave man, and he had the start of a good plan. I think General Bart has a better plan, and it may well work. But he gave me a hard role to play."

Shouting King Avram's name, his men made another lunge toward the eastern face of Proselytizers' Rise. A few more of them got into the trenches of the base of the Rise. Some of the ones who did came out again. Nobody seemed able to hold on there. *You are not here to win the battle*, George reminded himself. *You're here to keep the men on the wings from losing it.* Remembering that came hard.

"There's some sort of a commotion over to the north," Colonel Andy said.

"Well, so there is." George peered off in that direction, trying to figure out what sort of a commotion it was.

Andy's voice broke in excitement: "It's—it's the northerners running back from the slope of Sentry Peak, that's what it is!"

"Looks that way," Doubting George agreed. "And there's our men after them, too. Looks like Fighting Joseph has won himself a victory, it does, it does."

"It sure does," his aide-de-camp exulted. After a moment, Andy said one more word: "Oh."

George answered him with one word, too: "Yes." Seeing Fighting Joseph's men storming forward in pursuit of the traitors while his own soldiers impotently smashed themselves against Proselytizers' Rise ate at him. But then, with an effort he regretted but could not help, he said, "It's for the good of the kingdom. We always have to remember, that comes first."

"Of course, sir." Colonel Andy didn't sound as if he fully believed it, either.

*Fighting Joseph*, George thought with distaste. *I wouldn't mind nearly so much if it were Hesmucet, over there on the other flank. But he looks as though he's having as much fun as I am, or maybe even more.*

Part of it was his personal judgment of Fighting Joseph: overfond of gambling and spirits and hookers, the man would never be a gentleman. Part of it was his, and everyone else's, professional judgment of Fighting Joseph: having botched the battle of Viziersville, and having botched it in the way he did, why was he given another important command? General Bart probably had the right of that—King Avram didn't mind giving Joseph another command of sorts, so long as it wasn't anywhere close to Georgetown or the Black Palace.

"Send a messenger to him," George told his aide-de-camp. "Ask him if we can do anything to help in the pursuit."

"Yes, sir." Colonel Andy spoke as if the words tasted bad. Doubting George didn't reprove him. He hadn't enjoyed giving the order, either, however necessary he knew it to be.

Sooner than George quite wanted, the runner returned. After saluting, he said, "Fighting Joseph's compliments, sir, and he declines your generous request. He says he's quite able to do what wants doing all by his lonesome."

"He *would* say something like that," Andy sneered.

"Of course he would," George said. "He wouldn't

be the man he is if he were the sort who could be gracious at times like this."

"What do we do now, sir?" Andy asked.

"What can we do?" George replied. "We've done everything we can. We've served our purpose. In the north, Joseph *did* break through, as General Bart hoped he would. Maybe Lieutenant General Hesmucet can do the same in the southwest. I wish him the best."

"We can't break through here," Colonel Andy said.

"We're not supposed to break through. We're just supposed to keep the traitors too busy to send reinforcements anywhere else along the line," George said, trying not to think about the exact words of the order Bart had given him. "We've done exactly that. We wouldn't need just wizards to do more. We'd need . . . I was going to say real, live miracle-workers, but even they'd have trouble."

"For the sake of the men, I wish we could stay out of range of the enemy's engines and crossbows," his aide-de-camp said.

"So do I, but we can't," Doubting George said. "We wouldn't seem very dangerous here if we did." *Not that we seem all that dangerous here now.*

"I suppose you're right," Andy said. Whatever he supposed, he didn't sound very happy about it. A moment later, though, he had a thought that seemed to cheer him. "The battle looks as if it will still be going tomorrow. I hope General Bart will see fit to give us reinforcements."

"I don't, by the gods," George answered. "As best I can see, all we'd do if we had them is get them killed. Do you really think we can force Proselytizers' Rise?"

"It's our duty," Colonel Andy said.

Doubting George was glad his aide-de-camp wasn't in the line of command. If he went down himself, Brigadier Absalom would take over for him. And Absalom the Bear knew how things were supposed to work. Andy was excellent at details, not nearly so good at the big picture. George said, "No, no, no. Our duty here is just to keep the traitors busy. As long as we manage that, all's right with the world."

"If you say so, sir." Andy didn't sound convinced, and George was too worn to argue with him any more—and he wasn't convinced, either.

Instead of arguing, he watched the sun go down between Proselytizers' Rise and Sentry Peak. "We aren't going to accomplish anything more today," he said at last, and sent orders forward to have his men leave off fighting and encamp out of range of the northerners atop the Rise.

As they pulled back, a rather short man with a neat dark beard rode up on a fine unicorn. "Good evening, Lieutenant General," General Bart called.

"Good evening to you, sir," Doubting George replied. He held his salute as the commanding general dismounted. A trooper took charge of the unicorn's reins. George asked the question surely uppermost in everyone's mind: "What's your view of the battle thus far?"

"Up in the north, Fighting Joseph has done everything I could have hoped for, and a little more besides," Bart answered. "He's driven Thraxton's men as handsomely as you please, and I expect he'll do more tomorrow."

"Yes, sir," George said. "I gather things aren't going quite so smoothly in the southwest."

"Well, no," General Bart allowed. "Hesmucet and I looked over the ground ourselves before I ordered the attack, and—"

"Did you?" That impressed George. Few generals were so thorough.

"We did indeed. We looked it over, but we might not have done the best job in the world, because that Funnel Hill looks like a tougher nut than we thought it would. Hesmucet will have another go at things in the morning, too, and we'll just have to find out how that fares." Bart shrugged. "I still think we can beat the traitors here. It's a question of making them crack somewhere."

"Yes, sir." That impressed Doubting George, too. A lot of generals, having fought hard one day, were content to take things easy the next. Bart didn't fit that pattern. "What are your orders for me, sir?"

"For now, you're doing what you ought to do," the commanding general replied. "I have no complaints against you, not in the slightest."

"We'll see what happens tomorrow, then, sir," George said. "I think we can beat them, too. I hope we can." *We'd better*, he thought.

The campfires of Doubting George's men flickered down on the flat country below Proselytizers' Rise. Up on the crest of the Rise, the traitors' fires likewise showed where they were. General Bart studied those latter flames, doing his best to gain meaning from them. His best, he feared, was none too good. Thraxton the Braggart had men up there. He'd already known that much, but he couldn't learn much more.

"Colonel Phineas!" he called. "Are you there, Colonel?"

"Yes, sir, I'm here," the army's chief mage answered. He bustled up beside Bart. Firelight flickered from his plump, weary face. "What can I do for you?"

"What sort of sorcerous attacks has the enemy made against us in the fighting just past?" Bart asked.

Phineas licked his lips. "Actually, sir, not very many. For one thing, young Alva has kept the traitors remarkably busy down in the south."

He didn't sound altogether happy about that. Bart thought he understood why. "The youngster is strong, isn't he? I'd be surprised if he stayed a lieutenant very much longer. Wouldn't you be surprised, too, Colonel, if that were so?"

"Sir, deciding whom to promote is always the commanding general's prerogative," Phineas said stiffly. "I will admit, young Alva has proved himself stronger than many of his colleagues had thought he might." He didn't admit that he was one of those colleagues.

Bart almost twitted him about that, but decided to hold his peace. The less he said, the less cause he would have later to regret it. Sticking to business seemed the wiser course: "Does the northerners' quiet mean they won't be able to do anything much with magic tomorrow, or does it mean they're saving up to give us as much trouble as they can?"

"Obviously, you would have to ask Thraxton the Braggart to get the full details of their plans," Colonel Phineas said.

"But I can't very well ask Thraxton." Now Bart did let some annoyance come into his voice. "And so I'm asking *you*, Colonel. Give me your best judgment: what can we look forward to when the fighting picks up again?"

Phineas licked his lips once more. Now, on the spot, he looked very unhappy. The firelight probably made that worse by exaggerating the lines and shadows on his jowly face. With a sigh, he said, "My best judgment, sir, is that they're holding back, and that they still may try something strong and sorcerous against us tomorrow."

"All right," Bart said. "That's my best guess, too. I'm glad our thoughts are going in the same direction. Has Thraxton made any sorcerous attempts against me, the way he did against General Guildenstern up by the River of Death?"

"None I or my fellow mages have been able to detect, sir," Phineas replied.

"You so relieve my mind, Colonel," Bart said dryly. "You're saying that if he has tried to turn me into a frog, you haven't noticed him succeeding."

"Er—yes." Phineas didn't seem to know what to do with a general in a whimsical mood.

Bart decided to let the flustered wizard down easy. "All right, Colonel. I want you to go right on keeping an eye out for me. If Count Thraxton does try to get nasty with me, I want you and your mages to try your hardest to stop him—if you happen to notice him doing it, that is." He decided he didn't want to let Phineas down too easy after all.

"Yes, sir," the chief mage said. As best Bart could tell by the firelight, Phineas looked as if he wanted to hide.

Bart wasn't quite ready to let him get away, either. "And if you don't mind too much, be sure and let Lieutenant Alva know to keep an eye on the Braggart along with his other duties."

"Yes, sir," Phineas said once more, this time in a hollow voice. "Will there be anything else, sir?" He sounded like a gloomy servant in a bad play.

"That should just about do it, I expect," General Bart said. "You go get yourself a good night's sleep. We'll start bright and early in the morning." He nodded to show Phineas he really was finished. The mage bowed and saluted and fled. *If the traitors run as fast as he does*, Bart thought, *we'll win ourselves a great and famous victory tomorrow. Wouldn't that be fine?*

He thought about going back to his pavilion and getting himself a good night's sleep—thought about it and shook his head. He wouldn't be able to rest till the battle was decided. A yawn tried to sneak out of his throat. He stifled it unborn. He'd had practice going without sleep, and knew he could still come up with the right answers when he had to. He might take a few heartbeats longer than he would while wide awake, but the answers wouldn't change.

A quiet voice came out of the darkness: "Is that you, sir?"

"Yes, it's me, Colonel Horace," Bart replied. "I have a habit of prowling the field. You'll just have to bear with me."

"Yes, sir," his aide-de-camp said. "You would do better with some rest, sir."

"I'd do better if we'd driven the traitors just the way I hoped we would," Bart answered. "Nothing ever works out quite so smoothly as you wish it would."

"Fighting Joseph did well in the north," Horace said, though his tone of voice showed something less than complete delight.

Noting as much, Bart chuckled and said, "You sound like a man watching his mother-in-law fall off a cliff."

"I'm glad he won." Colonel Horace shook his head. "No, by the gods, if I can't be honest with you, sir, where can I? I'm glad *we* won. If we had to win somewhere, though, I wish it were at the other end of the line."

"Well, so do I," Bart said. "But Funnel Hill doesn't seem to be quite what Lieutenant General Hesmucet and I thought it was. He'll have another go at it tomorrow."

"And may the gods grant him better luck then." Horace coughed a couple of times, plainly aware he was opening a delicate subject: "What do you plan to do here in the center tomorrow, sir?"

"I'm still trying to make up my mind about that, Colonel, if you want to know the truth," Bart replied. "I think Lieutenant General George did about as well as could be expected yesterday, given what he was up against in Proselytizers' Rise. Still and all, though, I am weighing in my mind a larger demonstration against the Rise tomorrow. That should give Count Thraxton something to think about."

"Good." In the dim red glow of the campfires, Horace's face looked more aquiline than ever. "He doesn't think any too well. The more he has to do it, the better our chances."

"I don't believe that's quite fair," General Bart said. "It's not the Braggart's wits that land him in trouble. It's his temper."

"You're too kind, sir," his aide-de-camp said. "It's that nobody can stand him and he can't get along with anyone, himself included."

Bart chuckled. "I didn't say that. I'm not necessarily going to tell you I think you're wrong, but I didn't say that."

"Have you let Lieutenant General George know what you'll require of him, sir?"

"No, not yet." The commanding general shook his head. "I will want to talk it over with him before I give the order. If he doesn't think such a demonstration would serve any useful purpose, we'll probably try something else instead. He's the one who's been ramming his head against Proselytizers' Rise all day. He'll have a better notion of what will and won't work than I do; I'm sure of that."

"A lot of generals wouldn't care about their underlings' notions," Horace observed.

"I care. I care a great deal," Bart said. "That doesn't necessarily mean I'll do anything George asks me to. But I do want to listen to what he has to say before I make up my own mind. That last is the most important thing. I bear the responsibility, so I get to give the orders in the end. It's only fair."

"As may be, sir," Horace said. "By a lot of people's standards, you seem to bend over backwards to be fair."

"I try to see things as clear as I can," Bart said. "The way I look at it, that's how you do a job and get a fighting chance of having it stay done."

Colonel Horace plucked at his bushy mustache. "You may well have a point."

"And I may well be talking through my hat, is what you're thinking." Bart chuckled. "Well, perhaps I am. Everyone is strange in his own way: I'm sure of that. Take me, for instance. Here I am a soldier, and I have to have my meat cooked gray, for I shudder if they bring it to me all bloody."

"I'd noticed that," his aide-de-camp replied. "Seems a pitiful thing to do to a poor, innocent beefsteak, but that's your concern and no one else's. No accounting for taste."

"Which is what I just said, only all boiled down to a proverb." Bart set a hand on Horace's shoulder. "Why don't you go get yourself some shuteye, if

you're able?" He saw Horace hesitate. "Don't fret
about me, son. I'll sleep when I'm ready, I promise
you, but not until then."

"Very well, sir." Horace sounded grudging and
grateful at the same time. After a last crisp salute—
he seemed to do nothing that wasn't crisp—he strode
off, each of his strides almost twice as long as one
of Bart's would have been.

Bart looked this way and that, his head swiveling
on his neck as an owl's might have done. *Am I really
by myself at last?* he wondered. *Can I really get a
quarter of an hour to hear myself think? People have
been yelling at me the whole day long. How can I
hear what's inside my own head when I'm trying to
take care of everybody else?*

An owl hooted, somewhere off in the trees not far
away. In the distance, he heard the moans of wounded
men who hadn't been brought in yet. They didn't distract him; he'd heard them before, and was as used
to them as any man not dead of soul could be.

He paced along: one lean, medium-sized man in
charge of the destinies of more soldiers than anybody
this side of the gods. That it should be so struck him
as strange even now, but so it was. He'd rocked
Thraxton during the day, but he hadn't broken him.
That meant those soldiers were going to have to do
more work tomorrow, and he was the one, the only
one, who could decide what sort of work it would
be.

With a sigh, he murmured, "I'd better go see
Doubting George, the way I told Colonel Horace I
would."

Seeing Doubting George wasn't what he most
wanted to do. He knew the lieutenant general couldn't
care for his friendship with Hesmucet. And now

Hesmucet hadn't done what he'd set out to do—and, almost worse, Fighting Joseph *had*—and Bart was going to rely on George in a way he hadn't planned to do. If George wanted to throw all that in his face, how could he stop the man?

He couldn't. He knew it too well. But he walked toward Doubting George's pavilion anyway. The kingdom needed what they could do together, even if they weren't any too fond of each other while they did it. An alert sentry called out, not too loud: "Halt! Who goes? Stand and name yourself."

"I'm General Bart," Bart said, also quietly. "Is Lieutenant General George awake?"

"Advance and be recognized, uh, sir," the sentry said. When he did recognize Bart, he saluted almost as precisely as Colonel Horace had. "Sorry, sir."

"Don't be," Bart said. "Just answer my question, if you please."

"I'm awake," Doubting George said before the sentry could reply. He stepped out through the tentflap. "What can I do for you, sir?"

"I was thinking about what my whole army ought to do tomorrow, Lieutenant General," Bart said, "and I was also thinking it might help the cause if your men here were to make a grand demonstration against Proselytizers' Rise, as if they really intended to storm the heights."

"If that's what you need, that's what we'll do," George said at once.

"Do you think your men *could* carry the Rise?" Bart asked.

Again, George spoke without hesitation: "Sir, I don't think there's a chance in all the hells that they could. But if you give the order, they'll try with everything they've got in 'em."

"You're an honest man, Lieutenant General," Bart said. "Most officers would say, 'Of course, sir. My men can do anything.' "

"Maybe that's true," Doubting George replied. "And maybe, begging your pardon, that's how we keep sticking our dicks in the meat grinder, too. Of course, the traitors have lieutenant generals and brigadiers who say the same thing, so I suppose it evens out."

"I hope so," Bart said. The image, when he briefly let himself think about it, made him want to clutch at himself. With a distinct effort of will, he put it out of his mind. "Now let's get down to business, shall we? With any luck at all, we will be able to hang on to the trenches at the base of the Rise."

"Maybe that's true, but maybe it's not," George said. "We couldn't in today's fighting. The northerners up at the top of the Rise can shoot almost straight down at us when we're in those trenches. Still and all, we'll try at your command."

When the sun rose the next morning, the spectacle Lieutenant General George's soldiers made was as impressive as any man could have wanted. Four divisions formed in a line close to two miles wide. Flags fluttered in front of them. When horns called for them to advance, they did so in perfect step.

"They're well-drilled men," Bart said. "Thraxton won't dare pull any soldiers away to Funnel Hill with all that coming straight at him."

"No, indeed, sir," Doubting George agreed. "It's an expensive way to use them, I'm afraid, but I don't suppose it can be helped."

"Look at 'em go," Bart said. "They look as though they could roll over anything, like a great wave out on the Western Ocean."

"They're going to roll over those trenches, that's

certain sure," George said. "They got into them yesterday, too, but they couldn't stay."

"They're in them now," Bart said. He scowled as the enemy atop Proselytizers' Rise rolled stones and shot firepots and rained bolts down on the men. Then he ground out something startling and pungent, for he'd been shocked out of his usual impassivity. "Who in the seven hells ordered them to go *up* the Rise? They'll be slaughtered!"

"It wasn't me, sir," George said, "though your orders before yesterday's fight—"

"Never mind those," Bart said. "As you must know, those were for use if the lightning struck, and it didn't. I heard the commands you gave this morning, and they were just what I wanted. But if that charge fails—and what else can it do?—*somebody's* going to catch it, by all the gods. Can we do anything to call them back?"

Doubting George shook his head. "Not a thing, sir, not now. It's too late." Bart was dreadfully afraid he was right.

Normally, night suited Count Thraxton. Fewer people were awake to demand things of him and otherwise arouse his irascibility. *If only the rest of the world would leave me alone*, he often thought, *I would be the happiest man alive*.

But he was not happy now, and the world had no intention of leaving him alone. The world, in fact, was demanding things of him, and demanding things in a loud, piercing voice. The world, or at least what seemed like all the southrons in it, had spent the whole day doing their best to destroy his army, and their best had proved alarmingly good. Sentry Peak was lost, and Thraxton had no idea how to get it back.

"We haven't enough men," he grumbled.

"We might have, if you hadn't sent James of Broadpath away to hells and gone," Cabell of Broken Ridge said, his tone sharpened by the flask of brandy in front of him on the table.

Thraxton glared at his wing commander. "I suppose you will tell me next that Wesleyton does not need retaking," he said icily.

"I didn't say that," Cabell replied, and took another swig. "But if we lose here, what difference does it make whether Earl James takes Wesleyton or not? If we cannot hold our position, he won't be able to hold his."

"In that case, it is incumbent upon us not to lose here," Thraxton said. "Or would you disagree with me? Would you care to comment on how the southrons drove the men of your wing from Sentry Peak?"

"I can give it to you in half a dozen words, your Grace," Cabell of Broken Ridge snapped. *"We did not have enough men.* Is that plain enough?" His voice rose to a shout.

Thraxton growled something down deep in his throat. He turned away from Duke Cabell to Roast-Beef William, remarking, "Our right had no trouble holding, I will have you note."

"Our right is anchored on Funnel Hill, *sir*, I will have *you* note." Cabell put very little respect into Thraxton's title. "The ground I was charged to defend, unfortunately, did not offer us any such advantages."

Roast-Beef William coughed. In the firelight, his face looked not much ruddier than Duke Cabell's. A sheen of dried sweat did a good job of counterfeiting grease, though. He said, "Begging your pardon, sir, but my wing didn't have such an easy time as all that holding on to Funnel Hill. The gods-damned southrons look to have come up with a mage who's actually good for something."

"A showman. A mountebank," Thraxton said contemptuously. "I saw some of his little illusions from my headquarters here. He is good for frightening children; I have no doubt of that. But for doing anything that should seriously disturb a fighting man?" He shook his head. "I'm sorry, Lieutenant General, but no."

With another cough, Roast-Beef William also shook his big head. "And I'm sorry, too, Count Thraxton, but that's not what the mages attached to my wing say. As far as they're concerned, he's the nastiest son of a bitch to ever wear gray. Haven't you got their reports?"

"I've had more reports than I ever want to see," Thraxton said. "Since your wizards succeeded in neutralizing this terrible, terrible southron, I assume he couldn't be all that devilish, and I have other things to worry about."

"Such as what, your Grace?" Duke Cabell asked. "Such as *what*? What is the world coming to when the southrons assail us with sorcery and we do little or nothing to strike back? You are supposed to be a famous thaumaturge in your own right, are you not? Such talents are better seen than talked about, if anyone cares in the least for my opinion."

Thraxton knew that people who didn't care for him called him Thraxton the Braggart. Every once in a while, somebody like Ned of the Forest would do it to his face. Duke Cabell hadn't, not quite, but he'd come too close—especially since, with his rank, he was immune to most of the reprisals Thraxton might use.

And, to make things worse, Roast-Beef William

coughed once more and chimed in with, "If we ever needed some good, strong sorcery, now is the time."

"I shall give you everything that is in me," Thraxton said. "I have always given King Geoffrey everything that is in me. Our land would be better off if more folk in it could say the same."

"A free Detinan may say anything his heart desires," Cabell of Broken Ridge observed. "Whether it be the truth or something else, he may speak as he pleases."

William coughed again; he was beginning to sound like a man with a bad catarrh. "Your Grace, I do not think such comments aid our cause."

"Very well, Lieutenant General," Cabell said. "With your commendable" —he made the word into a sneer— "grasp of matters tactical, what do *you* think would aid our cause? How, being badly outnumbered as we are, do we lick the southrons?"

His sarcasm stung. But he'd asked a real question, an important question, even so. Count Thraxton leaned forward, the better to hear what Roast-Beef William would say. He hoped Roast-Beef William had an answer. *If he does, I'll steal it*, he thought without the slightest twinge of guilt.

But William only coughed yet again and muttered to himself. At last, impatiently, Thraxton coughed, too. Roast-Beef William said, "I'm sorry, your Grace. The only thing that occurs to me is that we might beat them with sorcery. Our manpower will not do the job, not even with the advantage of ground we hold."

Duke Cabell said, "That's the first sensible thing I've heard in this conference." He took another swig from his brandy flask.

"It's the first sensible thing *I've* heard in this conference," Thraxton said. "Certainly more than all the countless, senseless complaints I've had aimed at me."

"If you like, your Grace, we can continue this discussion through our friends," Cabell said. "Although you do not act like a gentleman, by blood you are one."

"As you undoubtedly know, regulations prohibit an officer of lower rank from challenging his superior," Thraxton said. "Nevertheless, however, I will be happy to give satisfaction at your convenience following the battle, if in truth that be your desire."

He spoke with a certain gloating anticipation. Duke Cabell licked his lips, suddenly not so sure of himself. He had a reputation as a redoubtable swordsman, but so did Thraxton. And who but a fool would challenge a mage to a duel? All sorts of . . . interesting things might go wrong.

"Gentlemen, please!" Roast-Beef William said. "I'm sure nobody meant any offense whatsoever. We're all just trying to lick the enemy as best we can, and we'd do well to remember that, in my opinion."

"Quite right." Cabell of Broken Ridge bowed to Count Thraxton. "My apologies, your Grace, and we can worry about carving each other's livers another time."

"Very well," Thraxton said. "I accept your apology, your Grace." Cabell looked unhappy; Thraxton offered no apology of his own. Doing so never crossed his mind. As usual, he didn't think he'd done anything to cause offense. He went on, "Our colleague is probably correct. We do need magecraft as both shield and spear against the southrons. I shall have the necessary spells prepared by the time fighting resumes in the morning."

"Can we rely on it?" Duke Cabell asked. He might not have known he was offending Count Thraxton with his question, but Thraxton was acutely aware of it.

Still, the commander of the Army of Franklin said only, "You can."

"May it be so." That soft murmur wasn't from Cabell. It came from Roast-Beef William, and hurt all the more as a result. William probably remembered Pottstown Pier and Reillyburgh, fights where Thraxton's sorcery hadn't done all it might have, where—however little he cared to recall the fact—it had come down on the heads of King Geoffrey's men, not on the accursed southrons.

"I do know what I am doing, gentlemen," Count Thraxton said. "Did I not prove as much in the fighting by the River of Death? Without my magic, we should never have won our victory there."

*We should have won more than we did.* Neither Duke Cabell nor Roast-Beef William said it out loud. But they both thought it very loudly; Thraxton could tell.

"We shall send them reeling back in dismay," Thraxton said. "We shall send them reeling back in defeat. We shall retake Rising Rock. From Rising Rock, we shall go on to retake all of Franklin."

"May it be so." This time, Cabell and Roast-Beef William spoke together. Neither one bothered keeping his voice down.

"May it be so, indeed," Thraxton said. "I intend to make it so."

"How, your Grace?" Duke Cabell asked.

"Never you mind," Thraxton answered. "My magecraft will find a way."

"Such claims have been made before, sir," Cabell said. Thraxton scowled at him. The quarrel seemed on the point of heating up again. Then Cabell went on, "And, if we know what your sorcery will be, what it will do, we can give our men orders that will let them take best advantage of it."

"That is an important point, your Grace," Roast-Beef William said.

"Perhaps," Thraxton said. But Cabell of Broken Ridge was right. Even if Thraxton couldn't stand the man, he knew as much. Grudgingly, he went on, "All right, then. What I intend to do is wait until the southrons are well involved in what will plainly be some important attack, then fill their spirits—which the gods must hate anyhow—with such fear that they can only flee."

"That will be very good," Roast-Beef William said.

"If you can do it," Duke Cabell added.

He got another glare from Thraxton, who spoke in icy tones: "I can do it, and I shall do it. Draft your orders, both of you, so that your men may exploit the southrons' terror and disarray."

"Yes, sir," William said dutifully. Cabell just gave a curt nod.

*You still don't believe me*, Thraxton thought. *I'll show you. I'll show everyone. Everyone who ever doubted me for any reason will know my might by the time this fight is done.* Aloud, he said, "Gentlemen, I dismiss you. I am sure that, when the morning comes, your men will continue to fight as gallantly as they already have. Now you must leave me to my sorcerous preparations."

Roast-Beef William left his headquarters in a hurry, as if he didn't want anything to do with magecraft. By the way Cabell of Broken Ridge departed, he didn't want anything to do with Count Thraxton. Thraxton could tell the difference. *Treat me as if I were a blond, will you? You'll be sneering out of the other side of your overbred mouth by this time tomorrow.*

He went to his sorcerous tomes with a grim intensity that would have alarmed friends as well as foes—had he had any friends nearer than King Geoffrey in Nonesuch. And he found the spells he wanted. The men who'd prepared them hadn't imagined that they could be aimed at a whole army rather than at a man or two, but that was their failure of imagination, not Count Thraxton's.

He forgot about sleep. He forgot about everything except the wizardry he was shaping. He didn't even notice it was growing light outside. He didn't notice anything except the pages in front of him till one of the sentries in front of his farmhouse headquarters exclaimed, "Lion God's claws, looks like every gods-damned southron in the world's lined up down there!"

That penetrated Thraxton's fog of concentration. His joints creaked as he rose from his chair. When he looked down on the enemy, he laughed. "So they think they can storm Proselytizers' Rise, do they? They might as well try to storm the gods' mystic mountain as ours. Let them come!" He laughed again.

Tiny and perfect in the distance, looking like so many toy soldiers, the southrons advanced toward the trench line at the base of Proselytizers' Rise. They'd come that far in the previous day's fighting, though they'd had to fall back. If they tried to come farther now . . . If they tried to come farther and then fear smote them . . .

Imagining thousands, tens of thousands, of panic-stricken men trying to tumble down the front slope of Proselytizers' Rise, Thraxton laughed yet again. That would be sweet, sweet enough to make up for all the embarrassment and bickering he'd had to put up with since the fight by the River of Death. "Let them come," he whispered. "Aye, let them come."

Come they did. The southrons might be—as far as Thraxton was concerned, they were—savages, ruffians, uncivilized brigands doing their best to pull down their betters. But they weren't cowards. If only they'd run from Merkle's Hill instead of standing fast . . . *But they had a good northern man—no, a bad northern man, for he chose the wrong side—leading them,* Count Thraxton thought. He wasted a moment sending a curse Doubting George's way.

Into the trenches at the base of Proselytizers' Rise swarmed the southrons. Before long, they had overrun them. And then, to Thraxton's delight, they did start storming up the side of Proselytizers' Rise, toward his men who were shooting down at them from above. Who could have given such a mad order? Whoever he was, Thraxton wanted to clasp his hand and thank him for aiding King Geoffrey's cause.

Thraxton peered down at the southrons scrambling toward him. General Bart's whole army seemed to be trying to pull itself up the steep slope of the Rise. Thraxton waited a few minutes more, then began his spell. Confidence flowed through his narrow chest as he incanted. No, nothing would go wrong this time. Nothing *could* go wrong this time. He'd been wrong before, perhaps, but not now. He laughed. Surely not now . . .

# XII

"Forward!" Captain Cephas shouted, waving his sword. His command was almost lost in the roar that came from the throats of hundreds of officers and the throats of hundreds of horns. And forward the men of Doubting George's army went.

"King Avram!" Rollant yelled. "King Avram and freedom!" He wasn't thrilled about moving once more against the base of Proselytizers' Rise, but nobody cared whether he was thrilled or not.

"We can do it!" Cephas said. Rollant didn't know whether they could do it or not. He wasn't going to worry about it very much, either. He would go forward as long and as hard as he could. If his comrades started going back instead of forward, he would go back, too— a little more slowly than most, so as not to let ordinary Detinans get any nasty ideas about blonds.

Beside him, Smitty said, "I hope the traitors up there at the top of the Rise are pissing in their pantaloons, watching us come at 'em."

"And the bastards in the trenches down below, too," Rollant added. "That'd be good."

"It sure would," Smitty agreed. Then he stared up toward the forbidding crest line of Proselytizers' Rise and grimaced. "Likelier, though, they're just sitting up there getting drunk and laughing their arses off at us."

Rollant thought that was pretty likely, too. All through the campaign, nobody in Rising Rock had said anything about driving the traitors from Proselytizers' Rise. The closer Rollant came to the base of the Rise, the more sense that made to him. It looked to him as if men who held the top could stay there forever.

The men in the trenches at the bottom of the Rise started shooting at the advancing southrons. They had a few engines with them, too, which hurled stones and firepots at Rollant and his comrades. A stone smashed two men to shrieking ruin only a few feet to his left. Something hot and wet splashed his wrist—somebody's drop of blood. With a soft, disgusted curse, he wiped the back of his hand on his pantaloons.

Then the southrons broke through the ditches and downed trees in front of the trench line. As it had been the day before, the fighting was fierce, but it didn't last long. The southrons had more men here today, and overwhelmed their foes. A few of the traitors got away, but only a few.

Having gained the trenches, what did the southrons have? Rollant had wondered that the day before, and still wondered now. The northerners on top of Proselytizers' Rise were free to shoot down at them to their hearts' content. And they galled the southrons, too, with their bolts and with the stones and firepots the engines up there hurled down.

"What do we do about this?" Rollant shouted to anyone who would listen. He hoped Smitty would have an answer, or Sergeant Joram, or Captain Cephas. If they didn't, he hoped the generals who'd sent the army forward—and who mostly hadn't come themselves—would. But no one said a word. A plunging crossbow bolt struck a soldier not far from him between the neck and the left shoulder and sank down through his flesh to pierce his heart. A surprised look on his face, the man fell dead. "What do we do?" Rollant repeated.

Afterwards, he would have taken oath that he heard someone with a great voice shouting, "Forward!" A few other men said the same thing, so he didn't think he'd imagined it. But he was never quite sure, for neither Smitty nor Joram nor a good many others recalled hearing anything of the sort.

What was plain was, the army couldn't stay there. It couldn't go back, not when it was only being stung, not unless it wanted to humiliate itself forevermore before General Bart and Doubting George—and humiliate George in the process. That left only one thing to do.

Rollant wasn't among the very first who started scrambling up the steep, rocky slope of Proselytizers' Rise toward the traitors at the crest line. He wasn't among the very first, but he wasn't far behind them, either. Anything seemed better than getting shot at when his crossbow lacked the range to shoot back.

"We're out of our minds," Smitty said as the two of them scrabbled for hand- and footholds. "They'll fornicating massacre us."

"Maybe they will," Rollant answered. "Maybe they won't, gods damn 'em. But we'll get close enough to hurt 'em before they do." A quarrel struck sparks from a stone a couple of feet in front of his face and harmlessly bounded away. *Maybe we'll get close enough to hurt the traitors*, he thought. *Maybe*.

More and more southrons were on the slope now. When Rollant looked back over his shoulder, the whole surface of the Rise below him was gray with soldiers taking the one way they could to come to grips with the foe. Even as he watched, a couple of them were hit and went rolling back down toward the trenches.

The spectacle of the southrons scrambling up the front face of Proselytizers' Rise was awe-inspiring enough from where he saw it. What did it look like from the crest, where the northerners watched a whole army heaving itself up the mountainside straight at them? Rollant didn't, couldn't, know. He just hoped he would make it to the top.

When he got about halfway up, he paused to shoot at the traitors peering down at him, and to reload once he had shot. He didn't know whether he hit anyone, but he'd come far enough to try. Another bolt spanged off a rock in front of him. *Lucky twice now*, went through his mind. *How much longer can I stay lucky?*

"They can't hit anybody," Smitty said, as obvious a lie as Rollant had ever heard.

Before he could answer, the sun seemed to dim for a moment, though no cloud was near. A breath of cold air went straight down the back of his neck.

Under his cap, all his butter-yellow hair tried to stand on end. He'd had those feelings before, back in his serf hut on Baron Ormerod's estate. "Magecraft," he whispered, putting all a serf's dread into the word. "That's strong magecraft."

Other voices, not all of them belonging to blonds, said the same thing or things that meant the same. The spell hovered over Proselytizers' Rise like a great bird of prey. Rollant shuddered, shivered, shook. *I must have been crazy to join King Avram's army, to go up against what the traitor lords can throw. Crazy? Worse than that. I must have been stupid.*

And the spell, after hovering for a few unbearable heartbeats, struck home. And the traitors atop the Rise howled like beaten dogs and fled, throwing away their weapons to run the faster.

Rollant stared up at the crest in delighted disbelief. That wasn't, that couldn't be, a bluff. That was real panic, and he knew exactly what had caused it. "Either our mages got a spell just right, or theirs botched one," he said as he scrambled forward.

"Bet on theirs botching one," Smitty said beside him. "Thraxton the Braggart's done it before."

"I know he has," Rollant answered. "It only goes to show that, every now and again, the gods do make sure there's some justice down here below."

"Maybe," Smitty said. "And maybe it just goes to show old Thraxton can't count past ten without taking off his shoes."

"Believe what you want to believe," Rollant said. "I'll put my faith in the gods. And I'll put my faith in getting to the top of the Rise before you do."

"That's what you think." Smitty made for the crestline as if propelled from a catapult. Rollant did his best to keep up, but found himself outdistanced.

Smitty waited, grinning, at the crest of the Rise. He gave Rollant a hand and pulled him upright. Somehow, it wasn't a race Rollant minded losing, especially when Smitty pointed west. "Will you look at those sons of bitches run? If they keep going like that, they won't stop till they get to the ocean."

"Good." Rollant brought up his crossbow to his shoulder and sent a bolt after the fleeing traitors.

More and more southrons, all of them whooping with the joy of men who unexpectedly find victory in place of disaster, came up onto the top of Proselytizers' Rise. And more and more of their officers, seeing Thraxton's men abandoning what had been the strongest of positions and running for their lives, shouted things like, "After them! Don't let them get away!"

Though still panting from the climb up the side of the Rise, Rollant was willing—Rollant, in fact, was eager—to go after the men who wanted to keep blonds bound to their land. And plenty of Detinans in the southrons' army went with him. Maybe they didn't care so much about serfdom, but they knew a won battle when they saw one, and they wanted to get as much as they could from this one.

"River of Death!" some of them shouted. "This pays you bastards back for the River of Death!"

The traitors who'd been on the crest of Proselytizers' Rise kept right on retreating in spite of the jeers from the southrons. Maybe, as Smitty said, they really would run till they came to the Western Ocean. When Thraxton's spells went wrong, they went spectacularly wrong. Rollant was glad this one hadn't gone right, or he would have been running back toward Rising Rock. But some northern soldiers finally formed lines to oppose the southrons. They were,

Rollant realized, the men whom Fighting Joseph had forced away from Sentry Peak the day before.

"See how thin they are, boys?" Captain Cephas called. "A couple of good volleys and they'll melt like ice in the springtime."

Rollant hadn't seen much in the way of ice before fleeing down to New Eborac; snow rarely fell near Karlsburg. But he was all for making the traitors melt away. That big, burly son of a bitch waving a sword, for instance. *Gods damn me if that doesn't look like Baron Ormerod*, he thought as he took aim with his crossbow. *Looks just the way Ormerod did when he almost put a hole in me.* Thinking thus, he aimed with extra care. He squeezed the trigger. The crossbow kicked his shoulder.

And the traitor dropped his sword, clutched his chest with both hands, and sagged to the ground. Rollant yowled in triumph. Whether it was Ormerod or not, he'd killed his man.

And Cephas had the right of it. There weren't enough northerners to stand up to the men facing them. After a couple of volleys, the company commander and other officers yelled, "Charge!" Charge the southrons did—and the traitors broke before them.

As Rollant loped past the man he'd slain, he looked down at him and whooped. "By all the gods, it *is* Ormerod!" he shouted, and kicked at the corpse. He missed, but he didn't care. "Tell me blonds can't fight, gods damn you." He hoped devils were doing horrible things to the baron's spirit down in one of those seven hells the Detinans talked about.

"Your liege lord?" Smitty said. "Did *you* shoot him?"

"I sure did," Rollant answered. "I just wish I

could've done it ten years ago." He paused. "No. All his Detinan friends would've caught me and burned me alive. Not now, though."

"No, not now," Smitty agreed. "Now we've just got to keep chasing all these traitor sons of bitches as far as we can."

More northerners kept coming forward to try to stem the retreat. They couldn't do it, but their rear-guard action finally did let the bulk of Thraxton's army break free of its pursuers and make its escape: the same role Doubting George's wing had played in the fight by the River of Death. By the time the sun set, most of the traitors were several miles ahead of General Bart's army, moving in the only direction open to them—up toward Peachtree Province.

Rollant and Smitty sprawled by a fire. Some of the soldiers ran up a tent for Captain Cephas, who'd kept up well but looked even more worn than most of his men. As Rollant was too tired even to get up and see what Hagen the blond had thrown into the stewpot, Cephas had to be truly weary. But when Rollant remarked on that, Smitty shook his head. "He wasn't too worn out to keep Corliss from sneaking in there," he said.

"What?" Rollant sat up, though every joint ached. "I didn't see that."

"Things happen whether you see them or not," Smitty said with a superior sniff.

"I know," Rollant answered. "*Bad* things are liable to happen on account of this." He glanced over at Hagen. As long as the escaped serf was busy dishing out supper, he might not have time to worry about where his wife had gone. For everyone's sake, Rollant hoped he wouldn't.

When Captain Cephas didn't emerge from the tent,

Lieutenant Griff ordered sentries out. "We have to stay alert," he said. "The traitors might counterattack." Rollant didn't believe it—the northerners were beaten men tonight—but he recognized the possibility. He also let out a long sigh of relief when Sergeant Joram didn't call his name. Making the most of the opportunity, he wrapped himself in his blanket and fell asleep.

He wouldn't have been surprised had Joram shaken him awake in the middle of the night to take someone's place on sentry-go. Getting jerked from sleep by a woman's shriek, though, took him back to the bad days on Baron Ormerod's estate, when Ormerod had enjoyed himself among the blond girls as he pleased.

For a moment, Rollant lay frozen. Back on the estate, he hadn't dared interfere. Few blonds did, and they all paid. But he wasn't on the estate, wasn't a serf, any more. A man's cry—no, two men's cries—rang out with the woman's. Rollant knew exactly where he was then, and feared he knew exactly what had happened. A cry of dismay on his own lips, he sprang to his feet and dashed toward Captain Cephas' tent.

Hagen burst out through the tent flap. He held a butcher knife, but hardly seemed to know it. He took a couple of stumbling steps, then fell on his face. Captain Cephas' sword stuck out of his back.

Cephas himself came out a moment later. "I got him," he said, and then something else, but the blood pouring from his mouth kept Rollant from understanding what. Cephas' left hand was clasped to his undershirt, the only garment he was wearing. He swayed, said one more clear word—"Corliss"—and crumpled as Hagen had before him.

"Oh, by the gods," Smitty said from behind Rollant, and set a hand on his shoulder. "Looks like you were right."

"I wish I'd been wrong," Rollant said. "Is she still in the tent?"

Smitty went inside before anyone else could. Rollant heard him gulp. "She's in here," he said, and his voice wobbled. "Hagen almost took her head off with that knife." He came out in a hurry, bent over, and was noisily sick. He might—he surely had—seen worse in battle. But you expected such things in battle. Here, after the victory was won . . .

"It takes the edge off," Rollant said. "It does more than that, in fact." He gulped, too, though he hadn't gone into the tent. What was outside was bad enough.

Smitty spat, swigged from his canteen, and spat again. "It does for us," he said. "But if you think the generals will care, you're daft." Rollant thought that over. Reluctantly, he nodded.

General Bart folded his right hand into a fist and smote his left palm, as much of a gesture of excitement as he ever allowed himself. The sun rose on as complete a triumph as the southron cause had seen in some time. He nodded to Doubting George, who was also just emerging from his pavilion. "Good morning, Lieutenant General. Now that we've whipped the northerners, let's see if we can run the legs off them and break their whole army to pieces."

"I wouldn't mind that at all," George said. "When General Guildenstern forced Thraxton the Braggart out of Rising Rock, he let him retreat, because he was sure Thraxton would run all the way up to Marthasville. He found out differently by the River of Death."

"Well, that's two lessons for us," Bart said.

"Two?" Doubting George asked.

"Yes, two," Bart replied. "The first is, pursue vigorously. The second is, keep your eyes open while you're doing it." He watched George consider that and nod. He would have been disappointed had the other officer done anything else. And he said what needed saying: "Congratulations to you and your men. They were the ones who cracked the Braggart's position and let us win our victory."

"Thank you very much, sir." George grinned wryly. "I would take more credit for it if I'd actually given the order that sent my men up the slope of Proselytizers' Rise, but thank you all the same. I do take no little pride in what my men accomplished, no matter who gave that order."

"If anyone did," Bart said. "Whoever he was, he's proved remarkably shy about coming forward and taking the credit for it." He hesitated, then went on, "Not to take anything away from whoever it was, or from you, or from your undoubtedly brave men, but Colonel Phineas gives me to understand that part of the credit for our victory and the traitors' defeat also goes to Count Thraxton for making a hash of a spell at just the wrong time."

"Yes, my mages told me the same thing," Lieutenant General George replied. "We hoped it would happen in the heat of battle, and it did."

"Give Thraxton the chance to make a mistake or make a man dislike him and he will take it more often than not," Bart said. He turned to a blond servant hurrying up with a tray. "Yes? What is it?"

"Your breakfast, sir." The servant sounded surprised he needed to ask. "Just what you said you wanted—

a cup of strong tea, no milk, no honey, and a cucumber sliced in vinegar."

"Perfect," Bart said. He dipped his head to Doubting George. "If you'll excuse me . . ."

"Of course, sir," George said. "What an . . . interesting breakfast."

"I eat it almost every day," Bart said. "I'm not a man of fancy tastes. I do as I do, and I am willing to let the men under me do as they do, provided they also do as I require when the time for that comes on the battlefield."

"You'd better be careful, sir," George said gravely. "Such judiciousness will get you into trouble." Only when he smiled could Bart be sure he was joking.

An aide said, "Lieutenant General Hesmucet is here, sir. Now that the traitors have left Funnel Hill, his men have occupied it."

"Good; that's very good." Bart resigned himself to eating breakfast in front of his subordinates. Doubting George said nothing at all to the aide. But Bart didn't need to be a mage to know what he was thinking. His men, who didn't have a reputation for boldness, had taken Proselytizers' Rise, while Hesmucet's soldiers, who did, had spent two fruitless days assailing Funnel Hill, and hadn't seized it till after the northerners withdrew.

Hesmucet gave the reins of his unicorn to a waiting trooper and hurried over to Bart and Doubting George. Without preamble, Hesmucet said, "Let's chase those traitor sons of bitches to the hells and gone. The less we let 'em up, the better off we'll be."

"I have no quarrel with that," Bart said.

"Neither have I," George said, "though I do think we would be wise to scout carefully out ahead of our main line of march, to keep us from running into trouble the way General Guildenstern did."

"Well, *I* have no quarrel with that," Hesmucet said. "I can't see how any sensible man would have a quarrel with that, although you never can tell with some people."

"Let's get on with it, then," General Bart said. "Soonest begun, soonest done, or so they say. I want to drive the Army of Franklin so far into Peachtree Province that it can't ever even dream of coming back to Franklin again."

"That's fine. Mighty fine, in fact," Hesmucet said.

"It will be fine indeed, if we can bring it off," George said. "Talking about such plans is always easier than making them work, though."

*He's not a coward*, Bart reminded himself. *He's a cautious man. There's a difference.* Hesmucet bristled at George's words, but didn't say anything himself. He wanted to go after the enemy, and was confident Bart would give him what he wanted.

Before Bart could make any remarks of his own, a scryer came up to him and said, "Sir, King Avram would speak with you from Georgetown."

"Would he?" Bart replied. The scryer solemnly nodded. Bart said, "Well, if the king wants to speak to the likes of me, I don't suppose I ought to keep him waiting. Take me to the right crystal ball and sit me down in front of it."

"Yes, sir. Come with me, sir," the scryer said.

Very shortly thereafter, Bart did sit down in front of a crystal ball from whose depths the long, bony face of King Avram stared out. "Congratulations, General, on the great victory you and your men have earned these past two days."

"Thank you kindly, sir," Bart said. "Thank you for

all the confidence you've had in me throughout this war."

Avram smiled a lopsided smile. Most of his smiles were lopsided. He was not, by any stretch of the imagination, a handsome man. Geoffrey and those who followed him made much of that, calling Avram a mistake of the gods and other, less complimentary, things. Handsome or not, though, Avram was engaging in a way the cold-blooded Geoffrey could never match. Seeing his smile, Bart had to return it; he couldn't help himself. Avram said, "I'd better be confident in you. You have the one quality I can't do without in a general: you fight."

"That's the point of the exercise, your Majesty," Bart said.

"You understand as much. It's second nature to you," the king said. "Too many men, though, think they've got their fancy uniforms for no better reason than looking pretty on parade. Now, if you'd be so kind, describe your present situation for me, and tell me what you plan to do next."

"Yes, sir." Bart obeyed. Avram had no formal soldierly training, but he'd learned a good deal about making war since he'd had to start doing it.

The king plucked at his beard. He'd grown it only after King Buchan died, perhaps to try to make himself look more regal. In Bart's opinion, it hadn't quite worked. But King Avram, though interested in Bart's views on matters military, had never given any sign he cared about the general's opinions on other matters. Avram said, "Had you planned to send your whole army after Count Thraxton?"

"Yes, sir," Bart said again. "Anything less would be asking for a nasty surprise like the one he gave General Guildenstern by the River of Death."

"Mm, yes, something to that, I suppose," Avram said. "At the same time, though, I am concerned about General Ambrose, over in Wesleyton. With James of Broadpath laying siege to him there, he could use some reinforcements, wouldn't you say?"

"Your Majesty, I'm not at all sure Earl James can go on with that siege now that we've beaten Thraxton the Braggart," Bart replied. "He has the last force loyal to the pretender left in the whole province of Franklin. If we were to go after him instead of Thraxton, we could crush him, and he has to know it."

"That wouldn't be so if he took Wesleyton before you got there, would it?" the king said. "I tell you frankly, General, I would be mighty unhappy if that happened. I've wanted to get an army into Wesleyton ever since this war started, and I don't care to see the chance lost before we can take advantage of it. Do I make myself plain?"

"You certainly do, your Majesty," Bart said with a sigh. "I still think you're fretting more than you need to, but—"

"But me no buts. That's what kings are for: to fret about things, I mean," Avram said. "Kindly take care of Wesleyton, General."

"I was about to say, sir, that I can send Fighting Joseph's wing in that direction," Bart said. "He has enough men under his command to meet James of Broadpath by himself, if need be, and enough to have a sizable edge on James if you add his men and Whiskery Ambrose's together."

King Avram stroked his beard again. After a moment, he nodded. "All right, General. Yes, I think that will do the trick." He raised one shaggy eyebrow. "I won't be sorry to see Fighting Joseph marching off into the middle of nowhere, either, and I've got a suspicion it won't exactly break your heart. Eh? What do you say about that?"

Avram might not have been a general, but he showed a shrewd understanding of his fellow man. "What do I have to say to that, your Majesty? I'd say you were right," Bart answered. "But I also have to say that, if I send Fighting Joseph off toward Wesleyton, it *will* delay my pursuit of Thraxton the Braggart."

"I'm willing to pay that price," the king said. "And, by the time the pursuit does get started, it may not be yours any more anyhow."

"Sir?" Bart said in surprise.

"One of the things I've been thinking for a while is that Detina hasn't had a marshal, an overall commanding general, for a goodish while, and that we need one right about now," Avram said. "Another thing I've been thinking for a while is that you're shaping pretty well for the job. That, I expect, would bring you here to the west to take charge of the fight against Duke Edward of Arlington and the Army of Southern Parthenia. What have you got to say for yourself?"

"Sir, if you think I'm up to it, I'll do my best not to disappoint you," Bart replied.

Avram nodded. "That will do. That will do nicely. What you try, General, you have a way of succeeding at."

*I have to*, Bart thought. *If I don't do well here, what can I fall back on? The spirits jar, and I'd fall into that, fall into it and never get out.* "Thank you kindly for all the trust you've placed in me," he said aloud.

"Thank *you* for not making me sorry I've done it,"

Avram answered. Yes, they understood each other well.

"Your Majesty, Detina's done a lot for me," Bart said. "The least I could do is give a little something back to the kingdom."

"General, what you and your men had given isn't a little something," the king said. "After what happened at the River of Death, I was afraid—I was very much afraid, though I wouldn't say so to most people—we would have to start the war in the east all over again, so to speak. Thanks to you, that isn't going to happen, and I thank you for it from the bottom of my heart. Good day to you."

"Good day, sir," Bart replied. In the middle of his words, the crystal ball went blank and empty. He turned and nodded to the scryer. "Thank you."

"My pleasure, sir," the young man said.

When Bart went out to Doubting George and Hesmucet, both lieutenant generals all but pounced on him. "What are our orders, sir?" one of them asked, at the same time as the other one was saying, "What did the king tell you?"

"We're going to have to send reinforcements to Whiskery Ambrose in Wesleyton," Bart answered. "That's what King Avram wants, and he is the king we swore to obey. It's not necessarily what I would do if I had a choice, but I don't."

Neither of the other officers made any effort to hide his disappointment. "That means we won't be able to chase the Braggart the way we ought to, gods damn it," Hesmucet growled.

"Whom will you send west to Wesleyton?" George asked.

*Will you send me?* he meant. *Will you get me out of the action after my men won your battle for you?*

Bart understood him as plainly as if he'd been shouting. The commanding general said, "King Avram and I talked that over. We agreed Fighting Joseph would be the best man for the job."

"Good choice!" Hesmucet said. Doubting George nodded. *Better him than me*, they both had to be thinking.

Bart coughed and then said, "There is some talk of my going west in the not too distant future."

"Congratulations, sir," George said. " 'Some talk' from the king is as good as an oration from anybody else."

He didn't ask whom Bart would leave in command in western Franklin if he did happen to be summoned to Georgetown. He probably already knew. Bart said, "I thank you. And I want everyone here to bear in mind that, even if we aren't going after Thraxton right this minute, that doesn't mean we aren't going to go after him at all. The day will come, and it will come soon."

"I'll go after Thraxton, if that's what needs doing," Hesmucet said. "I'll go after Marthasville, if *that's* what needs doing. But mostly, I aim to go after the traitors, grab hold of 'em, and shake 'em by the neck."

"Good," Bart said. "If King Avram calls me to the west, that's what I aim to do there."

"No, sir," the scryer who'd spoken to his opposite number in the Army of Franklin told Earl James of Broadpath. "There can be no possible doubt, not any more. The southrons have struck a heavy blow against Count Thraxton, and have forced his army off Sentry Peak and Proselytizers' Rise."

"Well, gods damn them," James said glumly. "I

wouldn't have thought a horde of half-divine heroes from the long-gone days could have forced an army off Proselytizers' Rise if it wasn't inclined to go, but what do I know? Did General Bart find some way to outflank our host?"

"No, sir," the scryer repeated. "They stormed Proselytizers' Rise from the front."

"*What?*" burst from Earl James. "How in the seven hells did even that imbecile Thraxton the Braggart— I beg your pardon, did Count Thraxton the commanding general—let such a thing happen?"

"As I understand, sir, there was a certain amount of difficulty with some piece of sorcery or another," the scryer said. "I am not certain of that, of course, but it does seem to be the most widely credited explanation."

" 'A certain amount of difficulty with some piece of sorcery or another'?" James echoed. The scryer nodded. "Oh, by the Lion God's claws!" James groaned. "By the Thunderer's prick! So he went and botched another one, did he?"

"That is my understanding," the scryer said primly.

"At least you *have* some understanding," James of Broadpath said. "By all the signs, that's more than Count Thraxton can claim." The scryer said nothing in response to that, which was probably wise on his part. With a sigh that sounded much like another groan, James asked, "What does Thraxton want me to do now? Does he think I ought to try to rejoin him?"

"No, sir," the scryer told him. "Count Thraxton believes the southrons are sending an army from Rising Rock in your direction, and does not find it likely that you could successfully evade it."

After a moment's thought, Earl James nodded. "Yes,

they'd do that. All right, then. I'll hold my position here in front of Wesleyton for as long as I can."

"Very good, sir. I shall report that to Count Thraxton's man." The scryer set about livening up his crystal ball once more.

James of Broadpath stood as if frozen in the scryers' tent for a moment. Then he exploded in a torrent of curses. They did no good at all. He knew as much. They did make him feel a little better, though. When he left the tent, he no longer felt like strangling the first man he saw in lieu of wrapping his meaty hands around the scrawny neck of Count Thraxton, whom he could not reach.

The first man he saw was Brigadier Alexander, who had charge of the army's engines. Alexander was young and cheerful and brighter than he had any business being. With a friendly wave, he asked, "How now, your Excellency?"

"How now?" James said. "I'll tell you how now, Brigadier, to the seven hells with me if I don't." He relayed everything he'd heard from the scryer, finishing, "*That's* how now, by all the gods. The Army of Franklin's wrecked, the southrons are sending an army of their own after us, and we can't break into Wesleyton. But for those minor details, all's well."

"He let the southrons storm Proselytizers' Rise against him?" Alexander said. "By all the gods, sir, an army of dead men could hold Proselytizers' Rise."

"That's what I thought," James answered. "In his infinite wisdom, however, the general commanding the Army of Franklin appears to have outdone himself."

"He's also left us in a hells of a pickle," Alexander remarked.

"Really?" James said. "I never would have noticed. I'm so grateful to you for pointing that out."

"Heh," Brigadier Alexander said. "What are we going to do, sir?"

"Try not to get squashed," James of Broadpath said. "If you've got any better answers, I'd be delighted to hear them."

"No, sir. I'm sorry, sir. I wish I did, sir," Alexander said. "How can we defend against the southrons moving on us from Rising Rock and from Whiskery Ambrose at the same time? Ambrose outnumbers us all by himself."

"I'm painfully aware of all that, too," James said. "I confess, I would worry more with, say, Hesmucet in Wesleyton than I do with Whiskery Ambrose. There are worse foes to have."

"Yes, the whole business of who one's opponent is can make a difference," Brigadier Alexander agreed. "Count Thraxton did rather better against Guildenstern than he did against Bart, for instance."

"Bart." James of Broadpath made a worried noise— had he heard it from another man, he might even have called it a frightened noise—deep in the back of his throat. "I know that man too well. Every day he is in command, he looks for a way to hit us. And he will keep on looking to hit us every single day, wherever he is posted, until this war ends."

"With our victory," Alexander said.

"Gods grant it be so," James said. "Meanwhile, back to our present predicament. I intend to hold our lines in front of Wesleyton with some of our force. I don't think Whiskery Ambrose will venture out into the open field against us."

"I'd say that's a pretty good bet," Alexander replied. "He's going to hold on to Wesleyton, and he's not going to do anything else." He sniffed. "The man has the imagination of a cherrystone clam."

James chuckled. "I won't say you're wrong. Even so, though, he does King Avram good and does us and King Geoffrey harm just by staying where he is. There's no doubt of that. He might do us more harm now if he came out, but he might come to grief, too, so I doubt he will."

"Thank you, Lieutenant General George," Brigadier Alexander said with a saucy grin.

"Doubting George would come out against me, because he'd be confident he could hold the place even if something went wrong," James said. "Whiskery Ambrose doesn't believe in himself so much. And he has reason not to, too." He went back to the business at hand: "Against Ambrose, I won't need the whole army. The rest I can move east, to try to hold the passes against the southrons when they come."

"Whom do you suppose Bart is sending against us?" Alexander asked.

"Maybe Hesmucet. I hope not—he knows what he's doing—but maybe." James stroked his beard. "Or maybe Fighting Joseph. The one thing you always want to do with Fighting Joseph is get him the devils out of your hair." *Count Thraxton must think the same of me*, went through James' mind. *Ah, if only I'd had the rank to send* him *off to Wesleyton. I'd have managed Proselytizers' Rise better. I could hardly have managed it worse.*

"Yes, Fighting Joseph," Alexander agreed. "That makes good sense to me."

"Bart has always been a sensible fellow," James said. "And now, if we're going to be sensible ourselves, we had better get moving, eh?"

He felt better in the saddle, riding away from Wesleyton on his robust unicorn. The fragment of his force that he left behind was smaller than Whiskery

Ambrose's—how could it be otherwise, when his whole force was smaller than the southron general's? The fragment he brought with him was bound to be smaller than the enemy detachment moving from Rising Rock against him. Whiskery Ambrose's inertia warded the part he left behind. The ground would, he hoped, do the same for the part he brought with him.

*Ground was supposed to protect Count Thraxton, too,* he thought, and wished he hadn't. His men were cheerful, at least till it started to rain—and rain, he hoped, would make things even harder for the enemy than it did for him.

"Stinking southrons can't whip us," one of his men said. "We're the Army of Southern Parthenia, by all the gods, and there ain't nobody in the whole wide world can whip us."

"That's right," James of Broadpath said. And so it might be, as long as the men believed it.

He didn't believe it himself. The southrons made good soldiers. They'd beaten the Army of Southern Parthenia down at Essoville just a few months before, beaten it badly enough to make Duke Edward fall back into Parthenia and stay there. The soldier who'd been boasting had probably fought at Essoville, and shrugged off the defeat as one of those things. The north probably did have better generals—some of them, anyway. *Of course, we also have Thraxton,* James thought. *He makes up for a lot.*

Brigadier Falayette rode up to him. "Sir," he said, saluting, "I don't think we can make a successful resistance against the southrons, not if they oppose us with even a halfway intelligent plan of attack."

"For one thing, there's no guarantee they will," James replied. "For another, Brigadier, have you got any better ideas? You don't seem to want to carry out attacks and you don't seem to want to make a defense, either. What *do* you have in mind? Shall we surrender?"

"I didn't mean *that*, sir," Falayette said stiffly.

"What the hells *did* you mean, then?" James of Broadpath demanded. "Did you mean you're sick of the war and you want to go home? By the gods, Brigadier, I'm sick of the war and I want to go home, too. But if you want to leave as badly as that, I can arrange it. I can dismiss you from King Geoffrey's service and gods-damned well *send* you home. Is that what you've got in mind?"

"No, sir," Brigadier Falayette replied, reddening. "I was merely pointing out the difficulties inherent in our position."

"I'm painfully aware of them myself, thank you," James said. "Whining about them doesn't help. Trying to do something about them possibly may."

He waited to see if Falayette had any real suggestions to make. The brigadier tugged on his unicorn's reins, jerking the animal's head around, and rode off. He was talking to himself under his breath. Perhaps fortunately, James couldn't make out what he was saying. Had he been able to, he might have had his friends speak to Falayette's friends, assuming the gloomy brigadier had any.

When they got to the pass Lieutenant General James hoped to defend, his own spirits rose, though he wouldn't have testified as to those of Brigadier Falayette. He summoned Brigadier Alexander and said, "Site your engines where they will bear to best advantage on the enemy."

"Yes, sir," Alexander said enthusiastically. "I hope the southrons do try to gore their way through. We'll make them pay, and pay plenty."

"That's the idea." James gave orders to cut down trees and move stones for field fortifications. The men worked steadily, plainly understanding what they needed to do and why they needed to do it. They did sometimes grumble about the rations they got, but James would have been surprised if they hadn't. Soldiers who had to stay in the field once the roads got muddy had to make do with short commons more often than not.

The southrons approached the pass two days later. By then, James of Broadpath had learned from prisoners that Fighting Joseph did command them. He wondered if Joseph would throw the whole southron force at his fieldworks. But the southron commander had apparently learned caution at Viziersville, if he'd learned nothing else. He tapped at the position in front of him, decided it was solid, and then settled down to figure out what to do next.

James of Broadpath didn't have time on his side. When Fighting Joseph was careless with a column of supply wagons, James sent out his unicorn-riders, captured the wagons, and brought them back to his own camp. He led a happier force after that. The northerners had done without luxuries such as tea and sugar for a long time, as southron ships held most goods from overseas away from their ports.

Fighting Joseph tapped at his defenses again a couple of days later, and again failed to break through. He tried once more, harder, the day after that, and did some real damage before deciding he wasn't going to penetrate James' line. James was more relieved than not when he gave up not long before sunset; one more hard push might have been enough to do the job.

Brigadier Falayette thought so. "If he strikes us

again, sir, we are ruined—ruined, I tell you!" he cried, striking a melodramatic pose.

But he'd been crying ruin and striking melodramatic poses ever since James' detachment moved out from Rising Rock toward Wesleyton, so all James said was, "Oh, quit your carping." He turned to Brigadier Alexander, whom he trusted to take a more sensible view of things. "What do you think?" he asked the officer in charge of his engines.

To his dismay, Alexander replied, "I fear my colleague may well be right, sir. If he comes at us with resolution tomorrow, we could find ourselves in some difficulty."

"Well, we'll just have to get ready to receive him in the morning as best we can," James of Broadpath said—hardly the ringing, inspirational battle cry he'd hoped to give. He rode along the line to encourage his men. All he succeeded in doing was discouraging himself. The soldiers seemed only too well aware that another attack might be too much for them to handle.

But instead of throwing in another attack the next morning, Fighting Joseph turned his own force around and marched off to the northeast, the direction from which he'd come. "Gods be praised!" Brigadier Alexander exclaimed. "He must have got orders to rejoin General Bart, which means we're safe for the time being."

"So it does," James of Broadpath agreed. He granted himself the luxury of a sigh of relief, but then unhappily added, "I fear we cannot say the same for the Army of Franklin, however."

The Army of Franklin had encamped in and around the miserable little town of Borders, near the

southeasternmost corner of Peachtree Province. There
Count Thraxton labored valiantly to put the blame
for the defeat—the disaster—at Sentry Peak and Proselytizers' Rise on anyone, on everyone, but himself.

King Geoffrey's long, stern face peered at him from
out of a crystal ball. Geoffrey, Thraxton knew, was
his friend. Nevertheless, the king sounded as stern
as he looked when he said, "I expected rather better from you, your Grace; I truly did."

"I quite understand that, your Majesty," replied
Thraxton, who understood no such thing. "I fear we
both erred in the conclusion for me to retain command here after the clamor against me."

He still hoped Geoffrey would tell him that had
been no error, that no one else could have done as
well as he had. But the king gave him only a curt nod.
"Yes, that was an error, and now I shall have to find
a new commander for the Army of Franklin under
harder circumstances than I would have before."

Rage boiled up in Thraxton. "By the gods, sir, I
would have done better—I would have won that fight,
sir—were it not for the bad conduct of veteran troops
who had never before failed in any duty."

"On what do you blame this failure, your Grace?"
King Geoffrey asked.

"In part, your Majesty, the men on Proselytizers'
Rise could simply see too much," Thraxton replied.
"They watched the swarm of southrons coming toward
them and they lost their nerve. And, in part, their
demoralization came from the effect produced by the
treasonable act of James of Broadpath, Dan of Rabbit
Hill, and Leonidas the Priest in sacrificing the army
in their effort to degrade and remove me for personal ends."

Geoffrey coughed a couple of times. When at last

he spoke, he plainly chose his words with care: "I have heard reports to the effect that one reason for our retreat from Proselytizers' Rise was the failure of our sorcery. How much truth lies in those reports?"

"Perhaps . . . some, your Majesty," Thraxton answered reluctantly. "I intended to cast a spell of terror on the southrons that would have sent them flying back to Rising Rock in rout and ruin."

"That did not happen," Geoffrey said, a truth so painfully obvious that Thraxton couldn't deny it.

That being so, he didn't waste his breath trying. "No, your Majesty, that did not happen, for which you have my profoundest regrets. But I must say, sir, that not a single one of the arrogant little manikins who claim I mistakenly cast the spell upon our own brave and patriotic soldiers has any true knowledge or understanding of the arcane forces at my control."

"I . . . see," King Geoffrey said after another pause. "You are not of the opinion, then, that a sudden burst of sorcerously inspired terror might have caused our men to abandon what should have been an impregnable position?"

"A sudden burst of sorcerously inspired terror might have done exactly that, your Majesty," Count Thraxton replied. "But any claim that I caused such a burst of terror among our men would be all the better for proof, of which there is none." *I couldn't have done such a thing, not this time. And if I couldn't have done it, why then, I didn't do it. It's as simple as that.*

Again, the king coughed. Again, the king paused to choose his words with care. At last, he asked, "If sorcery gone awry did not cause our men to abandon Proselytizers' Rise, what, in your opinion, did?"

"I have already alluded to the treacherous, treasonous conduct of officers formerly occupying positions of trust and prominence in the Army of Franklin," Thraxton said.

"So you have," King Geoffrey replied.

Thraxton didn't care for his tone. He had the vague feeling this interview wasn't going so well as he would have liked. Taking a deep breath, he went on. "I might also note that certain officers, Duke Cabell of Broken Ridge among them, are of less use than they might otherwise be, for they take to the bottle at once, and drown their cares by becoming stupid and unfit for any duty. This drunkenness, most flagrant, during the whole three days of our travail, contributed in no small measure to the disaster that befell us."

Geoffrey pursed his thin, pale lips. "So you blame your subordinates, both past and current, for the present unfortunate position of your army?"

"Your Majesty, I do," Count Thraxton said firmly. Relief washed through him, warm as spring sunshine. He'd been afraid the king didn't understand, but now he saw he'd been mistaken. Everything might turn out all right after all. Despite what Geoffrey had said before, he might yet hang on to his command.

But then the king sighed and said, "Yes, I was right before. I am going to name Joseph the Gamecock to replace you as head of the Army of Franklin."

"Joseph the Gamecock?" Thraxton said in dismay. "You must be joking, sir! Why, he's such a bad-tempered little man that no one can get along with him!"

"I have certainly had my difficulties along those lines," King Geoffrey said. "But your own judgment as to yourself was accurate; you should not have remained where you were, and you can no longer remain where you are. You have not the confidence of the officers serving under you."

"They are all a pack of jackals and jackasses!" Thraxton burst out. "You say I have not their confidence, sir? Well, they have not mine, either. By all the gods, I would dismiss every one of them were the power in me."

"I cannot dismiss every officer serving in the Army of Franklin," Geoffrey said. "I would not if I could. It would bring even more chaos than that unhappy army has seen up to now. You were in command, my friend, and you must answer for the shortcomings of those you commanded."

"Very well," Thraxton replied, though it was anything but. "Will you do me the courtesy of allowing me to resign the command on my own rather than being summarily dismissed from it?"

"Of course I will," the king said. "I will do anything within my power to let you down as easily as I may, but let you down I must."

"I *was* let down," Thraxton raged, "let down by those who should have done everything in their power to support me." His stomach twinged agonizingly. The healers had warned him he was liable to start puking blood if that went on. They'd told him to put less of a burden on himself, to demand less of others. But they hadn't told him how to do that while fighting a war, worse luck. He gathered himself. "How may I best serve the kingdom after leaving this army?"

As soon as he asked the question, he wished he'd kept his mouth shut. The king was liable to say something like, *Go home and never show your face in any public place again.* What could he do but obey? But he didn't want to fade into obscurity. He wanted a higher place than the one he had.

Instead of relegating him to the shadows, Geoffrey replied, "You know I always value your advice, your Grace. Come to Nonesuch after laying down your command there. Your insights into the struggle will be important to me, and if you serve in an advisory capacity you will no longer, ah, come into difficulties with other officers opposing Avram's tyranny."

"Come into difficulties?" Thraxton said. "Am I at fault if I have the misfortune of being surrounded by idiots?"

"Let us not delve into questions of fault for the time being," King Geoffrey said quickly. "Come to Nonesuch. That will suffice."

"I obey," Count Thraxton said. "I always obey." He gave a martyred sigh. "Would that others might say the same." Being a mage in his own right, he ended the talk with the king while giving himself the last word. He stalked away from the crystal ball with a horrid frown on his face and with fire scourging his belly.

His headquarters were in what had been a rich man's house in Borders. But the serfs had fled, and without servants the house seemed much too big for Thraxton and his aides. He strode inside, speaking to no one, found pen and ink, and wrote furiously. When he was through, he told a runner, "Fetch me Roast-Beef William at once."

"Yes, sir." The man hurried away. Thraxton's grim face probably encouraged him to escape all the faster.

Roast-Beef William arrived with commendable haste. "What can I do for you, your Grace?" he asked. If Thraxton's expression fazed him, he didn't show it.

"Here." Brusquely, Thraxton thrust the note into his hands.

After reading it, Roast-Beef William nodded. "I was

afraid this might be coming, sir. The king will know of it?"

"Oh, yes," Count Thraxton said bitterly. "The king will indeed know of it. He has appointed Joseph the Gamecock as my successor in command here."

"Well, that's good. That's very good," William said, which was the last thing Thraxton wanted to hear. "He'll make a first-rate leader, so he will."

"May you prove correct," Thraxton replied, in tones suggesting he thought the other officer was several slices short of a loaf.

If Roast-Beef William noticed that tone, he didn't let it anger him. Thraxton had had a hard time making him angry, and didn't know whether to admire or despise him for it. Roast-Beef William just went on with his own glideway of thought: "Yes, I do think Joseph the Gamecock will be just what we need. We won't be doing much in the way of attacking for a while—that's as plain as the nose on my face. And there's nobody better than Joseph the Gamecock at standing on the defensive, nobody in the whole wide world."

"Is that a fact?" Thraxton said coldly. In his own judgment, *he* was a matchless defensive fighter. He thought himself perfectly objective about it, too.

But Roast-Beef William soberly nodded. "Yes, sir, I think it is," he answered. "Remember when he was defending Nonesuch against the southrons after they came up the Henry River at him? He didn't even have half the men they did, but he held 'em off. He had people *playacting*, by the gods, marching men back and forth so they'd look like four brigades instead of just one."

"Folderol," Thraxton said. "Claptrap."

"Maybe so, but it worked," Roast-Beef William

said. "When you get right down to it, that's the only thing that matters, isn't it?"

Was he deliberately rubbing salt in Thraxton's wounds? Had William been any of several other officers, Thraxton would have been sure of it. With William, though, even his suspicious nature hesitated before laying blame. "May there be victory for us here," Thraxton choked out at last.

"Gods grant it be so." Roast-Beef William cocked his head to one side, as if remembering what he should have thought of long before. "And what will you be doing now, sir?"

"King Geoffrey has summoned me to Nonesuch, to advise him on matters military," Thraxton replied.

"That's good. That's very good." Roast-Beef William chuckled. "Keep you out of mischief, eh?"

Again, Thraxton couldn't decide if that was a cut or merely a witticism in questionable—very questionable—taste. Again, he reluctantly gave William the benefit of the doubt, where he wouldn't have for most of the men under his command. William had fought hard and stayed sober. And so Thraxton said, "Heh"—all the laughter he had in him.

"Well, good luck to you, sir," William said. "I'm sure you mean well." He went on his way: a sunny man who was sure that everyone meant well. Thraxton was just as sure he labored under a delusion, but what point to tell a blockhead that he was a blockhead? Off Roast-Beef William went, as ready to put his optimism at Joseph the Gamecock's service as he had been to offer it to Thraxton.

Off Count Thraxton went, too, off toward the glideway port. "N-no, sir," a startled clerk said when he arrived. "We haven't got any carpets departing for Nonesuch today."

"Procure one," Thraxton said coldly. The clerk gaped. Thraxton glared. "You know who I am. You know I have the authority to give such an order. And you had better know what will happen to you if you fail to obey it. Do you?"

"Y-yes, sir," the clerk said. "If—if you'll excuse me, sir." He fled.

Thraxton waited with such patience as was in him: not much. Presently, the clerk's superior came up to him. "You need a special carpet laid on?"

"I do," Thraxton replied.

"And it'll take you away and you won't come back?" the glideway official persisted.

"That is correct," Thraxton said. *Gods damn you,* he added to himself.

"Well, I reckon we can take care of you, in *that* case," the glideway man said. Thraxton nodded, pleased at being accommodated. Only a moment later did he realize this fellow hadn't paid him a compliment. To make sure he remained in no doubt whatsoever, the wretch went on, "Maybe they'll bring in somebody who knows what the hells he's doing." He smiled unpleasantly at Thraxton. "And if you try cursing me, your high and mighty Grace, I promise you'll *never* see a glideway carpet out of Borders."

Sure enough, that threat did keep Thraxton from doing what he most wanted to do. No, that wasn't true: what he *most* wanted to do right now was escape the Army of Franklin, escape his humiliation, escape his own mistakes, escape himself. And, as the glideway carpet silently and smoothly took him off toward Nonesuch, he managed every one of those escapes . . . except, of course, the very last.

✧     ✧     ✧

A runner came up to Lieutenant General Hesmucet in the streets of Rising Rock, saluted, and waited to be noticed while Hesmucet chatted with Alva the mage. Hesmucet could hardly have helped noticing him; he was a big, burly fellow who looked better suited to driving messengers away than to being one. "Yes? What is it?" Hesmucet said.

Saluting again, the runner said, "General Bart's compliments, sir, and he desires that you attend him at his headquarters at your earliest convenience."

"When a superior says that, he means right this minute," Hesmucet said. The runner nodded. Hesmucet turned to Alva. "You must excuse me. There's one man in this part of the kingdom who can give me orders, and he's just gone and done it."

"Of course, sir," the wizard replied. "I hope the news is good, whatever it may be."

"Gods grant it be so," Hesmucet said. Alva smiled a peculiar, rather tight, smile. Hesmucet was almost all the way back to the hostel that had headquartered first Count Thraxton, then General Guildenstern, and now General Bart before he remembered the bright young mage's remarks about how small a role he thought the gods played in ordinary human affairs. When he did recall it, he wished he hadn't. He wanted to think the gods were on his side.

Bart sat drinking tea in his room. "Good morning, Lieutenant General," he said. With him sat Doubting George, who nodded politely.

Hesmucet saluted Bart. "Good morning, sir." He nodded to George. "Your Excellency." Hesmucet wasn't an Excellency himself. If he succeeded in the war, he might become one.

"My news is very simple," Bart said. "King Avram is summoning me to Georgetown and to the Black

Palace, as he said he might. He also told me he intends to name me Marshal of Detina when I arrive there."

Hesmucet whistled softly. "Congratulations, sir. Congratulations from the bottom of my heart. It's been—what?—eighty years or so since the kingdom last had a marshal. If any man deserves the job, you're the one."

"For which I thank you kindly," Bart replied. He, Hesmucet, and doubtless Doubting George, as well, understood why Detina so seldom had a soldier of such exalted rank. A man supreme over all the kingdom's soldiers might easily aspire to the throne himself, and kings knew that. Bart went on, "I intend to deserve the trust Avram is showing me."

"Of course, sir," Hesmucet said—what else could he possibly say?

"No one could be reckoned more reliable than General Bart," George said. He was no particular friend of Bart's, but he didn't seem jealous that Bart had ascended to this peak of soldierly distinction. That took considerable character.

"When I become marshal," Bart went on, "I expect I'm going to have to stay in the west. If the king in his wisdom decides we need a marshal, he'll want that man to concentrate on trying to whip Duke Edward of Arlington and going after Nonesuch. If you're in Georgetown, if you're living in the Black Palace, that will seem the most important thing in the world."

Both Hesmucet and Doubting George soberly nodded. Ever since the war began, the cry in Georgetown had always been, "Forward to Nonesuch!" As Hesmucet knew, it was a cry that had produced some impressive disasters: the first battle at Cow Jog sprang to mind. False King Geoffrey's men might have gone on and captured Georgetown and split Detina forever if they hadn't been almost as disrupted in victory as Avram's army was in defeat.

Bart said, "That leads me to the arrangements I'm going to make for the armies here in the east. The fight here won't get the fame of the battles over in Parthenia. We all know that. I'm sorry about it, but I can't change it, and nobody else can, either."

"Oh, I don't know," George said. "King Geoffrey could have changed it if he'd sent Duke Edward out this way instead of Joseph the Gamecock. Joseph's a formidable fighter, but the bards and the chroniclers cluster round Edward like ravens and vultures round a dead steer."

"Pleasant turn of phrase," Bart said with a smile.

"Sir . . ." Hesmucet's driving ambition wouldn't let him sit around and wait for Bart to get to things by easy stages. He had to *know*. "Sir, what arrangements *have* you made for the armies here in the east?"

"Well, I was coming to that," Bart replied.

Hesmucet forced himself just to nod and not to bark more questions. He'd thought he had the inside track on higher command till his men banged their heads in vain against the strong northern position on Funnel Hill while George's, against all odds, stormed the slopes of Proselytizers' Rise. Of course, Count Thraxton's botched magecraft had had a good deal to do with George's success, but would Bart remember it?

The commanding general was looking at him. "One of the things I have recommended to King Avram, Lieutenant General Hesmucet, and one of the things he has said he will do"—he might not have intended to, but he was stringing it out, making Hesmucet wait, threatening to drive him mad—"is to promote you to full general, to leave no doubt who will and should be in command here in the east."

A long breath sighed out of Hesmucet. "Thank you very much, sir."

"General Bart—Marshal Bart—already told me what he had in mind along those lines," George said. "Congratulations, General."

"Thank you, too," Hesmucet said. "I expect we'll be working together closely to defeat the common foe."

"I expect you're right, sir," Doubting George replied. "Give me my orders, and I will carry them out as best I can."

"I'm sure you will, your Excellency." Hesmucet was also sure George had desperately wanted the command he'd just received himself. Some officers, in that situation, would try to undercut their superiors. Fighting Joseph would, in a heartbeat. Hesmucet didn't think Doubting George was a man of that sort. He hoped George wasn't. *But if he is, I'll deal with it—and with him.*

Bart said, "You will have charge of everything between the Green Ridge Mountains and the Great River. Take your station where you will, though I intend that you concentrate on Joseph the Gamecock's army, as I will concentrate on Duke Edward's."

"Yes, *sir!*" Hesmucet said enthusiastically. "That's just what I aim to do. If we can smash those two armies, King Geoffrey hasn't got anything left." He saluted again. "Thank you for giving me the chance to do this."

"Well, you won't do it all by your lonesome," Bart remarked.

*Ah. Now we come down to it,* Hesmucet thought. He asked the question the new marshal was surely waiting for: "What sort of arrangement for the armies under my command—under *your* command—have you got in mind?"

"First and foremost, I think you'd be wise to leave Doubting George here in command of the army that used to belong to General Guildenstern," Bart answered. "Since that'll be far and away the biggest army here in the east, he'll be your second-in-command. Does that suit you?"

"Yes, sir. It suits me fine." Hesmucet turned to George. "Does it suit you, Lieutenant General?"

"I tell you frankly, sir, there is one other arrangement that would have suited me better," Lieutenant General George replied. "But I'll do everything I can to whip the traitors, and that includes following your orders. From what I've seen, I think you'll give pretty good ones."

"Thank you." Hesmucet stuck out his hand. If Doubting George hesitated for even a moment before clasping it, Hesmucet didn't notice.

"Good. That's settled." Bart sounded relieved. *What would the new marshal have done for a second-in-command here if George hadn't cared to serve under me?* Hesmucet wondered. *Fighting Joseph? Gods forbid!*

"My next question, sir, is, when do you want me to get moving against Joseph the Gamecock and whatever's left of the Army of Franklin?" Hesmucet said.

For one of the rare times Hesmucet could recall, Bart looked faintly embarrassed. "It won't be quite so soon as you'd like," he replied.

"What? Why not?" Hesmucet demanded.

"Because I'm going to want your campaign against Joseph and mine against Duke Edward to start more or less at the same time," Bart said. "That way, neither one of them will be able to reinforce the other, the way Edward sent James of Broadpath here to the east. I'm going to need a while to get a grip on things there in the west, so we may well have to wait till spring."

"I want to move sooner," Hesmucet grumbled.

Doubting George inclined his head to his new superior. "Do you know, sir, if King Avram had had himself half a dozen generals who wouldn't be satisfied with waiting just a little while, with being almost on time, he'd have put paid to the northerners' revolt a long time ago."

"You may be right," Hesmucet said. Then he shook his head. "No, gods damn it, you *are* right. But I'll tell you something else. The king has got himself two of that kind of general now." He pointed to Marshal Bart, then jabbed a thumb at his own chest. After a moment, he said, "Make that three," and pointed to Lieutenant General George, too.

"I do thank you very much for the kind inclusion," George said. "But you two are the ones who count, and you two are also in the spots that count. Grand Duke Geoffrey won't have such a happy time of it from here on in, unless I'm wronger than usual, and" —his eyes twinkled— "I doubt I am."

"I know that I'm leaving the east in good hands," Bart said. "What sort of a mess I'll find when I get to the west—that's liable to be a different question. People back there have let Duke Edward cow them for too long. He can be beaten, I do believe, and I aim to try to do it."

"From what I've seen and from what I've heard, the soldiers there in the west go into a fight with Duke Edward wondering what he's going to do to them," Hesmucet said. "They don't think so much about what they can do to him. If you worry about what the other fellow is going to do, you'll wind up in trouble."

Bart nodded. "That's right. That's just right, I do believe. I aim to keep Duke Edward on too tight a leash to let him run wild the way he has a couple of times in this war. I don't know if I can do that, but it's what I'm going to aim for."

"Makes sense to me," Hesmucet said. "I will do the same to Joseph the Gamecock, as best I can."

Doubting George said, "Do one other thing, sir."

"And that is?" Hesmucet asked.

"Keep Ned of the Forest busy the same way," George replied. "We are going to have ourselves a devils of a long supply line as we move up into Peachtree Province, and we'll be depending on a handful of glideways to bring us food and bolts and firepots and such. If ever there was a man who knows how to hit a supply line, Ned of the Forest is the one."

"You're right," Hesmucet said. "You're absolutely dead right. That man is a demon, and I don't see how we can hold down the countryside until he's dead. I promise you, I'll trouble him all the time. He'll be too busy staying alive to bother us too much—or I hope he will, anyhow."

He'd wondered if he should speak sharply when Doubting George made his suggestion. Was the other man trying to sneak his way into command when he didn't have the rank? But what George proposed made such good sense, Hesmucet saw no way to disagree with it.

Bart held out his hand. Hesmucet took it. "Well, General," Bart said, "I look forward to working with you when spring comes. We're still on the same team, still pulling the same plow, even if we won't be side by side for a while."

"That's so," Hesmucet said. "And what we need to aim to do is, we need to plow up this weed of a rebellion. If the gods be kind, we can do it."

"I think you two can do it," Doubting George said, "and I congratulate you both." He clasped hands first with Bart, then with Hesmucet. *He* will *make a good second-in-command*, Hesmucet thought. *If he's jealous about having to serve under me, he's the only one who knows it. And that's the way it ought to be.*

Hesmucet left General—no, Marshal—Bart's chamber. A buzz rose in the hostel lobby when he came out of the stairwell. "Is it true, sir?" someone called. No mage had yet divined how rumor traveled so fast.

"It's true," Hesmucet answered, and the buzz redoubled. He added, "But I'll thank you not to pester me about it right this minute. I need to think." Unpestered—which would do for a miracle till a greater one came along—he strode through the lobby and out onto the street.

Men called to him there, too. Rumor had to be running wild in Rising Rock. But he ignored them. He ignored everything in this muddy town. His gaze swung toward the north and the west, toward Peachtree Province, toward the glideway center at Marthasville. He could see the city in his mind's eye as if nothing stood between him and it.

And nothing did—nothing except Joseph the Gamecock's army. Hesmucet threw back his head and laughed. "That's not so gods-damned much," he said, and began to think of how he, unlike Count Thraxton, might make such a brag come true.

# NOT QUITE A
# HISTORICAL NOTE

*Sentry Peak* is a work of fiction. Any resemblance to actual people or situations is purely a coincidence. It says so right there on the copyright page. Nonetheless, there are those who insist on imagining that art sometimes imitates life. For them, the following may perhaps prove of some minor interest.

In late summer 1863, Union General William S. Rosecrans flanked Confederate General Braxton Bragg out of Chattanooga, Tennessee. Bragg retreated south into northern Georgia. Reacting to the threat in the West, Confederate President Jefferson Davis sent a corps of the Army of Northern Virginia under General James Longstreet to aid Bragg against the encroaching Federals. Meanwhile, U.S. General Ambrose Burnside occupied Knoxville, in the mountains of eastern Tennessee.

Rosecrans thought Bragg had retreated farther

and faster than in fact was the case. Bragg, in northern Georgia, was spoiling for a fight. He lost the chance to strike the advancing columns of Rosecrans' army separately when his subordinate commanders would not move in a timely fashion, but, just after the Union army reunited, struck it a solid blow at Chickamauga. Rosecrans was forced to retreat all the way back to Chattanooga. Only the sturdy resistance of General George Thomas' corps on Snodgrass Hill kept Rosecrans' entire army from dissolving.

Nathan Bedford Forrest, who had commanded Bragg's cavalry, quarreled savagely with his superior (as did a great many men who served with or under Bragg throughout the course of the war) and left the Army of Tennessee, which did not help its cavalry at all. Even so, it laid siege, after a fashion, to Chattanooga. Having lost a quarter of his men in the victory at Chickamauga, Bragg did not see how he could mount an attack on the place. Not all his subordinates agreed. They sent President Davis what was in essence a vote of no-confidence in Bragg; Davis visited the front, but retained Bragg, who fired corps commanders with wild abandon.

Lincoln reinforced Chattanooga with 37,000 men, under Generals Ulysses S. Grant and William T. Sherman. They loosened Bragg's tenuous siege on the city and prepared to try to drive the Confederates back. Bragg, meanwhile, weakened his own army by sending Longstreet northeast to try to retake Knoxville; this failed.

On November 24, 1863, a Union corps under General Joseph Hooker cleared the Confederates from the forward slopes of Lookout Mountain, south of Chattanooga. Sherman's attack on Tunnel Hill to the east failed. On November 25, Grant asked General Thomas to have his men make a demonstration against Missionary Ridge, just south of Tunnel Hill. He did not believe the formidable position could be taken by frontal assault. Thomas' men moved forward—and kept swarming up the ridge, altogether without orders from above. The Confederates at the top of the ridge, perhaps unnerved by watching four divisions coming straight at them, panicked and fled where they could have cut the Union men to ribbons. Thus victory rested with the Union forces, though not exactly in the way Grant had planned. Bragg was removed as commander of the Confederate Army of Tennessee, to be replaced by General Joseph Johnston, who would have to try to withstand the next U.S. attack.